when the *West wind* moves

Drifters,
Book Fourteen

SUSAN RODGERS

Edited by Colleen McKie of Savvy Fox Author Services
Cover design by Alanna Munro. All rights reserved.
Book design and formatting by Valerie Bellamy, Dog-ear Book Design.

ISBN: 978-1-987966-17-6

Listen to the wind,
it talks.
Listen to the silence,
it speaks.
Listen to the heart,
it knows.
—Native American Proverb

Contents

Chapter One

"Arnie, you have my passport?"

Lucie hurried down the small hallway of the new condo. She stopped right behind her man. Arnie was posed in front of their large front room window with his legs apart and both feet braced firmly on the floor, muscular arms crossed, as if he needed the extra stability the assertive pose could offer. He didn't bother turning around when Lucie slowed before tiptoeing up behind him.

"When'd Murphy get new wheels?" he asked, his tone even and controlled.

Alarm skittered up and down Lucie's tiny frame. "I dunno," she shrugged. "A few weeks ago, I guess."

"Corrections must have given her some raise." Arnie pointed a shoulder at the window, in a direction Lucie interpreted as downward. After a furtive glance at him, she leaned a little forward and peered down at the street below. Her friend Murphy, a tall black woman who worked as a corrections officer at Alberta's Brody Pen, was leaning up against a pickup truck so new it literally shimmered in the midday sun.

"The hell if I know what she makes, Arnie. It's a federal job. I suppose she does pretty good."

"Good enough to leave her brand new truck here in Vancouver when she flies out to Brody every week to work? She must have another vehicle in Alberta." Arnie took a long, hard look at his woman.

Lucie made a point of staring down at Murphy, who was there to pick her up. The women were driving down to Seattle for the weekend to hang out in funky restaurants and cafés and make jokes about men. Ironically, one of the cafés they planned to target was Josh Sawyer's brother Zach's trendy Fat Cat Café, although Lucie was getting creepy vibes about going there now that 'the deed' was done, as Murphy put it when the women talked earlier.

"Arnie, I dunno. It ain't really my business. Do you have my passport or not?" It made more sense, from Lucie's point of view, to retreat on the offensive. Arnie was an astute guy. It wouldn't do to let him pursue this dark path any further.

"When did you and Murphy get so close?"

Damn, he's like a friggin' hound. Lucie was growing more exasperated by the second. *Doesn't give up until he gets all the answers.* Out loud she said, "She likes butter chicken. Murphy goes to the movies sometimes when she's around and she always stops by for her Indian food fix after. What business is it of yours anyway, Arnie? Where's my goddamned passport? I won't be gettin' through the border to the States without it."

Like his secrets—and there were many—Arnie kept the couple's important documents and papers close to his chest. He paid the bills, he knew their finances, he held onto the passports, he made the big decisions. Lucie felt like she was just along for the ride most of the time. For sex. To cook, to clean. As far as having him for a partner went, she was okay with that one downside to their relationship. Used to be he wasn't around much anyway. Lately, though, since leaving the Keating employ, Lucie's man was a somber, brooding presence in their home.

She switched gears, because he was growing more apprehensive by the second. Arnie had yet to look away from her. Those gentle, pale eyes of his, the ones that made women swoon when they were in his presence, were edging their way toward downright suspicion, growing cloudy and searching and menacing all at once. "You ought to go see her," she told him, backpedaling from his earlier questions about Murphy's newfound resources.

Arnie didn't have to think about whom Lucie was referring to. Nor did he bother saying it out loud. The tragic break in his stare, communicated with a surprised double-blink —was comprehension enough.

Lucie had to look away for a second. She moved toward the large window and spoke to the glass. "It's obvious you miss her, and she could likely use you right now, Arnie."

They'd gotten the call late the night before. Arnie was still pissed at Matt for not getting on the horn right after Josh was shot. As a rule, Arnie was not normally inclined to hang out on the Internet to regularly check Twitter or any other news feed. Nor did any of his boxing buddies think to contact him when they heard; they just all figured he'd be one of the first to get word from the Keating camp about something so sinister as Josh Sawyer getting shot.

In Lucie's experience, when Arnie's anger transmuted from outright hostility to the silent, seething kind, it was never a good idea to stick around. Hence the planned excursion with Murphy. Regarding Arnie just before she'd averted her eyes away from his probing stare, Lucie considered just tiptoeing away. She wondered if he'd notice. Arnie's bottom lip was curled down. Arnie's bottom lip was never curled down. He was the calmest person she knew.

His voice took her by surprise. Flat. Emotionless. As if all the energy Arnie had before the upsetting call came in was sucked into some nefarious black hole, left to wither and die. "I'm the last person Jessie wants to see, Lucie," he said.

Ah. So that's why you're upset. You weren't there to save Josh. Lucie could see Arnie's reflection in the glass, his body wavering in the sunlight, the edges wavy and distorted. The way Arnie was punishing himself for this thing with Josh…*God save me if he ever finds out I had anything to do with it…hooking up Josh and Murphy so Josh's wishes could be pipelined via Vaughn directly to Morgan at Brody…*

Lucie stuck a fingernail between her teeth and started to chew.

Hunkering up her nerve, she dove in again. Pleading with Arnie's reflection, she almost whined. "I got to go, Arnie. Murphy's waiting for me. I need my passport."

Arnie bore a hole into his woman's petite back. Shortly, he flicked his gaze over to her eyes in the glass—distorted, warped, flicking uncertainly in little jerking motions. He grunted his displeasure. With one last disdainful look down his nose to Murphy's shiny new wheels, he uncrossed his arms and marched across the room to the condo's open concept kitchen. Picking a key out of a drawer by the fridge, he strode down the hall to the bedroom he'd repurposed as a home office. Lucie held her breath until he returned with her passport. Holding on tightly to it as he held it out to her, Arnie forced her to work hard to nudge it out from between his thick, callused fingers.

"I'll walk you down," he told her, when she finally yanked the small black booklet from his grip. "You ready?"

Seriously? Lucie started tapping the small black passport against her thigh. *I don't need Arnie and Murphy within eye or earshot of each other. Not now, and not freakin' ever.*

"Okay. Thank you," she managed anyway, because there was no backing down from Arnie when he was in this state. Hell, there was no communicating with Arnie when he retreated into his head like this and went into surveillance mode, all serious and introspective like a chess player trying to figure out his next move.

Sticking out a finger, Lucie pointed to her wheeled suitcase, which was sitting by the door like a cat waiting to be let outdoors. Arnie grabbed the handle and held the condo door open so Lucie could pass through.

Outside on the street below, he didn't bother rolling the bag across the asphalt to where Murphy, sheltered by the truck's open driver's side door, was waiting in tight pants more suited for a midnight romp on East Hastings than for standing here modeling shiny new wheels. Instead, Arnie picked up the bag outright and carried it across the street, narrowly evading a pricey Beamer as he moved.

Cursing her husband's stubborn penchant for silent, stealthy probing, Lucie trailed along behind like an obedient puppy, jogging to keep up in the tipsy high wedge shoes she'd chosen for this warm mid-September day.

Lifting Lucie's bag, Arnie positioned it in the large back seat of the big truck, and gave it a sturdy final push to settle it into place.

With a huff, Murphy shoved the back door closed. "Vaughn wants to know when he's gettin' his song from Jessie Wheeler. He's been doin' what you asked."

Not wavering from Murphy's curious gaze, Arnie leaned, on one straight, muscled arm, against the back door of the truck. "Last I heard she was working on it."

Lucie watched Murphy systematically take in Arnie's challenging stance. The woman was as astute as he was when it came to scrutinizing opponents

"Jesus Christ. Jesus fucking Christ." Arnie couldn't bring himself to look at his wife. A slow quake started up his body. At his side, his grip on Lucie's arm tightened. Pressing his free hand to his jaw, restlessly pawing at it, he growled at Murphy, "What'd Vaughn do?"

Most people facing off with Arnie Sylvester would, in this case, take a step backward. Murphy just spit out the truth, evenly and with no real emotion. "What you were asked to do," she replied with a casual nonchalance that pissed Arnie off even more. "He went to Morgan, on Josh Sawyer's behalf, that's what he did. And I went to Vaughn for Josh so poor little rich boy could broker a deal." She may as well have just stolen candies from a convenience store instead of bartered away a cherished man's life.

Arnie was choking. One of the most trusted and respected men of the Downtown Eastside was losing his shit. "Do you have any fucking idea what you have d-done?" he stammered.

Lucie wasn't tough like her new rich friend. She took a step backward. "Arnie, let go'a my arm. You're scaring me." She glared at Murphy, who shrugged, shifted her weight to her other leg, and fiddled in her bag, which was gaping open like a wound on the driver's seat in the big truck. Retrieving a small plastic Tic Tac container, Murphy snapped back the lid and popped two of the green mints into her mouth. "Ah. S'got that new car smell. I fuckin' love it."

Arnie had to forcibly beat back the urge to raise an arm and slog that righteous, petulant smirk right off Murphy's smug face.

Completely unconcerned, after tossing the Tic Tac container back into her purse Murphy refocused on her new BFF's man. "What the hell do you care?" she tossed over at him. "You don't even work for them anymore. The rich bastards."

"Don't go there, Murphy," Lucie warned, nervously eyeing Arnie in her peripheral vision. "You're not from here. You don't know what Jessie Wheeler means to the Downtown Eastside."

"Sawyer's intentions were noble," Murphy bit off to Arnie, ignoring Lucie altogether. "He earned Vaughn's respect by that deal he made with Morgan. The way we see it, Sawyer stepped up while everyone else around him sucked ass. He did it for his family. To end the terror."

"Did he end it? Is it over?" Arnie struggled to grasp this new truth. The whole thing was unbelievable.

"It's over. His family's debt to Morgan got paid."

"Bullshit. Not entirely."

"The kid?" A slow, confident leer settled on Murphy's attractive face. Waving an arm idly toward the truck, she crunched on her Tic Tacs. "What do ya think this is?"

"The price of a Sawyer child," Arnie bristled. "Is that what it is?"

"Partially. Vaughn calls it my finder's fee. I don't know where he stashed the rest. Morgan don't seem to want any of the money. He's a lifer, anyway. What would he do with it? He ain't got no family to give it to." She said that like Morgan didn't have Rice Krispies on his shelf for breakfast. The way she was talking…Arnie wondered what kind of woman could disassociate herself this way, from something so vile and terrible as a man losing his family the way Morgan did. Losing his hold on life, at that, or at least his reason to live.

The thought brought Arnie back to Josh. "And if Josh survives?"

The way a mother gazes lovingly at her child, Murphy was fondly appraising the truck. Considering Arnie's question before she looked back at him, she shoved a nail between her top two front teeth and picked at a tiny gap. Since Arnie was known on the streets as a particularly composed, cool guy, she was rather surprised to see that he was shaking. Her response was petulant and defensive. "This is business. Morgan's team negotiated good."

"Meaning?" Arnie was barely hanging on. He'd have to work the strain off by going twelve rounds with his gym's youngest, most fit boxer. In these few tense seconds, however, he had to focus on retaining some semblance of control. This delicate matter required answers, answers he wouldn't get by going all postal on this suffocating, detached woman.

"Meaning they agreed to take cash instead of the kid. But Josh Sawyer made a deal. And he's gotta keep his end of the bargain." She grinned slyly at Lucie. "Or else it ain't over. Right, Luce?"

That was it. Murphy's offhand sideways look to her friend was Arnie's breaking point. Lucie knew it before he even captured her in his furious, exploding eyes. She took a second step backward and wondered how ugly the bruise on her wrist, underneath where his fingers were so tightly clenched around her arm, was going to be. *It's too warm to be wearing sweaters or long-sleeved shirts,* she contemplated anxiously, teetering on her new heels. Although she'd worn long sleeves in hot weather lots of times long before Arnie came along, before he rescued her, before he found something compelling about her worth saving, like the messy blonde updo she almost always fixed in the mornings. Well, that and her gutsy, fierce determination to survive.

She pulled up some of that ferocity. "Let me go, Arnie. Now." Lucie narrowed her eyes. "You're hurting me."

"What part did you play in this, Lucie? You got your eyes on some new wheels too?"

"I don't, Arnie, you know me," she whined. "I don't care about money. I got all I need."

Murphy jumped in and further illuminated Arnie. In utter disbelief, he listened. "She brought Josh to me after he approached her and asked for help. That's all. Lucie didn't have anything to do with the negotiations. I took Josh's request to Vaughn, and he met up with Morgan. Lucie did shit-all. She had no clue what Sawyer was really after."

"Lucie," Arnie bit off evenly, his hard gaze fixed on his woman, "knows what that family means to me."

"Oh. So, I get it now. That's why you came home from Calgary. Why you quit. Because you didn't...you didn't..." Lucie stuttered.

"Josh tell you he came to me first?" The hot red anger wasn't just washing over Arnie's cheeks now. It was coming from inside his too cool body. Alarmed, Lucie held her breath. "On a night he was drinking?" Arnie added. "You're damn right I didn't agree to help him out, Lucie, if you're referring to me going along with his crazy scheme. The guy is—was—so damn scared he couldn't piss straight."

The old streetwise fight Lucie grew up with came back. She launched into a tirade. "And you couldn't save him. If you're standing here judging me— and Murphy here—for catering to the wishes of a man desperate to save his family, then you're a two-faced bastard, Arnie! Because I've seen you carrying out your shady work, I've seen you procure guns and help people disappear, yes, Jessie included. You think you're so almighty stealthy and quiet and above the law because people down here respect you, but you have your own rules and your own law, and you use them to play God. You choose who you want to help and why."

Poking a finger into his hard chest, she lowered her voice. "You didn't want to go along with Josh's wishes because you, like the rest of her highness' little harem of love-struck guardians, didn't want to see Jessie get hurt. Well, I've got news for you. Josh didn't ask for anything you haven't already been involved with. He was already dying. His spirit was *begging* for a break from the pain."

Arnie's lips were trembling. Everything Lucie was spouting back at him was true. In the past, yes, he'd helped many a man even the score, or end his life, if need be, usually by virtue of supplying a weapon. There was a kind of agony on the Downtown Eastside that a man like Arnie was far too often privy to, that he could respect, even, that warranted that kind of release. But Josh? What made him different from anyone else?

Jessie. The children. Lucie was dead right. That's what made Josh different. The others? They, like Morgan, had nothing left to live for, to ground them to the earth. Josh had anchors. Addictions would stalk him forever, but he had a steady light the others didn't have—four lights, in fact, plus a new baby on the way—that, at least in recent years, kept him tethered to the earth. This thing he engineered, this unfathomable deal Josh brokered with Murphy and Vaughn, and therefore with Morgan and likely his hired ape, Caulfield, was only out of the norm in that Josh had too much to live for.

And Jessie, yes…she would be lost without Josh. Lucie was right about that too. She would be inconsolable.

"I can see you thinking this through, Arnie." Lucie was near tears now. Her man was a quiet man most of the time, but he was not immune to letting little signs flicker here and there, in his eyes, in his surface exhalations, that allowed her the ability to read him. And now his brain—and his heart, his big, tough, impenetrable Downtown Eastside heart—were on fire, she could tell. Lucie could almost see steam rising from the aching pores on Arnie's weathered body. "I know you care about them, about all of them. Josh was your friend—"

"Is," Arnie snapped through clenched teeth, "my friend."

"Then you should care enough about him to let him go. To let him have this, this—peace. In my books, he's a hero. Most men don't have that kind of courage."

"Courage is a funny thing, Lucie," Arnie snarled. "Sometimes it's wrapped in fear. And when it is, it can come out looking like cowardice."

"What do you—oh, you mean Jessie. That's how your precious Jessie is going to see this. Like her husband is weak. Like he gave up."

"No. Jessie won't see it that way because, to her, this is just a hit. It's another one of Morgan's attempts to even the score. And neither you, nor Murphy," he stated, staring Murphy down so hard that she, too, finally backed away, "will ever let her know otherwise. She doesn't need to know that her husband chose to end his own life in some whacked-out attempt to save her. To save their kids. She'd only see that as Josh choosing to leave them all behind. And there's no heroism to be found in that."

Wrenching her arm away from Arnie, Lucie finally loosed herself from his brutal grasp. Wincing, she rubbed her wrist until Arnie faced her full on, his eyes sparking with anger. "Move out of the condo," he demanded. "I'll be gone when you get home. It'll buy you a week or so to pack."

"What? Why? Arnie!"

Arnie stormed back across the busy street, leaving Lucie at a loss.

Halfway across, he turned back around to her. Nearby, a Mercedes coasted to a stop and waited for him to pass by. Rooting himself to the center of the street, Arnie yelled back over to Murphy's blood money truck. "I respect what Josh hoped he could accomplish by this, and I know all about living with the demons of addiction that got him there, but I'm disgusted by his choice to give up. There might have been a way…there had to have been a way…you needed to come to me with this when Josh approached you. This was too damn big a secret to keep from me, Lucie."

"Arnie," Lucie rather indignantly informed him, "you gave up first! You walked away when Josh reached out to you, when he needed you. If you thought there was another option for Josh, for his family, then why'd you leave them?"

Arnie stopped cold. The Mercedes driver got annoyed, beeped the car's horn, and eventually skirted around him. An Audi TT driver laid on the horn too. When he finally passed Arnie, he accompanied his hollers with a third finger salute. Arnie didn't bother dignifying the guy's anger with a response.

Murphy touched Lucie's arm. "Hop in, honey," she instructed. "He's too damn close to that family. But this kind of thing isn't new to him. Your man will come to his senses."

"I don't know…"

Lucie wanted to run after Arnie, but Murphy saw the desperate look and shook her head. "Not now, Lucie. A man like him needs to cool down. Give him the weekend. You and me will go turn Seattle red. Too much coffee during the day, too much vino at night."

Lucie and Arnie were at a standstill. Neither was moving. Theirs was a comfortable, easy relationship based on mutual granting of space, and a lack of nosy interest in each other's business. Now the tide was turned. Now they knew too much about each other. And there was no going backward.

"No," Lucie said to Murphy, still staring at Arnie in the middle of the street, "he's right. We're done."

"What? You're giving up too easily, girlfriend." Murphy slid up into the big truck and slammed the door. Her window was closed so she didn't hear what Lucie said next, and nor did Arnie, but he understood his woman's body language loud and clear.

Proudly, she raised her head so that she was almost looking down her nose at him. "Life is big, Arnie," she said. "It was too big for Josh. By introducing him to Murphy, I did what I thought was right. For him." Hunching up her shoulders, she added, "Normally you'd be all over that. You'd be doing what you could for a man in that much pain." Staring at him across the beeps and horns, she swayed and had to take a quick step to keep her balance. *But this isn't about the man,* she considered as she rooted herself more firmly to the earth. *This is about a girl who used to be homeless, whom you've made it your mission to protect. This is about the woman.*

Most days, Arnie understood body language. Today he wished to hell he didn't. Whipping around and storming his way back across to the entrance of his building, he added a post script to the thoughts he knew Lucie was transmitting to him. "This goes far beyond death. This is about life, the lives of Jessie and her children. And for Jessie, there is no life without Josh."

Lucie had to pull herself up into the hulking truck with arms that weren't quite strong enough to easily master the trick.

Murphy looked back over her shoulder to scout for a break in traffic before she pulled away from the curb.

"Where will I go?" Lucie moaned. "I have no place to go."

Murphy flashed a smile toward the passenger seat. "I know a ninety-year-old woman who could use a full time live-in. A caregiver. And she loves butter chicken. You just gotta cut it up real tiny for her. Little itty bitty pieces."

"Thank God." Slipping lower into her seat, Lucie stared straight ahead. Murphy navigated them down Hastings Street toward Highway one. "I'm gonna miss him," Lucie complained. "He's all man, that one."

"Arnie's a good guy. You two did good by each other for a while now. Maybe he'll come around."

"I wasn't talking about Arnie, Murphy." Looking over at her friend, Lucie sighed sadly. "I was talking about Josh."

"Don't second guess yourself, honey. You did the right thing. Jessie Wheeler and her kids can move on in peace."

"Maybe he'll come around."

"You talking about Arnie this time? Or Josh Sawyer?"

"Josh." It was a whisper.

"Lucie?" Merging into traffic, Murphy pointed the big truck east.

"Hmmm?"

"You better hope not. You just better hope not. Cuz if he comes around, the hell he's been living in won't be over."

Seattle awaited. Lucie steeled herself for a forced good time while, back on Hastings, Arnie made a call to Air Canada and booked a flight to Calgary.

Chapter Two

Charles eased his tired body down onto a small coffee table and faced Jessie. Reaching out, he took her hands in his. Her eyelids fluttered, and opened. Despondent, she'd melted deeply into an uncomfortable sofa hours ago, and hadn't moved since.

"You need to go to the condo," Charles told her. "There's nothing you can do here, Jessie. Josh will sleep for a while." He was right. In surgery yesterday, skilled trauma surgeons had cut Josh open and dug around a lung for a bullet. Today, keeping him medicated was affording Josh the rest he needed to recover. "I just talked to one of the doctors," Charles continued. "Josh must have an angel watching over him, or a whole passel of heavenly creatures. They think his body turned slightly just as the sniper fired. It minimized the damage; made it less significant than it could have been. It, uh, it missed his heart. He's a strong guy. He's hanging on."

"He's not so strong." This was the first time Jessie spoke since arriving at the hospital the day before. Her voice was gravelly and raspy from disuse. "It's bullshit, thinking he's strong. And I'm not talking about the fact that he's incredibly susceptible to infection. The whole 'got knifed so don't got a spleen thing,' remember, Charles?"

Charles blanched at the hard steel of his girl's eyes. She hadn't slept last night, none of them had, but there was more than bone-weary fatigue at play in the soft baby blues everyone loved. There was a seething cauldron of anger.

Using her hands to leverage her body, Jessie sat more fully upright. "I want to see my babies."

"They're on their way to Calgary now," Charles responded with an air of caution. "Charlie and Deirdre are taking good care of them. Sam and Alin are with the kids as well. Honey…Dan's at the jet. He called an hour ago. It's secure and ready to go."

"Fine. Let's go." Jessie didn't move. Her eyes, however, did. They flicked up past Charles' left shoulder and landed on Matt. Her best buddy was leaning against the far wall of a hospital room, where the three of them were quietly hovering over Josh as he rested. Snugged into the far corner past the door, Matt, too, hadn't moved or spoken in a while. Nor had he taken his eyes off of Jessie, apart from a few tedious minutes when Shanda stuck her head in earlier and forced a chai tea into his hand.

Catching Jessie's eyes on him now, he straightened.

Twisting around, Charles studied him.

Red-eyed and drained, Matt was stooped over from the weight of this latest drama. His grief-stricken gaze remained locked on Jessie.

A tired sigh pulled Charles back to his superstar. "I meant for the children," he explained heavily. "The jet. Not you. We need to get the children back to Vancouver, to a place where they feel safe."

"I'm going with them."

"Josh needs you here, Jessie."

"Apparently only Josh knows what Josh needs. And it doesn't seem to be me. Or our kids."

Confused, Charles probed further. "What are you saying?"

Jessie's eyes flicked back to Matt. "Ask him. He knows."

"Matt?" The tone Charles used left no room for argument.

Resigned, Matt shoved himself away from the wall and made his way across the polished floor. There was a deep chair closer to the door. Grabbing hold of the top back rail, he dragged it across the floor. At the width end of the coffee table Charles was sitting on, Matt swung the chair around and eased down onto a worn cushion.

Bending forward, he rested his forearms on his thighs and clasped his hands in front of him. "You're wrong," he said intently to Jessie. "I know what you're thinking, but you've got no reason to believe that."

Staring at the ceiling, Jessie let out a long exhale before she raised her free hand to her forehead and rubbed the fingertips over her skin. "He was up to something, Matt," she determined. Refocusing her eyeline in his direction, she elaborated. "Josh admitted that he was planning something. I thought… I thought…"

She couldn't finish. How could Jessie say out loud, to these two strong men she respected so deeply, that over the summer she'd wondered whether her husband might be considering ending his life by his own hand? There were nightmares about that, about those dark, unfathomable thoughts, but the bad dreams faded once Josh seemed to settle into a kind of easy contentment as the summer progressed. In Jessie's mind, filming *Sacred Peace* and caring for the kids and the ranch seemed to have renewed his focus and given him hope.

"I guess we were living life on autopilot, Charles, at the end," she admitted. "We thought…I thought…that we would be okay. That Josh was okay. He was so calm, so…happy. So at peace. Obviously I was just being duped by an Oscar winning actor."

The peace part didn't entirely ring true. Josh, toward the end of the summer, was withdrawn and quiet most of the time, but he wasn't angry and he wasn't drinking. Jessie felt she could reach him if she needed to, at least on some level. Sex wasn't necessarily happening as much as she wished, but she attributed that to the pregnancy and Josh's lack of interest in the new baby. Still, they always touched when they passed each other. There were secret shared smiles here and there, usually over silly things the kids did, like over the new puppy Josh brought home to Emily-Grace once she seemed ready to try puppy ownership again. And over Dylan's natural skill at riding the pony.

Matt lowered his tone. "Jessie…Josh would not have arranged to have himself shot. This has got Morgan's stink all over it."

"What?" Charles had to bend over and gasp for breath. "Is that what you think?"

Jessie ignored him. She pointed her hurt and anger at her best friend. "He was planning something," she said again. "If this is what it was, if Josh did arrange this, it's a fucking coward's way to go, Matt. Think about it. You want to end your life, all you really need's a goddamned gun or a thick fucking piece of rope. Why stage a big show? To throw everyone off the truth? To make them think you're some heroic martyr?" Eyes narrowing into angry slits, Jessie took a sharp breath to keep from crying. "You sure as hell don't need to hire a hit man. If Josh did that because he was too damned chicken to pull the trigger himself, and because he wanted to go out a hero, then I'm sick with disgust. Face it, Matt. Josh coulda had his pick of self-inflicted exits. He's got guns."

Matt bent over and rested his chin on his clasped hands. "Josh is no coward, Jessie," he said quietly. "You're taking yourself down a shadowy road you've got no reason to be on. That's not fair to Josh."

"You're jumping to conclusions," Charles determined before Jessie could jump all over that. Gently, he squeezed her damp, limp fingers. At the same time, a flicker of warning careened through his tired eyes. With a sigh, he softened. "You're beat and you're worried, honey. Let Matt take you back to the condo so you can rest in peace. Jon went back there for some shuteye. You can switch off with him."

"Rest? In peace? Well said, Charles." She rolled her eyes. "Jesus. If I go anywhere, it's to the jet so I can fly out of this hellhole and start again. Preferably with someone a little less volatile and a lot more stable."

Charles let Jessie's fingers float out of his. Standing, he rubbed a hand over and over his balding head and stepped over to the window.

Concerned, Matt watched him for a few minutes before he lifted his body out of his chair and took Charles' place in front of their troubled girl. "You're not leaving Josh, Jessie. He needs you to be here when he wakes up. Your kids need to be in Vancouver. Let them go."

"I can't, Matt." The limpid eyes were bubbling over. "They outnumber Josh. They need me more than he does right now."

"They're healthy kids, Jessie. They have a lot of love around them. Deirdre and Carlotta are both spoiling them rotten as we speak. Your husband needs your strength right now. Let the kids go. When Josh is stable we'll move him to Vancouver."

"That's the thing, Matt." Jessie wrinkled her eyebrows and forced a steady determination into her wet, weary eyes. "No matter how many times I go over this, I always land at the same answer." Her voice trembled when she spoke again, "I don't think Josh will ever be stable. Even if he does pull through. Don't you see? Jacob was right all along. Josh will always be a flint waiting for a spark. He'll always be that unpredictable guy I should have let walk out of my life that very first night instead of following him out to Charlie's garbage. What the hell was I thinking?" Jessie leaned into the safe tent of her best buddy's arms and covered her face with her hands.

Matt's soothing voice drew her back to her senses. Cupping her chin in his right hand, he spoke with an assurance he was struggling to feel. "What you were thinking way back then was that you could have years of a deep, passionate, shared love with that man if you gave him a chance, that's what you were thinking. You were thinking about future children with beautiful souls nurtured by the deep love that man has for you and for them. You need to release this negative energy and give Josh the benefit of the doubt, Jessie. There's no way he did anything wrong here. He may have been planning something, and some day we'll know exactly what, but this was not it. This was another attempt by Morgan to wring vengeance and hate upon a family that has already suffered far too damn much."

The ice blue eyes were leaking, but the flow was slowing. Jessie hiccupped her way back to strength. Wiping her right eye with the sleeve of a sweater the hospital's cool temperature required, a pretty pale yellow cashmere sweater Shanda had thoughtfully brought in for her, Jessie treated Matt to a sad but hopeful smile. "He'll be okay, right Matt?" Afraid to let go, she held tightly to his elbows. "Tell me he'll be okay."

"Of course he will." Forcing a smile, Matt bent forward and brushed his lips against Jessie's cheek. He spoke gently in her ear. "Of course he will. But you have to help him. No more negative stuff. Only the good stuff from here on in. Especially in this room, where Josh might hear you."

"Rainbows and sunshine," Jessie murmured back. Slipping her hands up Matt's arms and wrapping them tightly around the trusted shoulders, she inhaled deeply. "You smell like a memory, Matt," she whispered softly. "A good one. There are far too few of those these days, honey."

Melting, Matt tried not to crumble in the loving arms. But he couldn't avoid sending a little love back. "You smell like a memory too, sweetheart," he told her, hoping Charles wouldn't notice just how long their sweet embrace was lingering. Matt wanted this moment. Moments like these were sacred; they were what carried him through each day. Like beacons in the night, he relied on them to light the darkness. He tossed more lightness into the heavy day. "But you need a shower."

A low giggle warmed his sorrow.

"Sweet girl," he murmured. "It's not what you think, with Josh. It'll all be okay. Trust me."

Jessie didn't answer. She buried her face in Matt's warm neck, breathed him in, and closed her eyes.

When Jon landed at the hospital an hour later, Zach and Wes were trailing him. Jessie was alone; Matt had walked Charles down to the cafeteria for a cup of tea. Josh's older brother was bearded and wiped out; the faded green wool sweater he'd thrown over a wrinkled button-down shirt gave him an even more rumpled aura. When the light changed at the door and Jessie looked up to see the three, she couldn't help but wonder what they all could have done differently to keep a lonely little boy from becoming a sometimes solitary, frightened man.

Zach nervously tugged at his nose before he stepped forward and enclosed his little brother's wife in his arms. "How you holding up?" he asked.

"Swell," Jessie declared, proudly throwing her shoulders back before letting go of Zach. "Just hunky-dory. Seeing the three of you here together doesn't do anything for my confidence, though. Specially you two." Raising an arm in a half-assed salute, she treated Jon and Wes to a half-hearted wave. "When's the last time the two of you were even in each other's company?"

"We made our peace over the years, Jessie." Jon was as businesslike as usual. "We learned from the best."

Jessie's cheeks pinked up, just a tiny bit. She managed a small frown, which was supposed to come out as a smile but which failed miserably.

"Do I get a hug?" Wes opened his arms.

Jessie bit her lip before she moved to him. In her eyes, and in Josh's now, too, Wes wasn't all bad. He was just a confused man who spent a chunk of his life trying to figure out how to raise his wife's love child. Dylan sprang to mind. Jessie almost crumbled. Sometimes even now, watching Josh—and Jacob—try to navigate those murky waters was still heartbreaking. But they were trying, all of them, and nobody was more determined to make the whole co-parenting thing work than Josh. So far Dylan was responding, the way all little boys respond to sincere and abundant love. Dylan's choice of parent for the times when he needed security, like when he was overtired or sick, was always Josh, even when Jacob was in the room. What drew Josh and Dylan together, Jessie figured, were the similar circumstances of their births. What kept them together was a beautiful man's devotion and patience with a high-spirited, rowdy child.

"It's good to see you, Wes," Jessie mumbled. Letting go of him, she turned back around to Zach, who had wandered over to Josh in the hospital bed and was standing quietly with a set of white knuckles wrapped around a bed rail, staring at his brother's beleaguered, resting body. Far too often since Josh hooked up with Jessie, Zach had been called to his younger sibling's bedside. It was a humbling thing. Wrapping her arms around her growing middle, Jessie shrank back into herself as she pondered that difficult truth. "Is Hilary with you?" She asked the question in a raspy, thin voice.

A light came on in Zach's dark eyes. "No," he said, adding by way of explanation, "Kayla went into labor. Hilary dropped me off at the airport and is, as we speak, on her way to Vancouver. Driving. Actually, she's likely there, depending on how long she had to wait at the border. I ought to check in with her." He reached deep in a baggy jeans pocket for his phone, but left it there when Jessie pounced on the news about Kayla.

"Kayla wanted to come here but I guess Jacob wisely talked her out of it. Not like there'd be anything she could do, anyway," she said. The words came out with an anxious, uncertain huff at the end.

Trying to keep things cool for Jessie, to help keep her calm, Zach made a point of relaxing the tension in his jawline and easing his grip on Josh's bed rail so the blood could work its way back into his fingers. "It's promising though, right Jessie?" he asked. "Wes and I got the scoop from Jon. It sounds like my little brother will get past this latest shit. Thank God."

Jessie raised her arms higher on her body and tightly crossed them. The anger in her eyes sparked again. Since the second Josh got shot, her emotions had started cycling through her sea-pearl blues like socks in the washing machine, only instead of going through soak, rinse, spin, they rotated through hurt, frustration, and anger. In place of detergent was a heaping tablespoon full of unrelenting worry. "Depends on how you choose to interpret 'get past this latest shit'," she said.

"What?" Zach, Jon and Wes all went on high alert. They didn't have a chance to pursue the troublesome comment, because Matt and Charles were just returning, extending hands to shake in greeting.

Jessie removed herself from their immediate company and dropped back down onto the sofa. Turning her toes in so they faced each other, she bent over her baby belly and wrung her hands together the way Emily-Grace did when she was scared.

Pushing his way through the throng of bodies clustered around the door, Matt made his way over and plopped down next to her. "Charles and I saw the doctor," he announced. "Josh is stable. He's doing okay, Jessie. You watch, they'll have him awake and up walking in a day or two, big tough guy like him."

"La di da. How freaking wonderful."

"Hey. What'd I tell you?"

A low grumble was all Matt got from Jessie. With a heavy sigh, he leaned back and raised an arm to place around her shoulders. "Charlie has the gang at the jet. How about you and me go out to see the children?"

Jessie made a small nonsensical *mmphhff* sound, but she laid a hand on Matt's thigh, which she used to ease herself up to a standing position. He took that as a yes, and helped her rise before he stood himself.

"We need to get some food into you," he told her. The piqued face and troubled eyes were breaking his heart. "You've got to think about that baby you're carrying, sweetheart."

"We need to call Jacob, Matt. I was hoping, you know…to be there for him and Kayla. I was planning to head west the second Kayla's labor started."

"The baby's coming?" Matt missed that news when he approached the Sawyer men a few minutes earlier.

Jessie's breaking point was significantly lower than usual. Instead of answering verbally, she teared up again and nodded before shoving a thumb and forefinger into the outside corners of her eyes.

"Deirdre will go when she gets back to Vancouver," Matt tenderly assured her. "She'll be there for the two of them. They won't be alone."

"I know. Hilary's there now too. Kayla gets the girls, and I get the guys. Lucky me."

Hesitating, Matt said, "Shanda's dropping by after she wraps today, Jessie. Charles and I will take the men out for some famous Alberta beef so you and Shanda can talk girl talk. Although I really wish you'd go to the condo and grab some shuteye."

"I will. Later. Just not for a bit, okay?"

Matt rewrapped his arm around Jessie's shoulders as they started to move through the others. He caught Charles' eye. "We're going to the airport," he informed him. Two uniformed security were hanging around in the hallway, keeping an eye on Josh's room. There were more at every entrance and exit, inspecting bags and generally watching for trouble.

Burying her face in the coveted hollow of Matt's neck as they walked, Jessie recoiled at the sight of them. "I can't stand this," she moaned. "I'm so goddamned sick of it. No wonder Josh—"

"Look," Matt interjected, "stop with that train of thought, Jessie. Josh doesn't deserve it."

"Yeah, let's just shove that stupid theory under the proverbial rug and stick our noses in the sand." Raising her head, she angled her body away from Matt and studied one of the more burly security crew as they passed. "Although you might want to tell Charles he's wasting the gazillions of dollars he pimped outta me and my husband. You don't need security for guys who just wanna shuffle off this mortal coil. Way I hear it, if that's what they want, they'll damn well find a way."

Chapter Three

They left the hospital and walked in silence toward Matt's sleek Audi. In the car, he hesitated before putting it into drive. "Promise me something," he entreated, glancing over at her, all small and curled up into a sad little ball in the big leather seat.

Chewing on her thumbnail, Jessie looked over at him. Leaning her head back against the seat, sideways so she could meet Matt's concerned gaze, she waited, shrinking back, her luminous big, scared moist eyes accompanied by shallow breaths.

"Your children," Matt said quietly. Twisting a little to reach out his left hand, he did what he often ached to do. Lifting Jessie's maternity top, he laid his palm on her swollen skin. Responding to his touch, Jessie covered Matt's hand with hers and exhaled slowly. "Including this one," Matt continued. "I know how awful this is, Jessie, all of you have been through so much, but—"

"I know," she answered, cutting him off. "Whatever happens now with Josh, with me, with Morgan…the kids have to come first."

"The kids have to come first. Yes. And that means love and cuddles and not worrying them."

Jessie linked her fingers through Matt's and focused on them. "They're not stupid, Matt. They've been through hell and back. They know we're being hunted. They know their father's weaknesses."

"And, little girl," Matt smiled and looked down when the baby kicked under his warm hand, "they know their mother's strength."

"He's kicking." Jessie allowed a small smile to sneak through the seemingly never-ending chaos of fear and worry.

"He's kicking because he agrees with me." Matt looked up again. "Sweetheart," he said, eyes suddenly alight, "you said 'he' again."

"I did, didn't I?" Jessie chuckled. "Emily-Grace will not be impressed. We better hope Kayla has a girl, at least."

"Text Jacob to see how they're getting along," Matt ordered, easing his hand out from underneath Jessie's and grasping the steering wheel. "I'm running us through a drive-thru somewhere. Maybe what your baby's trying to tell us is that he's hungry. He wants his mother to eat something."

Shortly, with less than half of a chicken fajita pita in her tummy, a text from Vancouver lit up the screen on Jessie's cellphone. "Finally," she growled, her eyes scanning the screen. "Hmm. Kayla's still in the early stages of labor," she proclaimed. "She's got a doula with her, one of Vancouver's best. Jacob's losing his mind, though. I wish to heck I was there."

"I'm sure Jacob does too, Jessie. And Kayla." Taking her hand, Matt adjusted his grip on the steering wheel as he navigated his way through the busy Calgary traffic. At his side, Jessie yawned widely and struggled to keep her eyes open. Matt frowned. "Grab a few winks," he demanded. "It's a slow drive today. I'll wake you when we get there."

"Maybe." Sinking deeper into her seat, Jessie crossed her arms over her chest and let her eyes close over. Through her mind slid visions of her babies when they were born, all perfect little bundles of joy and bliss.

At the airport, picking their ways up the steps of the luxurious Keating jet, the three somber, scared Sawyer children waited for their mother to come and tell them their worlds would balance out again, and that everything would somehow be A-okay.

⌒⌒

"David." Despite the overhanging sadness, Emily-Grace was being her usual bossy self. "Put Fluffy's toys on her bed." Aware of her demanding tone, the little girl added a less serious, "Please."

The three children were alone on the jet at the moment. Even Victoria was outside conferring with the adults, which only served to concern the children more. They were generally never left alone.

A sigh from the tips of her toes worked its way up Emily-Grace's body as David gently laid three small puppy chew toys on the round bed the family kept in the jet, once for Snow and now for her cousin, Fluffy. Emily-Grace set the new puppy carrier down on the sofa at the back of the jet, and oversaw David's careful movements. Dylan reached for the carrier, but Emily-Grace's hand shot out and slapped him away. Flinching, the littlest Sawyer protested with a loud, "Owww!" He rubbed one hand over the other and perched his small butt on the edge of the sofa.

"I'll do it. You're too rough all the time." A few seconds later, Emily-Grace sat down next to Dylan, reached into the carrier, and took out the small bundle of quivering fur. Cradling the newest puppy in her arms, she contemplated the tiny paws and lightly touched a front one with a sorrowful finger as Snow's innocent, loving eyes passed through her heart and slipped away.

David padded over to the empty space on his sister's right side and sat down. The carrier was behind him. He shoved it away. It was purple, not at all like the one Snow was drowned in, but none of the Sawyer kids could ever look at it without thinking about their beloved first puppy and the horrible way she died.

Extending a hand, David drew his thin fingers through Fluffy's white fur, on her tiny head. The puppy was awake. She peeked up at him from her sweet and soulful damp puppy eyes. David smiled. His bony shoulders relaxed, and he swiped a long swath of hair off his forehead and tucked it behind his ear.

Emily-Grace turned partway around and stared out of a small window. The grownups were in their usual serious huddle. None of those grownups were her father or mother.

David drew her back to him. "Other kids don't have jets, you know," he announced smartly. "Some of them don't even have cars. Stella told me." He was still gently touching Fluffy's head. Dylan was tenderly petting the puppy's rump.

Emily-Grace was holding the precious dog like a fragile egg. In her soul she knew Fluffy was just about the only good thing binding her and her two brothers together, anchoring them to the earth while the rest of their world shattered into pieces, flinging all three children into a sort of unified but detached hopelessness while this new madness haunted their family.

"I know," Emily-Grace sighed. "I'm glad we have the jet. I don't ever want to come back to the ranch. Ever. Ever ever ever."

"I don't want Daddy to come back to *Sacred Peace*," David added. "Ever. Ever ever ever."

"Ever ever ever," Dylan echoed.

"Emily-Grace…" David got lost in thought. The way the puppy was looking at him, laying her head on her tiny paws, trusting all of them, was making his heart swell. David almost cried, little Fluffy was so beautiful and perfect and loving. "Is Daddy gonna be okay? Nobody's saying."

Shoring up her body, Emily-Grace wriggled herself more toward the outer edge of the sofa. Bending over the puppy so her brothers couldn't see her eyes, she said honestly, "I don't know. I don't know what's going on. I don't care. I just want to go to La Casa and live with Grammie forever."

Little boy fingers left the puppy's rump and wound their way through Emily-Grace's arm. Dylan snuggled in close. "I want Daddy," he whispered. His small Jacob-eyes, blue as the sky in late afternoon but far less hopeful than usual today, buried themselves in his wise sister's much paler blues.

A lump formed in Emily-Grace's throat. She was the oldest and therefore the most senior of the Sawyer children. She may as well have been thirty. Or eighty. "It's okay, Dylan," she said in her worried high-pitched little girl voice. The assurance came out like a song, all up and down and melodic in a sacred kind of way, as if her words were gospel truth. "Sawyer Strong, Momma says. Remember?"

Nodding, even though he hardly understood what she was telling him, Dylan laid his head against his sister's shoulder and studied the fragile puppy in her arms. He watched his brother pat the soft white fur and wished he didn't have to leave the ranch that his sister hated. To Dylan, it was deeply loved because it had a pony, and a saddle with an intoxicating leather smell, and it had safe places to run to and hide in. At the ranch Dylan could wear rubber boots all day if he wanted to instead of those stiff black dress shoes his grandmother made him wear to his momma's and daddy's special events, and if he felt like it he could lie in the grass forever and stare up at the clouds and wonder why some of them looked like dinosaurs and why others looked like turtles.

A shuffle at the front of the jet got the instant attention of all three children. Their mother appeared, a hazy silhouette in the gray light from the open door. The kids watched as she turned to someone outside—Matt or Charlie, they thought knowingly—and said, "Give me a few minutes, okay?"

To Jessie, the sight of her three children snuggled up together with their beloved 'second chance puppy' was almost enough to do her in entirely. The hardest part of parenting, she'd learned the hard way, was in trying to put on a brave face when all she really wanted to do was sink into her children's cherished young arms and let them be the ones to offer comfort and healing. It was excruciating for it to be the other way around.

Sucking in a breath for courage, she tiptoed down the short aisle toward her babies, and dropped down onto the ottoman in front of them.

Outside, everyone grew silent, expectant. Collectively, they all held their breath and waited and wondered. If Jessie lost it, somebody would need to go running. Charlie eyed Matt carefully. He didn't think the guy would be capable of holding Jessie up if she needed help. Shadowed crags under Matt's eyes were running circles around themselves. His shoulders were slumped in exhaustion. Little did Charlie know, he was in every bit as rough shape as Matt. They were all just barely hanging on.

Inside, Jessie smiled sadly and laid a hand on Fluffy's miniature white head. The puppy sniffed into the air and looked over at her. Unable just yet to meet her children's eyes, Jessie glanced over to the side. On the floor was a cozy nest Emily-Grace had created for the little furball. Jessie ran her eyes over the soft bed, the puppy's food and water dishes, the tiny toys all laid out so carefully…

Such childish wonder, such innocence and hope, all wrapped up in the sweet love of a puppy.

Josh…Jessie's mind catapulted back to Josh, the father of these scared children, the giver of the puppy. Of both puppies.

You knew. A wave of nausea passed over Jessie. *Josh, you bastard,* she cried inwardly. *You knew these children would need this puppy.* Such confusing feelings…Jessie wanted to kill him herself for doing this to her, to their children, for putting them through this new hell.

Matt's quiet warning flitted across her mind. *Okay, Wheeler,* she warned herself inwardly. *Get your shit together. These babies need you. Besides. You could be wrong. God, I hope I'm wrong.*

None of the kids had uttered a word. The Sawyer children knew they were different from other kids, that their family was different. The way people always treated their mother and father as if they were somehow special made the kids believe that they were. Although out of everyone, they saw the real sides of their parents. The damaged sides. The sides that hurt.

"Kids," Jessie started, finally looking up and into three sets of frightened eyes, "you've done such a good job taking care of Fluffy. Fluffy is the most spoiled puppy on the planet."

"Thank you, Momma." Emily-Grace was the children's spokesperson. Besides, in her mind, Fluffy was her responsibility. Daddy had given the puppy to her, really, not to the boys. But she was willing to share the furball love. To spread sweet Fluffy's peace and hope around.

"You're wondering about Daddy," Jessie said, squeezing David's shoulder as she talked, and laying her other hand on Dylan's knee. "Grammie told you he's doing okay, right?"

"Charlie did."

Jessie took in David. It was Emily-Grace who had spoken again, but under her hand Jessie felt David tense up. Drawing her fingers along his cheek, moving that rogue layer of hair that bugged him as much as the longer swath drove the kids' father nuts, Jessie allowed a tiny light to filter into her eyes. "You look so much like him," she said softly. "Like your daddy. Those beautiful eyes," she added, a little afraid to look at Dylan, who hadn't yet quite figured out his biological parentage and how it affected his place in the family.

"Can we go now?" The look in Emily-Grace's eyes, like a cornered animal, was disconcerting. She was telegraphing a sheer, desperate need to fly away, to outrun her troubles.

"Like mother, like daughter, huh?" Jessie spoke in a serious, low tone.

Emily-Grace snuggled the puppy up a little tighter, and leaned toward her mother. "I don't ever want to come back here," she stated firmly. "I want to live in Vancouver all the time."

"Right now, honey, so do I." Bending forward, Jessie drew her daughter to her and kissed her forehead. "And guess what, you three? I have some really good news." Instantly, the three brightened. Good news to them was like a drug right now. They needed it the way Fluffy needed food and water.

"Auntie Kayla is having her baby as we speak. And I know Grammie will take you to meet the new little one."

"And soon we'll have a new baby too." Emily-Grace was almost, but not quite, smiling.

"We will, indeed. Get lots of sleep these nights, all of you, because soon our new little one will be waking us up."

"In Vancouver?" The usually quiet David was talking now. His lips were pursed and thin.

Jessie noticed that he was still absently running his little boy fingers through the puppy's soft white fur. "You bet, sweetheart. We'll be bringing Daddy back to Vancouver as soon as he is feeling well enough to travel. Hey, David, you're reading so good these days. When you get back, why don't all three of you pick out some books you know Daddy likes, so you can read to him? He'll need some quiet time when he gets home."

Dylan piped up. "What about me?"

"You can show him some pictures, honey. Daddy and you will have lots to talk about, I know it." Tapping him lightly on the knee, Jessie had to fight the urge to break down again. It kept sneaking up on her, as if a wind kept coming up and stirring up waves of grief, trying to unsettle her, to throw her off her feet once and for all. Gathering all three children as close as she could, Jessie sighed into their young bodies and murmured a silent prayer for their safety. Letting go, she struggled through the sorrow of sending them off to Vancouver without her. Without their father.

Fretfully tossing her curls, she rallied. "Now, I want all of you to have a really good time with Grammie Dee. Don't be on your electronics too much, you know she doesn't like that." Leaning forward, Jessie whispered conspiratorially, "She's old. But don't any of you tell her I said that."

"Grammie always says she's young at heart, Momma." Again, David. Emily-Grace had grown quiet.

Laughing, surprising herself, Jessie nodded in agreement. "And she is. Truly. Grammie Dee is a special lady. Now, all of you be good, and when you meet your new cousin, um," she glanced at Dylan, "when Dylan meets his little brother or sister, you make sure you send me and Daddy lots of pictures. We'll be looking for them."

With one last hug, Jessie rose and let her anxious gaze drift over her children. All three were silent and watchful. She, their mother, was tired and worried. And they took their cues from her.

A few minutes later, Jessie stepped carefully down the outside stairs of the jet. She landed in Deirdre's arms. "Please, please, please don't give them too much sugar," she begged tearfully, sneaking a sideways glance at Carlotta. Pointing a finger, she added, "And that means you, Mizz 'we always gotta be baking' lady."

"They'll be fine," Deirdre asserted, calling forth some hidden strength she didn't know she had. "We'll take care of your children. You take care of my man. And yours."

"Of course." A small smile worked its way across Jessie's face. "I'm sending Charles back to the condo for sleep as soon as I get back. After he has steak with Jon, Wes and Zach, that is. A small steak for him. With salad on the side. And Matt, too, Matt will be with them too." A wistful glance toward the quietly watching Matt eventually drifted sideways to Charlie. "And Charlie. You guys need to eat too, you know. And sleep. Y'all look like shit."

Twenty minutes later, the jet was airborne. There were no more tears left to shed. A sick, aching knot in her gut was all consuming, but Jessie swallowed new tears away and proudly raised her chin. "Come on," she said to Matt and Charlie. "Back to the darkness we go."

As the jet with her children on board disappeared into the clouds above the western prairie city, Jessie wished, with all her might, that she were on it too.

Inside, all three children stared out of windows and watched their mother disappear.

Chapter Four

Later in the day, as impending night rolled its twilight warning over the city in unhurried blue-black grace, Jessie brought her feet up on the end of the sofa in Josh's hospital room and laid her head on Matt's comfortable lap. "Glad you decided to skip the steak and stay with me," she said. From where she lay on her back she could see Josh, although her view of him was distorted since she was lying with her feet in the same general area as his head.

A subdued grunt was Matt's tired answer.

Throughout the long day, Jessie had watched the men around her circle constantly, like crows looking for places to land. With the exception of Matt, none of them seemed capable of sitting for longer than two minutes. Instead, they spent most of their day in the cafeteria until Charles and Charlie finally took the lead and escorted everyone out to dinner. They left with a murmured directive to Jessie to stay put and not go wandering.

"We're bringing Shanda back with us," Charlie promised as if Shanda, a woman who loved two of the same men Jessie did, could possibly be any great comfort. Jane had popped in earlier while her two children passed the time at *Sacred Peace's* on-set daycare, but she was home in Canmore now, likely settling Lucas for the night and getting Stella bathed and ready for school tomorrow. Just thinking about their uncomplicated lives made Jessie wince with a regretful, wishful ache.

Now, Jessie was almost drifting off to sleep—it helped that Matt was lovingly brushing his fingers along her cheek and back along her hairline as she dozed—when a new shape filled the doorway. Half-expecting to see Shanda there with Charlie, Jessie and Matt both looked over at the same time.

It was Arnie.

Jessie sat up, a little too quickly given her lack of both proper nutrition and adequate sleep. The room spun. "Whoa," she breathed, picking a spot out on the floor and begging it to stay still, grabbing Matt's knee with one hand and gripping the edge of the sofa with the other.

"That's it," Matt decreed. "You're going to the condo, missy."

"Not yet I'm not, bossy pants." Lifting her head, Jessie managed to fit a sense of Arnie into her spinning mind. Slowly, the room came back to order and his image stabilized. She sat back while Matt worriedly assessed her for signs of an impending faint. In one brusque motion, she pushed him away. "I'm fine." Arnie didn't get off so easily. To him, Jessie mouthed off. "Hello, Mr. Downtown Eastside Savior. Too bad you can't save them all. But then again, you actually have to be in a person's general vicinity if you want to keep them from getting shot."

"Easy, Jessie," Matt warned, rising and reaching out a hand to greet Arnie. "Arnie. Surprised to see you here."

"I'm not." Jessie stood but she wavered unsteadily. Both Matt and Arnie were at her side in a second. "Leave me alone," she ordered and backed away. She had the sense to at least sit back down. "If I'm sitting, you guys are sitting," she snapped, and kicked the chair Matt dragged over earlier in the day in Arnie's general direction. He stopped it with his foot, moved in front, and eased his body down. Matt was a little more tentative before eventually easing down next to Jessie.

Arnie gestured toward the prone Josh. "He gonna pull through?"

"He damn well better. Cuz I've got a few things I want to say to him before he joins some random angel choir. And none of what I have to say is nice." Jessie sent Arnie her best surly, pissed-off frown.

Matt shot her a hard look before he turned back to Arnie. "He's on the mend. The doctors are optimistic."

"Mmm. I see." Shuffling his feet, Arnie avoided Jessie's accusing stare.

She jumped on him. "What the hell are you doing here, Arnie? What's the point of you now?"

"Jessie—"

"Shut up, Matt. I want to know what the hell kind of purpose Arnie has in coming here. You," she blamed, pointing a trembling finger at her old buddy, "should have been here when Josh needed you."

"To do what?" Arnie sniped back. "To leap in front of that bullet? The way I heard it, none of you knew it was coming."

"At least one of us did. I think. Although I'm not sure he knew exactly when. Musta been a helluva thing, waiting to get shot."

No surprise registered on Arnie's face. Not a flicker. But Arnie didn't have a chance to retort. Carrying two large trays of take-out sushi, Shanda wafted into the room on a low pair of orange Converse Trainers, and in a drifting haze of coconut Body Shop lotion.

"Scoot," she said to Matt, and squished down between him and Jessie. "Eat," she demanded.

Groaning, Jessie turned her head away. "Not hungry."

Matt deflated. When Shanda held sushi out to him, he, too, shook his head.

Arnie caught Matt's eye just as Charles and Charlie strode back in to check on things. Quick to realize that Arnie's serious, light eyes were three shades darker than usual, and narrowed in earnest but silent communication, Matt leveraged his hands on his thighs and stood upright.

"Give you ladies some time for girl talk," he muttered, and signaled to all three men to follow. "I need coffee. Shanda, get some food into that girl and her baby."

"Yes-suh." Irreverence wasn't generally Shanda's specialty, but her eyebrows darted up into a question mark when her man left the room without so much as a touch. "Wow," she said, settling back against the sofa. "Who's that scary guy, and what did he do with my boyfriend?"

"Down, girl." Leaning against the far side of the small sofa, Jessie exhaled to a count of six and rested her chin on a crooked elbow on the armrest.

Shanda followed her gaze over to Josh. "We'll help him through this," she promised softly.

"If only you could," Jessie sighed. "Help's not his thing. My man's the lonely cowboy sort. He prefers to ride his ranges alone, or haven't you noticed, Shanda? Of course you haven't," she answered herself. "You're too busy screwing."

The shock factor no longer worked on Shanda. Jessie's nasty jibe was not a complete surprise. "I'm not going to apologize for loving Matt, Jessie. He's a very good man. But I gather you know that. Far too well, in fact."

"He's a satisfying fuck, if that's what you're hinting at."

"Jesus, Jessie, you're well past high school. Can we not do the jealous drama queen thing while your gunshot husband is lying in a bed right next to us? And while the man I love spent pretty much the entire last two days—and a night—holding your hand?" Shanda lowered her voice when a nurse who hurried in to check Josh's vitals gave her a stern look. "I care about Josh too, you know. A lot. And I had to go to work today and run lines that, for once, I didn't give a shit about."

Shanda had been trying to focus on eating some of the sushi herself, but now she tossed the takeout dish down onto the low table in front of them. It skidded almost to the end, where it might have fallen off and made a huge mess, but neither woman even flinched. On days like today, messes were totally subjective.

Jessie stared over at Josh and wished she could disappear. The kids were safe at La Casa now, likely settling the puppy and getting ready for bed. Grateful for the kind of support Charles and Dee always offered when she needed it, Jessie was glad to focus on them for a minute instead of on the constant woes that consumed her. "I'm sorry, Shanda," she said. "Honestly, I am. Matt's been great, he's always great. I can't say I would be functional at all if he wasn't around. And that's relative. Because I don't feel very damned functional. I appreciate you not demanding that he leave me. I needed him. I—need—him."

"This is the thing, Jessie." Tucking a foot up underneath her butt, Shanda turned her body around so she faced her sort-of friend. "I need him too. Matt works far beyond the call of duty when it comes to you." She softened. "Look, I recognize that the last few days have been hell, but honey, Matt's my guy. Not yours. Tonight he's coming home with me. Okay? He needs to sleep, and he needs me to make him sleep."

Closing her eyes, Jessie swallowed back a rush of fear and worry. A night alone in the hospital without trusted Matt by her side was inconceivable. Yet she was well aware that Shanda was absolutely correct in assessing Matt's devotion as 'beyond the call.' "Okay," she whispered. "I get it."

Jessie never felt more alone. More abandoned.

In the bed, Josh moved. Something beeped. Both women tensed, but the nurse was still there; calmly, she pushed a button on a monitor. Josh relaxed, and remained asleep.

Reaching beside her, Jessie grabbed Shanda's fingers and held on tight.

Chapter Five

$\mathcal{M}$att was the last one to enter the small conference room where Charles led the men.

Charlie strode to the window and closed the blinds. Turning around to Matt, sending a confused look to Arnie, he raised his arms in question. "What?" he asked. "You looking to get rehired, Arnie? You're a goddamned gunshot too late."

Charles walked by Charlie and clapped him on the shoulder. "Let's sit," he said. Nobody moved.

Arnie had yet to speak. Clearly he had something to say, and it was serious. Punctuating the grim nature of his visit, he chose to remain standing. Eventually Matt crossed the room, leaned his butt against a window ledge, folded his arms over his chest, and waited. His tentative movements gave permission for Charlie to take action. Shoving out an all-purpose metal-framed chair, angling it toward the other men, Charlie sat on the table and rested his feet on the chair seat. Charles took his cue from Arnie and remained standing, but he laid a hand on the end of the table as if it could somehow carry his burden.

Once they settled, Arnie didn't keep them in suspense. He nodded at Matt. "What's Jessie thinking?"

Matt bristled. "About what happened? Darkness. That's what."

"Elaborate."

Hesitating, Matt eyed Charlie before he spoke. Charlie leaned forward and listened in uneasy earnest. "She thinks there might be a connection between Josh getting shot and some, uh, plans he spoke of over the summer. Plans Josh wouldn't expound upon."

Arnie grimaced. "Jessie's right. She knows how to read Josh. He set this up."

"Jesus Christ." Charlie white-knuckled the back of the chair. Tilting it toward him, he laid his forehead on his fingers. "I'm gonna be sick."

Charles was confused. "You're nuts. Why would Josh do such a thing?"

Matt uncrossed his arms and gripped the window ledge. Turning a sickly shade of green, he picked out a worn spot on the rug to stare at.

Arnie focused on Charles, since he was the only man who seemed capable of maintaining eye contact. "Josh brokered a deal. He thought he could call off the dogs, if you will, if Morgan got what he wanted."

"But Morgan didn't get…Jesus, the kids, Arnie!" Charles vaulted for the door, but Arnie grabbed his elbow and stopped him.

"According to my source, the perceived debt for Morgan's kid has also been paid."

Matt's head darted up. Charlie closed his eyes and concentrated on not puking by silently counting.

Arnie went on. "In cash. The deal Josh brokered involved cash for a kid and, well," he shrugged, "himself. Josh was supposed to die."

"He's going to pull through, Arnie." Charles was white.

"S'why I'm here. We need to work this out. We need to take advantage of this."

"Always lookin' at the bright side, are ya, Arnie?" Charlie finally raised his weary head. "Lookin' to shine up that halo, are you? Seems it got a little rusty when you bailed on Josh."

Arnie's voice thickened. "You wanna know why I bailed on Josh, asswipe? I'll tell you why. He asked me to hire a hit man, that's why. For him, to kill him. Let me repeat that. He wanted me," Arnie shoved a pointy finger in his own chest, "to hire a guy to point a gun at Josh and pull the goddamned trigger. Tell me, Charlie, would you have done that? To Jessie, to the kids?"

Straightening, Charlie reassessed the older man in front of him. All of them were still, and rendered almost immobile in a kind of respectful shock. "You've done this before," Charlie stated blankly.

Arnie stared him down. "Ya think?" he retorted disrespectfully. "Jesus, Charlie. You're so fucking naïve."

"And you're so goddamned wound up." Throwing back his chair so that it teetered, Charlie leapt off the table and gave the muscled guy a shove. "What the hell do you think you're doing, marching in here like some fucking know-it-all and telling us that Josh ordered a hit on himself that almost killed him?"

"Take it easy, Charlie." Matt launched himself forward and clutched a handful of Charlie's jacket. Hauling him backwards, he said to Arnie, "So if you refused to set this up for Josh, who did?" He didn't bother wading into the other unconscionable topic Jessie raised earlier, which was why would Josh not just kill himself, if he thought it would end Morgan's vicious need for vengeance. There would be time to go deeper into those murky shadows later.

"Morgan did." Warily eyeing Charlie, Arnie added, "His goonie, I mean. Caulfield. On Morgan's behalf."

"The guard."

"And Josh got to them how?"

Squinting at Matt, Arnie ran two fingers over his chin. "That's privileged information."

"Bullshit." Charles entered the fray. "Talk, Arnie."

"Look," Arnie growled, elbowing past Charlie toward Charles, "we have more important things to consider right now. Talking is wasting time."

Oddly, it felt like the air pressure in the room was intensifying. To Matt, it all of a sudden felt like he was breathing through a tube. He had to push the words out. "Josh will survive. Morgan didn't get his end of the bargain." His voice was quiet, even. Controlled. Disconnected. "This insanity isn't over." *Jessie…could she still be a target?*

Charlie's eyes were wild. Rifling fingers through his hair, he almost moaned aloud. "We've got security everywhere," he said, almost to steady himself as opposed to calming the others. "Nobody's getting to him, right? Or to Jessie."

Charles' eyes were latched into Arnie's. "That's not it," he decided. "That's not why you're here."

Respectfully, Arnie nodded at him. "We've been handed an opportunity here, boys. We can end this unholy war and save this family."

"How?" Charlie was losing it. "Morgan's got way too much power. Even behind bars he's got a long fucking reach."

"Easy," Arnie answered. "What is it you guys do every day, huh? Think about it. You're always devising positive conclusions. Happy endings."

"What?" Backing up, Charlie leaned against the wall. "You talking about *Sacred Peace*?"

Arnie swiveled around to him. "You got people on your team you can trust?"

Charlie blanched. "What the hell can *Sacred Peace* do to help Josh and Jessie? Their lives are not a fucking television show."

Matt grunted. Everyone looked at him. "Arnie thinks we should write ourselves an ending."

"Meaning?" Charles asked.

Waiting a second to be sure he was reading Arnie right, Matt studied his face and then spoke directly to him. "You think we should hide Josh."

Arnie shrugged in confirmation. "Morgan needs to believe Josh is dead, Matt. That's the only way this game will end."

"And how the hell do we accomplish that? Josh is recovering. Morgan will know, hell, the whole world will know that Josh survived." That was from Charlie, who was starting to see this whole thing as a whole new level of some already incomprehensible nightmare.

"We're moving him soon, are we not?" Charles said, clueing in. The pieces were clicking into place. "If the world has to believe Josh is dead, there are ways we can make that happen. We'll be the ones arranging his death this time. We'll be in control. Josh should have come to us instead of trying to figure this thing out on his own."

As Charlie digested that, Matt dove in again. He took them down another dark path by firing a new question at Arnie. "What'd Josh pay for, uh," Matt choked on the bile that rose in his throat, "uh, to save his child? What'd that cost him?"

"Don't matter," Arnie responded. "I don't know, anyway. I just know he paid. A lot."

"We'll get the money back. We have ways," Charles said. "Connections."

Arnie shook his head. "No, we won't. Let it go. Josh doesn't need the money. Jessie alone is worth millions. Let Morgan think he got his vengeance. Let this thing end. It's the only way. Even the shooter, it doesn't matter if he ever gets caught. He got paid for a job. Period."

"Jesus, your lot sees your own damn shades of black and white, huh, Arnie?" Sickened, Charlie reclaimed his seat on the table, clasped his hands, and bent over them.

Lifting a thumb and finger to his chin, Matt started a slow back and forth pacing in front of the back window. "Jessie can't know; about Josh, I mean, about what he did. We have to convince her that she's wrong. Otherwise she'll never trust him again."

"And what about hiding Josh? She'll have to go too. She's done. She's finally getting what she wanted. Does she have to die too? The kids?" Charlie was near tears. So many dreams coming to an end…and not by choice. Not really. If they went through with this new plan, Charlie's best friends would essentially have to live new lives under some made-up Keating version of the witness protection program.

Stopping, Matt pondered that, what it would be like to never see Jessie sing on stage again, to never again see her work her magic over a crowd. "No," he determined. "Jessie doesn't have to travel with Josh when he, uh, dies. That means she can continue on with her life on some level, although she'll slow down. She'll have to anyway, at least for a while because she's having the baby. That'll buy her some unquestioned down time. She can still do shows. Films. Just…Josh can't. He'll have to stay undercover. Jessie will have to go along with that. The way she presents herself to the public will have to be that her husband is dead. She won't have a choice."

"The kids?" Charlie was wild. "They're too young. They can't keep this kind of secret."

"Until we can safely move them to be with Josh, how about this," Matt posed. "At first their father will simply be missing. That way there won't be any need for them to lie. And they can be tutored in Vancouver to keep them from having to answer painful questions."

Charlie waded back in. "And how's Jessie supposed to keep the secret that Josh is still alive? We can't let her think he's dead. I don't care how nasty all of this is, that would destroy her entirely."

"Simple," Arnie suggested. "Jessie's a multiple Oscar winning actor. This, my friend," he clapped Charlie on the shoulder, "will simply be the role of a lifetime."

"It'll work. It'll give them peace. Finally." Heaving out a long, low sigh, Charles shrank into a chair by the table and rubbed his tired cheeks with both palms.

A subdued voice broke the contemplative silence that followed. "Peace, is it? You think this will give them peace? I think you're forgetting something, guys." Matt shoved his hands in his pockets and stared glumly at his friends, at the men who had the power to change Josh's and Jessie's lives—and his own—by virtue of snapping their fingers. By virtue of removing the much-loved Sawyer family to some secret location far, far away.

"What?" Charlie straightened as Charles looked up and lowered his fingers to pick nervously at his tie. "What have we forgotten? If you're thinking of *Sacred Peace,* we've already got the writers going full tilt to rewrite the last episode of the season without our star."

"Did you think about season three yet, Charlie?"

Gulping, Charlie had to draw deep to try and play the tough guy. "We'll have to recast the lead."

"And how happy do you suppose that will make Josh? He must have made some kind of peace with ending his life. What do you think will be running through his head when he comes to and discovers that he's suddenly got to live a life he'll hate? A life without work? Where he can't be himself?"

"Jessie did it. I guess she'll have to help him figure it out."

"And when Jessie goes to work? I hate to be the downer here, fellas, but this may not be the answer we're all hoping for."

"No," Charles agreed, meeting Matt's eyes. "But right now, it's the only answer we have."

Arnie stirred, and all eyes turned to him. "How soon can we 'move' Josh to Vancouver? When will he be stable enough to travel?"

"And when should we tell Jessie what we're planning and why?" Charlie was shrinking by the second. He didn't have the nerve to look at Matt or at Charles. The reality of living a life without Jessie close by was unfathomable. Above and beyond that, there was a sneaky, manipulative feeling about all this…about playing God and 'burying' Josh while formulating a plan that would keep Jessie, at least occasionally, in their lives and on the stage.

"In the immediate future, we don't tell Jessie," Matt decreed. "Not until we determine it's safe for her to know. And not until we think she can handle it." Matt stared Charlie down. The hard look was a warning—*Don't you dare.*

"How're you going to do it, Matt? How are you gonna live without her in your life every day?"

"Easy," Matt said, lying through his teeth. "I'm going to marry Shanda. That's how."

Whipping open the door to the small space, he strode through the doorway and turned right—away from Josh's room, away from Shanda, away from the men who now held the Sawyer family's hope in their hands. The last few steps were jogged, out of the main door and around the corner to a quiet place behind the trauma center where he could puke his guts out undisturbed.

Above him, the stars in the night sky were big and expansive, but Matt could barely see them. The skies were clear, but the light pollution from the city below made the stars cloudy anyway. Hanging his head, clutching his thighs, Matt leaned back against the brick and bent over his knees. He rarely cried, but when he did it seemed it was always over Jessie, over some new loss of her, over the lack of control he felt he had over her. When Matt shed tears, more often than not they were over those sweet, pale blue eyes he first spied at La Casa all those years ago when Jessie was young and scared and lonely and silent. Tonight was no exception.

To Matt, Jessie was still in the submerged Lexus, placing her fingers up against the glass of a window, pleading with him…Like a mute ghost, still asking him to help save her and her daughter.

Once again, Jessie was unreachable. And once again, she was about to disappear into a dim nothingness.

$\mathcal{A}$ rustle in the bed alerted Jessie to the fact that Josh was stirring. She was alone—it was almost eleven. Shanda and Matt were still around the hospital, down at the café grabbing decaf coffees, holding hands and stealing kisses, she supposed. Didn't matter. Nothing seemed to matter. Fatigue and worry had stolen Jessie's capacity to care about the two of them, although she missed like hell Matt's trusted presence and gentle touch.

A low moan drew Jessie to her husband's bedside. Peering down at him, it occurred to her at first that Josh didn't know where he was. Late that afternoon, the ventilator that eased his breathing had been removed, but to help keep his lungs inflated he still had a chest tube in place to evacuate air and residual fluids from his chest cavity. Sore and confused, in that hazy place between reality and a drugged sleep, the only way Josh was really capable of communicating was by virtue of setting his intense, scared eyes on Jessie's.

Jessie wrapped her cool fingers around his warm ones. Matt's voice echoed in her brain. *Stay positive, Wheeler,* she demanded of herself. *Offer comfort.* Still, in her heart was anger along with a sense of betrayal she couldn't quite wrap her mind around. Didn't matter what Matt said. Everything about this latest catastrophe just felt wrong.

Pushing the unsettled feelings aside, Jessie managed a solemn, "Hey, there."

Josh blinked up at her and tried to talk, but all that came out was a garbled mumble.

"You're at the trauma center in Calgary, Josh," Jessie told him, leaning down so he could more easily focus on her. "You got on the wrong end of a…a bullet." Even saying the words was excruciating. "I guess I kinda pulled you to one side just as the bullet left the gun, because it was meant to kill you. And it would've. Instead, you're gonna have a sore lung for a while. You and me, we're, um, well, we're getting too comfortable with hospitals, Josh. We gotta stop hanging out in hospitals."

Josh's eyes flitted down to Jessie's belly. She moved closer. Lifting his right hand, Jessie held it to their growing baby, back-on, with her fingers wrapped around his. She stared at the hand she used to count on to be strong. "So I guess you'll get to meet this little guy." *Whether you want to or not.* "I say guy because it feels like a boy to me, I don't know why. Just does."

Drawing in a long, nasally breath, Jessie swiped a fist at the outer corner of each eye. She was still lost in Josh's big hand against her belly, wrapped securely in her own fingers. "I'll be honest with you. I'm glad my Montreal film got recast, because it's been a busy summer and I just want to be with my family right now. We're moving you back to Vancouver, to Vancouver General, okay? Because of the whole no-spleen thing you may have to stay a little longer in the hospital, Josh. Between the rest of us we're gonna get the ranch closed up. Charlie was by earlier and he says *Sacred Peace* is doing some rewriting to end the season the best way they can. He'll likely bring you in for pickups, I suppose, to try to get something shot, um, er, filmed, to wrap up the storyline, but I don't know if I want you coming back here. I honestly don't know what I want right now. I'm just so…confused, Josh."

Stealing a glance up at him, Jessie sniffled and wiped her eyes with the sleeve of Shanda's borrowed sweater. "We've got things to talk about, Sawyer, when you're feeling better. For now Matt says I need to let you sleep. Good old Matt, huh? Always looking out for us, although I've got orders from Shanda to loosen up and let him wander free more. You'd think I have the guy on a leash or something."

The soft shush of hurrying shoes swept into the room. Jessie watched a big, slightly stooped black male nurse aptly scroll through readings on the monitor on Josh's other side. "He was awake for a minute?" the nurse asked.

"Um, yeah, he is, uh…" Looking down, Jessie saw that Josh had drifted back off to sleep. "Well, he was." She deflated. "I guess he didn't want to listen to me ramble on." She tried to smile. "I was definitely rambling. I don't have a clue what to say to him right now. I don't even know what to think."

"He'll sleep a lot over the next few days. He's got a lot going on in that body right now. Quite a battle."

In his mind, too, Jessie thought. *You have no freaking idea.* She took a closer look at the nurse and decided the big guy was in his early to mid thirties, super efficient, and always in a hurry. He had nice eyes; they were dark but were flecked with just enough light to lend an air of compassion and kindness.

Out loud Jessie came back with, "I know, uh…new antibiotics partly because of the spleen thing, and pain meds." She crumbled. "My husband doesn't do well with drugs. This sucks, for so many reasons. And it's not gonna get any simpler when he heals." For some reason, it was easier to unload her worries on this stranger who, by the way he was cautiously smiling at Jessie, seemed willing to engage in conversation.

Jessie lifted Josh's fingers so she could brush her lips across them before she laid his hand back down on the bed. A second later, like a little girl being scolded by a parent she bowed her head and started twisting and retwisting the bottom hem of the yellow cardigan.

"I hear the two of you have a trusted counselor back in Vancouver," the nurse offered. "Make the time to see her."

Jessie looked up. "Trudy, yes, we're lucky to have her. But still…" Memories of the breakup after the whole Langley thing rose up and choked Jessie. She coughed them away. "There's never a quick fix. Not with this man."

"Do you mind if I speak frankly?" The guy's voice was caring but firm.

It startled Jessie. People didn't usually speak to her this way. Instead, they were usually deferential and nervous, second-guessing everything they said or else just blurting out stream-of-consciousness stuff. Waving a hand to accentuate her words, she said, "Please. Be my guest."

"Addictions are a life sentence. I think you know this."

"Sucks," Jessie agreed sadly. "So fucking hard. But it's like we never get to just be normal, to fight the way most people do. To stay on an even keel so we can try to find balance. We're always climbing up a goddamned cliff. We're always off balance. Sorry." She ducked her head again. "I don't mean to swear. The words just sneak out sometimes."

The nurse bent over Josh and fussed around the chest tube, checking the bandages and whatever else, *for infection maybe,* Jessie thought as she watched, somewhat repulsed and at the same time curious. "It can't be easy for you," the guy was saying as his large hands capably adjusted the tube. "But I think that if you wanted to walk away from this guy you would have done it. The greatest courage a person has, in my opinion—and it's just my opinion, Jessie. A lot of people tell me I'm too outspoken, especially with patients and their families, but I can't help it, it's who I am. The greatest courage," the nurse continued, "is sticking things out to the end when they seem insurmountable. When life seems insurmountable. Not quitting. That's courage. That's strength."

"Sure," Jessie replied. She released her hold on Shanda's sweater and curved her fingers over the bed rail. "I get that. People are always trying to tell me I'm courageous and strong when I'm pretty damned sure I'm the most cowardly and broken person of all. But…" Jessie squinted at the nurse's name tag. "Um, what's your name?"

"Kalon. With a K."

"Um, Kalon, sometimes it's hard, you know? When you have to be strong for," she raised two fingers, "two people. When it's hard enough being strong just for yourself." *Just ask Matt,* she thought. *Ask Matt with his dark circles and slumped shoulders just how hard it is. And he's got all of us Sawyers to worry about. A whole big pretend family.* The new baby crossed her mind. Jessie touched her belly, and immediately let her fingers float away on empty air.

Done checking on Josh, Kalon circled the end of the bed and reached for Jessie's hand. She stiffened, but let him touch her. Holding her hand high, he spread two fingers apart. "V," he said. "Make them a V. Victory. Next time you think about how hard all of this is, picture a positive result. Picture a day when you and your husband are both healthy and happy. Create your future. He's been substance free for a while, right? He's doing okay?" Kalon let go of Jessie's fingers and reached down to tidy, on the side Jessie was on, the light cotton blanket covering Josh.

"Ha!" Jessie jumped on the reference to substance abuse. "I guess you missed the social media frenzy over my man's two-night bender late last spring. I'm pretty sure all of Calgary came out to freeze-frame that one for the sake of posterity."

Kalon looked over at her. "After your accident."

"After I was deliberately run off the road, you mean." A haughty chin-raise coated the remark with disdain and a deep, simmering anger. There was fear there, too, caught up in Jessie's declaration like dust in the wind.

"That'd be hard on a man."

"Jesus. If you're asking me to cut him some slack, I did."

"Jessie…"

Idly, Jessie pondered the fact that Kalon was calling her by her first name. *Everyone always thinks they know us. It's like we somehow belong to them.* "Mmm?" she replied, angling her head at him.

"If you're asking yourself hard questions about all this, about your life with this man, then cut *yourself* some slack. Try asking yourself the easiest questions. The common denominator ones. In my experience I find that these are usually black and white."

Jessie shifted her weight and waited. She watched Kalon for clues.

"Do you love him?" was what he asked her. "Does he love you?"

"Ah. So if this latest disaster is too much for him and Josh goes off the rails again, it's that simple, is it?"

"I told you I was outspoken. And opinionated."

"I've got kids. We've…got kids."

"Then make sure they're protected, but show them the true meaning of love. Show them the down and dirty, gritty truth of what it's like to really, truly love someone. Who says love is a Hollywood romance?"

"You're forgetting one thing. You're forgetting how hard it is to watch someone you love hurt so bad."

"Maybe you're forgetting the sweet joy of holding up someone you love. Of watching them grow past the bad stuff to find peace in the every day."

A tiny smile eked its way forth. "Why do I get the feeling you know true love?"

"I used to."

"Oh. Shit. I'm sorry, Kalon."

"Don't be. We had some good years. Cancer," he admitted, his voice growing thick. "I won't lie to you. It was almost a relief when her suffering ended. She passed on about a year ago."

"Freaking cancer. I'm so, so sorry." Hesitant, Jessie tossed in a question. "Do you have kids?"

"No, I do not. Unless you count the people who come unwittingly through these doors and land on my floor. They're my kids."

"I'm glad you had love."

"Is there anything better? It made the bad times harder, I agree. But it made the good times crazy sweet. I'll never forget my woman, Jessie. But I'll get another taste of love one of these days. All the pain…it's worth it, eh? I'll see ya." Humming a happy tune, Kalon started to move toward the door.

"Kalon?" Jessie called after him.

Resting a hand on the door frame, the big guy stopped and turned back around. "Uh-huh?" he asked.

"I don't want to let him down. I really don't. But there's something…there might be something that…I don't know if I can handle."

Kalon wasn't new to nursing. He wasn't new to the trauma unit, to gunshots. Heck, people didn't generally just randomly land on his doorstep with bullet wounds. Usually there was some nefarious reason to intentionally put a patient into the delicate balance between this world and the next. Still, something about this woman and her music, her films, her family, all of her very public struggles, brought a certain calm knowing to Kalon, even if Jessie couldn't see past her pain today to see it for herself. A warm smile lit up his compassionate eyes. "You're a John Lennon fan, right Jessie?"

The curve ball threw her. "Yeah, I am," she admitted.

"Call me corny if you want to, girl, but there's not a problem in the world that can't be solved with love. Love is the answer, girlfriend. Faith in the future. You'll see your way past this. You and your man. You'll be fine."

And with that, Kalon shuffled his way back out into the hallway, whistling this time. The light tune faded with the waning sound of his soft-soled shoes as he moved down the hall, and Jessie heard him greet some other struggling family member in a room not all that far away.

"Yeesh," she thought. "Spiritual healer disguised as nurse." Looking away from the door back at her prone husband she saw that Josh was awake again. Almost carefully, he was watching her, his half-lidded chocolate eyes struggling to stay open.

Only you know the truth, Jessie considered as she leaned sideways against the bed rail and took his hand in hers again. *And only you can set it—and yourself, and us—free.*

Chapter Seven

By midnight, with assurance from Kalon that he'd call if anything changed, Jessie finally relented and let Matt and Shanda take her back to the condo Charlie shared with Josh. Charlie had texted earlier that he'd be down the hall in Charles' unit when she arrived, so Jessie planned to take advantage of the quiet and tuck herself into Josh's bed and try to grab a few *zzzzs*. At the boys' door, when a young uniformed security guy from the Calgary firm Charles and Matt trusted stepped cautiously out of the way for a moment, Matt touched Jessie's hand and asked if he could have a word.

Leaning against the door with her fingers wrapped around the handle, Jessie gave Shanda a quick scan to see if she was okay with it. "I'm already on her shit list for soaking up your time," Jessie grumped as Shanda, with a surreptitious backwards glance, cruised on down the hall to her own place. "Come in, Matt. What's up? I suppose Shanda asked you to talk to me, to call me off you or something, huh? Jesus, you'd think she'd ease up for a coupla days, at least."

"That's not it." Closing the door behind them, nodding a serious thank you to the hired security first, Matt didn't step any further into the condo than just a few feet.

At first unaware that he wasn't following her to the sofa, at least, like he usually did, or to the stools in the kitchen area, Jessie spoke over her shoulder. "Let's have a drink before you split, Matt. Although I suppose Her Highness might smell it on your breath. Orange juice. Are you allowed to share OJ with me? Are you allowed to make any of your own choices anymore?"

"Jessie, settle down, would you?" Annoyed, Matt's harsh tone got her attention.

Jessie turned. Cocking her head to one side, she said, "Well, then. The master has spoken. This must be serious."

Matt wasn't moving. Running a palm over the stubble on his cheek, which felt foreign and strange and for some reason brought back his summer in Darnley, P.E.I. with Catherine, Matt waited for Jessie to sidle back over to him.

She did, but it took her a minute. She employed a cocky swagger. The look on Matt's face…his hesitancy to come further into the condo…they frightened her. The swagger seemed a good defense. "What is it, Matt?" she asked, fighting against the new icy chill racing up her legs.

"This isn't about Shanda," he said again. "It's about Arnie."

"Oh." After digesting that, a second later Jessie repeated herself, infusing the simple word with a quieter, confused quality. "*Oh*. I figured he had some big reason for showing up. What'd he tell you, Matt? Let me rephrase that. Do I wanna know what he told you?"

There was a moment when Matt considered opening up. For most of their years together, he was often the one to lecture Jessie on always telling the truth. *You spin webs, you get caught up in webs. You lie, and then you wonder why everything gets so messed up when the truth comes out.* There was no way around this latest corner that could save the Sawyer family without bending the truth, however. And part of the truth twisting meant creatively omitting Josh's part in the whole, grand scheme. Earlier, the decision making men of the Keating-Sawyer camp, minus Ulysses since he was now with Deirdre in Vancouver, had agreed to let Matt tell Jessie what they all felt she needed to hear in order to set Josh free from her speculation and worry. Technically, it meant Matt had to lie.

Watching him from just a few feet away now, Jessie was practically swaying from exhaustion. Her eyes were so droopy Matt thought she might fall over. Sitting wasn't an option. Matt knew if they sat together at all, anywhere, that he'd pull her into his arms and hang on for dear life.

He started carefully. "Jessie, what you've been thinking about Josh, what you think he might have done…Arnie got validation from his guy at Brody Pen that this was a directive straight from Morgan."

"Oh. Okay. So. Sweet Jesus. You sure, Matt?"

"I'm sure." Matt blinked, and followed it up with a timid swallow.

Furrowing her brow, Jessie contemplated Matt's equally bone-weary fatigue. "You mean Arnie heard this from Vaughn? That guy? The one I'm writing the song for? Or, um, the one I'm supposed to be finishing a song for?"

"Yes, sweetheart. Vaughn. He got word to Arnie that Morgan orchestrated this. Whatever Josh was planning…" He drifted off.

Jessie finished for him. "Only Josh knows." She sighed. "Oh, thank God. Really." Collapsing with relief was on the agenda—Jessie's knees were shaking—but Matt's intentions were clear. He was not moving further into the room, and so Jessie felt she had no choice but to brace her feet and hold her ground. She rallied. "So what now, Matt? Josh will survive this, the doctors said, thank God. It's just one more vicious, unsuccessful attack that's gonna piss Morgan off even more."

The helplessness wading through Jessie's swimming, pale eyes worried Matt. "Damn, I wish I didn't have to leave you tonight," he murmured. "I'm going to send Charlie down right away, okay? I don't want you to be alone."

"Ha. That makes two of us. Jesus, Matt, I think Shanda's awesome, and the two of you are really great together, but you don't think she'd let you stay tonight? You can sleep on the sofa bed. Heck, you and Shanda can both stay there, although I gotta tell you, tonight I wish you could snuggle up with me. Doesn't have to mean anything or go anywhere," she added hastily. "Just… you're my best friend. I need you. I know you need to spend less time with me and more time with her but tonight, well, this is the worst, Matt. I don't even want to be here. I should be in Vancouver with my kids, or back at the hospital at least. Those nurses, that Kalon guy, they're super amazing, but let's face it. They can't be at Josh's bedside all the time the way I can."

"Slow down, Jessie." Reaching out, Matt took a firm grip on his superstar charge's shoulders. Underneath his hands, she felt frail and weak. Bony, even. "First of all, you do a great job of taking care of everyone else, sweetheart. But tonight you need to grab a few winks of your own. If you feel even remotely guilty about it, think about that beautiful new child you're carrying. You need rest."

"Matt, I…" Hesitating, Jessie pulled up a reservoir of strength and peered deeply into his gentle eyes. "If Josh survives, then…" She gulped. "This isn't over. And what about…what about the kids? Will any of us ever feel safe again? Ever?"

A few well-chosen words were all Matt needed to pull up. He had the power to set Jessie's worries free, to let loose at least some of the heartache that seemingly stalked her every second of every day. "You will, Jessie," he lied, "because Vaughn told Arnie that Morgan considers the debt paid."

"What? How?"

"He called off his minion, that Caulfield guard everyone's apparently afraid of. Morgan told Vaughn that Josh took the bullet and that it was enough. He's leaving the rest up to the universe. As for the kids…sweetheart, your accountant would have come forward with this eventually but Arnie was also told that Josh paid the other part of his debt." He could hardly say the words. "His perceived debt, I should say. For Darin. Morgan's child. In cash."

"He gave Morgan money? H-how much was our child worth, Matt? I think I'm gonna be sick. This all just makes me sick."

Shanda be-damned. Unable to help himself, Matt took Jessie in his arms and offered what comfort he could by virtue of the safe embrace they'd both come to trust over their many years together. Murmuring in her ear, he admitted that he didn't know. "But Arnie and I talked about it, with Charles and Charlie too, Jessie, and we all think it's best just to let it go. The two of you don't need that money."

"What if word gets out at the prison that Josh paid for one of our children's lives? What then, Matt? Everyone will want a chunk of us!"

"Look, we've got a plan. I can't…I don't know the details yet, but when I do…" Pushing her face away from him, Matt held Jessie's cheeks in his palms. "Jessie, it's a good plan. It will take some sacrifices on your part and on Josh's, but it will work. Your family will be safe. Once and for all, you'll all be safe."

Jessie took that in with despair and surrender, visibly melting under his gaze. "I hope so, Matt. I'm so glad…you know, about Josh. God, what he said when he was shot…about being so tired…about wanting me to just let him go…" A low sob accented the shock of hearing those words that, in remembrance, almost sent Jessie to the floor in a crumpled heap.

Matt brought her back to his body and held her close. "I have no doubt that Josh was tired, kid," he said in a tender way he hoped would sound encouraging. "Why wouldn't he be? Look what he went through. Look what all of you went through. When you went into the river, it scared the hell out of him. It was a jolt for all of us, to start thinking about how we could end this thing, or even if we could. I hate to say it, but with Josh being shot, we now have an opportunity we didn't have before. Not really, anyway."

"I don't think I want to know." The words were muffled against Matt's chest.

"Not tonight, you don't. Sleep, my sweet girl, please. What time do you want to head back over to the hospital in the morning?"

"Oh, I dunno…maybe around seven?" Jessie peeked sadly up at him. "You sure you can't stay?"

Fondly, Matt brushed his lips against her cheek. "I wish I could. I really do. Shanda's been very understanding, but tonight I think she's reaching the end of her rope. I'd better head down that way."

"If it's a good lay you need, Matt, I—" Jessie backed up and threw her arms out to the sides. "I've been known to provide."

"Not funny. Although given the circumstances I admire your attempt at humor. I'll see you in the morning."

"Nite, Matt. Thank you. It helps hearing that about Josh. Really, it does. I can't tell you how much it helps. I feel like a big gust of wind just blew in a whole bunch of fresh oxygen."

Matt paused at the door before he found the nerve to turn the handle. Jessie looked so small. She was doing that thing she often did, turning her ankle over and sulking a little so that she appeared childlike and scared. It occurred to him that she was also trying to be brave standing still like that, watching him turn the handle and disappear for the darkest part of the night.

"I'm glad this is all coming to an end, kid," he said, putting a postscript on the late night chat. "It's time."

"I can't…I'm gonna need some time for all of this to just sink in, Matt. Truth? I honestly don't think I'll believe this can end until there are no more notes. No more threats. No more so-called accidents. I suppose, Matt, that I won't truly believe we're safe until I die."

The word almost sank Matt. "You'll feel safe again, Jessie. I swear. You'll see."

"This plan of yours, huh?"

"Ours. We're working it out."

"And I don't get a say?"

"You trust me?"

"You know I do. With my life. With all of our lives. I just don't see how… I don't see any kind of opening, or light here, baby. Not with Josh having paid for our child's safety. It opens too many scary new doors."

"Please, Jessie. Trust me. And while we're on that…the trust thing…" There was one more thing Matt needed to say. "Jessie…Josh getting shot…"

She knew where he was going. It had to come up at some point. Jessie shook her head. "Not your problem, Matt. You had no control over what happened. None of us saw it coming. There was no time to do that 'leaping in front of bullet thing' you do so well. Don't beat yourself up about it."

"You know I would have done what I had to, to help him. You know that, right?"

Taking a few steps toward him, Jessie hooked a finger over his belt, at his side. "Matt, baby, the thing is, you used to just be security. You're so much more than that now. I wouldn't want you in front of that bullet any more than I wanted my husband there. There's no question about how I feel about you." Lifting her fingers, Jessie undid the top two buttons of Matt's shirt as he let go of the door handle, turned to face her, and let her. She slid her hand under the thin fabric, and laid her palm against the New York scar. Underneath the warmth of her skin on his body, Matt tensed, and watched her eyes float away from his to land on the pinched and wrinkled skin as Jessie tenderly ran her fingertips over the scar. "You and me, we're one, remember?" she rasped, her voice heavy and hurting. "There are gonna be pieces to pick up when this all shakes down, when Josh comes home. I need you, Matt. I can't do any of this without you."

There were no words big enough to cover that kind of trust and need. Laying a hand over Jessie's on his skin, Matt choked on what he couldn't say. The times in his life when he lived away from Jessie were excruciating. He was so embroiled in her existence now, in her family's existence, that it was incomprehensible to consider putting distance between them again. He consoled himself with the pretty blonde woman waiting down the hall, the one with the slim, touchable body and pretty, bouncy Marilyn Monroe curls. Plus there would still be events maybe, for Jessie—concerts and the occasional film, he hoped. Would she be happy living a reclusive life? Didn't matter. To the Keating security team, there was no other choice. An opportunity for peace had presented itself. There was now a brass ring of hope, and they had no choice but to grab it.

"Nite, honey," Jessie said softly, brushing her lips against Matt's cheek and staying there for an extra few seconds, closing her eyes as he tipped his face just the slightest bit toward her and buried his hand in her hair, against her head, so he could hold her close. Jessie could feel his warm breath on her cheek. It was a life force, one she counted on, and it gave her strength. "I'll be okay," she sniffled. "I promise."

In the hallway, as the door *shumphed* closed behind him, Matt had to struggle to compose himself before he could speak. Wiping a fist under his nose, he started purposefully down the hallway before he called over his shoulder to the local security, "It's Mathieu tonight, right?"

"Yes, sir." Straw-blond Mathieu was fit and trim. Muscled tattoos danced on the forearms peeking out from below the black jacket that identified him as security.

Matt stopped. "Quebec French or East Coast French?"

"I'm a New Brunswick Acadian. Moncton."

Gesturing toward the door he'd just exited, Matt said, "She'd like that. The east coast connection. A bridge away from her cherished island."

Mathieu grinned. "A long bridge, sir. I used to cross it many times for hockey." He shrugged. "Tournaments, when I was a kid. It was always a thrill to travel over the Confederation Bridge."

Strangely enough, knowing that an east coaster was watching over Jessie tonight helped Matt move his feet further down the hall. There was just something about the hardy stock of people known as Maritimers that engendered trust. As he walked, Matt got down to business. "Come get me if you need to,

Mathieu, if. . .well, just if." Inwardly he silently wondered what might end up requiring his attention overnight. In his mind he pictured Jessie scrunched up alone into a tiny, helpless ball on Josh's bed, quaking from loneliness and fear. It took every reserve of willpower he had in him to compel his feet to keep moving forward, and not to spin around and go back to her. It helped to have the friendly New Brunswicker at Jessie's door.

When he approached Charles' condo, Matt gave the door a good solid rap. A yawning Charlie opened it. A crystal tumbler of bourbon was balanced in one of the actor's hands; the bourbon's amber liquid, reflected in the dim overhead light, was moving in waves and ripples—*like a liquescent, nocturnal animal*, Matt thought weirdly. He shook his head to restore clarity to his muddled brain.

Matt leaned on the door frame on one high, raised arm and tried to relax into Charlie's comfortable, inquisitive scrutiny. "She's here," he said. "Can you leave the *Sacred Peace* paperwork and go down and stay with her, Charlie?"

Rocking back on a heel, the bourbon hovering at his side, Charlie gave Matt a sympathetic half-smile. "Big boy's got his dog collar on tonight? Got your ears cuffed, did ya?"

"Shut it, Deacon," Matt snapped. "I just don't like the idea of leaving Jessie down there alone. She's wiped out."

Charlie's eyes darkened. "You tell her?"

Shadowy and exhausted, nursing his own soothing brandy, Charles appeared. He took a sip and listened.

Matt fisted a hand at his side and answered Charlie. "If you mean did I lie my ass off, yes, I did." Thinking about looking into Jessie's frightened eyes while he lied outright jolted Matt into an even deeper wretched, regretful mess. He forced the rest of the words out. "This is one secret that I hope all of us will be taking to our graves. I get why Josh did what he did, but let's face it, Jessie never will."

"You're wrong," Charlie stated with a knowing finality Matt needed to hear. "Jessie understands Josh better than anyone, Matt. She might surprise all of us. She knows that boy's hurts."

"I don't know. Maybe." Grabbing Charlie's glass from him, Matt finished the bourbon. The heat of the alcohol sliding down his throat, warming his sickened stomach, was desperately welcome. He gulped twice before airing the rest of his thoughts, shifting his feet as he talked. "She's angry, and anger twists and turns and boils until it spews over. It doesn't translate well to marriages, and it won't serve a pregnant, worn-out mother well. For now, Jessie needs sleep and nutrition, and I intend to see that she gets both." He shoved the empty crystal tumbler into a slightly bemused Charlie's chest. "Go to bed. Charles needs his beauty sleep too. *Sacred Peace* will sort itself out."

Saluting him, Charlie barked, "Yes sir, Matt sir. Will do. Sir."

"G'nite, both of you." Frustrated, aching to go where he just insisted Charlie go—back to Jessie—Matt made his way to Shanda's condo, and let himself in.

Chapter Eight

At three a.m. Mathieu rapped sharply on Shanda's door.

In bed, where he was curled around Shanda's lithe body, Matt abruptly awoke. Snapping his head up off the pillow, still in a fog from only a few hours of sleep, at first he wondered if he dreamt the knock, but it came again, louder, insistent. Shanda mumbled something and lifted her head just as Matt swung his legs over the side opposite her and groped around in the dark bedroom for the jeans he left on the floor the night before. Blood started to pound in his ears; shoving his legs into the jeans, he hopped-dressed his way to the condo's main door.

Swinging it open, he expected to see Jessie standing there teary-eyed and desperate, in need of comfort or a ride to the hospital. *Maybe that male nurse, Kalon, texted Jessie and asked her to come,* was running through Matt's frazzled brain.

She wasn't there. Matt poked his head through the doorway and looked to the right. Agitated, Mathieu was pacing the hallway.

"She took off, sir," he explained, his breathing shallow and his eyes wide. He stopped his interminable pacing and faced the important man in front of him. "Told me she couldn't sleep. She didn't want to bother you."

"What? Jessie left?" Matt was still trying to force himself fully awake. When he left Jessie earlier and sank into Shanda's embrace, a vigorous love-making session—reconnection, Shanda called it—had borrowed a precious hour of coveted slumber. Matt was beyond tired. "Damn it," he cursed. Jessie's hardheadedness, and disrespect toward the guy hired to keep her from wandering off alone—or, God help them all, from becoming another victim of Morgan's vicious game of reprisal and revenge—was disconcerting and frustrating. "Why didn't you go with her?"

Mathieu's words emerged panicked and fast, almost spilling over themselves in his haste to get them out. "She took off running, sir. I tried. She got ahead of me, ran down the stairs, was in the truck before—"

"The truck?" Matt interjected harshly.

A nervous swallow preceded the rest of Mathieu's explanation. "She took her husband's truck, that big Ford, a King Ranch, I think? *Sacred Peace's* transport department drove it back here today."

"You should have followed her, damn it. Why the hell didn't you follow her?"

"Sir, I live two blocks away. I walked here. I don't even own a car. I use car2go when I need wheels. Car sharing."

"And that's great for the environment, good for you, but it's not helping me now." Rifling his fingers through his hair, Matt prodded for more. "Did she say where she was going?" Backing into the condo, he raised a hand to his unexpected middle of the night guest and signaled for him to enter. The door shushed closed behind Mathieu. Swinging around, Matt dispatched himself into the bedroom to grab more clothes.

Hoping he wouldn't get fired, Mathieu added some volume to his voice so Matt could hear him in the bedroom. "Back to the hospital, she said. They didn't call her or anything, she just said she couldn't sleep so she might as well be there."

Shanda was up now, in pink checked pajama pants and a black T-shirt with a large cartoony pink heart printed on the chest. Wide-eyed, she moved into the front room just as Matt appeared at the door, pulling a T-shirt followed by a forest green cotton sweater over his head.

While he was speaking, the young New Brunswicker shyly averted his eyes from Shanda. Catching on to his nerves, Shanda crossed her arms over her breasts and blushed.

Matt's fingers moved quickly to his belt, to buckle it at his waist. Almost running, he disappeared back into the bedroom and grabbed his phone. A quick study of the screen revealed a text from Jessie. He halted by the bedroom door, next to Shanda.

Don't kill the messenger. I didn't give the kid a chance. I'm fine. Stay there with Shanda. Sleep, baby.

Chewing on one corner of his lip, Matt's heart warmed and then quickly sank at the affection he read into the typed endearment, 'baby.' Turning his back to potentially spying eyes, he speed-dialed his rogue girl. "Gonna kill Charlie for not keeping a better eye on her," he mumbled unhappily. At the same time, he found himself rather jealously contemplating whether Jessie might have asked Charlie to lie down with her. If so, Charlie would likely know sooner rather than later that she'd left. Alternatively, since Charlie and Josh shared the condo and Charlie had his own bedroom, if Jessie had lain down alone there was a good chance Charlie had no clue that she'd even flown the coop.

Jessie answered on the first ring. In the background, Matt could hear sirens. Jumping to conclusions, he prayed they had nothing to do with her. Her hoarse, tired voice put him at ease right away. She didn't bother with a greeting, and just jumped in with, "Matt, don't yell at me. I needed a drive, that's all. I got a text from Jacob—Kayla had the baby. It's a girl! They called her Lily, I think the name means 'a new start' or something like that."

A great inhale accompanied by relieved, closed eyes, settled Matt's racing nerves. "That's great news, Jessie," he breathed back to her. "Really. But you need to slow down, girl. You promised me you'd sleep."

"Can't. Tried. My head's spinning. Every time I close my eyes all I see is chaos. In case you're interested, chaos looks like blood and sounds like a piercing single gunshot accompanied by screaming. Which is always coming from me. Chaos behind one's closed eyelids is very disconcerting when one is alone in a silent bedroom engulfed by a big black nothingness."

A long, low *pfffttt* zipped through the phone. Matt rubbed his head, hard, as if by manipulating his short hair around and around on the outside of his skull he could somehow change the energy in his brain and restore his faith in the possibility of a lifetime not peppered by fear. "Fine," he grumped, upset with himself for not having the guts to stand up to Shanda and stay with Jessie overnight. "I'll be there in twenty minutes."

Anticipating Matt's intention, Jessie countered instantly. "No, you won't. Kalon texted a while ago. The hospital made up a cot for me in Josh's room.

I'll lie down when I get there. Stay with Shanda and nose your way back into her good side."

With a start, Matt realized he had almost forgotten where he was, that Shanda was even in the condo, never mind just a few feet away from him. He was so caught up in concern for Jessie that it hardly even occurred to him to consider Shanda's feelings if he took off. Swallowing slowly, he felt like he was at the center of a tug-of-war rope, with Shanda at one end and Jessie at the other.

In his mind he took a large, wide step toward Jessie.

"I'll see you in the morning, then," he said with the awareness that Shanda's eyes were boring holes in his back. The response felt forced. Letting the phone drop to his side, Matt made a mental note to give the hospital security a shout to confirm Jessie's safe arrival. With Morgan still acting as puppeteer, letting Jessie wander around on her own was risky. It occurred to Matt that after what he told her about Vaughn communicating to Arnie that the 'game' was over, she likely had a false sense of safety.

"Damn it," he cursed again. Turning to Mathieu in the condo behind him, Matt muttered, "You might as well go home. We'll be in touch."

Mathieu shuffled his feet but otherwise didn't move. The guy was obviously star struck in Shanda's presence, awed by his close proximity to the stunning *Sacred Peace* star. Unwillingly, he compelled his eyes to leave Shanda's perfect form and shifted his gaze to Matt. "I'm really sorry, sir. Mizz Wheeler is kind of a handful."

Matt wondered if the guy was as awed by Jessie as he was by Shanda. That would explain Jessie's ease in getting away. He made a mental note to talk to Charles about bringing Dan in from Vancouver although, if Jessie wanted to, she'd darn well manipulate her way past him, too. A low chuckle from Matt caught the embarrassed Mathieu by surprise. "I won't deny that," Matt agreed. "She's a handful, all right. Jessie's given me the slip more times than I can count. It wasn't your fault that she took off alone."

"Thank you, sir. Good night. Good night, Mizz Ellis."

After Mathieu left, Matt faced Shanda. "Let's go back to bed." He started to pad back into the bedroom, taking her hand loosely in his on the way.

She gave him a little tug so he'd turn around. "Go if you need to, Matt. I understand."

Oh, how badly did he want to go…

In a few short days Jessie's life would be topsy-turvy and upside down, and once more she and Matt would no longer be in each other's visible company. Nauseated at the thought of it, Matt pushed a growing anxiety back into the pit of his stomach and laid his free hand gently on his girlfriend's slender hip. "I'm good here," he said with an assurance he couldn't quite sincerely muster. "I'll call our security at the hospital in a few minutes just to make sure she got there okay. She'll be with Josh. It's where Jessie's meant to be, Shanda. Me hanging on to her, and the other way around, only serves to keep the apron strings too tight. You're right. I have to let her go."

"Have to, huh?" The light in Shanda's eyes sizzled and fizzled into a halting nothingness. "But you don't want to."

Matt studied her before he replied. He knew he should play the peacemaker card, but instead there was overt frustration in his response. "Not now, Shanda, okay? It's three in the morning. It's been a helluva long few days. Can we just go back to sleep?"

There was a long pause while Shanda tried to come to terms with her man's interconnectedness with Jessie. Matt watched the emotions play around Shanda's face; watched her bite her bottom lip and consider what to do, how to feel. In the end, he sighed and took matters into his own hands.

"Shanda," he started quietly, "don't compare how I feel about Jessie to how I feel about you. It's not the same thing. In a few days it's not going to matter anyway."

Alarm jumpstarted Shanda's brain while, at the same time, her heart did a double take. "I know it's not the same thing, Matt," she countered hotly. "And I honestly don't think you and I will ever get to where you and Jessie are because, let's face it, I hope you never have to save my life. I do, however, think you'd better explain what you mean by saying it won't matter in a few days."

Shaking his head, Matt gave Shanda an answer he hoped would satisfy her for now. "They're going back to Vancouver." The declaration was almost savage in the way he uttered it, like a wild thing Matt felt compelled to let loose but was downright terrified to close the corral door behind, for fear he'd never regain control of it. "For now," he inserted. With a hope he couldn't quite muster, he added, "Things will eventually settle back into some kind of normal." He didn't bother speaking aloud what he was also thinking—'without me.' That unacceptable reality completely disarmed him.

Pivoting away from Shanda, letting her fingers drop from his, Matt steeled up his strength, went further into the bedroom, and lowered his weary body back down on his side of the bed, the side by the wall. He set his cellphone on the nightstand for easy retrieval so in a few minutes, when Jessie would likely be back at the hospital, he could call security to confirm her presence.

Matt turned his back to Shanda and buried his nose in his pillow, which he crushed to his body and hugged tight in a vain attempt to fill the empty hole inside his arms. It was bad enough when Jessie was in another condo down the hall from him. Now that she was across the city, the emptiness was even more profound; he was incapable of protecting her when she was not close by. The anxiety, the lack of control, was overwhelming.

Snugging his nose deeper into his pillow, Matt squeezed his eyes tightly shut and took a few yoga breaths to try to ease the angst. Hoping to calm him, Shanda curved her body around his. Although her presence should have brought comfort, Matt found himself seriously ticked off at her for getting in the way of the treasured time he had left with Jessie.

He tried to picture Jessie parking the big truck and trudging into the hospital alone, ducking her head to avoid anyone clueing in to her celebrity. After a few minutes he raised himself up on one elbow, grabbed the cell, and made the call. As he expected, Jessie had arrived where she said she was going, and all was well.

Letting his eyes close over, Matt sighed, put his phone back on the nightstand, hugged his pillow again, and tossed and turned throughout the remainder of the interrupted, lonely night.

Chapter Nine

Jessie passed Kalon at the nurses' station and treated him to a slow, re-lieved smile. "Working a double?" she asked as she drifted by.

"Just keeping an eye on your fella for you," Kalon winked. "He's doing great, Jessie."

"Thank you, Kalon. I can't tell you how relieved I am to hear that."

The sincerity in Jessie's tired voice and the sad little light in her eyes was worth triple the pay Kalon was getting for staying overnight. He was the kind of guy who went out of his way to help anyone, no thanks necessary. Moments like these, when he could ease the minds of worried wives, or husbands or parents, depending, made the fatigue absolutely worthwhile. Watching Jessie disappear into Josh's room, Kalon smiled and got back to filing patient notes.

Tiptoeing her way inside the small space, Jessie did a double take. Zach was propped up on the sofa on the far wall, about as awake as could be expected in the middle of the night.

He lifted a hand to his mouth in a half-assed attempt to stifle a wide yawn. "What are you doing back here?" he asked kindly. Nudging his butt over on the small sofa, he patted a spot to the right and raised an arm.

Jessie scooted over and cozied up to him. Zach let his arm drape down over her shoulders. "I could ask you the same question," Jessie said. "Couldn't sleep either, huh Zach?"

Wiping back a slicked bit of long hair—which was darker than Josh's, and stylishly greased back with some trendy hair product—Zach shrugged. "Just playing this all out in my mind. Dad and I got a briefing from Charles and Jon at dinner. Charlie, by the way, was oddly quiet. They seem to think the bad stuff has come to an end."

"So they say."

"You think so?"

Sighing, Jessie curled up her legs and leaned into Josh's older brother's side. She glanced over at Josh in the bed. He appeared to be resting comfortably. "I'm actually trying not to think. Not about the bad stuff, anyways." Brightening, she sat up straighter and smiled at Zach. "Were you talking to Kayla?"

"I was. A new little baby girl. That's awesome."

"So we now have something to celebrate. I shoulda got us some champagne. I can't wait to meet her."

"That makes two of us." Curious, Zach strained his neck to peek over at the doorway. "Where's your shadow?"

A wave of sorrow passed over Jessie. "Moving on. Righteously so. Matt needs a life of his own."

"He adores you."

"Feeling's mutual."

Zach's arm tightened around Jessie's shoulders. He chose to steer around the desolation in his sister-in-law's voice; soaked in mourning, it was the kind of declaration best left to stand on its own. "Jessie…" he started, deking left, turning a half-corner in his thoughts, "how is Josh doing these days? At dinner the guys brought up that bender Josh went on a few months back. The one that dominated social media. Has he been okay since? As far as the drinking goes, I mean."

"Sure, yeah. He's been okay. It was a one time thing."

Zach braked a hard right. "It's just…you and Matt…maybe you don't realize how it comes across, but you seem awfully close."

"Umm…" Jessie looked back up and over at Josh. He looked so frail, so defeated, attached to monitors and tubes like that as if they were the only things tethering him to the earth, to his life. She ran a fingernail over and over her bottom lip and posed an almost heated question to Zach without looking directly at him. "What are you saying, Zach?"

Zach's arm around her shoulders stiffened further. Jessie edged away from his side. "Don't get defensive on me, Jessie. I'm just saying that I don't think I'd be able to handle that, if Hilary had a friend like that, someone she leaned on the way you two lean on each other." He softened his words. "Josh is your husband. He's supposed to be the guy you lean on."

"Well, this is the thing, Zach." Jessie's voice got a little thin as she reflected on why she and Matt were as close as they were. "A lot of times in the last few years it's been tough to lean on Josh." Another furtive glance in the general direction of the bed affirmed that Josh wasn't eavesdropping on their conversation. Jessie lowered her voice anyway. "He tries, but a lot of the time I feel like I'm holding him up, you know? All this fear we've been struggling with…I mean, I think he's doing really great staying sober, apart from that one time. It's just that for guys like him I think it's such a damn internal battle every goddamned day that it's tough to be strong for someone else. And I'm sorry, Zach, but there are days when I just really need to feel supported in ways Josh can't deliver. We're good, we really are, apart from the insanity of our everyday existences, I mean. And you want to know something? The best part, Zach, is that Josh leans on Matt too. Matt holds us both together. In fact, sometimes he's the guy telling Josh and me to smarten up and hang on."

"Matt's a good guy."

"Ah. I can hear a question in your voice. Before you ask, no, I'm not sleeping with him."

"But you did. You slept with him." At Jessie's silence, Zach looked over. He wiped a fretful hand over his trimmed beard. "Sorry. I know this is none of my business, but I've been sitting here for hours watching my little brother once again have to face a helluva recuperation, physically as well as emotionally, spiritually, all that shit, and Jessie—I see you with Matt and I wonder who will be lifting Josh up through all of this."

Jessie made an annoyed *puh* sound. "You know I'll be there for him, Zach. I'll never let Josh go. I will always be by his side. And he'll be by mine. We promised each other." Anger and confusion colored her voice; hard and painful emotions Jessie didn't quite know how to compute. Chalking them up to residual fears left over from the earlier terror that Josh had maybe chosen to leave her and her children behind—now abated somewhat because of Matt's assertions that her theory did not ring true—Jessie tried to talk herself into relaxing.

Zach apologized. "Hilary and I aren't much help to you. I should have set up my coffee biz in Vancouver."

Lifting her right hand, Jessie exerted a gentle pressure on Josh's brother's fingers. "It's okay, Zach. I get it. You needed a new start in a different city all those years ago. Josh just hides by rebranding himself as a new person with every acting job, and Kayla loses herself in music. The Sawyer kids have found ways to cope with their confused childhood." Lowering her hand, she poked him in the ribs. "There're too many damn coffee shops in Vancouver, anyway. I mean, there's not a street corner left. Add in the yoga studios and medicinal cannabis shops every ten feet and there ain't no room for you!"

"You think Seattle's any different?" Throwing back his head, Zach laughed. "I supply beans to a lot of Vancouver's cafés anyway. We're joined at the hip. So I guess I didn't completely run away."

They were quiet for a few minutes, each lost in difficult memories, in old times that were gone but definitely not forgotten. After a bit, Jessie took them down a new road. A rough road. "Zach," she wondered aloud, "what was Josh's childhood like? He doesn't talk about it. All Kayla admits is that he got a lot of well-earned stitches."

"Ah," Zach said with a perceptive glint in his eye and a determined set to his lips. "You're wondering about Wes. You really you want to go there? It's not pretty."

Jessie curled back into his side. "I'm glad they've made their peace. Josh is making up for whatever Wes did to him by spoiling Dylan rotten, but sometimes when I see him disappear into himself, I wonder where he goes. I know things were bad." She hesitated. "Is this okay? Is it something you can talk about?"

"I'll talk about it if you're sure you want to hear it, but I think you've got enough on your plate already, Jessie."

Resorting to her little-girl voice, Jessie spouted off an over-confident, "You'd be surprised how much I can fit on my plate." Without even realizing she was doing it, she started digging fingernails into a hand.

Zach glanced away from her, over to the far wall, as he considered how much Josh would be comfortable with him sharing. In the end he decided honesty might actually help his little brother. Maybe with this hard road the two were traveling, talking about Josh as a kid would give Jessie a better understanding of the things that made him tick. And maybe, just maybe, delving into Josh's mixed-up childhood would gas up Jessie's bleeding heart for the bumpy road ahead.

"You already know there were bad times," Zach said, reaching his left hand down to pull Jessie's fingers apart, saddened to see crescent-shaped scars spotting the backs of each hand. "Good old Wes didn't know how to cope with raising his wife's love child. There was this one night…" Shifting his butt on the sofa, Zach tilted his head back against the wall and closed his eyes.

Perking up her ears, Jessie nestled more comfortably into him and laid one now idle hand on her growing belly. The baby was quiet, as if listening for clues on how to interpret its father—an often quiet, introspective man.

Continuing, Zach spoke in a subdued tone. "I don't remember there really being a reason. But this one night at dinner, old dad Wes was in a piss-poor mood. And our mom, all she did was try to appease him." Opening his eyes, he stared at Josh in the bed. "'Do you need butter? Salt? Pepper? Seconds? More beer?'" Glancing over at Jessie, he added, "In our household, us kids learned early on when to be quiet, when to zip up our lips and shut up." Exhaling, he picked out a spot on the floor before going on. "Kayla, she was only maybe about six then, she had this stuffed animal at the table. She always brought it to dinner. It was a rabbit, I think. She'd set it by her plate at every meal, facing her, so it could watch her eat, I suppose."

Remembering, Zach paused and reached for the words. He was still focusing on the floor. "Dad didn't like it," he finally said, navigating around a memory that still made him cringe. "I can't imagine why a stuffed bunny was any threat to him, but at one point he grabbed the thing and pitched it across the room. Kayla was afraid to move 'cause usually she was our father's little princess and this outburst of anger didn't fit the usual vibe. So she sat there with these big, slow tears running down her cheeks, squeezed her eyes shut, and started counting under her breath. I could see her lips moving, but she was too scared to let her voice be heard."

"Poor Kayla. Yeesh, Zach. What'd you do?"

A rumble escaped Zach's chest. It was a low guffaw. "Me? Chicken shit me?" He glimpsed at Jessie at his side and quickly looked away again. "As the older brother my job was to watch everyone and try to keep the peace. Mom was too freaked out to move, much less speak. Wes could be a tyrant when he wanted to be. Kayla was disappearing into some safe little world."

"I bet she was counting dance steps," Jessie said wisely. "Or singing some song."

With a sideways look, Zach's eyes grew wide. "I bet she was. I never thought of that."

"I hum." Peeking shyly up at him, Jessie allowed a small smile. "Not around my dad, though. Didn't need to. In our house, it was my mom that scared me."

"Was it. I see." Zach grinned sadly. "Well, I'll give you one guess as to how the rest of that infamous Sawyer dinner went down."

"Hmmm. Josh, huh?"

"Yep. Little brother saved the day, for Kayla at least. But he paid dearly for it. Dad didn't like Jon's kid rescuing a Sawyer woman, I suppose," he added dryly.

"What'd he do?" For some odd reason it gave Jessie a tiny thrill to hear this story of her husband as a child mustering up the courage and strength to go to his sister's aid. These days, both—courage and strength—sometimes seemed hard to find in him.

Zach rubbed his jaw before he went on. "He shot Dad a dirty look, slid off his chair, and picked the stuffed bunny up off the floor. Not only did Josh set it back in its place by Kayla's plate, but he did this little hop-hop-hop thing with it that made Kayla smile, but that—"

"Incensed your father further," Jessie cut in. "Do I detect an ouch in here somewhere?"

"Many. Dad should have been arrested."

That was humbling. "Jesus, Zach." Jessie held her breath. "He beat him?"

"Took him by the hair and dragged him out of his chair. Shoved him into this little closet where Mom kept her bucket and mop, kicked him two or three times, and slammed the door on him. Jessie…" Zach made a little idle pop-mutter sound before he went on, then he took a deep breath. He couldn't look at her. "I'm ashamed to say that none of us had the guts to go rescue Josh. Mom held Kayla's hand and told her to finish her dinner. But she was crying, our mom was, just sitting there in silence letting her tears drip onto her uneaten food."

It was easy for Jessie to picture. Thinking about Josh as a child, alone and hurt, curled up into himself in a dark broom closet, helped Jessie reconcile the sometimes broken spirit she saw in her husband today. "What happened after?" she whispered. She needed to know that little-boy Josh wasn't left entirely alone that long ago night. That somehow he came out okay in the end. Until the next time…

"Nobody dared open that door until our dad was asleep in front of the television. For over an hour we tiptoed by the door, wondering what to do and why Wes was always so hard on him."

"This happened a lot?" Jessie was blinking back tears.

"Josh learned from a young age that our dad had a hate-on for him no matter what he did. So after a while he got his back up and just started pushing Wes' buttons. When Josh was strong enough, he fought back physically. But as a kid…" Zach deflated as the memory of the mystery behind that closed door came back to haunt him. "It was Kayla who finally went to Josh that night. She opened the door, and…"

Nervous, struggling with the difficult recall, Zach licked his lips. "I was looking over her shoulder. Mom was nowhere around. I think she was in her bedroom crying. She did that a lot. So Josh, he was just sitting there in the dark, all scrunched up into himself, his big eyes looking out at Kayla, but kind of past her as if he wasn't really seeing her, or," he sighed, "or he couldn't bring himself to look at her, more likely. He'd been crying, you could see the tear streaks on his face, but I swear to God we never heard him. He didn't move. He just sat there, kinda lost in himself, I guess. He was angry, I could see sparks in his eyes, but his anger wasn't directed at us. My guess it was at the whole injustice of getting treated the way he was so often treated, knowing he was always being singled out by our father for some crime he didn't even know he committed. Which, we eventually realized thanks to Jon coming clean, was just the crime of being born. Of being conceived."

"Yeah." Picturing Josh's confusion as a child, trying to sort out a life that made no sense to him, Jessie let out a long breath. "Jon loved your mother. He would have been good to Josh back then, if he had the chance."

"Woulda, coulda, shoulda," Zach intoned darkly, before he went on with his difficult telling. "So Kayla, seeing that no way was Josh coming out of that closet until he made up his mind to come out on his own terms—he didn't want to be rescued—climbed in with him. She was so small. She wrapped her arms around his neck and kissed his cheek and told him she loved him. And by God, he smiled. It was a crappy night in the annals of Sawyer history, but there was still light. By all accounts today, a child abused the way Josh was, physically and emotionally, should have been removed from the home. But he got through it, supported mostly by his baby sister, and by me when I had the guts, and by Mom as long as Wes wasn't around, for the most part."

Zach smiled wistfully at his sister-in-law. "And now, Jessie, I gotta tell you sometimes I think it's a miracle Josh ever opened up enough of his soul to allow himself to be loved by a woman as special as you are. I think Kayla gave him that grounding. She let him know that he was loved, and so now he responds to love. But I think you can see why I worry about you and Matt. If what the guys said at dinner is true, and Josh is disappearing inside himself again…"

"He isn't," Jessie countered. "Not…not really, Zach. Not to the extent you're thinking of, anyway. Things have been weird, but Josh is still here. He's not inside some dark place refusing rescue. He still likes to do a lot of things on his own terms, I'll give him that, and yes he's been withdrawn, but he's doing okay. He's functioning."

"And the new baby? I guess that's helping. He must be excited."

That threw a curve ball. "Oh. Well. Not so much. But he will be. He just needs to meet the little guy." Josh's reticence to bond with the as yet unborn Sawyer baby hurt to acknowledge. Still, Jessie hoped Josh would come around. Once again the old dread that Josh was refusing to connect with their new child out of some fear that Morgan would somehow take the child away made Jessie double over.

"You okay?" Zach leaned over her, and pushed back her hair. "Jessie?"

"Nerves," she declared mournfully. "Just nerves. And fatigue."

"Well, you better rest up," Zach decreed staunchly. "Steve messaged me earlier. He's coming in the morning. He'll be here by seven."

"Steve, huh? I'm glad he's coming. Josh could use a dose of his buddy's humor. Sleep. I think maybe I could sleep now, Zach. Will you wake me if your little brother needs me?"

"You bet, although I'm not waking you unless I really need to." Rising, Zach took Jessie's fingers in his and helped her stand. He led her to the cot that, earlier, Kalon had orchestrated orderlies to set up by the far wall. Tucking a cotton blanket around her tired bones, Zach said, "You've got maybe three hours, Jessie. Make 'em good ones. Sweet dreams."

"I'm pregnant, Zach," Jessie smiled mischievously. "I'll be lucky to get an hour in before my bladder blows up like a balloon."

Something about being in the dimly lit room alongside big brother Zach, with Josh sleeping nearby, gave Jessie the sense of closeness and security she needed to slow down her racing brain enough to doze off.

Zach wandered over to Josh's bedside for a quiet study of his sleeping brother before laying his head on the sofa back and crossing his ankles on the small table. A maddening wave of sorrow made a tedious, slow journey up his body and established a steady hold on his heart as he watched Jessie slip into slumber on the tiny cot. Dredging up the nasty memories of a confusing, sometimes frightening childhood in the old Sawyer household did nothing to ease his worry over how Josh would cope with this latest injury. Some days when he paused to reflect on Josh's past, Zach thought it was a wonder that his baby brother was dealing well at all, much less thriving in his celebrity lifestyle as an actor, as a husband of a superstar, no less, and as a father.

An unwanted thought catapulted across Zach's brain. *The layers of sadness Josh grew up with are often exacerbated and inflated because of Jessie.*

It was as if when cracks in Josh's soul opened up and he let light in—Jessie being the light—dirt got in too.

Letting his eyes close so he, too, could doze off, Zach pondered the hurtful reality Josh was living, and the idyllic one he wished he could live. There was a new child in the Sawyer family now—Kayla and Jacob's baby girl— and a new baby coming. There were other small children to contemplate, to keep safe, to teach and nurture and love so that they, some day, would be fully functional emotionally healthy adults. Already the world Josh and Jessie inhabited was an insane glass fishbowl of fame and celebrity. They were prey, not just on behalf of Morgan's wicked team, but also from everyday people who wanted a piece of them.

At the top, watching over them, was a powerful couple that had made no secret of not wholly accepting Josh as Jessie's husband. Alongside, fully in the Keating-Sawyer fold, was Matt—the man Zach questioned Jessie about because of their obvious bond.

Clearly, Matt was at Jessie's beck and call. There was a sweet adoration and connection between them that made Zach wonder how Josh even stood to have the guy in his life. Matt was strength personified, and now Josh was once again weak. Jessie, about to have a new baby in the next few months, was somewhere in the middle. In Zach's presence she made a big show of appearing strong but there were leaks in her bucket. That digging her nails into her hand thing? The way she blinked and tried to smile and didn't even go to Josh's bedside tonight? Zach saw right through her. She was quite obviously lost and scared. Which way would she go? To whom would she turn?

She won't abandon my brother, Zach reasoned.

But in the future when Jessie would need someone to lean on, Zach knew it would be Matt.

Sinking further into the sofa he groaned, swallowed past the pain of forever seeing his little brother hurting, and slept.

Chapter Ten

*O*nly a few short hours later Matt edged out of bed and took his clothes into the washroom so he could dress in there after his shower and not wake Shanda. It was seven a.m. Reprimanding himself for not wanting to face his girlfriend, which Matt admitted was a pathetic, cowardly move, he exhaled with relief when he finally closed the condo door behind him and strode down the hall toward the elevator. Passing Charles' suite, and then Josh and Charlie's, he contemplated knocking on both doors to see if the *Sacred Peace* producers were up and wanted to go for breakfast, but in his hurry to get to the hospital to make sure Jessie was safe and coping, Matt chose to walk on by.

Not long later, hands shoved deep in his coat pockets, he was standing at the entrance to Josh's room watching Jessie sleep when a lanky body wandered up behind him.

Steve. And he had a welcome tray of Starbucks coffee suspended in one hand.

"You're a sight for sore eyes." Taking a proffered cup, Matt tried to grin. It came out lopsided. "Good to see you, Steve."

"I'd say I'm happy to be here, but…" Steve waved the tray at Josh in the bed, hooked up to a chest tube and a monitor, but seemingly at peace. "This guy pisses me off. He ought to know to stay out of the path of trouble."

"It's ending, Steve," Matt said as he took a sip of hot dark roast and wondered when the last time he had his usual tea was. "Josh and Jessie will get that peace they deserve."

"Care to elaborate?"

"Not at the moment." Matt raised his white cup in a greeting aimed at Zach.

On the sofa, Zach was stretching as he awoke. After a look to Josh and a surreptitious peek at Jessie on the cot, he lumbered his way on dragging feet to the doorway. Out of respect for Jessie and Josh, who were both still asleep, the guys moved out into the hallway to continue their chat.

It wasn't long before Jessie eased her body up on one elbow and looked around. Josh's monitor looked fine, at least as far as she knew to look in terms of blood pressure and heart rate. Josh was pale as usual and his eyes were closed.

A low rumble in the hallway was a cue to look that way. Rising, weaving at first from the effort to force her tired body to stand, Jessie spotted the guys nursing their Starbucks. With a cry she vaulted into Steve's arms. At the last second, Matt rescued the tray with its one remaining coffee.

"Whoa, girl," Steve laughed, surrendering the tray. "Down, girl. Down!" After a long, steady study of his old *Drifters* co-star, he enclosed her tightly in his embrace.

"You calling me a dog?" Jessie said into his neck. "If I didn't have to pee so bad right now, I'd prove you right and lick you all over. Okay, not all over." She colored. Pulling back from Steve, holding him at arms' length, Jessie instantly brightened. "Damn, I'm glad to see you, Steve."

"I'm glad to see you too, girl, but just a heads up—this visit will have to be short but sweet. I've only got one day off. You've got me til dinnertime, okay?"

Her smile flipped upside down. "Zach's leaving tonight too. Sucks that we have to visit this way."

"We'll plan a better visit next month, when Josh is up and around again. Deal?"

"You got it, Steve. Deal."

Apprehensive, Zach was eyeballing Matt. Jessie had yet to greet him. Unaware that he was the object of scrutiny, Matt fidgeted with the tray and nervously swiped a sleeve across his mouth. His eyes never left Jessie's face, yet Zach found a curious relief wash over himself in the way the man was studying her, as if Matt was uncertain of his place in her life. Zach had no way of knowing that Matt was already trying to disconnect from Jessie, to memorize her, to grieve the loss of her from his everyday life once more.

Momentarily Jessie took Zach's hand and brushed her lips against his cheek. "Good morning, Josh's brother." She smiled. "I'd give you a hug but I might just pee here and now if I put any more pressure on this preggo bladder of mine." Taking a slow, deep breath, she swung slowly around to Matt and met his searching eyes. "Hey," she said, letting go of Zach's fingers and taking his.

Steve reached over and took the last cup out of the Starbucks tray. He tossed the tray as well as his own cup into the garbage, and held onto the last cup—chamomile tea for Jessie—while Jessie spoke to Matt.

"You shouldn't be here," she was telling Matt. "As you can see, I'm not alone."

You will be. A dark shadow flitted across Matt's eyes. Out loud he said, to counter the sudden shock of worry he saw crisscross Jessie's face in parted lips and a slight tilt to her head, "Shanda was snoring. I took that to mean she was super tired. I let her be."

"You snuck out on her? Aw shit, you're totally gonna be in the doghouse now, Matt. Which means so am I. Do I gotta teach you how to treat that woman?"

The quick downturn of Matt's lips brought a more compassionate response. Leaning in for a similar welcome to the one she gave Zach, Jessie whispered in Matt's ear, "But I can't right now. Teach you, I mean. I really have to pee. I'm glad you're here, my friend. Shanda will eventually recover from the shock of waking without her beautiful man next to her."

A restrained groan was Matt's response. Aware now that Zach was watching him, he turned his head to the side and blinked stupidly at the floor.

Jessie wrinkled her nose in consternation. But her bladder was calling. "I'll be back," she told the guys, and wandered off to the private washroom in Josh's room.

"I'll stay," Matt determined, recovering his senses. "Go take her for something to eat. I'll keep an eye on Josh."

"I could eat," Zach agreed. "You in, Steve?"

"Fill me in on how my buddy is doing first, will you?"

"We'll talk on the way. You sure, Matt?" Zach stifled a yawn.

"Yeah, sure. Go. Make her eat, even if you have to force feed her."

"Will do."

A few minutes later, Jessie emerged from Josh's room. She was practically skipping, she was so happy to see Steve. Hooking one arm in his crooked elbow and the other in Zach's, she exuded light as the three of them strolled off down the hallway.

Behind them, Matt caught the eye of one of the security guards on duty outside Josh's room. "Go," he mouthed. The big quiet guy nodded his understanding and followed the trio.

With a sigh, Matt wandered back over to Josh's room. Caught off guard, he jumped when he saw Josh's eyes on him. "Hey," he said. "Welcome back to reality." It was hard to maintain Josh's gaze. Matt had to swallow away his disappointment and worry at Josh's unbelievable single-minded decision, the one that had them all gathering at the trauma center this morning. There would be time later to let Josh know how he felt about the decisive—and in many ways, still final—action.

Josh blinked his way to a more aware muzzy consciousness.

"Something I can get for you, Josh?" Matt asked, moving deeper into the room.

"Sit up," Josh groaned. He was trying to move but his arms were trembling and wouldn't quite support his body.

Glancing behind him, Matt saw Kalon saunter casually over. "Can we have a hand?" Matt asked. With Kalon navigating tubes and Matt helping to maneuver Josh, the two of them managed to help their patient find a more comfortable position. Kalon chatted amicably while he adjusted things, then he raised a hand in a wave and left Josh and Matt alone.

"I even…fucked this up," Josh mumbled, avoiding Matt's stare.

The hairs on the back of Matt's neck prickled. *Okay, so we are going there right away after all.* "I heard," he said.

Josh angled his heavy head toward Matt. "Arnie?" he rasped.

Matt nodded his affirmation. "Yeah. He's got a guy at Brody, that Vaughn guy from the Downtown Eastside. Your, uh, broker."

"Jessie know?" Josh's eyes closed over.

"She thought she did. I talked her out of it."

"I had a reason."

"I realize that. It wasn't good enough." Matt's voice was knife-edged sharp. He tried to bring it back to a more normal tone, but it was tough. The anger and fear that started swirling around his brain and heart the second he realized how Josh chose to deal with his family's plight just plain sickened him, despite the supposed inherent honor. In truth, Matt didn't have a clue how to feel. Or how to deal.

"I needed…to save my family."

"So you bargained your way out of responsibility. You were just going to leave her here alone to deal with the pile of shit you left behind."

Josh's eyes opened and locked onto Matt's. "Not alone."

"Me?" A pitchy chuckle escaped from between Matt's thin-pressed lips. "Jesus, Josh. Jessie doesn't want me. The only man she will ever love is you. You know this about her."

"You're…wrong. She'll change her mind when…she knows."

Matt almost choked. "She'll never know."

"She needs…a stable man. One who…she can trust…to keep it together. Anyways…I can't be here. I made arrangements…to pay my debt."

"I know all about your arrangements, Josh. They're being countered as we speak."

"What? How? Matt, I…I made my peace. I have a lot of faith. Please…"

"Jesus, don't go there, Josh. Don't try talking anyone into helping you take this thing to fruition." Matt had to grab the rail and hang on. He wondered if Kalon should be notified to keep a real good eye on Josh. But could he be trusted not to leak the story to the media? No. The big male nurse seemed like a great guy. But no. Not yet, anyway. Resolving to stand guard himself, Matt decided the best course of action was to call Charlie and get him to step up their plan.

"Trust me," Matt said to Josh. "We've got it figured out. Please, Josh. Trust me, okay?"

"You'd be…good for her, Matt. Jessie loves you. The kids love you."

"They love their father." Matt's voice was hoarse. In his mind he reached for Jessie's mantra, the one about hope. It gave him the strength to rouse up some courage of his own, enough to at least transfer hope to Josh. "Hang on, buddy," he begged. "You're not alone anymore. We're going to see this through together. All of us. And it's going to end with you and that beautiful woman of yours raising your family safely and in peace."

Josh's eyes darkened. "Don't make promises…you can't keep, Matt."

"I intend to keep this one. Now sleep. Steve's here, and Zach's lurking around. Rest up before they get back."

"Jessie?"

"Yeah. She's here too. And you better fucking look her in the eye and give her some strength she can rely on, Josh. Give her some faith in you. Don't let her think about what…" Matt gulped. "Just don't let her think anything bad. She's always had your back. Prove to her that you've been worth it."

Not one more second could Matt stay at Josh's side. Looking into those defeated eyes scared the hell out of him. There was no hope there, only pain and loss and frustration. *We're sending them away,* Matt thought as he walked away. *There's no way Josh will cope with the life we have planned for him. And if he can't cope, how will Jessie fare? With all of those kids? A new baby?*

Turning so his back was to Josh, Matt stood outside the door for a good half hour just thinking until, to his surprise, Shanda strolled up. Straightening, he scanned her face to see what secrets she was hiding—was she about to rail at him for bailing on her this morning?

She didn't. Cocking her head to one side she adopted a sympathetic, loving lilt, and took him in her arms. "Matt, you carry the weight of the world on your shoulders, you know that?" she breathed. "Why don't you for once let me share the load?"

It's going to be okay, he told himself, burying his face in Shanda's curls. *I'm not alone. Josh is not alone. It's going to be okay.*

Down the hall, Jessie, Steve and Zach were making their way back up to Josh's room. Zach was talking; he fell silent when he saw Jessie stop short and take a quick breath. Following her gaze, he spotted Shanda and Matt embracing just outside Josh's door. It seemed like Matt's shoulders were shaking. The man was crying.

In street clothes, Kalon was on his way by, finally going off-shift. Zach grabbed his arm. "Josh?" he croaked.

With a concerned look behind him toward Matt and Shanda, Kalon said, "He woke about a half hour ago. He's doing fine."

Jessie was immobilized. She closed her eyes. A hand reached down and gripped her fingers.

"Hey," Steve said. "He's beat, Jessie. That's all that's going on. Your Matt's just beat."

My Matt. Jessie couldn't look at Zach. By virtue of his silence, she was aware that he was reading much more into Steve's 'your Matt' comment than was warranted. For her, once she knew Josh was okay, the jarring pain that ricocheted through her body upon seeing Matt lose it in the comfort of Shanda's arms was just too much. Matt's pain came from her—from Jessie and from her family. It was unbearable to see him hurt this way on account of her.

Feeling eyes on him, Matt looked up to find himself caught in Jessie's tragic stare. The shock of seeing her there watching him break down disarmed him. Taking a step back from Shanda, he shoved a fist across his eyes but kept his second hand tightly clasped around Shanda's fingers.

Jessie's eyes darted over to Shanda. Like a great wall a long pause stood in the silence, delaying the motion that finally carried Jessie and the guys forward. When they drew close, Steve tapped Matt's elbow to acknowledge the burden he carried, and Shanda tried to leave Matt to follow the quiet Zach inside Josh's room, but Matt wouldn't let her go.

"Take the day off," Jessie pleaded, eyes wide and scared. "Please, Matt. Go to work with Shanda today. Think about other shit besides us. Do other shit."

He nodded. Words would choke him if he tried to speak. Looking up at Shanda, who offered a tiny, sad smile of agreement, Matt touched Jessie's arm and walked away from her. It was everything he could do not to lose it again as he crossed the floor with his fingers entwined in Shanda's, in the knowing that Jessie's anxious eyes were surely latched onto his back.

Matt had a job to do. He would find Charlie and Charles on set; Arnie would be there too. They'd find a corner to set up in, and they'd fine-tune their plan to set the Sawyer family free.

Trouble was, Matt knew that the new freedom, as hard earned as it was for all of them, was going to end up feeling just like a prison.

Brody River Penitentiary was hopping, but not all of it. At least, it was hopping no more than usual when one considers the volatile prison population and all its subcultures and layered tiers of political maneuvering. No, the area that was busiest at the present time was the lunchroom—specifically Morgan's table, where Vaughn had settled himself for a chat. Standing guard nearby was Caulfield, chewing on a peppermint—an unusual wintergreen this time, green in color yet tasting kind of like a pink one, which disappointed the steely-eyed man every bit as the fact that Josh had survived the agreed attempt on his life.

"We got the money," Vaughn was saying to Morgan. "So we can let this shit go."

Morgan's gaze drifted over to Caulfield, against the wall. Something about Caulfield's narrowing eyes unnerved him. With one easy, slow movement, Morgan dragged his fork across his plate and scooped up some mashed potatoes. Lifting his fork to his mouth, he dumped the potatoes in and swallowed. Earlier in the day he had been expecting a big, juicy steak to be delivered to his cell in his home range. But it hadn't come. It was supposed to be in celebration. Its absence was how Morgan knew that Josh Sawyer was still alive. This unexpected conversation with Vaughn confirmed it.

Caulfield held the cards, though. Morgan was powerless. He knew that Vaughn had no idea about that, about how many cards the self-righteous corrections officer held, or how potent they were. How despicable, how utterly dangerous they were.

This game hadn't ended. It wouldn't end until Josh—or maybe Jessie, Morgan supposed—was dead. Glancing sideways, Morgan took a good look at the hefty black man next to him. Vaughn had almost as much control in the prison as Caulfield did. And thanks to his association with Arnie, Morgan thought, and Vancouver's Downtown Eastside neighborhood, Vaughn seemed amenable to letting the Sawyers live in peace, regardless of the fact that Josh's deal backfired. Maybe there was another deal that could be brokered…

Groaning, Morgan shrank under Caulfield's hair-raising stare. *Forget it. I can't win against that creep.* "It can't be over," he said to Vaughn. He didn't take his eyes off Caulfield. "Until…"

"Arnie says they're moving Sawyer to Vancouver in the morning."

It wasn't true. It was a ploy. Josh's medevac flight was happening tonight under the encapsulating, protective darkness of a midnight sky. The move, as far as Vaughn knew, was to the west coast hippie city. That's all Arnie shared with him. For some reason Arnie seemed to want Morgan to know what the Keating clan was up to. There was more at play here than Vaughn understood, but when all was said and done he didn't care all that much. He was waiting for a song from Jessie Wheeler, one with his name written all over it. He'd do whatever the hell Arnie asked of him although, to be honest, his patience was running thin.

"Okay, then." Morgan just wanted the big black guy to go away so Caulfield would take his mean-spirited gaze over to some other unlucky bastard's table.

"Tell Caulfield," Vaughn demanded. "We got more than enough money. Jesus, what's a man supposed to do with that kind of money anyway besides rot in hell with Catholic guilt? I went to church once or twice. I know what them kinda white folks say about money. It's over. Sawyer's going home."

"I'll tell him." *But I know what he'll say. I know what he'll do.* Morgan winced. His fork fell from his hand and rattled onto his plate.

Vaughn got up. Fisted in one hand was his homemade knife. On Morgan's leg was blood. "Glad ya listen so well, Morgan," Vaughn said, a haughty frown making his big face look every bit as dangerous as his reputation decreed. "I'll see ya."

Watching him amble away, Morgan kept his eyes locked on the knife in the big, hulking fist.

Until Caulfield dropped down next to him.

Oh, Jesus. Sucking up his courage, Morgan looked over. At the same time, he moved to pick up his fork but he dropped it again. His shaking fingers couldn't quite manage to grasp it firmly. It clattered to the floor, quickly forgotten.

Caulfield was red-faced. "What'd he tell you?"

Morgan bit down so hard on a corner of his lip that a pinpoint of red blood appeared, and he turned away.

Chapter Eleven

"I need a few minutes with Josh alone," Charlie said to Charles, Arnie and Matt, later in the day after Matt's return to the hospital from set. "For starters give me five or ten minutes with both Josh and Jessie, and then come get Jessie."

"I'll come by," Matt said. "She's been here all day. She needs a walk."

"Thanks, Matt, I appreciate that. I'm going to miss my buddy. I've got some stuff I want to say to him."

"Fair enough. I'll get Jessie in ten."

Charlie had drawn the short end of the stick. Now that the day was coming to an end, and Steve and Zach had both said their goodbyes and headed home, Keating security was getting down to business.

Charles patted Charlie on the back and wished him well. Arnie shoved his hands in his pockets, narrowed his eyes, and gave Charlie a serious, curt nod. Matt placed both hands on his hips, angled himself sideways away from Charlie, raised his chin and idly watched a blonde nurse make her way to the nurses' station with a clipboard in hand. When Matt looked up from her, his eyes met Kalon's. The dark-skinned guy was focused on Matt and the Keating crew who, this evening, were grouped over by the entrance to a small kitchen.

Kalon waved Matt over as Charlie numbly stared at his feet and sauntered on down to Josh's hospital room fifty feet away.

Matt didn't initially speak to Kalon, not verbally at least.

Kalon was antsy; he jumped in quickly. "We're all set," he said. "Transport will be ready at midnight."

"You're sure about all this, Kalon?" During the day while he was at the

Sacred Peace set with Shanda, hiding out with Charlie in his upstairs office, Matt had enlisted his most trusted RCMP buddy to do a thorough background check on the male nurse. Following a tense mid-afternoon interview with the guy—who had only managed a few niggling hours of sleep prior—and references from various hospitals, Kalon was enlisted to travel with Josh on the medevac plane. Thing was, though, he signed up for a helluva lot more than just a simple trip to Vancouver.

"Apart from working here, I've got nothing keeping me in Calgary," he told Matt now. "As I told you when we talked earlier today, what's left of my family is in Kenya. I haven't been in touch with them for years. I could use a new start."

"Couldn't we all." Blowing out a slow stream of air, Matt studied the newest member of the Keating team. "Whether we want it or not, in some cases."

"I'll be here and ready for you, sir, at midnight. I did everything you asked, which is virtually nothing." Kalon grinned.

"Just call me Matt, okay Kalon? We're a pretty informal group. No 'sir' stuff. And thanks for that, for your prep work, I mean. Under no circumstances can this look any more planned than a short day trip to Vancouver and back."

"You got it. See you later."

"All right." Lightly slapping the top counter of the nurses' desk, Matt shoved himself away from it and wandered over to Charles and Arnie. "We're good to go for midnight," he told them. "Kalon's been versed on protocols. Tonight's the night."

The men were quiet. Nobody really wanted tonight to happen. What they had planned would change everything. Even so, it wasn't the change that was most disconcerting. It was the fact that Jessie and Josh would have no choice in the matter. And right now it was up to Charlie to tell them.

When Charlie moseyed into Josh's room, he found Jessie on her left side on the bed next to her husband, leaning on one elbow, a hand supporting her head. Her right hand was moving slowly over Josh's bandage on his chest. By the look of her, sad and despondent, she was mulling over the darkness that seemed to always hold them captive. Awake, Josh was watching her. They were half-sitting up—reducing the chance of blood clots was imperative, and Josh was well enough now to be raised to a sitting position to help mitigate that possibility.

"Hey, Charlie," Jessie said as he wandered up to Josh's left side. "I'm tracing his scars. They suck. There're too many."

Charlie stole a look up at Josh, who met his eyes for only a second before he exhaled heavily and turned his head away. Josh had laid his left hand over Jessie's as she moved her fingers over his skin. He let the hand drop to his side.

Peeking more closely up at Charlie, Jessie flipped herself around on the bed so she was sitting with her back to the pillow. Challenging Charlie, she laced her fingers in Josh's, his right hand this time, and spoke in her little-girl voice. "So, Mr. Deacon, I gather today's an important day. The way y'all are tiptoeing around us, it's obvious something's up. What's worrying the heck out of me is that none of you are your joyful, bouncy selves. Matt's been dragging his feet since he got back from set. There's a groove in the floor from all his pacing. I'm gonna start calling him Eeyore."

Charlie let his eyes wander over his two good friends, sitting on a hospital bed holding hands, scanning him for clues of what their future held. He licked his lips and rubbed a hand over his stubble. It was going to be hard to find the words, yet he was glad this difficult job had fallen to him. Charles was done-in, and the man didn't need the stress. Arnie was still angry at Josh—they all were, on some level—and Matt was a mushy mess. Grappling for strength, Charlie illuminated Josh and Jessie the easiest way he could, parceling them morsels of information in bits and pieces.

The easiest thing to start with seemed to be the transportation arrangements. "You know Charles," he started with. "He always wants the best for you guys."

"Harrumph," Josh grunted. "For one of us."

"Down, boy," Jessie warned. "Let doofus here speak." Her eyes were wide and afraid. Jessie's intuition was kicking in big time. Something was up— the mysterious plan Matt told her about back at the condo, maybe—and her gut didn't like it.

A quick look at Josh, and Charlie went on. One hand was resting on the bed rail as he spoke. Jessie's eyes latched onto his fingers. Charlie was gripping it so hard that his knuckles were white, yet he was trying to speak casually.

"It was our choice to move you back to Vancouver, Josh," Charlie said. "The hospital wasn't able to offer its usual medevac service, and Charles being the great man that he is, hired a private service. You'll be transported to the airport and loaded into a Learjet air ambulance for the trip to, uh, for the trip to Van. One of Charles' old college buddies, a retired physician, is coming along for the trip. A Dr. Westfield. Him and Kalon, actually. You know Kalon. He's agreed to come along."

"Kalon? Oh. Well, that's good." *Phew. They wouldn't be planning anything weird with Kalon along.* Jessie relaxed. Charlie couldn't meet her eyes. "I don't know about you guys," Jessie added, "but I can't wait to get back to Vancouver. I need to see our kids."

Josh was watching Charlie intently. Something else was at play here…he and Charlie had acted opposite each other on *Sacred Peace* for two seasons now. Josh could read the guy. Thankfully Jessie was lost in thoughts about the children. To Josh's eye, she didn't seem too concerned.

"So, Jessie," Charlie went on, "you'll have access to the studio on Robson to rehearse with Jacob for the set the two of you are doing at the latest of your domestic violence awareness concerts, the one in L.A. in two weeks. You can be close to the kids."

"Sounds good to me. What about, um, well I hate to bring this up, but what about Morgan? What's the latest?"

"Nothing new. We're moving Josh tonight just so we can do it on the down low. We're hoping nobody will notice. Only the people here at the hospital who need to know, know."

"All stealth-like. How exciting." Jessie was frowning, though, and with her right hand was twisting the hem of the cotton blanket that covered Josh to the waist. She trained her sea-pearl blues on the movement. "I hate this," she whispered. Tossing her hair, she looked up and searched Charlie's eyes.

Sucking in a breath, he had to look away.

"Charlie?" Alarm jumpstarted Jessie's heart. The twisting screeched to a halt.

A voice came from the doorway. Leaning against the side was Matt, one arm outstretched above his head so that his toned body took up most of the space. "Walk with me, Jessie," he demanded. "I need a coffee."

"I guess," Jessie replied, uncertain. Striding into the room, Matt lowered the bed rail and took Jessie's elbow to help her down. Josh had yet to say anything substantial. Jessie turned back to him. "Are you okay for a bit?"

Josh's body was healing but his spirit was still a confused, uncertain mess. A bitter bewilderment was burning in the chocolate eyes Jessie adored.

Shoulders sinking, she bent forward and pressed her lips to his. "I won't be too long, babe. Can I bring you anything?"

Shaking his head, Josh muttered a hasty, "No thanks," and squeezed her fingers as she left under an arm Matt raised for her.

Still watching the doorway after Jessie and Matt slipped through it, Josh lifted a finger and pointed. "He didn't even look at me," he said weakly to Charlie. "What the hell's going on? And what about *Sacred Peace*? I only shot the first few days of the last episode."

"Like you care?" Wary, Charlie found himself relieved that some of the old Josh seemed to be coming back. There was spite in what Josh was saying, which meant there was also some fight left in his good friend. "Fuck it," he said at Josh's stunned silence, and scratched his head thoughtfully.

He refocused. "Look, Josh," Charlie started, "we have crew moving on to other projects. We have a deadline. Jon's on set now, supervising the last few days. He'll be around here later to see you. We had no choice—between the footage we got, some quick rewriting, and your stunt double, we managed to pull an episode together that'll finish the season off in a way the audience will accept."

Josh groaned. "Charlie, come on. Let me finish it, man. I'll be on my feet in a few days."

"No can do. We gotta move you, Josh. Tonight. I'm sorry. We don't think Morgan has a ton of reach. You'll be safer when you're out of the province."

"Just so you know, you guys suck. You should have let me finish the goddamn season. Can I see the script? So I know what to expect in season three?" There it was, a reference to the future. A tiny light. *Hope.*

Sick to his stomach, Charlie had to look away again so he could compose himself. When he finally let his gaze drift back over to his buddy, he had to shove a thumb and a finger in the outer corners of his eyes. "Josh, look. You want to know what sucks, buddy? Season three. That's what's gonna suck."

Still medicated, Josh was a little slow to catch on. There was real fear in the way Charlie was looking at him through moist eyes, in the way he was stooped over the bed rail now as if he didn't trust his body to hold him up. When Josh clued in, his body stilled. Later, he would think to himself that his heart almost literally stopped. At the very least, his blood seemed to stop flowing.

"Jesus, Charlie. What'd you do?" The question was worded in such a subdued tone that Charlie had to bend an ear to hear better. In Josh's mind, simply uttering the words made what he was starting to clue in to, real. But it didn't make it any easier to accept. "Tell me you didn't write me out. Tell me you didn't fucking write me out of *Sacred Peace.*"

"I'm sorry, buddy. I'm real, real sorry. We didn't feel we had a choice, Josh, I—"

"Bullshit. You always have a fucking choice. Charlie, no! *Sacred Peace* is everything to me."

Charlie turned around in a circle; coiling up the fingers of his right hand, he slammed the pinky end of his fist against the wall. He counted to ten before he spoke again. "It's so everything to you, Josh," he said in as cool a voice as he could muster, "that you arranged a hit. On our set. *Sacred Peace* is so everything to you that you were willing to say goodbye to it, to make your exit ON SET in a blaze of glory the entire cast and crew will never, ever forget."

"You don't understand. It's not your family that's at risk here."

"Well guess what, Josh." Charlie pointed a trembling finger at his friend and co-star. "You survived the hit. You know what that means, huh buddy?"

Lifting a hand, Josh rifled shaking fingers through his hair. He didn't answer, although he held Charlie's accusing stare.

"It means," Charlie elaborated, biting off the words, "that Morgan is still after one of you. We know about the deal you made about your kids, Josh. We know you paid him. At least a sweet million, I take it. Although what the hell he will do with it in prison is beyond me. Morgan knows you survived the hit. We told Jessie he called it square, because she doesn't deserve this; we also told her that the hit was Morgan's doing, not yours, and she better never fucking find out otherwise, you hear me?"

Pressing his lips together, Josh nudged deeper into the pillow and listened.

A hot rage had taken over Charlie, the result of worrying and planning plus dealing with all of the repercussions to *Sacred Peace*—his baby—and it was erupting.

Charlie continued on with a firm and steady, but low voiced, bitterness. It would not do for Jessie to come back and overhear, nor would it help any of them if a random nurse walked in and took some of these truths out to the press, who were all hungry for whatever titanic information they could gather. "So this is what's happening, Josh," he said. "Listen closely because I'm only going to say this once. It might not be you who Morgan goes after next time. We have no clue where he will turn next. Arnie's guy Vaughn can't get any concrete shit out of Morgan. We're scared."

Watching Josh to see if he was paying attention—he was, his eyes were somber but attentive—Charlie took in a breath and hammered on. "Tonight," he stated darkly, "you're not going back to Vancouver. We've arranged a little detour."

"Detour? What? Where?"

"Josh, listen. I hate to do this, buddy. We're all hating this. But you have to agree—it's the only thing that will guarantee any kind of ending for this terror you and Jessie and the kids have endured. It's the only way we can see to make the bad stuff go away."

"What the hell, Charlie? What's the only way?"

Charlie waited for Josh's muddled drug-riddled brain to catch up.

"Secreting me away for a while?" Josh asked, wrinkling his brow. "What the hell good's that gonna do? It won't accomplish anything other than putting Morgan off for a while, that's all. He won't stop until his debt is paid. I may as well stay here and finish *Sacred Peace* and let fate play out the way it's meant to."

"You're not listening to me, Josh! Goddamnit!" Losing it, Charlie gave the bed rail a hard shake followed by a shove before he whipped around and slammed a full fist into the wall this time. When he turned back to his friend, his face was red, his handsome cheeks spotted with anger. "Jessie! You hear me? It could be her next time!"

Josh went silent. He trained his eyes on his hand, opening and closing his fingers into and out of a fist until he finally murmured, "Jesus, Charlie.

Why'nt you all just let me go, then? I told you. Sending me away for a while will not end this nightmare."

"No Josh, but—" The fury was subsiding. Charlie's body started to quake. Facing Josh fully, he spat out the words he knew would destroy what little was left of his good friend's already low spirit. "Like you already figured out…killing you will."

Josh stared at Charlie. Then he let the morbid thought slide away. It slithered off into the corner like some evil creature, leaving behind a rancorous trail of damp, pathetic despair. "Jesus Christ," he whispered as the despair crackled its way into his spirit. "You're going to tell the world I'm dead."

"What else would you have us do, Josh? What other options do we have? This will end things. It'll all be over. You can live in peace."

"Where? And do what? You call that living? Charlie, I…where? What about Jessie and the kids? How can I…" He fixed a slow, hard stare on Charlie. "How can I work…if I'm dead?"

Charlie's eyes hardened. He said nothing.

On the bed, Josh groaned and closed his eyes. "You're joking, right? Tell me you're joking, Charlie."

Hurrying footsteps alerted them to the fact that someone was heading in their direction, likely one of the nurses dropping in to check Josh's vitals.

Leaning toward Josh, Charlie issued a final clarification. Josh blinked his eyes open, narrowed them into angry slits, and listened. "Jessie has a show in L.A. in two weeks. She doesn't know this yet, but she'll be playing the role of a lifetime, acting like a grieving widow. We'll tell the kids you disappeared so when we bring them and Jessie to you after the L.A. show they won't be any the wiser, and they'll be happy as shit to see you alive and kicking. Nobody will find any trace of the plane; we're hiding it in an abandoned barn someplace up north. If you're wondering whether Jessie will work again, I think she won't for a while until things settle, and then it will be her choice. Knowing her, I wouldn't be surprised if she decides not to work ever again. And your names? Start thinking about who you want to be for the rest of your life, Josh. Because Josh Sawyer is dying tonight. And he won't be coming back."

"You can't do this. I need some say in this. It's my fucking life, Charlie!"

"We can. And we are. And before you ask? Jessie doesn't know a thing.

Let me rephrase that—she knows something's up but she doesn't know what. It's all lies and deceit again in the Keating camp. Let's hope we all get out of this web in one piece. And Josh? When she gets back today, do me a favor and don't tell her. This day is hard enough on all of us. We don't need to be picking her up off the floor today too. Just tell her you love her and hold her hand. It'll be a good few weeks before you see her again."

With that, Charlie gave the bed one last shove, stepped back, took a long look at his hurt, furious friend, swiveled around, and bolted from the room.

Sinking deeper into the pillow, Josh closed his eyes and moaned. The small blonde nurse strode in and asked if he was feeling okay.

"No," Josh said. "Not even close." Turning his head away from her curious stare, he swallowed back a whole new fear and wished to hell they had let him die.

Chapter Twelve

Jessie was arguing with Matt when they made it back to Josh's room after their walk.

"What kind of jet is it? There's bound to be room on it for family. Come on, Matt, I want to travel with Josh." That was about all Jessie got from Matt when she tried digging into the men's somber silences and down-hearted looks—that she and Josh would be flying on separate aircraft during tonight's move to Vancouver.

Kalon was in the room at the time, checking Josh's surgical wound. Glancing up, he caught Matt's eye. Shrugging, he said to Jessie, "Honey, don't take this the wrong way, but there's never enough room for families in those things. Look at me," he gestured to himself. "I may as well be an elephant. You really wanna squish in beside this smelly manly hulk?"

"Take the Keating jet." Josh's empty-sounding croaked demand was final.

The way he said it, as if he didn't want her near... Jessie shuddered. "Damn it, Josh. Kalon's big fingers are nowhere near as soft as mine."

Recalling Charlie's hurt and anger, Josh made an effort to lighten up, for Jessie's sake. "You'll be more comfortable with a big chair to stretch out in. Kalon was telling me about the medevac jet. It's got a narrow aisle. It'll be crowded with me in there on a stretcher."

"Okay, fine. Whatever." Nervous, Jessie took a long look at Matt. He made a point of watching Kalon's adept fingers navigate Josh's bandage.

Wincing, Josh curled his bottom lip down in distaste. At least the tubes, minus a lingering IV, were all out now, including the awkward and uncomfortable chest tube. Hospitals and their assorted mysterious paraphernalia were becoming far too familiar.

Matt touched Jessie's arm. "There's security outside the door, and Arnie's around. I'm going to head back over to set for a few hours."

Taking his fingers in hers, Jessie winked at Matt. "Gawd, she must be some good in bed. Josh, you might be sorry you never tapped your female co-star after all."

"Not funny, Jessie." With a tiny, forced smile, Matt brushed his lips against her forehead. "I'll come back in a few hours and drag you back to the condo so you can pack. Evelyn's supposed to land later with clothes and a few things the kids asked for from the ranch, too. See you in a bit."

The ranch.

As he turned to go, Matt let himself dwell for a second on Josh. He didn't have to wonder how well the conversation with Charlie went. Josh was paler than usual—tinged with a weak, sickly green. The mention of his much-loved ranch just now obviously didn't sit well, either. The man wouldn't even have a chance to stroll its grounds, to walk its creek, to touch his horses, to say any kind of proper goodbye.

I'm sorry, Matt wanted to say to him, but for Jessie's sake he kept his mouth shut. Josh looked so diminished in the bed, at the mercy of Kalon to change his wounds and to help him piss. Matt could only hope that Josh would someday see the blessing in all of this. *You'll meet your new baby,* he thought. *You'll see your children grow older, you'll see them fall in love, marry. You'll get to hold this amazing woman in your arms again, and make love to her the way I...*

He cut his thoughts short. There was no point in going there now. Jessie would soon be far away again. Shanda, however, would stay near.

"Bye, Matt," Jessie breathed to Matt's departing back as he left the room.

Kalon smiled at her on his way by. He had been told that Jessie knew very little about what was going to happen in her life, about this new direction in which she was being taken. She would soon need all the smiles she could get.

Uncertain, Jessie let a finger rest on the footboard of her husband's bed. Resting most of her weight on one foot, she tilted the sole of the other foot up against her ankle, in a sort of treelike yoga pose, and angled her head at her prone husband. "I'm getting a freaky vibe, Josh," she admitted fairly casually. "Are you?"

There was a moment in which Josh thought of blurting it all out, all the shit Charlie told him. But seeing Jessie standing there that way, so cute, so naïve and innocent in all of this, already having been hurt so much by Morgan and Nadia…Josh couldn't do it. Even now after all these years of being with her, he saw what everyone else still saw in Jessie—the reason why Arnie, Charles, Charlie and Matt were all so downhearted and sorrowful today. It was her simple beauty and effervescent hope—her extraordinary music; it was the way she brought them all to their knees again and again with gorgeous melodies; it was her determination to see light during times when most people were capable only of getting lost in darkness.

You better hope you can still see light now, Josh considered, *and in the days to come, sweet girl. Because shit is about to get real.*

As if him getting shot wasn't real enough. As if him brokering a deal to get himself shot wasn't real enough, even if it was meant to save his family.

"You're so beautiful," he told her now in that murmured way of his that Jessie often got lost in. Josh let his eyes land on her pregnant belly.

Instantly forgetting about the odd vibe that was freaking her out, Jessie lit up and made her way to Josh's side, where Charlie stood shaking earlier. She took Josh's hand and caressed his strong fingers. "We ought to be thinking about baby names," she chided him. "This little one's only gonna percolate for a few more months, Josh. Got any ideas?"

Will the world know about our baby? I guess they will, Josh thought. *I have no idea how this is going to work. I don't see how it can work at all.*

He swallowed. Not since he was made aware of this new child had Josh really stopped to consider it as a person. All of that time, pretty much, was devoted to pretending the baby didn't exist, to trying to find a solution to the dark forces that haunted the Sawyer family day in and day out. Now, though, this baby was the one small perk in the plan Charlie revealed earlier.

Jessie saw the change come over Josh's face. "Scoot over." Brightening, she lowered the bed rail so she could climb back on the bed and snuggle with her husband. "If it's a girl," she decreed as she settled on her side next to him,

"I was thinking about Sarah, with an H, kind of an ode to my sister but still keeping her own personality."

"Hmm. Sarah. That's pretty." Wrinkling his nose, Josh pushed thoughts of the unknown away. *Where am I going? Will I ever work as an actor again? What about the kids? How can we change their names? They are who they are...* With a shake of his head, he tried to focus on baby names. "And if it's a boy?"

"Not sure." Jessie averted her eyes from her husband. Looking down, she played with his fingers. Inside, she ran a name over and over and over her tongue. *Micah.* It was not a name she could say out loud just yet. In her mind it was sacred, a name that recognized Matt's devotion to her and to her family. At this point in time Josh was not likely to recognize that just yet. He may not ever, in fact. No, if the baby was a boy, the name Micah would have to be carefully whispered and explained in the hope that Josh would also respectfully recognize Matt's value to the family without thinking Jessie chose the name simply for her love of him.

"We'll know when we see the baby what he or she should be called, Jessie." Tenderly, Josh let his fingers twine around his wife's. Lifting their hands, he placed them over Jessie's swollen belly. "Ah," he said, when her abdomen moved underneath his touch. "Another fighter, huh? What is it you always say?"

"Sawyer Strong," Jessie whispered, watching Josh's big hand move over her belly. Tears pricked at her eyes. "Josh, do you realize this is the first time you've even tried to touch this baby?" She peered up at him from underneath damp lashes.

"I was scared," he murmured into the pale blue eyes he loved. "I'm sorry, Jessie. I'm so, so sorry."

Jessie's heart abruptly hitched in confusion when Josh said that, but she screwed up her courage and forced it away. This moment was too precious to let slide by in a splatter of bewilderment and tears. Softly, Jessie breathed back, "It's okay, Josh. We're good now. We're all good. The bad stuff is over. You know that, right? We made it through, babe. You and me. Our kids. We made it through."

"You bet." They were almost nose to nose again. Josh closed his eyes and prayed that Charlie was right, that he and Jessie could somehow regain their equilibrium and raise their family in safety. Still, the dagger that sliced his gut in two at the thought of starting a whole new life away from their friends, away from the celebrity and fame and incredible acting jobs he loved, may as well have been really, truly, slicing through his skin, the pain it left behind was so acute.

Jessie thought he was emotional because things were wrapping up, coming to an end. She had no way of knowing just yet that Josh was aware of things she had yet to discover, and that the future, as far as she could see it—paved with gold, perfect and safe once again—was, in fact, reducing her husband to a whole new level of hopelessness.

Chapter Thirteen

"There was room on the medevac jet for me! Jesus, Matt, didn't you already get laid today, in Shanda's dressing room or wherever? Why'd you want me all to yourself?"

"Settle down, Jessie. Sit down, damn it!" They were airborne now, powering through the skies just beyond Calgary in the Keating jet. Jessie was so angry at Matt for not letting her travel with Josh that she couldn't see straight. Speaking was not an option until now. Even so, shutting her trap and fuming in silence had only served to heat up Jessie's anger so that when she finally let loose on poor Matt, she didn't bother holding back. Now, pacing the narrow aisle of the Keating jet, Jessie was rattling Matt's last nerve. Wisely, Victoria had stepped quietly up to the cockpit to sit with her pilot husband. The amiable flight attendant left a cloud of her usual jasmine fragrance behind; although the scent was calming, it wasn't sedative enough to convince Jessie to stand still.

Matt had a clear understanding of where Jessie's angst was coming from. When Josh and Jessie were separated, there were always uneasy hours—or days—to fill until they were back in each other's company. Factor in the events of the last week and of the tumultuous year before that, and it wasn't a stretch to see why Jessie was so upset.

She turned to him. He was sitting on the sofa at the back of the jet, not reclining with his feet on the ottoman as usual, but pitched forward, his head in his hands, which further ramped up Jessie's weirded-out vibe. With a final *grrrr*, she plunked herself down on the ottoman in front of him, and took his hands in hers.

Matt looked up. The beloved gentle hazel-gray eyes captured Jessie in their worried gaze.

"You're really freaking me out now," she declared, shuffling forward on the ottoman so that she could be closer to him. "Tell me what the hell this is all about, Matt. The only person close to Josh on that medevac flight is Arnie and let's face it, they're not even talking!"

"The three stooges had to stay in Calgary for *Sacred Peace*, Jessie. You know that." Matt was starting off slow. Safe.

"Yes I know, but Zach might have stayed if we asked him to, instead of flying home. And think about the carbon footprint. Jesus, Matt, both you and I could have gotten on that plane with Josh! Kalon's a big guy, but he's not that big!"

"Jessie…"

"What in hell are you not telling me, Matt? What don't I know?"

Forcibly moving her aside, Matt stood up, took over the aisle, and started pacing. He thrust one hand down to his hip and used the other to anxiously wipe—over and over—the top of his hair so that the usual gelled tips got all disorderly and jumbled, as if they'd had a good drunk and weren't yet sober. With one last swipe of the now unruly hair, he planted his feet and faced his friend.

"You trust me, Jessie? Do you trust me?" He was almost crying.

"What?" Standing, moving past the ottoman to face him, Jessie started to tremble. "I've seen you during some pretty bad times, Matt. You're usually composed and in control but this last little while you've been a different person. On our walk you were quiet and remote. Josh and I being on different jets right now makes absolutely no sense. I'm scared. You need to talk to me. You need to tell me what the hell's going on!"

"What's going on, Jessie? You really want to know?" He loaded his gun and fired. "I lied to you. That's what's going on."

She crooked her head. "Wh-what? When? About…" She swallowed and got super quiet. "About what, Matt?"

"At the condo, I told you it was over. That Morgan considered the debt paid."

"Yeah…so?"

"You heard me, Jessie. I lied."

The dull roar of the jet filled Jessie's head. Beneath her feet was a steady vibration she'd gotten used to over the years, a gentle, even pulse that felt like home. It was always a sure and stable heartbeat. Now the roar was unwelcome. It morphed into a thunderous reverberation that stuffed Jessie's head with cotton; that dulled her senses. The continual vibration escalated into a foreign, unwelcome thunder.

The jet was now a trap. It was inescapable. How swiftly things changed, how quickly life became a plunging marauder, a villainous brigand.

Sinking backward, Jessie floated back down to the ottoman in a confused daze.

Regarding her from a distance, Matt stayed put. Locking his jaw tight, he clenched his hands into fists at his sides and spoke through gritted teeth. "I—we—didn't want you to worry. You had enough to worry about."

"And Josh?" Jessie looked up. The hardened steel of her eyes braced themselves for a fight, narrowing into pipes of accusation that spoke legions. "Did he plan this?"

Hanging on to his nerves and his pride, Matt walked to Jessie, squatted down in front of her, took her fingers in his and dug himself a deeper hole, a pit so big it would take a backhoe to dig him out. "Josh getting shot was Morgan's nasty project, Jessie. Let it go. We're taking care of things."

"So you guys think Morgan will still go after Josh. Because he survived the shooting."

"Yes," Matt whispered.

"You're spiriting him away, aren't you, Matt? Josh? He's on a different plane because he's not landing in Vancouver."

"There's only one way to end this thing, Jessie. I asked you if you trust me, and you didn't answer."

"I trust you." It was a whimper, accompanied by a fierce pride and softly trailing tears. "You know I trust you."

Reaching up, Matt used the backs of his fingers to erase his girl's pain. "Sawyer Strong," he said, but he, too, crumpled.

Pulling him close, Jessie felt him tip forward onto his knees as he buried his face in her shoulder. His body was electric, taut and trembling. "Oh,

God," she breathed, awakening to his 'last chance' plan. "It's not just Josh! You're spiriting all of us away."

"Jessie," he said, rocking back so he could place his palms on her cheeks and force her to meet his heartsick gaze, "This has not been an easy decision for us, for any of us. I am truly, truly sorry."

"I don't get it, h-how…?"

Matt didn't answer. He waited for her to grasp at straws and figure it out for herself. It only took her a few seconds.

"Jesus, Matt." Jessie laid her hands over his on her cheeks. Her palms were sweaty, her eyes unfocused and glazed as they put two and two together. "You want Morgan to think Josh is dead. Is that it? You want us…to pretend he's dead? Jesus. Does Josh know about this?"

"He knows. Charlie told him while you and I were out for our walk."

"Where are you taking him? Matt, where are you taking him?"

Matt had to still his racing heart before he could summon up the nerve to tell her. Reaching deep, he called forth the professional, take-charge side of him. "The medevac will turn off all communications near Chilliwack, over a mountain known as Slesse Mountain. Planes have been known to go down there and not be found until spring."

"Jesus Christ." Jessie shrank away from Matt but he grabbed her shoulders and pulled her back to him.

"Listen to me. You need to know this. He'll be transported by an ambulance to a remote cabin eight hours north."

"Eight hours?" Jessie's voice was dull and afraid.

"He's got Arnie with him, and Doc Westfield and Kalon. They've got everything they need. The jet was stocked. Josh will lay low until he's well enough to be moved independent of a medevac flight, a week or two, maybe. Charles has a friend he trusts who has a house on some tiny isolated Caribbean island, an underdeveloped place the tourists leave alone. We'll fly you and the kids out after your show in L.A. You'll have sun and waves and your family."

"But…but…the baby… Charles and Dee…Charlie, Jane, everyone…" Inhaling deeply, Jessie almost collapsed before the one word Matt needed to hear the most escaped her lips—"You."

He did okay until that word was uttered. When she said it, Matt lost himself in her eyes and she lost herself in his. Time was no longer a thing; in its place was eternity, past, present and future, non-linear, all caught up in that one simple word, 'you,' as if by holding their shared gaze Matt and Jessie could control time, could make it freeze, could make the intense moment last forever.

The illusion was shattered when Matt gathered his wits and said brusquely, "I will be fine this time, Jessie, and so will you. You and Josh will no longer need security. You will no longer fear for your lives. If you need one of us, we are a phone call away. Charles is making sure the place is connected, although I've been told to warn you that the Internet may be spotty. We can come visit, all of us. A lot of people live that way, away from the people they love. In your case it's a matter of life and possibly even death. Jessie," Matt lowered his voice, "Morgan has to believe Josh is dead. That's the only way out of this."

"I've always wanted this…a normal life…but why doesn't it feel right, Matt? Why does it feel so wrong?"

He didn't say it, but Matt thought it. It *felt* wrong because it *was* wrong. Jessie had lived a lonely life long enough. Now, not only would she suffer from the disconnects and the lies they would all have to face in order to endure this, but she would also have to support a lonely, disconnected husband too. Not to mention confused and frightened children, as well as a brand new baby.

"You'll be fine, sweetheart," he told her, doing his best to maintain some kind of control over his emotions. "You are the strongest woman I know."

Jessie tried to look away. "It won't work, Matt. I respect all of you for trying, but it won't work."

Grabbing her chin, Matt turned Jessie's face back toward him and made her look into his eyes. Without a second thought, he bent forward and pressed his lips to hers. She tasted of the one coffee she allowed herself that day in her pregnant state, and she kissed him back.

When they separated, Jessie licked her lips as if by doing so she could bring him inside her, inside her mouth so he could be a part of her forever. She shook her head slowly from side to side. "What was that for? What was the point of that? Was that your goodbye?"

Matt didn't answer. His eyes were solemn pools of pain.

On the ottoman, Jessie slid her hands underneath her butt. "Or was that your way of asking me to hang on?"

"You can't," he murmured. "There's nothing here to hang on to."

"I never get a choice," she whispered, her eyes dewy, flickering vaguely as if their light was about to go out. "It's my life, but I never get a choice."

"Then blame me," Matt demanded. "Blame me, Jessie. Because I want you on this planet the same way you want your husband on it. Sweetheart, maybe some day this game will change. But right now, this is the only way."

Eyes widening, Jessie sat up taller. "No. No, it isn't, Matt. There's one more…Arnie once said…we could…" Deflating, she closed her eyes.

Matt placed his fingers on the sweet lips he'd just so tenderly kissed. "Shhh. No. You wouldn't be able to live with yourself."

Eyes blinking open, Jessie looked back up at him with a childlike hope. "If Morgan doesn't exist, the debt is paid."

"You don't know that, Jessie. He has that Caulfield guy on his side, the corrections officer. If any of that crew ever thinks Josh is alive, it may never end."

"I see." Jessie sucked in a hitch-like half breath. "So. Into exile we go. How the hell do we explain this to our children?"

"Make a game of it."

"Sure. You look into Dylan's precious eyes and tell him his revered daddy has disappeared. You keep Emily-Grace from the vultures in public restrooms who will all tell her how sorry they are that her father is dead."

"We'll talk to the kids, Jessie. We'll prepare them as best we can."

"Fine. Have at 'er. While you do that, I'll be in the music room practicing my new angry Metallica vibe."

Matt tossed Jessie's little hissy fit away. He changed course. "Listen, sweetheart, when we land, news will come out that the medevac plane has disappeared from radar. Are you prepared for this?"

Blinking hard, Jessie swallowed. "No, Matt! No. How could I ever be prepared to pretend that my husband is dead? I may be an actor, but I'm not that good."

"You're not alone, sweetheart."

"Ha!" Jessie chortled. "Famous last words, Matt?"

While he tried to figure out how to respond to that, Victoria appeared at the top of the aisle. "Fifteen minutes," she warned gently. "Would either of you like a drink of anything before we prepare to land?"

"Yes," Jessie moaned, eyeing Matt as he stood and helped her rise so they could make their way to the relative safety of seats and seat belts. "Jim Beam. With a little funky smoke on the side." She held up three fingers. "Make that three." Before Victoria could respond, Jessie bit off, "Three drinks and three smokes. On the double."

Sinking into the wide second seat she usually used on the jet, Jessie fixed her gaze on the small window and contemplated how her life seemed to once again be taking a turn she had no time to prepare for.

Shaking his head at Victoria, who busied herself at the front of the plane, Matt slid down next to his girl.

"Black hole," Jessie lamented. "My life. It's a fucking black hole. I suppose you'll marry Shanda the first second you can, eh Matt?"

"Does it matter to you? Really?" His face bleak, Matt stole a cautious glance at his seatmate. Pale and trembling, Jessie looked about ready to keel over.

She turned to him. Her eyes were as serious as Matt'd ever seen them. It only took Jessie a few seconds to make that excruciating short jaunt from Calgary to Vancouver even more unbearably absolute. "I take back what I said earlier," she bit off. "This thing about me not ever having choices? It's a damn good thing. Because right now, I gotta tell you. Facing a life alone with a man as unstable as Josh, in a place where I'm about to have a new baby and won't have any support, really tips the scales in your direction." Jessie's anger and the hopelessness of this new situation—that in all reality had yet to fully sink in—emerged without any kind of filter to soften the blow to a man as devoted, and in love, as Matt. "A little west wind moving at my back to keep me in Vancouver, living a life I know with stable people I love nearby? S'all I need. If I had a choice, that'd be it."

At that, Jessie shoved earbuds in and cranked her iTunes up as high as she could stand. A haunting old Sarah MacLachlan tune came up when she hit the *shuffle* button on her favorite playlist. *I Will Remember You* filled her head, while shocked silence emanated from Matt's seat.

It didn't last long. Heartless, he roughly yanked the earbud from Jessie's closest ear. With a high-pitched yelp, she pulled out the second and sent him a scathing look.

"You are not playing that game with me, Jessie." Furious, Matt gripped the earbud tighter when Jessie tried to grab it from him. "You and Josh are everything to each other. The whole time you were with Jacob you were mourning Josh. You took vows. For better or for worse. This is for worse, I agree, it sucks, but this is the way it is. You will never be happy without him by your side, and it's goddamned nasty of you to pretend otherwise. Now if you'll excuse me, I think you've broken enough damn hearts. Leave mine alone."

Bracing his arms to give himself a hard shove upwards, Matt tossed the earbud back at Jessie who, in surprised despair, was cringing away from him. Matt wasn't quite finished. "You," he fumed, "are a selfish, spoiled bitch. You have never suffered alone, not since you entered Jack Deacon's door all those years ago. Always, there has been a whole host of people shedding tears for you, for Josh, for your family. Do you think any of us want to see this happen? Any of it? None of us really know how it's all going to go down, Jessie. None of us. We're doing the best we can here, on very short notice. If you want to save your husband, you need to hold up your end and stop with these endless games!"

"You bastard!" Rising so she was kneeling on the seat facing him, Jessie pointed to the back of the jet and cried, "You kissed *me* back there! Not the other way around! And for the record, the other night was one of the darkest nights of my life and you went down the hall to fuck Shanda! You left me alone then, Matt, and you're sending me off to deal with my depressed husband alone. Is it so bad to want some security, some stability in my fucked-up life? In the lives of my kids? You know who used to give that to me, Matt? Huh? You, you goddamned bastard! You."

Victoria was starting to stress out. The jet was already descending. It was one-thirty in the morning Alberta time, although only twelve-thirty Vancouver time, and everyone was tired and at their wits' end. The lights of Vancouver were shimmering below them; there was snow on the peaks of the mountains to the north, although all that seeing the lights of the Grouse Mountain ski area served to do was make Jessie feel even more defeated. She couldn't even remember the last time she had a good ski, or took her kids out for a casual Sunday afternoon romp. Did Matt say they were moving Josh to a Caribbean island, where she and the kids would join him?

Skiing wasn't even going to be an option anymore. One less choice she—and Josh—got to make.

"Sit, please, buckle up." Victoria was insistent. "Matt, please. Sit."

He did, but before he sank back down—behind Jessie, on the sofa at the back—he planted his feet in the aisle and fired off one last volley of spiteful remarks fueled by uncertainty and worry. He spoke quietly, with a firmness he had to strive hard to pull up from the depths of his weary soul. His words emerged soaked and weak . "You know what, Jessie?" he started. "This stability and security you speak about?" Raising a finger, he pointed to himself. "I want it too, sweetheart. I fucking need it. All these years with you… you exhaust me. With all your talk of hope you could be a rainbow, but the thing about rainbows? They always come with rain. Shanda's a rose in the goddamned rain. When the rain goes away, long after your rainbow disappears she'll still be a rose, stuck in the dirt, grounded, as steady and dependable as they come. You're a flighty mirage still fighting for space in the sky."

After he stormed the rest of the way down the short aisle and buckled in, Jessie was shaking too hard to even attempt to do up her seatbelt. Victoria, usually a calm and pacific person, marched over to her and knelt so she could help buckle it under Jessie's baby belly. Victoria attempted to fire a nasty look at Matt, but he had buried his head in a hand and wasn't looking.

"Thank you," Jessie said softly to Victoria as she started to come back to herself. "Do you know what's happening, Victoria? To us? To my family?"

Victoria was still kneeling by Jessie. "Some," she replied carefully. "I don't think I know everything, honey. But whatever it is, I get the feeling it won't be easy."

"Not for him, either, Victoria. Okay? Go easy on him. I saw that look you gave him. It's his fear talking. What he's losing is doing his talking for him. It's not just me. It's a whole little family."

Deflating, Victoria smiled sadly. "You are really something, Jessie," she said. "If my husband said those things to me, I wouldn't speak to him for a week."

"Well, I might not speak to him for a week." Jessie tried to smile, but it came out crooked. "But, Victoria?" She held up two fingers. "One, he is not my husband. And two? I think I'm damn well gonna need him this week."

The truths were accompanied by a new round of slowly moving tears, which trickled down Jessie's pale cheeks in dribs and drabs. Wiping them away with a fist, she straightened and inhaled deeply for strength. "Into the breach," she managed as Victoria stood. "Now go buckle up, Victoria. It just might be a bumpy landing."

The flight path had the jet coasting beyond the land and out over the dreamlike Pacific Ocean, where it banked into a wide 180-degree turn before it was cued to land. The turn took Jessie and Matt back toward the city, over humungous logs spread out in the water, all cut and ready for processing by some unknown sawmill; over pools of silken moonlight that caressed the ocean with illusory magic and lent it a shimmering depth and mysticism Jessie hoped to never really know. The snow-tipped mountains were on the left now, since they'd flown out to sea and turned back inwards. Pondering them, and the miles and miles and miles of invisible mountains Jessie knew were behind the ones she could see, she let her mind wander back to her husband.

Sitting back, she laid a hand over the unborn baby in her tummy and wondered how Josh was faring on his journey. *Where will you be landing?* she silently asked as teardrops landed on her top. *And when will I see you again?*

Behind her, alone on the sofa, sorry for unleashing such heated words on an unattainable woman he'd loved now for a very long time, Matt shrank into the creamy leather, and wished to hell he could be the one to disappear.

Chapter Fourteen

What really struck Josh about his short time in northern British Columbia was the debilitating claustrophobia brought on by isolation. For the first few days, apart from stunted short conversations with his caregivers, Arnie included, he passed the time by staring out at trees from a window of the small log cabin he was told Charlie had sourced out via a trusted producer buddy. If it was warm enough, in the afternoons Kalon and Arnie helped him navigate his way to a mini verandah, where he wrapped up in a cozy quilt and watched the wind breathe life into the blanket of greenery surrounding the foursome's northern refuge; coniferous trees, like soldiers on watch, lined the clearing of the mountainous terrain where the cabin was situated.

Josh had been removed to a place that felt like the center point of a thousand staring eyes. The cabin was in a valley; higher ground eclipsed it, stretching upwards and outwards for as far as Josh could see. There were only forest sounds here, and wind, and the occasional call of a bird or howl of a four-legger somewhere off in the woods. When Arnie or Kalon cooked, or when Doc Westfield tossed carrots and potatoes into a pot where stew beef slowly roasted, Josh welcomed the homey clinks and clanks of normal mealtime prep. Apart from the low hum of the mens' idle chatter—not his, he rarely spoke—the place was ghostly, its natural beauty stunning but stifling to a man accustomed to a busy, noisy film set, or a household filled with industrious children.

Several days after he was officially declared missing, he finally got up the nerve to corner Arnie and ask questions. There was a small single cot along the east wall of the cabin, tucked into a corner of the kitchen next to a simple wooden table. Leaning against the wall, with a pillow supporting his back, Josh got Arnie's attention while Kalon and the doctor were out strolling the nearby woods.

Arnie, just back from a nearby town where he couriered a note Josh wrote to Jessie—using an alias on the return address, with a newly whiskered Arnie telling the courier company that he was a fan and the letter was a sympathy card—was shoving split wood downward into the round hole of an ancient stovetop, prodding the bits and pieces with an iron handle usually used to maneuver the burner tops. His back to Josh, he was so used to his friend's silence that he jumped when a low voice cut through the sizzling of the wood pieces as they were consumed by flames.

"How long are we staying here?" Josh asked, his voice raspy with disuse. He was staring at his fingers, intently studying the nails as if they could provide some clue to the mysteries of his new, unwanted life.

Arnie turned. After a moment, he looked back at the stove, replaced the iron fitting over the hole he was pushing wood through, and snugged the bottom of the handle into a small square where it would sit until it was needed again. Rubbing his hands together, he walked the few steps to a 1920's glider rocking chair that was facing the cot Josh was resting on, and eased himself down into it. "Another few days, or a week at the most, maybe," he replied, watching Josh for clues of his thoughts on the subject. "The weather's unpredictable up here this time of year. We need to get out before we get snowed in."

"So why here? I heard you guys say we're near some old ghost town."

"We didn't have a lot of time to figure things out, Josh. A friend of Charlie's once shot a film up here. The old ghost town was a company-owned asbestos mining town. It was, for the most part, abandoned and bulldozed and burned to the ground when the mine closed down in the early 90's."

"Where're we going when we leave here?" It was so weird, not having any say in his life. Josh was looking at Arnie now, up from underneath a long layer of hair so that he appeared naive and frightened.

Arnie sat back against the rocking chair and gave the end of the cot a little push with his foot so he could rock while he talked. Outside a window at his left, a gust of wind circled down through the verdant valley and set the tops of the trees dancing. "South. Caribbean," he elaborated. "I kind of wish we could winter here, though. I like the solitude. I thought I'd hate it, after Vancouver, you know, and Calgary. But we're not geared up enough to make it through a long, snowy winter."

"We'd drive each other nuts," Josh said. "Four big guys in one small space? You'd miss Lucie. You'd miss getting laid."

"Yeah. Lucie." Arnie stared out of the window again. A certain calm passed over him. "I sent her packing, Josh."

"What? Why?" The admission set Josh's teeth on edge. He caved, and stopped fidgeting with his fingers. "Oh, I get it. Because of me."

"It wasn't so much what she did, Josh. It was that she lied. On the Downtown Eastside, lying is enough to get a man killed."

"Apparently. Or at least it should be."

Josh's attempt at black humor only served to rattle Arnie's nerves. "Yeah, Josh, if I had known my wife had anything to do with your dark scheme, I would have strangled the truth out of her and knocked some sense into you. If you had listened to me in the first place, the whole world wouldn't be mourning your supposed loss right now, and you might possibly have been able to sign on to season three of *Sacred Peace*. Never mind how fucked up you've left everyone else."

"I couldn't see how, Arnie…" Josh confessed quietly. "I couldn't see how we could have kept on going the way we were going. I couldn't see an out."

"What you did was not an honorable thing, Josh. I'll never forgive Lucie for her part in it."

"Who said anything about honor? Honor was never my strong suit, Arnie. I just wanted to save my family. I wanted Jessie and the kids to move on, to live their lives in peace."

"You honestly think any of them would have found peace without you in their lives, Josh? Especially Jessie?"

"Matt would have helped her."

"Matt's planning to marry Shanda. Jessie's already losing her hold on him."

Slowly, Josh shook his head. "He'll never let Jessie go. Not fully."

"Jacob did. Charlie did. Both of them let her go and moved on. Matt will be doing the same."

"Because we're going to be living under the radar in God-knows-where. Out of sight, out of mind. You think she wants this?"

Arnie had to think for a minute. Outside his window, some kind of brown bird he didn't recognize was skipping over the ground, oblivious to the ruffled feathers the wind was tossing around without mercy. "No, I don't think she does. I think your wife will be in shock for a while over how quickly her life is about to change. What we're hearing from the Vancouver crowd is that she's on auto-pilot these days."

"Arnie, I think…" Josh rubbed his jawline. Shaving was not a thing, out here living this rustic life. His new whiskers were itchy. He looked up and met Arnie's gentle, thoughtful eyes. "I think Jessie needs to be able to make her own choice. I think she needs to know what she's getting herself into, if she chooses to come live with me. More or less in exile, I mean."

"I don't agree, Josh. There's no point in sending her down a path laced with misery. She's got enough to deal with. Besides," Arnie added, buoyed by the positive energy with which being ensconced in nature was infusing his spirit, "you survived this deal you brokered with Morgan. Things are different now. He thinks you're dead. You can move around at will as long as you're cautious."

"As long as I pretend to be someone else, you mean. As long as I never accompany my wife and kids anywhere where they can be themselves. Ever."

"It's the lesser of two evils, Josh. You need to make this work."

"Look, Arnie, this is the thing." Josh's eyes faded from an intense liquid brown to a more dull-like finish, as if he added a photographic filter to de-saturate the color—the life—from them. "It's enough to have to change my own life. To give up my dreams, the work I love, the respect I was finally building for myself after all those years when people hated me. I can't take on Jessie's pain too, her losses. And the kids—Emily-Grace has been a struggle from the time she lived with Jacob in New York. She'll hate me for being the reason she has to leave Stella, and Jacob and Kayla, their new baby…"

"Jessie's an amazing woman, Josh. She has the strength you need to help you start focusing on living again."

"How is hiding from myself 'living,' Arnie? Tell me how that's living."

"Reframe your thinking, Josh. Find new ways to live. There is joy in other things besides acting, especially with your wife and kids safe by your side."

"That's the thing. We'll never really be safe. Not really. Someone might figure out who we are. And then what?"

"Then we move you."

"And we start again. How many 'start agains' do you think we have left, Arnie? Jessie and me?"

"A thousand, if that's what it takes. You've made it this far."

"I can move around easier on my own."

Arnie stared at Josh. He stopped moving the rocker with his foot. "But you won't. You won't want to live your life without your wife and children in it."

"Say some random day down the road Jessie inadvertently finds out the truth. I don't want to live my life seeing resentment and shame in her eyes every time she looks at me. She won't understand why I did what I did. She deserves to know now, before she and I see each other again."

"So how would telling her the truth be any good?"

"It'll give her a choice. She'll feel like she has some semblance of control and it'll give her some time to process the big shit."

"She'll choose you. Jessie will always choose you."

"I don't know, Arnie. I honestly don't know. I just know that I can't look her in the eye wherever we end up, with this kind of secret hanging over us. She deserves to know what she's getting into."

"You'll destroy her."

"Maybe not. Like you said, she's strong. She's stronger than any of us."

"So. How do you propose to tell her?"

Josh paused. "It's done, Arnie. The wheels are already in motion. That envelope you couriered to Jessie for me? The one you sent to the L.A. venue?"

Silently, Arnie studied Josh. A certain peace was settling over the man's eyes, which startled him. There was nothing left to say out loud that could bring any kind of resolution to this confusing, difficult situation. Inwardly, Arnie said a prayer; he directed it to the hopeful cloud-dotted blue skies he could make out above the tops of the secretive, whispering trees.

Arnie let out a long, meaningful sigh, and turned away.

Chapter Fifteen

A few hours after Josh and Arnie had their difficult heart-to-heart, Jessie had one with Kayla. They were in the nursery of Jacob and Kayla's large condo in Vancouver's sedate Olympic Village, overlooking False Creek. It was ten o'clock, and the three Sawyer children had finally bedded down, all snuggled up together down the hall in the guest room in a king-sized bed. In the condo's expansive front room, Jacob was entertaining Matt and Shanda.

After taking her newborn from Jessie's arms and laying her down to sleep, Kayla stood by the nursery's crib and gazed lovingly down at her baby.

"You're glowing," Jessie said from a comfy, cozy spot in a window seat lining the far wall. "Mommy-hood looks good on you, Kayla." Watching her, Jessie reflected on the way Kayla was smiling softly at her baby girl. From this perspective, essentially a three-quarter profile, it was easy to see Josh in his sister, in the way Kayla moved and in her radiant expression as she watched Lily's small body in rosy-baby slumber.

Kayla was resting one hand on the crib's rail. Lifting her hand, she trailed it along the top edge as she moved over to Jessie and lowered herself onto the cushioned bench seat next to her sister-in-law. "She's a good baby." Twisting two fingers together, she held them up. "Fingers crossed. I've heard some horror stories about colic and stuff."

"That's just boys," Jessie replied, leaning her head back against the window. "And it stays with them for life. Trouble, I mean."

A sideways glance at Jessie took Kayla's momentary happiness and squashed it. "Speaking of boys, how are you holding up this week, Jessie?"

"I suppose that depends on what you consider holding up. And which boys you're talking about."

Kayla's voice softened. "I hear that you said no to any kind of memorial service."

Jessie jumped on her. "Why the hell would I want to hold a memorial service for a man who isn't dead?"

If things were different, Kayla would have taken offense to Jessie's quick retort. As it was, she just shrank back against the window. "The world needs a chance to grieve," she offered after a brief hesitation.

"Ha. Hypocrites. It took them forever to even see what an incredible man your brother is, Kayla. Let them do their own grieving." Rubbing her swollen tummy, Jessie blinked back tears and said, "This is hard enough on the kids. I'm not putting them through a service that's just gonna scare them even more. Besides, Jacob and I will be doing the *Sacred Peace* ballad at the concert in L.A. Everyone can cry their eyes out while my husband gives Shanda an orgasm on screen behind us while we sing. Good 'ole Shanda," she added with a liberal dose of sarcasm, and rolled her eyes. "Shanda the shadow."

Warm fingers locked themselves around Jessie's, on her belly. "I'm guessing all this is pretty hard on the kids' momma, too. You haven't left this room since Charlie and Jane said their goodbyes an hour ago. I don't think you even said hi to Matt and Shanda when they got here."

"I have nothing to say to either one of them right now. I can barely think, Kayla." Looking over at Josh's sister, Jessie asked in the almost inaudible, defeated voice she used when life just got too big for her, "Is it okay with you if I just stay here for a little while? We—meaning this new little Sawyer in my belly and me—apparently aren't going to be able to get to know Lily the way we'd like to. I kinda just want to be close to her right now."

"Of course," Kayla replied, brushing back a loose wisp of hair with one hand and giving Jessie's fingers a squeeze with the other at the same time. "Stay in here as long as you like, Jess." She was about to get up to go, when Jessie's voice stopped her.

"I've been thinking about Sandy a lot this week, Kayla." Jessie was staring down past her belly, trying to sit back and inch her feet forward so she could see them past baby Sawyer. Her voice was lost and hollow. "I don't know why. I think maybe I was wondering what my life would have been like if he hadn't died, if we could have spent our lives together like we planned."

"Maybe you've been thinking about him because of Josh. Because Josh survived."

"I guess so. I'm so grateful, Kayla. I can't even tell you how much. I barely remember my life in those first years after Sandy was killed. But with Josh… I'm so damn conflicted. I'm so glad he's okay, but it's this strange world out there now, a one that thinks he's…dead." She twisted her lips into a grimace. "I can barely say the word. We were out this afternoon, with Sam watching over us, and David wanted this toy—some kind of Marvel action figure— and so, I don't know, I kinda forgot all this shit that was going down. I pushed it away, I guess, and focused on the kids, and so I pulled into a Toys "R" Us. Sam was trying to caution me, but you know stubborn me, I wasn't listening. In we go, the kids and me, and before I know it Emily-Grace is white and Dylan's crying. Poor David, he just silently takes it all in, this crazy world he ended up in."

"Did someone say something?" Kayla was rubbing Jessie's fingers, offering a calm, cautious support in the only way she knew how. "Did something happen?"

"Ha! Did something happen. Hell, yeah, although in truth nobody needed to say a word. It was just the way they were all looking at us, and whispering and pointing." She took a breath. "We were in the action figure aisle. Dylan spotted that toy of Josh from the Marvel film we did together a few years ago, and he grabbed it. This one woman lost it, right then and there. Before I knew it she was hugging Dylan, sobbing her heart out. Her friend had to pull her away. I couldn't move. Sam didn't have a clue what to do. In the end, he picked Dylan up but the damage was done. Kayla…" Looking up, finally, Jessie wrinkled her eyebrows. "Even if we change our names and our hair and become new versions of ourselves, the kids aren't going to forget who we were. We'll go into stores and see our faces on magazines. We're not just going to disappear."

"Of course not," Kayla said staunchly. "Just keep the communication open. Talk to the kids so they'll know how to handle those kinds of situations."

"Matt never would have let me take them inside that store today. In Sam's defense, he tried to stop me but Matt would have made damn sure I stopped and thought about what I was doing."

Kayla smiled sadly. "Matt's got a built-in radar for how to navigate the tough corners where you're concerned, doesn't he?" Taking a chance, she hesitated and then sent them down the previous path. "You never talk about Sandy, Jessie. I'm surprised to hear you mention his name today."

Alert now, Jessie took a long look at Kayla. "That's because nobody ever asks about him. Or about Rachel." Jessie seemed surprised. In the crib, Lily made a cute snuffling noise. Both women looked over, and they shared a small smile.

Kayla let go of Jessie's fingers, sat back, and hunkered up her shoulders. In a daring sort of way she said, "Tell me about him. What was he like?"

"Sandy? Oh. Hmmm." Biting her lip, Jessie cocked her head and tried to bring her first serious love back to the surface. "Well, when I first met him he was adorable in that tanned surfer beach bum kind of way. It was his eyes, though, that really got me. Kind of like Josh's. Not in color, but with this gentle, sad intensity. Sandy put on a good act, this tough guy kind of act like a lot of guys do, but it was easy to see through to the deeper part of him. Jacob has those eyes too." She sighed wistfully at Kayla. "I've got a soft spot for men with sad eyes, apparently."

"Matt doesn't. Except sometimes when he looks at you. Usually his eyes are rock hard, and they have this power that just screams 'don't mess with me.'"

A low chuckle slid out from between Jessie's lips. Unable to help herself, she trembled slightly. "I love that about Matt. The way he stands with his hands in his pockets and his legs apart with that concentrated stare and not a hint of a smile, with his lips almost turned down at the corners in a serious kind of way…it just makes me totally awestruck. It's his wall. You know that, right Kayla? On the inside Matt's every bit as vulnerable as the rest of them."

Kayla laughed. "I have to admit, he used to scare the shit out of me when I first started dancing in your company."

"Awww, he's a softie at heart. My GQ buddy is all bark and no bite."

"Liar. Stop protecting him. He has a bite. I've seen him yell at you."

Jessie's voice got a little less playful. Lacing her fingers over her belly, she focused on them. "Whatever you've seen in the past, Kayla? That was nothing compared to the way Matt lost it with me on the jet the night we left Calgary. Just ask Victoria. She's probably still shaking."

Edging sideways on the window seat so that her arm touched Jessie's, Kayla asked, "Is that why you've been avoiding him? Why you won't come out to join us by the fireplace tonight?"

"Our fight? Yeah, I guess. We both said things that I suppose we'd both been thinking, but that we never really shared until the shit hit the fan, as they say. He told me what was happening, and I admit that I didn't deal very well with it." Making a gesture by her lips, splaying her fingers outwards, Jessie lowered her voice. "You know me and my verbal diarrhea, I just spew out whatever comes to mind without processing it first. It set him off."

"You said something that hurt him."

"Yup. Because, you may have noticed, he hasn't spoken to me all week either."

"I don't think that's it."

"I don't suppose it is, either. Not entirely."

"You'll see each other again, Jessie. Things will settle. We'll all be together again."

"No offense, Kayla, but let's not forget that for all intents and purposes your brother has been declared dead."

"Not dead. Missing. There's an elemental difference, my dear sister-in-law." Kayla wagged a finger at Jessie. With a smile, she added, "Which means, dear girl, that Josh could reappear some magical day."

"If we survive our lives in exile, you mean."

"You will." Bending sideways, Kayla brushed her lips against Jessie's pale cheek. "You and Josh are gonna love the peace and quiet of your new lives. You'll never want to work again, either of you. Think how lucky you are that you won't have to, unlike most folks."

"One of us will have to work. It'll look weird to outsiders if we don't."

"I don't know how that will go," Kayla chuckled. "I can't see you as a secretary."

"This conversation's over." Groaning, Jessie closed her eyes and sank lower into the window. "I feel sick."

Rising, Kayla tried to pull on Jessie's hand. "Come on, sister. Come spend some time with us."

"In a bit. I just need some space right now, Kayla, okay?" Jessie's eyes blinked open.

Kayla was saddened to see that they were moist and worried. "All right, sweetheart. I'll come get you when we break out the salty chips and dip. Deal?"

A wan smile followed her to the door. "Deal."

Disappearing around the corner, Kayla had to grab her stomach and hang on to the wall until she regained her equilibrium. In the open-concept kitchen, she wasn't surprised to see Matt and Jacob having a similar conversation as they opened wine and organized beverages.

"None of that for me or Jessie," Kayla ordered as she stood before a chair at the island. "Although we both need it. Desperately."

Quiet footsteps approached. Shanda dropped down into a seat. She raised a hand. "I'll take the bottle." Matt's reproachful stare had no effect on her. Reaching out, Shanda grabbed a vintage Malbec after Jacob removed its corkscrew.

With a wry look to Kayla who, amused, was watching Matt adopt a defeated but noiseless sulk, Jacob pushed a wine glass over to Shanda and raised his arms in humble surrender. "It's all yours," he said, wondering why Matt wasn't saying anything. To Kayla Jacob said, as he retrieved some Evian water from the fridge and poured her a glass, "Where's Jessie? Bathroom?"

"Nope." Kayla moved over a few steps and scooted into a seat next to Shanda. She peeked up at Matt, who was now watching her, but he looked away the second he found her eyes on him. "She needs some alone time."

Nobody said anything. Matt was opening a beer. His hand froze on the twist-off lid.

After a minute of uncomfortable silence, Jacob eyed Kayla. "I'll go talk to her," he announced. "In Jessie's world, being alone translates to being lonely."

"She's got a lot to process, Jacob. She's gonna be lonely no matter what. For a long time, if I know her." Cautious, Kayla let her gaze move sideways to Shanda, who was sipping her wine now, and then up to Matt again. She caught a new sad vibe from Jacob, who accented it by leaning both forearms on the island and laying his chin on his hands. A wave of sorrowful love passed through Kayla, an energy that captured Jacob's attention.

His puppy dog eyes latched into hers. "What?" he asked, his curiosity piqued.

She got all serious. "Jacob, Jessie said you guys are planning to play the *Sacred Peace* tune in L.A. The one with all the video from the show playing behind you guys on stage."

"News to me." He straightened.

"That's not a good idea, Jacob," Matt said, unable to look at Shanda. "Talk her out of it."

Watching them, Shanda narrowed her eyes at Matt. "Why not?"

Three pairs of eyes landed on her at once.

"Uhhhh," Jacob started, eyeing Kayla in a desperate search for rescue, "it's a heavy tune. It takes a lot out of Jessie when she's feeling good. She's hormonal, people will be crying, she's still reeling from all this crap with Morgan, and she knows how much saying goodbye to *Sacred Peace* is gonna kill, uh, er, hurt Josh. Trust me. Jessie will not have the strength to get through that song."

"You know," Shanda mused, "I find it interesting how everybody always tiptoes around her. Like they're scared she'll break if someone says or does the wrong thing. If she wants to sing the damn song, let her sing the damn song."

"Shanda, easy." Matt wasn't saying a lot, so those two simple words immediately caught Shanda's ire. Didn't help that they were tersely edged.

Sitting taller, clutching the stem of her wine glass, she waved an arm at him. "You're the worst one. You've been moping around all week. What the hell'd you two fight about this time, anyway?"

A quick glance to the hallway assured Matt that Jessie wasn't, at least as far as he could see, standing there taking in the conversation which, to Matt, was deteriorating quickly. He tried to regain control. "Fear of the unknown, essentially. Nothing serious. Knee-jerk reactions from all this shit that's going down, that's all."

"I'd hate to see you fight about something serious, then." With a righteous smirk, Shanda slipped off her chair. "Come on, Kayla," she ordered. "Let's talk babies." Hooking her arm in Kayla's, she led her toward the fireplace on the far wall.

Matt stared down at his newly opened beer. He only poured half of it into a glass before setting the bottle down with a resigned *thwunk*.

Taking it from him, Jacob poured the rest into the glass. "Matt, the secret to relationships, as I've discovered with my amazing wife, is to keep the lines of communication open. Don't be moping around and keeping things from Shanda. That kinda stuff drives women nuts." Raising a hand beside his head, Jacob spun a finger around in the air. "Makes 'em start to imagine things, to create their own version of what their guy might be thinking. You don't want that, trust me."

"No," Matt grumped, lifting the beer to his lips and taking a long pull on it, "I sure as hell don't. But Jacob," he said, deflating, "some things are not meant to be shared. If you can figure out the balance here, feel free to fill me in."

Clapping Jacob on the shoulder, Matt started around the island toward the girls. After a moment to ponder what the hell Jessie and Matt might have fought about, Jacob followed.

⌒ ⌒

Well after midnight, Matt took Shanda by the hand and pulled her upright. "C'mon, sleepyhead, it's time to go," he declared. "Early morning."

"For sssome people," she slurred. "Sssome of us get to sssleep in."

"Tomorrow, yes," he agreed. "But on Monday you're back in Calgary at *Sacred Peace*. You should get up early tomorrow so Monday's five a.m. call doesn't come as such a shock." Winking at Kayla, who shared an amused look, he grinned.

Kayla had Lily back in her arms. The new baby was gurgling in contentment after feeding. Jacob had slipped into the nursery to get her and had come back to report that Jessie was sound asleep, curled up on the window seat cushion. Dylan was snuggled up in the curve of her body. It broke Jacob's heart to pick Lily up out of the crib and leave his son and his son's mother alone in the moonlit room.

Matt shook Jacob's hand. "I'll see you in a few days," he said. "Enjoy a quiet day off tomorrow." He was alluding to the rehearsals that would ramp up in the Robson Street studio on Monday, prior to Friday's trip to L.A. for the much-anticipated concert. Holding Shanda's fingers lightly in his, he started toward the door.

"Seriously, Matt?" Jacob shot him an annoyed, questioning look. Gesturing toward the hall that led to the bedrooms, he said, "You can't leave her without at least saying goodbye."

Shanda was tipsy enough to warrant grabbing Matt's fingers with both of her hands. "Sure he can," she mumbled rather gleefully.

Kayla sucked thoughtfully on a lip. "Shanda," she offered, "let's get you a glass of water. And you should probably pee before you two love birds head out. The last thing you want is to get halfway home and have to go. Right?"

"Fine. I know when I'm being manipula—uh, manipula—uh, coerced. Go say goodbye to the little princess, Matt. I'll be here when you're ready to return to real life." She wandered off with Kayla, suspiciously eyeing Matt over her shoulder as she moved away.

"I'll come get Dylan," Jacob offered helpfully to Matt, "so you and Jessie can make friends again."

At the entrance to the long, wide hall, Matt gripped Jacob's arm.

Jacob stopped and faced him.

"Don't let her leave on her own this week, okay Jacob?" Matt said. A new despair was settling into his eyes, one that he managed to hide in Shanda's presence. "Don't let her take off and go on one of her long drives unless you plan on going with her."

"She won't," Jacob assured him. "She promised us. Besides, Jessie's sticking pretty close to the kids these days. They need each other big time while they try to sort all this out."

In the nursery a few minutes later, Jacob was sorry to wake Jessie, but he didn't want her sleeping on the window seat all night anyway, for fear that she might fall off or, at the very least, wake in the morning with a crick in her neck. Squatting down in front of her and Dylan, he kissed her forehead lightly before he slipped his arms around his son. Soothing him quietly, he lifted Dylan and carried him past Matt out of the room.

At the flutter of air along with suddenly empty arms, Jessie stirred. Blinking open her eyes, she spied Matt easing his body down onto a nearby rocking chair. Sitting up, she pushed some loose hair out of her eyes and looked sleepily over at him. "You have your coat on," she blurted out.

Raising his chin he said, "It's late. You missed our little gathering."

"I didn't miss a damn thing." Jessie swiped a wrist across her tired eyes.

"Don't do this, Jessie," Matt said, his voice subdued and afraid. "Don't leave Vancouver like this. Mad at me, I mean."

"Duh, you sat out there all night and never even came in to say hi. I suppose Shanda brought her cuffs from *Sacred Peace*, huh, and forced you to stay at her side?" Spitefully, her eyes narrowed. "Do you two have as much fun with those props as Josh and I do, uh, as we used to?"

A semi-disgusted guffaw broke the angry silence that followed the jealous gibe. "You've got to learn to let things go, Jessie. Hanging onto this kind of negative energy is only going to give you ulcers."

"Ulcers would be the least of my problems. I'd welcome them. They'd be a minor speed bump in my fucked-up life."

"Jesus, girl. I came in here to say I'm sorry. Look, I said things I shouldn't have said. And I should not have kissed you on the jet."

Jessie hooted. "Oh, can I yell that out? Where's Shanda, is she still out there? Mind if I yell that out to her, Matt?"

"Damn it!" Slipping a hand over Jessie's mouth, Matt followed the quick motion by vaulting up out of the rocking chair and landing on the window seat next to Jessie. Grabbing at his hand, she struggled against him. "Jessie, you're a lot of things," he growled, "but you're not vindictive enough to hurt me by going after Shanda. I know you."

She stopped wriggling. Slowly, carefully, Matt let his hand slip down from Jessie's mouth. He let his fingers linger on her chin, and gently brushed his thumb over her skin.

Angling her head sideways, Jessie buried her nose in his shoulder and slipped both arms around his waist. Inhaling deeply, she soaked up the familiar spicy aftershave that washed over her trusted friend like the softness of a welcome cloud. Mingling with a slightly sweaty male musk, at first it raised her spirits, but then it sent her spiraling into a new-old depression, one that spoke of loss and that cried defeat.

"Okay," Matt whispered tenderly into his superstar charge's curls. "This really hurts."

"You need your ass kicked," came a small voice that tickled his arm. "You haven't spoken to me all week, you bastard."

"And you've been downright open to talking to me," he chided. "I can't stand it," he breathed, wrapping his arm tighter around the body Matt knew had the power to disarm him when it wasn't close enough to hold, to protect. "I'm losing my mind, Jessie."

"Don't talk to me about losing your mind, Matt. The world at large is mourning my husband, and my kids are so confused they're barely going through the motions. The worst part is that I don't have a clue how to help them."

"One more week," he said lovingly, as Jessie lifted her head and peered at him through wet lashes. "This time next week you'll be on the jet on your way to Josh. Children are resilient little creatures. They'll bounce back."

"Our kids? They'll be messed up for life, Matt."

He shook his head slowly, accompanying the head shake with slightly upturned lips. "No. Your children have a lot of love on their side, Jessie. They'll be fine."

"Go," Jessie demanded. "I can't do this 'take days and days to say goodbye' thing. What you said to me made a lot of sense, Matt. It hurt like hell but I know it's true." She gulped. "Shanda's stable."

"She likes her wine."

"Lucky you. Your woman will be frisky as hell when you get home tonight."

"Either that or she'll fall sound asleep." Matt laughed, a solemn, serious laugh that was colored more with worry than with actual amusement. "All right," he said, wiping his eyes with the sleeve of his coat, and getting up. "I'm going. I'll see you at La Casa for dinner tomorrow night."

Jessie's heart plunged. "You're not picking us up here tomorrow morning?"

Matt was halfway across the room before she got the words out. Turning, he dismally studied Jessie. In the moonlight she appeared ghostly, apparition-like. Against the window, she seemed already lost to him, suspended amongst twinkling stars in a mystical, haunted sky.

"No," he managed, unable to say more.

"Umm. I see. Your minions are picking up the Sawyer slack. We've become dregs. Duty."

"No, Jessie. I'm meeting with Charles and Charlie bright and early in the morning. We'll be reaching out to Arnie up north. He drives into a nearby community every day to access cell service."

"Better not tell me where. This place may be bugged."

Her tone was haughty, but Matt knew where it was coming from—a lack of control. He chose to ignore the biting comment. "I'll see you at dinner," he said again.

"Hey, Matt? Don't bring Shanda, okay? Every time she looks at me I see victory. It's like she couldn't have Josh, so she scooped you up instead. You're the booby prize, as Jacob used to say." Saying that, spitting out the angry comment, Jessie's voice broke. Tears were liberally rolling down her cheeks as she tossed her curls and set one last merciless comment free. Only this time, it was more pain than an attempt to be mean, and it was meant for both of them. "You've already let me go. In your head and in your heart you've already separated yourself from me. That's why you were so mean on the jet. It's easier to build nasty walls than it is to hang on to crumbling stones. Or should I say lead weights, Matt?"

Speechless, Matt couldn't move. His jaw worked as he tried to sort out what he could say that would possibly give any kind of honor to the untenable, raw, aching predicament in which they found themselves after Josh's seemingly thoughtless actions sent them all spiraling downward. Shifting his weight to one foot, he lingered there and let his gaze drift over Jessie. She was hovering, almost, against the blue-black sky—*memorizing me*, he thought.

"I'll miss you, kid," he finally murmured. "And you're right. I've already moved on. You need to do the same."

He stopped at the washroom on the way out. It wouldn't do to let Shanda— or Jacob and Kayla—see him so destroyed.

In the nursery, Jessie turned her head to the side and let her eyes go unfocused as she picked out the white rails of Lily's crib. The baby would sleep in a bassinet by Jacob and Kayla tonight, so the crib would be vacant. Jessie was glad, because from this vantage point, in the eerie late night light, the crib brought to mind the rails of a prison cell. Morgan passed through her vision, and with his image a new nausea worked its way into Jessie's body. Turning sideways, she lifted her legs up onto the window seat, laid a warm cheek against the cool window, and trembled until Jacob came in ten minutes later, took her by the hand, and tucked her into a comfy sofa bed in his and Kayla's den.

"Sleep, and dream of good things to come," he directed her.

"Sleep, and escape," Jessie said to herself after he left the room. Closing her eyes, she melted away.

Chapter Sixteen

The following week Jessie was hanging the light jacket she wore on the trip from Vancouver over the back of a chair when a light knock came at the door. She was at the L.A. venue of the domestic violence concert, alone in her assigned dressing room. Hollering, "S'open," she looked up to see Sam hold the door ajar for Jacob. Just seeing Sam there instead of Matt was disconcerting. Matt was on the trip, but he and Charles were off discussing security with the local crew. Deirdre was meeting with the stage manager and the kids were settling into the hotel with Carlotta, who had Dan and Alin along to help and to keep watch.

"Hey, Jacob," Jessie called to her visitor. Turning, she half sat on the high chair, which was positioned in front of a long counter to help facilitate makeup and hair for the show tomorrow. A mirror bordered on three sides by light bulbs was across from Jessie, behind her back after she used a foot to leverage the chair around so she could face Jacob.

"You sound cheery. Should I be nervous?" Greeting her, Jacob brushed his lips against his old girlfriend's forehead. He hadn't seen Jessie yet today, since he and Kayla, with their new baby, had flown in the evening before so he could spend the morning doing interviews with the media. Jessie had opted out—rather, Charles and Deirdre had opted out for her. These few weeks were hard enough without having to face the harsh scrutiny of news-hungry interviewers.

Jessie frowned. "I'm happy to see you. That's all. Can't I be happy to see you?"

"Ah. Now there's the woman I know and love." Backing up two steps,

Jacob sank into a chair similar to the one Jessie was sitting in. He studied her. "You've got black circles on your black circles."

Ignoring him, Jessie deflected the comment by tossing her head and asking where Kayla was.

Jacob motioned to the left. "In my dressing room next door. She's feeding Lily." A slow, sad smile widened across his face. "As tired and worried as I know you are, you are radiant, Jessie. Adorable, even."

A pink flush spotted the tops of Jessie's cheeks. Always, she would regret the sorrows Jacob suffered when she left him to go back to Josh. One bright light in this latest madness was the sheer joy he exuded these days as a man in love with an amazing woman, and a new baby to cherish. "You know, Jacob," Jessie said, reaching out to hold his fingers in hers, "I know I put you through hell. But I'm glad we had our time together."

"Our times," he half-joked. "Plural. Edinburgh and New York."

"Yeah. Times." She waited a beat. Their old electric spark passed between them, not in any threatening way, just to remind them they would always mean something to each other. Blushing, Jessie changed the subject. "Kayla told me you guys will be coming to see us lots. And you'll bring the kids back to Vancouver with you to visit sometimes, right?"

"Starting next week," he replied amicably. "We'll spoil them rotten before Charles and Dee fly them down to you and Josh."

"It's good of the two of you to take all three," Jessie ascertained. "Josh and I are gonna need a week to learn to relax around each other again, I think."

Careful, Jacob waded in a little deeper. The intense cobalt blues of his eyes were a Caribbean summer sky, shimmering with remembered love as he fixed Jessie solidly in his gaze. "I haven't wrapped my mind around how all this is going to work yet, Jessie," he divulged. "Communicating and traveling and all that, without..." He couldn't finish.

"Without alerting Morgan's cronies to the fact that Josh is alive, you mean?" Jessie whispered the last bit.

"Yeah, that." Swallowing, Jacob gave Jessie's fingers a gentle squeeze, which she returned.

"Ulysses told me that this Caulfield guy, the guard who coordinates the, uh, retribution and vengeance on behalf of the inmates, isn't all that sophisticated. His work resonates more with the hit men of the prohibition era than anything technological in orientation. He hires 'em and they're physically present to do their shit, like beatings or whatever." She gulped. "Caulfield, at least as far as the goons linked to him in the past go, who Matt's RCMP buddies found and coerced into talking, said they've never heard of anyone on his team who is very deeply connected to technology. I think good old Keating security is counting on that."

"And on the fact that everyone thinks Josh is likely dead."

"As long as some overzealous reporter doesn't start digging for airplane ruins next spring, we should be okay. Do you remember my blogger friend, Gabrielle? From Calgary?"

"Yep. What about her?"

"She's got a lot of power. She doesn't know the truth, but I've been in touch. She's leading the charge. I give her statements that I work out with Charles and Dee, and Matt and Ulysses, more Ulysses than Matt these days," Jessie sighed, "and she runs with them. The other media, who I don't want to talk to, have to go to her if they want a voice they believe is me."

"How many people know, Jess? The truth?"

"You're wondering about our *Drifters* friends, Maggie and Sue-Lyn and Carter."

"It just seems dangerous to me, the more people who know…"

"Well," Jessie wriggled her butt deeper into the chair and stared, unsee-ing, at the door beyond Jacob's right shoulder, "none of the general *Sacred Peace* crew know, and some of those are *Drifters* alumni. Um, obviously our security all know, and Patin, Alin's brother, because he came back to Van to tutor the kids and to help me sort out some kind of a home-schooling plan before we leave. Dan's wife? Ulysses' gal?" She shook her head. "We've even asked Alin and Patin not to tell their friends or parents. Carter knows. He and Josh became pretty good buddies again on *Sacred Peace*. Obviously Steve and Zach know. Maggie and Sue-Lyn? Carter's going to tell them in person. There are some people on our radars whose suffering will soon be alleviated. But I'm with you. Too many people know, in my opinion."

"How many people will know where you are?"

"Do you know where we're going?"

Jacob shook his head. "No. Kayla has no clue."

"Nor do I. I don't even know. At least not exactly."

"Then that's good."

"To a point." Shrinking, Jessie hunched her shoulders and ran her fingers over Jacob's hand. "God, I'm gonna miss all this…playing music with you… hanging out with everyone…"

"But right now you miss Josh more. It'll be worth it in the end, Jessie."

"Will it?" Looking up at him, Jessie ran a finger over her bottom lip, again and again. "My husband is gonna require some serious TLC to get past this one. I just can't picture Josh being happy if he can't work."

"Just…geez, Jessie, I don't know how to say this without pissing you off." Shuffling uncomfortably, Jacob sent Jessie a look of pure concern. The cobalt eyes were no longer dancing and alight. They were dark and serious, a black lowland swamp instead of an indigo blue sky.

Jessie's low voice eased into the silence. "Just say it, Jacob."

"It's just…" He glanced at the wall separating Jessie's dressing room from his own as if Kayla, who was in there feeding Lily, could hear what was being spoken between him and his musical soul mate. "I feel like I'm being traitorous to Kayla, saying this, since Josh is her brother, but Jess…look, if things get bad with Josh, if he goes down another dark road with addictions or whatever, you'll come home, right?"

Jessie's face fell. There was no argument from her, though, as there would have been back in the New York days. Too much solid proof, too much water under the proverbial bridge, was her stark reminder that Jacob's long ago warning about Josh was, distressingly, right on the mark.

Jacob hunkered up his courage and went on. "Look, kid, you and I both know that Josh is a great guy. But being suspended in some kind of false reality where he doesn't feel like himself is not going to put out that fire that haunts him, the one that only a cold beer or some crushed percs can put out. You'll have four beautiful children counting on the two of you to keep it together, Jessie, with no help…" By the look of her face, pinched and solemn now, Jacob realized he'd likely gone too far. Going silent, he held tightly to her hand with both of his while he waited for her to respond.

Jessie was lost in his warm, concerned eyes; lost in the sweet friendship and deep love she shared with Jacob dating back to the old Scotland days. Trust was what she spied there, not anger or remorse or hatred or shame or even fear, like over the years when Jacob was so desperate for her to love him back the way he felt he deserved.

"I love that man, Jacob," she told him, with a strength and passion she almost had to fight to dredge up, because they were fraught with tension and a lack of control over what Jessie would face in the next while. "I know Josh is not always the man I wish he was. But honey, I knew that the night I met him. I saw his demons then, how they haunted him without remorse, how they played in the surface of his eyes and threatened to destroy him. You're right about the kids, it's not just me and him now, it's not just me that he can hurt. And if it ever gets to that point, the way it was back when I fled to New York, I know that I may have to walk away again. If it means protecting my children," she sighed, and exerted a little pressure on Jacob's fingers, "*our* children, meaning your Dylan included, then I will do what I feel is best. But Josh deserves the best that I can give him in terms of support. I'm not saying it will be easy. But I know we've got to try to find a way to make this work."

"Just promise me that you'll call if you need to. Someone. Anyone."

"Ulysses said last night that he thinks Arnie might be staying around for a bit, just to make sure Josh and I've got a handle on things." Letting go of Jacob's hand, Jessie sat back and forced a smile in Jacob's direction. "The rest of you are worrying so much about all this that I almost feel like I have to start calming y'all down instead of the other way around."

"I'm sorry. You've got enough to worry about. You don't need me looking over your shoulder adding weight to your burden, Jessie."

"Just take care of Kayla and that new little baby of yours. Keep them safe, and stay away from protesters. Keep doing awareness shows like this, and those lectures you do around the country, and be a stand-up guy, Jacob. It's enough for me to be worrying about my husband. I need you to stay deliriously happy."

Sliding off the chair, Jacob said, "Kayla and I don't know what life will throw at us next, Jessie. There's no way to guarantee that everything will always be this perfect. Is there? You know it better than anyone."

A depleted chuckle made its way into the space. Jessie followed it up with a, "Is that what you really wanted to say to me? That sometimes life just really sucks? That you're waiting for the other shoe to drop? Because that's not the way to live your life, honey. Talia wouldn't want you to just remember the bad times, how things ended with the two of you. Sandy wouldn't want me to focus only on the tragedy of our last few days together."

Blinking back tears, Jessie gave Jacob a light punch in the arm. "Look at you and me. All the shit we lived through together, and what I think of when I'm standing here by you now is how much I love you, and all of the good times we had. Including," she added into his curls as she drew Jacob's comforting body close and held on tight, "the incredible music we've made over the years. Which," she smiled, "we'll continue to make. I'll send you stuff. Somehow." She frowned. "I don't know about Internet yet, whether that'll be a thing, like, safe and all that, or even whether we'll have any kind of dependable connection. More likely I'll be sending you stuff in person, when I travel or whatever."

"Fair enough." Jacob hugged his old girl back and let her go with a few last optimistic words. "Tomorrow night, then," he said, "when we do this show and get to sing together, we'll focus on the good times, okay Jessie? Let's try to do that. We'll make it a celebration of all the good stuff."

"You got it. Let's rock today's rehearsal and show the world that we can get past bad stuff. Let's ride the top of the wave, Jacob, and coast our way to happiness. I don't see any other way."

"Me too." One last hug, and he was out the door. "I'll see you in half an hour for rehearsal. I hope this gang is organized because I want to get out of here on time to hang out at the hotel with you tonight, you and the kids."

"I second that," Jessie agreed. She was just about to close the door behind Jacob when an older member of the venue staff came striding purposefully toward her.

Sam extended an arm and blocked the guy's way. Their visitor was a Caucasian guy, in his fifties maybe, with stylish mirrored-arm silver glasses perched on his nose. He was nervously tugging at a bowtie that accented a gray sweater he wore over black jeans. In short, he didn't appear threatening in any way but he seemed like a very serious worker bee type, so much so that Jessie and Jacob exchanged small knowing smiles.

Sam maneuvered his lean, muscular cyclist's body between Jessie and their visitor. "Yes?" he asked.

An arm whipped out. At the end of it was a white couriered cardboard envelope. "This came a few days ago for Mizz Wheeler. I meant to leave it in the dressing room before you," he peeked around Sam to eyeball Jessie from behind the dazzling spectacles, "arrived, Mizz Wheeler. I got busy. Please accept my most sincere apologies."

"Umm, it's just Jessie," Jessie responded in a soft, gentle voice that instantly calmed the man who, they were all amused to see, was almost vibrating with the seriousness of his duty. She stuck a hand out past Sam's strong body.

Accepting the friendly shake, the man cracked a tiny smile. "It's a pleasure to meet you, Jessie." The smile did a quick reversal, and flipped upside down. "I'm real sorry to hear about your husband."

Jessie's attempt at lightening things up came to a crashing halt. Her bottom lip quivered. "Thank you," she croaked, and let her hand drop to her side.

Sam took the couriered envelope. He echoed Jessie's comment. "Thank you." It was a rather curt dismissal. Their visitor nodded, pivoted around, and strode away. Looking down, Sam studied the handwriting and the return address. The envelope was from a post office box in northern B.C.

Peering over his shoulder, Jessie whispered, "Is it fan mail or do you think it's from our guys?"

Sam had been apprised that Arnie sent something to them here since Morgan's minions could potentially monitor their home mail. In the fuss of settling in he'd forgotten about it and was glad the serious guy thought to bring it around, although it was likely Matt would have grabbed it at the main office at some point. "I think it's likely," he answered Jessie, "but with your permission, I'll open it." At her nod, Sam pulled the tab across one end and reached inside to grab the cardboard envelope's contents—a single white envelope with Jessie's name handwritten on the front.

"Josh's writing," Jessie murmured so nobody but the three of them could hear. "Thank God. I can't stand not being in touch with him."

A light rub on her back from Jacob was accompanied by a sad grin. "You mean you can't stand not being touched by him."

"Duh. Goes without saying, doofus." Taking the envelope from Sam's proffered fingers, Jessie winked at him and playfully nudged Jacob aside so she could go back into her dressing room and read the letter in peace. "I might be a mushy mess when you come get me for rehearsal, Jacob," she said. "I'm just warning you in advance."

"As long as you're focused," he cautioned, wagging a pointy finger at her. "I don't want to be here a second longer than I have to be today."

With a light laugh, Jessie pushed the dressing room door open. At the last second, she wheeled around and further opened it by pushing her back against it and taking a few backward steps. "Thanks, Sam," she said, holding up the envelope. "This made my day."

Sam caught the door as it started to close. "Happy reading, Jessie," he said. "I'll knock when the stage crew calls for you and Jacob."

Forty minutes later, he did just that.

Jacob, approaching, was less than impressed that they were already starting the ensemble rehearsal late. It further annoyed him that Jessie wasn't answering her door.

Unconcerned, Sam thumbed in the dressing room's general direction and said to Jacob, "She must be in the washroom."

"Well, she is pregnant," Jacob said, amused now. Depressing the handle, he pushed the door open. "Kayla lived in the bathroom the last few months before Lily was born."

As he wandered into the room, the door clicked shut behind Jacob. Sure enough, the door to the private restroom was closed. Sauntering over so he could hammer on it and maybe toss out a few teasing gibes, Jacob grabbed a few grapes off Jessie's well-stocked craft table as he passed by. At the same time, the hair on the back of his neck prickled and stood straight up when he discerned the sound of low sobs emanating out from under the closed door. Fixating on the gray light bleeding out into the room from under the door, Jacob stilled and stopped chewing, another grape halfway to his mouth. Then he remembered Jessie's half-joking comment about being a mushy mess after reading Josh's letter.

Giving the handle a downward thrust, he nudged the door open. "Come on, kiddo," he called into the shadowy grayness of the small room. "Suck it up. You'll see your big stud soon."

Inside, his eyes took a few seconds to adjust to the dimness. Eventually he picked out Jessie who, with Josh's letter dangling from her fingers, was curled up into a ball on the floor at the far end of the shower stall. The envelope was at her feet, forgotten. It lay by the drain as if waiting for water to soak it so it could shrink up and disappear and no longer be associated with whatever bad news it communicated.

Jacob crouched down and studied his musical partner. "Jessie," he said, his heart starting to race, "if this is a mushy mess, I'd hate to see you have a complete meltdown."

"You've seen those," she hiccuped as she sobbed. "On a scale of one to ten, you've seen me have a fifteen. This one's more like fifty."

"What the hell?" Jacob reached for the letter.

Clutching it to her chest, Jessie white knuckled the damp paper and twisted her body away from him. "I was right, Jacob," she cried, pressing her cheek against the far end of the shower stall. "About the hit, I mean. He ordered the goddamned hit."

"Who? Who ordered the hit? I thought you said the letter was from Josh? Is it from Morgan?"

"No, goddamnit!" Jessie struggled to speak past a new round of convulsions. "It's from Josh. He ordered it. He ordered the goddamned hit! On himself!"

"What? Why the hell would he do that?"

"He says it was the only way. He still thinks it's the only way! For all of us to be safe, I mean." Turning to Jacob, Jessie pleaded with her eyes for him to somehow help, to take away the nauseating pain of this new truth that, in all reality, wasn't a complete surprise. In all honesty, the possibility—now outlined and written in Josh's own careful script on the paper Jessie was holding against her heart—had been niggling at her all along, from the moment Josh was shot in the first place.

Jacob was white. Dropping down next to Jessie, he glanced over at the toilet and fought against crawling over to puke into it. "Why would he tell you this just before you're supposed to fly out to be with him?"

"Easy," she wept. "I'll tell you why. The other night I told Matt that he was already distancing himself from me, from us Sawyers. Well, Jacob, looks like Josh was doing the same all along. He started disappearing the day the Lexus was forced into the river, in fact. He can't deal. He'd rather be dead than deal with this, this bullshit!"

Jacob lowered his voice. "Is he asking you not to go, Jessie? Does he want to be alone?"

"Not in so many words." Trying to compose herself, Jessie held the disturbing letter away from her chest. Laying it on her thigh, beneath her growing belly, she started to fold it. It was damp from tears, and from the sweaty moisture on her hands. "No more secrets, he said. He doesn't want me to go down there and look him in the eye and have to feel like he's withholding the truth from me. As if he didn't do that the whole time he was planning this shit in the first place!" A new round of gulping sobs overtook her.

Sighing deeply, Jacob lifted an arm and pulled his old girl close. "He must have felt he had no choice, Jessie. What he said rings true. Josh would not have done this if he didn't think there was no other way. Jesus, he almost lost you and Emily-Grace. That'd be enough to terrify a man into taking drastic steps to ensure his family's safety."

"We're a team!" Pounding a finger harshly into her chest, Jessie choked, "Us! Me and Josh! We're parents, together we make choices. Together! Not alone! And not choices that mean one of us gets to go to sleep forever and never have to face the kind of fear you and I were talking about earlier, the kind of fear that makes a person sick with worry every Jesus day! What gave him the right to be the one to back down, to run away?"

"Why a hit, Jessie? Why wouldn't he just…you know…"

"Stretch a rope over a goddamn tree branch? He's weak, like you said. He's a damn coward. Oh God, Jacob. Drinking himself into oblivion is one thing. Am I going to have to be watching him every day for this now, too? Because if that's our new reality, then I don't want any part of it. I can't do that. How can anyone be expected to live that way?"

Gently grasping a fistful of her hair with his left hand, forcing her to turn her face back around and look at him, Jacob offered assurance. "You won't,

Jessie. You know how I know? Because you are going to be hidden, all of you, and so Josh has nothing to prove to Morgan. The world will think he's dead. Morgan got even. It's over."

"You're forgetting one thing."

"What's that?" Jacob sounded more confident than he felt.

Jessie held up the now-folded letter. "He already made his peace. Josh said his goodbyes. In his head, he's already gone. I knew it'd be hard for him to face a life without meaning, Jacob, but this…" Jessie shook her head. "This is so much more than that. He talks like he has nothing left."

"Then it's up to you to bring him back, Jessie. Help him find that spark again. And don't talk to me about meaning. He's got you—the woman I wanted, who I know Matt still wants…"

Jessie cringed.

"And he's got those beautiful children, and another about to pop in the next few months. Josh has a lot to live for."

"That's the thing. Don't you get it? He knows that. He loves us so much he's terrified to be with us. He's been hurt so bad he's scared to let down his walls and just love us from day to day, from moment to moment."

"Let me give him a piece of my mind," Jacob steamed. "You, my amazing girl, are still here, on this planet. Your daughter, your other kids, are still here. What you said earlier makes sense to me. You and I, we've lost, big time. But Josh has not. He has to keep going, he has to choose to keep going. And he has no real reason anymore to worry that Morgan will ever stalk any of you ever again."

"It's a lot, Jacob. It's so damn much to process. I can't…I just can't… right now…"

"The show?"

As if on cue, a hasty knock came at the washroom door. Sam stuck his head in. "Everything okay in here? They're waiting for you guys."

"Give us a minute, Sam," Jacob said, and Sam nodded and sauntered away. Bending his head, Jacob nuzzled his old girl's hair. It tickled his nose. "Let's go do this," he said quietly. "Music makes everything better, Jessie. Let's go get lost in music."

She shook her head. "I can't, Jacob," she hiccuped. "Not right now, babe, okay? Please…just tell them I'm sick. Nobody, especially not Charles and Dee, needs to know why. Don't tell anyone why."

"You got it, kid. Look, I'll get Sam to arrange to take you back to the hotel." Jacob started to leverage himself back upright.

Jessie grabbed his arm and tugged on it. She buried herself in the eyes she loved and trusted. "Not yet, Jacob. The kids…I can't…"

"You can't stay here," he admonished. "Not on this cold floor."

"I want to go home." New tears threatened and started to trickle. "I want to go back to Vancouver."

Jacob held firm. "Not an option, Jess. What'd I just tell you, huh? Let me remind you. It was a repeat of what you told me earlier."

"I need some time to process this. Please. Tell Dee I want to go home."

Digging around his back jeans pocket, Jacob pulled out his hotel key card and held it up in front of Jessie. "This is for mine and Kayla's room. I'll get Sam to take you back there. Sleep for the afternoon, take a load off and just sleep. Kayla and I won't be back for a good few hours."

Slowly, Jessie started to calm. Soul level gratitude moved in one giant wave across her eyes now that she had a safe place to hide. "All right," she agreed. "Thanks, Jacob. Really."

"You got it." Crushing Jessie to him, Jacob kissed her forehead before helping her stand. He got her to the couch in the main part of the dressing room before Sam stuck his head back in the room again.

With Sam by her side, Jessie was cruising through the streets of L.A. on her way to be safely wrapped up in the big duvet on Jacob and Kayla's hotel suite bed before Charles, Dee, Matt and Ulysses, who were all sitting in the audience waiting for the rehearsal to start, even knew she was gone.

Chapter Seventeen

Because of Jessie's anxious state, Sam's first priority was to get her back to the hotel where she could feel safe, and so it was Jacob who agreed to initially notify Matt. He did so with a text that he hastily typed as he walked toward the stage for rehearsal.

Just after Matt vaulted up from his seat with a reassuring, "Just wait here," to Charles, Dee and Ulysses, his cell rang. To the annoyance of other watchers sitting in the same row, he took the call while he shuffled past knees and feet to get to an aisle. It was Sam, finally calling from the limo he'd pressed into service; it had been on standby, waiting at the theater's backstage entrance until it was needed.

Sam was careful. Seated next to the limo driver, there wasn't a lot he could say with the exception of, "Jessie's under the weather." He didn't know the whole truth anyway. And there was no need to alert some random limo driver that Jessie was perfectly fine until she received a letter that was purportedly from Josh.

Before he hailed himself a cab, Matt texted Ulysses so Charles and Dee would stay put and not rush out to see what was bothering Jessie. In twenty minutes he was at Jacob's hotel suite door, only a few minutes behind Jessie and Sam. Sam was standing outside in the hallway, pulling a chair from the suite through the open doorway.

"What's up?" Matt barked, eyes flashing. "This came on rather abruptly, did it not?" He added the 'did it not' because lately, with him not really being around Jessie the way he usually was, Matt wasn't, to be honest, really sure how Jessie was feeling earlier in the day. Excuses to find other things to do were easy enough to come by. Putting Sam on 'Jessie duty' was a breeze, despite Alin's sad eyes when she and her man were separated.

"She got that letter from Josh that Arnie told us was coming." Sam's eyes were wide. He had no clue what was in the letter, but judging from the look of pure fear in Matt's eyes at the proclamation, it was clear Matt had some idea.

"You see it? The letter?"

"Not the contents."

"Stay out here."

"Sir…" Sam stood by the chair in the doorway. Matt couldn't get by.

"What?" Reaching down, Matt hauled the chair through and started to slide by it.

Sam took a chance and grabbed his arm. Matt whipped around. "She doesn't want to see anyone."

"What? She'll see me." Shaking off Sam's hand, Matt started to move forward.

"Matt, pardon me, but Jessie explicitly said she doesn't want to see anyone. Your name, in particular, was mentioned."

Matt took two brisk steps back toward Sam. "I appreciate you communicating her highness' wishes, Sam," he said, his jaw set and his eyes flashing, "but Jessie is supposed to be on stage rehearsing with an ensemble cast for a very big show. This is one time that I need to overstep her wishes." In his heart he knew why Jessie was likely unwell. She was reeling from something Josh communicated to her; something that Matt guessed rightly could only be a truth he had hoped would remain buried forever. He wondered if Arnie knew and why he chose not to warn them if he did. Knowing Arnie's hardened nature, he likely just felt it wasn't his business, Matt supposed.

The show…thinking about it, Matt figured it wouldn't be a bad thing to force Jessie out of hiding and back into music, although for Jessie hiding in her tunes would only be a whole other escape route.

"Yes sir. I'll stay here," Sam was saying while Matt digested the chaos likely reverberating through Jessie's mind.

"Thank you, Sam." Disappearing inside, Matt let the door slam shut behind him.

He found Jessie in the bedroom, arms crossed and one booted toe tapping impatiently, for all intents and purposes waiting for him.

"I heard ya," she grumped. "Poor Sam. You didn't give him a chance. The kid will think I'm pissed at him because you snuck in."

"What was in the letter, Jessie?" Matt wasn't in the mood for pissing around. Someone was gonna catch hell from Charles and Dee, and he didn't want it to be him.

Jessie narrowed her eyes. Her voice was a low, throaty growl. "You fucking lied to me *more*. That's what was in the letter. Bastard. You knew, didn't you?"

Silent, Matt dug his heels into the lush carpet of the lavish suite and pocketed his hands in the trim, stylish canvas jacket he was wearing in the temperate L.A. warmth. Shifting his weight to one foot, his intense stare spoke volumes.

The expected outburst wasn't long in coming. Jessie marched toward him and gave him her trademark shove. Matt grabbed her elbows to try to keep her from wailing on him, but Jessie got a few good hits in anyway. "You fucking bastard! You just can't stop lying to me, can you? You told me it was Morgan's hit! Why? Why?! You should know by now that you can't protect me! You cannot protect me, Matt, if that's what your intention was by not telling me, because lies always have a way of finding their way to the surface!"

Backing up, Jessie wrenched her arms out of Matt's strong grip. His eyes were watering, but he swallowed bitterly and held his composure. "I wasn't trying to protect *you*," he confessed, his words a poison he had hoped never to taste on his tongue. "I was trying to protect your marriage, Jessie."

Jessie was seeing spots; the blood in her ears was pounding harder and harder now that she had someone physically in front of her to punish for this latest travesty. "That's hilarious. You're a fucking clown, Matt," she hollered back at him, "because in a roundabout way, that's exactly what Josh said in his letter. He said that we can't keep those kinds of secrets from each other, you know, the," she raised her fingers in quotes, "killing kind, because they'd erode away at our marriage, and he doesn't want that. Imagine! He doesn't want to keep those kinds of secrets because they'll kill us, although he's already half dead! In more ways than one."

Half crouched over now, clutching her belly as she unleashed her torment,

Jessie let Matt have it. "And you, you fucking bastard, you say you're trying to protect my marriage, but that's crazy talk considering I think Josh's intention by writing that letter was likely to give you back to me. As if you're some kind of pawn in a vicious game, some kind of trump card! Like Josh says, 'Look at me, I'm half dead and I don't see how I can be any good to you and to our kids, because for one, some day Morgan might find out that I'm still alive, and for two, in my mind I've already said goodbye to life, to living.'"

"Hold up, Jessie," Matt interjected, reaching for her. As if his hands had the power to burn her, she jumped back. With his eyes Matt pleaded with Jessie to understand, to settle, but she just shoved the heels of her hands into her own baby blues and went on.

"So Josh made damn sure I got that letter," she said, sniffling, "and thank God he and Arnie, that traitor, got it sent here on time because I was gonna get on that jet none the fucking wiser. And now," Jessie backed up and swiped an arm under her nose, "Josh wants me to stay in Vancouver, I think, because that was his plan in the first place."

Tilting her head, narrowing her eyes, she gave him a cocky, arrogant nod. "You know that, right Matt? That all of this comes down to you? Josh once told me that if anything ever happened to him, I was supposed to go to you. So now that his diabolical plan got all fucked up, likely because I made the goddamn mistake of taking his hand in mine in the ambulance to try to bring him back to me, he's all messed up." She threw her arms up and guffawed loudly. Jessie's voice got all loud and pitchy, all thin and wiry. "He doesn't know what he wants, he just knows that you would take care of me, of the kids and me, whereas if he and I try to stay together, someday, somehow, either Morgan and his cronies will find out that he's still alive—they'll follow one of you when you travel to see us or something, I don't know—and we'll end up losing anyway, or else we won't survive because this is too big to get past. All of it, I mean—what Josh did, and going into exile and not working and missing everybody, and just all of it, the big whole fucking shebang! We can't win, Matt! No matter what, we still can't win! And you know something else? The sickest, most disgusting, most terrible part of this whole thing?"

Defeated by the sharp edged truths Jessie was throwing into the room like daggers, Matt let the weight of the world bear down upon his shoulders and said, in a barely there whisper, "What, Jessie? What could possibly be—"

Soundly, Jessie cut him off. She lowered her voice although a concentrated, hot anger still drenched every word with kerosene. She was like a flame about to ignite into a full-out explosion. Her eyes were pits of darkness. "If he had died—if Josh had really died—we could have moved on. At least, I could have moved on and the kids could have started to heal. Because then we could have had a funeral and there would have been a—" She gulped, and swallowed hard. "A body. There would have been a body that people would have seen, damn it, and you know what they say, a picture's worth a thousand words, so the whole damn world would have seen for themselves that Josh was dead, and so Morgan would have seen it and known it and once and for all he would have let us go. So what does this all come down to, in the end, Matt? Right now? Huh?"

Jessie didn't bother waiting for an answer. Stooping lower as if it simply hurt too much to stand upright, she whispered out a truth that hurt far too much to attempt saying louder. "I'll tell you what," she forced herself to say. "He was right. That's what. Josh. He—was right."

During the entire tirade, apart from a few garbled attempts at edging in, Matt mostly listened in a confused, terrified, stricken way, half ready to go to Jessie's rescue; to grab her and hold her in his arms and keep her from falling to the ground in a heap, but she surprised him. She held on and fought for dominion over her body, over her brain, and over her heart, and it kept her standing, although she was wavering.

And she still wasn't quite done.

Raising a finger, she pointed at him. "The only thing Josh fucked up on, I mean really fucked up on, was thinking that I could go to you. Because you're with Shanda now and no matter which way I turn I'm going to be alone. That's something Jacob warned me about a long time ago, in New York. He told me that if things didn't work out with Josh, I might just end up alone. And I gotta tell you, Matt, if I get on that jet and I fly down to be with Josh, I'm damn well gonna feel alone. Because I don't know how to look that man in the eye knowing that he did all the choosing for me once again. That he chose to leave us instead of trying to find another way, and that death was the reward, and now that his plan backfired and he's still here, there's a damn good chance he doesn't want to be." She shoved a pointy finger in her chest. "Here, I mean. With me. With our kids. With this new baby he and I made together because we love each other. How do you look a man like that in the eye and ever possibly think that everything will eventually be okay?"

Matt waited a good few minutes before he dared speak. All he and Jessie could hear in the meantime was the odd ticking of the in suite refrigerator, and the distant vacuum a maid was pushing around somewhere down the hall. Even the traffic noises outside were muffled as if they were in some distant dimension and only fractionally real. "Are you done?" he finally asked between Jessie's sniffs and hiccups as she tried to compose herself. "Have you said everything you need to say?"

Looking over to the foot of the bed, Jessie followed her glance and slowly sat down on the very edge, as if she were wavering between two worlds. "Y-yep," she wept, giving in to the fears that seemed to constantly dog her and her family. "I'm so fucking done, Matt. With everything. I'm sick of it, of all of it. And that means I'm done with you and your fucking lies too, and your fucking attempts to shove me under some goddamn rug so you and Shanda can get on with your 'stable' lives."

"Are you going to go? On Sunday?"

The nasty look Jessie gave Matt when she finally got up the courage to stare him in the eye would have curdled milk. "What do you fucking think, Matt? And pardon me for adding, what do you fucking care?"

"You need me to spell it out for you, kid?"

"Don't you dare fucking say I'm lost without him. Don't you think I know how fucking goddamned 'lost' I am without him?!" Grabbing a pillow, Jessie fired it at Matt. Standing, she followed it up with two more. "Get the fuck out of here! Leave me alone! Just leave me alone, and tell Charles and Dee to leave me alone too! I don't want to see anybody. I just want to be alone."

Matt didn't bother bringing up the show. What would be the point? Jessie had worked herself up into such a state of anxiety that she was no longer capable of seeing straight, much less participating in what would surely be a tedious rehearsal. Tomorrow night? For the actual show? How could she possibly offer any kind of compassionate understanding and hope to hers and Josh's grieving fans in the audience—and those watching on TV or streaming live—when she was no longer able to find any compassion to give to Josh or to herself?

Spinning around on one heel, Matt bent and picked up one of the angrily fired pillows, and threw it back over to the bed. Narrowly missing Jessie, he added one last directive. "You stay here," he told her. "Don't be pushing Sam around. If you go anywhere it's to see those beautiful children of yours down the hall. And don't go see them until you get your shit together. The last thing they need is more confusion and uncertainty."

"Goddamn you, Matt. You and your fucking self-righteous pity. You don't think I see it? You don't think I look into *your* eyes and see judgment and shame when you look at me? Whatever happened to the man I loved, huh? Whatever happened to the wise man I trusted with my life? You treat me like a caged animal, like I ought to be drugged and tossed aside like some wild creature that's too dangerous to be let loose."

Matt stopped at the door to the bedroom. Laying a hand against the door frame, Jessie saw, from as far away as the bed, that it was trembling. "You aren't?" he asked her. "Funny. Because you're the wildest creature I know, Jessie, with all your accusing and blaming and hurting people who love you, including Josh, whose actions maybe we will never fully understand, but who doesn't deserve the shit you're throwing at him. And calling you wild, in case you're wondering, is by no means any kind of compliment." He paused. "Maybe you should have spared everyone all this pain and just stayed on the streets."

A mighty roar followed him through the door, but Matt escaped the next catapulting pillow by pulling the French door to the bedroom closed behind him. He stood a few feet beyond that, his body quaking with the adrenalin unleashed by the angry words both he and Jessie threw at each other on a day that should have been sacred by the very nature of its L.A. concert, which was designed to be about forgiveness and awareness, and which had become a vigil of celebration for a man who was supposed to be dead but who, when all was said and done, was really just pretending.

Chapter Eighteen

Charlie and Jane arrived that night along with Sophie and Steve, Carter and Ashley, Maggie and John, and Sue-Lyn and her latest partner, Elizabeth. It was important to all of them to attend this concert—the media, for one, would notice if Josh's good friends were not present. Already the entertainment news shows were buzzing about why Jessie walked out on rehearsal. They were blaming it on grief.

Jacob's suite was large. Some of the gang gathered in his living room later in the evening when it became apparent that Jessie was staying sequestered in Jacob and Kayla's bedroom and was not interested in spending time in their direct company. Secretly, everyone present hoped she would emerge from her cocoon and take comfort from them, but only Matt, Charlie, Steve, Jacob and Kayla understood the level of her anger and thus her need to be alone.

After a while, Carter and Ashley left with the others from the old *Drifters* days. There were truths to tell the grieving Maggie and Sue-Lyn. Steve shook Carter's hand and wished him well, following up with a promise to connect the next morning for breakfast.

Charles and Dee retired early. They had tried to see Jessie earlier, but after railing at Matt she had nothing left to give. The next day's concert was a mystery insofar as to whether or not Jessie would rebound enough to perform. The planned trip on Sunday? When pressed, Matt could only shake his head. He had no clue whether Jessie would go south to be with Josh, who was now safely squirreled away in the Caribbean, or not.

Left in Jacob's suite at ten that night were Charlie, Steve, Matt, Jacob, and Kayla. Lily was asleep in a travel bed at Kayla's side. Shanda had arrived but had left with Sophie and Jane to indulge in a bottle or two of robust wine and some welcome heart-to-heart girl talk. Kayla stayed behind to be with her new baby, but almost wished she hadn't. None of the guys knew what to say to each other and so the conversation was sporadic and random. Between awkward exchanges, renewed sobs were heard starting back up in the bedroom. Jessie was apparently awake again. It seemed all she could do was cry. In the living room, an extended, renewed silence was suddenly deafening.

Glum, Matt only grunted when anyone spoke to him. After a while, Charlie kicked him lightly in the ankle. Matt glared darkly at him. "What?"

"What the hell's your problem?" With a defensive stare back, Charlie gave him a directive. "Go work your magic."

Matt threw up his hands. "She doesn't want to see me."

"Why not?"

"Might have something to do with lying to her," Matt mumbled. "Twice."

"Jesus, I wish I knew how we could help her." Charlie leaned forward and rested his forearms on his thighs. He picked out a piece of the rug to stare at, a large pink rose that decorated the center. The rose seemed far too beautiful for the gloomy way their day had turned out. "I can't stand this helpless feeling. I can't stand not knowing what she needs."

Hesitant, Jacob reached across to Kayla. A soft smile spread across her face at his touch; it was the same kind of intuitive, electric knowing he once shared with Jessie when they were lovers, and that Jacob was well aware Jessie shared with Josh. He brightened noticeably at his wife's reaction, and spoke out loud in a quiet tone that was so serious, yet gentle, that it got the guys' attention too. They all perked up at his words, even though Jacob's eyes were locked on Kayla when he spoke.

"I know what she needs," he murmured, and stood. "Keep an eye on Lily for us, guys," he ordered, although there was no urgency in the request. As a parent, Jacob was confident that his newborn would be fine in the company of the experienced fathers in his midst. As a friend, and as a past lover of the woman whose every heart wrenching sob was gutting all of them, he had a bigger priority at this time than watching his baby sleep, although these days it was indeed one of his greatest pleasures.

Tugging on Kayla's hand, he urged her upright. Astounded, Charlie, Steve and Matt watched as Jacob walked Josh's sister to the French door leading to their occupied bedroom, slid it open, disappeared inside, and closed it behind them.

Inside the room, the interior drapes were still open so a pale, wanton moonlight was bleeding over the floor and bed, softened by the gauzy sheers that dominated the large window. Jessie sensed the presence of someone approaching beside her; she didn't know it was actually two people until Jacob lay down on the window side and Kayla flanked Jessie on the opposite side. Jessie's blotched, teary-eyed cheeks were facing Jacob. Weary, spent, hugging a pillow, she blinked despondently at him.

"Hey, pretty girl," he said, and lifted his right hand so he could brush away her tears with the backs of his fingers. "We think that's enough pain for one day."

"Who's we?" Jessie sobbed back at him.

A careful, solemn smile spread across Jacob's face. Jessie was talking. Talking was good. At least, it precluded crying. "Me, Kayla, Charlie, Steve and Matt," he answered.

"Funny you didn't add Shanda in there."

"Shanda went down to Jane's suite—or to Sophie's, I'm not sure—to get wasted."

"Lucky her."

"Hey. This thing with Matt, Jessie, you gotta let it go. It's eating him up inside."

"Nope. That bastard lied to me. Again. Plus he said some things that really sucked."

"You won't have to keep worrying about Shanda at this rate. She'll dump Matt's ass if he keeps stewing over you the way he stewed over you all day today."

Perking up a little, Jessie sighed. "Well, I don't want that. He's gonna need her."

"Mmm. So you're going. We were wondering."

"Honestly, Jacob?" Jessie said, picking at the hem of the pillowcase and twisting it around a finger, "I don't know. I'm so scared." Turning her nose into the pillow, she started to cry again. "I'm terrified to be alone with Josh right now. I don't want to have this baby on some backwoods Caribbean island without Dee, without Carlotta…I'm so angry…and so damn scared…"

"Okay. Stay with us a while longer, then. Go see Josh when you're ready, even just for a weekend to start, maybe, to sort some things out."

A small arm wrapped itself around Jessie's shoulders. Jessie kissed the fingers and held them tight against her chest. "Kayla," she said, "I'm so, so sorry. This must hurt you too."

"I've known my brother longer than you have, Jessie," came Kayla's small voice from behind Jessie. "I watched him struggle all through his childhood, and through his teen years. To be honest, some days I'm actually surprised he's made it this long."

"He did it for us, Kayla. I really, truly believe that he thought he could save us but it still makes me so damn angry. I can't wrap my mind around it. And there's a bigger problem."

"What's that, honey?"

"The bigger problem," Jessie wept, "is that I just don't know if I have the strength to save him right now."

"Of course you do, sweetheart," Kayla replied confidently. "You've always been the only one who could save Josh. After our mom passed away, I mean. You just got thrown for a loop today. Add pregnancy hormones in there and you didn't have a chance."

"I guess." A small whimper muffled its way outwards from the pillow. When Jessie turned her head more sideways, she was almost nose-to-nose with Jacob. The deep blue eyes she'd once loved with an intensity that sometimes saved her in the past, were startling. Sighing, Jessie lifted her left hand and laid a palm against Jacob's cheek. It had been a long time since she was close to him this way, lying prone on a bed. "God, you look so at peace, Jacob," she whispered. "I can't tell you how happy that makes me, babe."

His eyes danced up to just behind Jessie's head. Kayla was holding her sister-in-law close, her own Josh-like eyes filled with light and smiling down at her husband past Jessie's mussed-up hair. Still watching Kayla, Jacob leaned forward and pressed his lips to Jessie's. Tensing, Jessie let him kiss her. Kayla seemed okay with it; she started gently running her fingers through Jessie's hair.

A few blissful, peaceful moments later, Jessie pulled away. "Jacob…" she started softly.

Touching her lips with his finger, he murmured, "It's okay, sweetheart. Kayla's here."

Jessie took a breath. "I know. I know, and I know you guys are more open than Josh and me when it comes to this stuff, but you and me…we shouldn't…after what happened…"

"We've made our peace, Jessie. We're good people who've made some crappy mistakes. It's time to stop carrying the world's judgment on our shoulders."

"And no more hiding from the people who love you." Wriggling closer, Kayla spooned her body tightly against Jessie's. "You're not alone, honey. Let us help you shed some of that pain."

Kayla started stroking Jessie's cheek. Her feather-light touch brought an inadvertent gasp from Jessie, whose fuzzy recall of Caryn's loving ministrations all those years ago brought a desperate need to the surface—a need for the kind of love that came with touch.

Kayla added, "And what better time to bring forth healing than the night before a concert designed to create awareness?"

"Oh, God." Stuffing her nose back into the pillow, Jessie tried to breathe. "I could…I mean, I want…I need…" She looked back over at Jacob. For so long, she'd trusted him. He was once her partner, her lover; he was also the father of one of her children. Kayla was here, apparently supporting some kind of coupling between them. Nervous, unsure, Jessie rolled onto her back and peered anxiously up at Kayla. Outside in the living room, the guys relaxed and started to talk quietly. What a relief it was to hear quiet voices coming from the bedroom instead of the desperate, soul level crying they were privy to earlier.

Kayla bent to Jessie. Tenderly, she ran a finger over her lips and kissed her. "Relax and enjoy this," she commanded lightly. "Let go of the pain, Jessie. Stop fighting everything. Trust Josh."

Jessie gulped. "I'm not sure how Josh would feel about this." She tried to smile but her worried eyes squished it.

"Somehow," Kayla whispered, "I think he would understand, Jessie. Today, at least, after sending you that letter, I think Josh would be glad to know that you're with Jacob and me. That you can turn this hurt into the most beautiful kind of pleasure." Leaning over Jessie, she pressed her mouth to hers again. She tasted of strawberry lip gloss. A low moan passed through Jessie's lips, originating from someplace deep inside her body. Arching her hips just slightly, she turned back to Jacob, who lifted his hand to caress his wife's hair before he focused his attention on the woman he once loved with a passion and fervor he thought might have the capacity to destroy him.

To Jessie, pregnancy was a beautiful, natural thing. Generally to her, with the men— and the woman—she loved over time, so was sex. It had been so long since Josh touched her intimately, and actually he'd never—apart from that brief time in the hospital—run his hands over her growing belly. Jacob had missed out on being with Jessie when she was expecting Dylan. Now his much-loved hands caressed her pregnant belly lovingly, as did Kayla's.

It was easy for Jessie to let go of the things that hurt; to trust these two while they loved her, while they touched the sweet spots on her body with experienced fingers, and with mouths capable of creating quickly mounting desire as they trailed over her thighs, teasing her. Parting her legs, Jacob and Kayla took turns lingering on the special warm, damp place at the apex of Jessie's thighs, urging deep, animal moans from a place in Jessie's spirit that she longed to connect with again, that she desperately missed.

In the other room, Charlie was the first to realize what was going on. He kicked Steve's leg and shot him a look that meant, 'what the fuck?'

When Steve clued in he laughed and shook his head, but the serious bend to Charlie's head—his way of studiously ignoring Matt—was a warning. Steve silenced his amusement with a trip to the washroom at the far end of the suite at about the same time Matt raised his head at the new, raw sounds coming from the bedroom.

Matt went cold. Ice rocketed through his veins.

Charlie was speechless.

It seemed like forever, but it was only a few minutes before Matt's hurt heart got the better of him. When he stood, the movement was sudden. Knocking his knee against a glass coffee table, he inadvertently cursed. Distracted, Matt was too late to catch an empty beer bottle that tipped over and skittered across the table. Frozen, he stood immobile as, inside the bedroom, he listened to Jessie accept Jacob's and Kayla's love with increasing moans of pleasure. Distraught, he rifled his fingers through his hair and passed Steve as he took a brisk walk across the room and whipped open the door to the main floor hallway. Immobile, he stood there, unable to bring himself to leave.

Inside the bedroom, when it came time Jacob gently and tenderly took Jessie from behind to accommodate her comfort with the growing baby, while Kayla murmured lovingly to her and caught the last of Jessie's tears. There was a kindred, special beauty in their shared lovemaking. It was born of love and brought to glory by a deep trust fueled by a lonely, confused, desperate need.

There were regular cries now, mounting in intensity and volume as a much-missed desire escalated. Sweat trickled down Jessie's forehead; Kayla's lips against her cheek hummed a quiet vibration of love and support. Jessie clutched Kayla's fingers while Jacob groaned and moved inside her, slowly at first and then faster, urgent. Soon the hunger for release grew and a dizzying, explosive ecstasy ricocheted through Jessie's body. The room spun and her eyes went black; a sheer, perfect, unexpected pleasure soared through every nerve and hurtled through every frantic, aching particle of Jessie's skin. With a fervent, unrestrained, "Oh, God! Oh, Jesus!" followed by a climactic cry, gasping, she turned her flushed face to Kayla, who absorbed the loudest, most freeing, of Jessie's primal moans with passionate, searching kisses.

The main door to the suite slammed.

"I'd go too," Charlie complained in the living room in a low voice when Steve raised his eyebrows and dropped back into a seat next to him, "but I guess someone's gotta keep an eye on this baby."

Steve reached for another beer and unscrewed the cap with one quick twist. Tipping it back, he laughed outright before he drank. "Fucking Jacob kills me," he said. "Even married, he gets Jessie. With his wife's approval, apparently."

"Approval? Outright participation, you mean." Catching Steve's eye, Charlie raised a bottle and pointed it toward the bedroom.

Inside, Kayla was lying on her side. As Jacob released Jessie, he encouraged her to lie on her side as well, facing Kayla. He lay down behind her so his body could cradle hers. His and Jessie's breaths were fast and shallow, but Kayla was still wriggly, still wanting; her moist, hungry eyes communicated this to Jacob over Jessie's twitchy, slightly convulsing body, so Jacob took Jessie's fingers in his and slipped them down inside Kayla's leggings, where together they cupped her and touched her and brought her to a sweet climax too.

In the living room, Charlie rose with a tired groan and sidled over to the window. Parting the drapes, he stared at the ground below, where red taillights and bright low beams from headlights created energized colored trails up and down the street. His senses were on fire. What was happening in the bedroom was nothing new to him, but not since his years with Jessie, and just after, had he been privy to this kind of free-spirited sex. A part of him wished he'd had the guts to act the way Jacob did…but then, Jane would not be open to this kind of shared lovemaking. And there was one other person to consider.

"Josh doesn't deserve this," he tossed over his shoulder to Steve. On behalf of his buddy, Charlie was, on some level at least, mortified. "Shouldn't we be pissed?"

Sobering, Steve lowered his beer and narrowed one eye to scrutinize Charlie's back. "She stopped crying," he explained to his friend. "Let her have this. If Josh were here to see her, to listen to Jessie cry like that all day…" He shook his head. "He'd be the first one to beg Jacob to dry her tears. This is his doing, Charlie."

Shoving a knuckle in his mouth, chewing thoughtfully as he walked back to Steve and dropped down again, Charlie only partially agreed. "The hell it is," he grumped. "It's fucking Nadia's doing." He had one more thing to throw into the mix. "Let's see how long those tears stay away," he wondered aloud. "I wonder how far Jacob's miracles extend."

"The show, you mean?"

"Yeah. She's gotta get through tomorrow night."

"She missed the rehearsal. Can she even do the show?"

"Deirdre made arrangements for her to have a 'fly-by' rehearsal with Jacob at ten tomorrow morning. But I guess we'll see if Jessie's feeling better enough to even give it a try." Following Steve's example, Charlie reached for a new brew. After twisting off the cap he managed an incredulous chuckle and raised his bottle. "To Jacob," he toasted.

Leaning forward, Steve tapped the neck of his bottle against Charlie's. "To Jacob," he agreed and added, "the lucky, spoiled, cocky, asshole son-of-a-bitch."

Inside the bedroom, Jessie closed her eyes, tucked Josh's sister's face into the hollow of her neck and chest, and soaked in the love and afterglow of unexpected but divinely satisfying lovemaking.

In the hallway outside the suite, Matt leaned against the wall, sank down until his butt reached the floor, and hung his head in his hands.

Chapter Nineteen

Josh was safely in the Caribbean by the time he got the news that Jessie had received and read his letter. Arnie communicated it to him after he found Josh down by a wooden dock inspecting a sleek speedboat that, to Josh's welcome surprise, got his adrenalin pumping at the simple sight of it. The boat, a 250 horsepower yellow and white twenty foot Bayliner Bowrider, jump started some long lost desire to feel the wind in his hair and the sun on his face. Eyeing it, Josh was reminded that his beloved Harley was now lost to a life he'd left behind. The few roads on this tiny, hidden island were the last place to ride a big bike, unless you were talking about the pedal kind.

Arnie braced his feet on the dock next to Josh and tilted his face back so he could soak up the glorious rays of the sun. "A guy could get used to this," he announced agreeably, while Josh digested the intel that Jessie now knew the truth about what happened on his fateful final day on *Sacred Peace*.

"At least you have a choice. I gotta get used to this." Grumbling, Josh adjusted his forlorn stare to bypass the one bright spot in this new day, the pretty speedboat. All he could see for miles was an endless ocean, although if he looked to the sides there were quarter mile juts of land both right and left. They were a little hilly, yet treed, all lined by white sand beaches.

"I'm not in a hurry to get back to civilization," Arnie told him. "Neither's Kalon. Even incognito." Since Josh was officially on the mend they'd left the doctor back in B.C., sworn to secrecy and living in his own kind of agreed exile up north, but both Kalon and Arnie were sticking it out with Josh. Neither wanted to leave him alone, although Josh was right—they could both leave if they wanted to, and start reworked, secret lives wherever they wanted. They were on the 'missing' plane with Josh and so they, too, had to 'disappear.' Josh was a prisoner in his life in a way they weren't, however. He was a hunted man prior to the medevac flight's disappearance. His options, although not non-existent, were extremely limited if he wanted some guarantee of safety for himself and for his family.

"So," Josh said to Arnie in a monotone voice, without looking at him, "is she still coming here tomorrow?" Beneath their feet, small wavelets were cozying up to the wooden pilings of the dock, making themselves known with tiny bell-peal splashes that, in better times, would have been comforting. Now, Josh could barely breathe. If Jessie didn't make her way to him tomorrow as planned, time would become an enemy. The more time that passed, the less chance he had of ever having his wife and children at his side in this serene, private sanctuary.

Arnie took a moment before answering. The tropical sun's warmth on his skin was peaceful, invigorating. Calming. He prayed Josh could somehow let his fears and worries go so that he would feel its healing balm. Eventually he told Josh what he knew. "She's doing the show tonight, Josh. That's a good sign."

"A sign of what?" Josh bit off. "That she's willing to say goodbye through song?"

"That she's functioning. That's what."

Not surprised, Josh stole a sideways glance at his bodyguard and friend. "So I take it she wasn't functioning for a while."

"According to Ulysses, no. You know Jessie. She sequestered herself in a bedroom for a night, but apparently this morning she pulled herself together and went down to breakfast in the dining room with your children. Ulysses called her 'quietly determined.'"

"Whatever the hell that means."

"You know something?" Arnie shifted his feet for better balance. "She once told me she was stronger than all of us guys put together. Kind of hollered it at me, actually. Your wife will do the right thing, Josh."

"Arnie…"

"I'm listening."

"If she doesn't come tomorrow…Jessie shouldn't be flying much longer, is the thing. And once the baby comes…" Josh let the tide carry his final, grave thought away.

"If she needs a little time to adjust to the baby, Josh, then she'll land on your doorstep as soon as the new little one is cleared to fly. Don't doubt her. You and Jessie have been through a lot of tough times, and through all of them you've both proven that your love for each other trumps all the other crap."

"I just wish I could talk to her. I don't even care if she loses it with me, in fact I expect her to. I'd just like to hear her voice, Arnie. And I need to see my kids."

Studying him, Arnie silently agreed that both of those things would be beneficial to Josh. He was still pale and was standing in the middle of the dock with both shoulders slumped, and his hands shoved deep in the pockets of trademark faded denims. Barefoot, Josh appeared to be digging his toes into the old wood as if he needed the extra hold on the earth to keep him upright. More concerning was the way he was speaking, in a drone, almost. Barely a flicker passed through his eyes. For a second Arnie was hopeful, thinking he saw a spark of fight in the liquid chocolate eyes of Jessie's man, but he soon realized it was the reflection of the water that he saw moving across Josh's somber expression, and not any kind of inner contentment.

"We'll stream the show tonight, Josh," Arnie said, although a trace of doubt snuck into his hopeful plan. The Internet was spotty at best here on this desolate island. Still, he was optimistic. The younger Kalon was technically savvy. After talking at length with Ulysses via untraceable cellphone before they left Alberta, the hired nurse had stocked up on 'toys' they agreed might help boost reception. He was busy playing with them now, up at the large white beach house some rich American had built ten years ago and almost immediately sold to a record producer Charles knew. Charles had rented the house under a false name and via an account he and Matt had set up so the money and paper trails couldn't be traced to the island. Not that they thought Morgan and his crew were savvy enough to do a lot of digging, but they weren't taking any chances.

Arnie dropped some honey in the evening plans. "You'll hear her sing," he said.

Josh had perked up at Arnie's note about streaming Jessie's show. Watching

Jessie on stage was always a breathtaking ride. Best of all, she communicated through music. He wondered what message she would send him tonight, soaked as she was in the inconceivable, shocking new knowing about his dark deed. "She'll have a rough go of it tonight, Arnie," he decreed flatly, as he considered how Jessie must be feeling. "As much as I hate to admit it, I guess I'm glad she'll have Jacob by her side and Matt watching over her."

Arnie harrumphed. When Josh raised his eyebrows and looked over, he said, "From what Ulysses said, Jessie's pretty pissed at Matt, and vice versa. They're not talking. I don't think they've said two friendly words since Calgary."

"What'd he do? Is it because of this? Hiding me?" That was not, in any way, good news. As much as Josh sometimes struggled with Matt's deep involvement in all of their lives there was, and always would be, a guarantee that he'd keep Jessie and the Sawyer children close to his heart, and as safe as he could possibly keep them. Even more so, Matt was Jessie's confidante, her best friend. On a day like today, Josh hoped Matt would be an even keel for Jessie, a wise ear, a warm body to hold her if she needed to let loose and cry. The last thing Josh wanted Matt to be was a distant, silent voice.

Interrupting Josh's anxious thoughts, Arnie clapped him lightly on the back. "I don't know. You know those two, they're always intense." He turned a corner in his thoughts. "What do you say we put the darkness aside for a bit and take this little sweetheart out for a spin? Give her a little test run?" He nodded at the Bayliner.

A tiny smile pricked at the corners of Josh's lips. Arnie relaxed. "Keys are in 'er," Josh said, wondering if the fresh salt breeze could possibly have the capacity to ease his troubled mind the way wind passing over the Harley did. "You wanna drive, city boy?"

"No, sir," Arnie said, wandering over to the speedboat. "I just want to soak up some rays. You're the adrenalin junkie. You take the wheel."

"We need some brew, Arnie." At Arnie's sudden silence, Josh chuckled. "Kidding," he teased, to Arnie's relief. "I promised Jessie I wouldn't go there again, and I won't."

You sure about that? Arnie thought as he took a good hard look at Josh's muscled body while Josh stepped over the side of the boat and settled himself behind the wheel, one bare foot on the boat's bottom, and the other leg bent at the knee, his calf resting on the white leather seat of the sporty little powerboat. He couldn't help but notice that Josh was wearing, around his neck on its leather thong, the J pendant Jessie gave him years ago. 'The night Josh first asked me to marry him,' Jessie had once explained to Arnie, in happier days.

The boat wasn't unlike one Josh had rented in Prince Edward Island the summer before he and Jessie were finally married. Josh's small smile widened when he turned the key and felt the hopeful little boat roar to life and settle into a light tremor in its tropical home.

After Arnie let off the lines, he too climbed in. He stretched out on the passenger seat next to Josh, hands behind his head and face once again tipped up to get the best of what the sun had to offer. Josh pointed the Bayliner into the light waves and let the bow rise up in steadfast hope as he took them on an exploration of the sunshiny place he now had no choice but to call home.

～ ～

It was well after midnight in the Caribbean when Jessie took the stage in Los Angeles. Kalon, Arnie and Josh made themselves comfortable on the stylish floral furniture in the beach house's expansive cathedral-ceilinged living room. The awareness concert was an ensemble cast kind of thing so by the time Jessie was finally introduced toward the end of the show, all three men were anxious and curious, and none more so than Josh.

To newbie Kalon, Josh appeared stoic and calm, but Arnie knew better. A close study revealed the cracks. It was the telltale nerve on Josh's sunburned cheek that gave away his angst; it twitched every now and then and was punctuated by occasional rapid swallows, and highlighted by wide, nervous eyes.

Jacob was the one to introduce Jessie. When she strode onto the stage she locked her eyes on him and didn't so much as wave to the crowd in the Kodak Theatre, their venue for the televised, streamed concert. Josh almost nodded as he watched his wife take her place behind a microphone. There was no guesswork as to how she was feeling. He discerned immediately that Jessie was in control and not just going through the motions in some kind of forced paralytic daze, as he had worried she might.

No, this version of his wife was strength personified; she carried an air of angry, determined grit Josh knew well, as Ulysses had communicated to Arnie earlier that day. Looking out at the audience would crack that determination, would break down the walls that Jessie had soundly constructed around her body and soul. To acknowledge the audience's presence would be like putting a bullet through a wall of imagined bulletproof glass. Connecting with eyes, any eyes besides Jacob's, would shatter the invisible wall Jessie built up around her in the dogged hope that it would help her remain invincible, that it would protect her and keep her safe.

Tonight millions of bleeding hearts were watching her for signs of breakage. The concert was a dual-purpose show. In the midst of trying to heal Jacob's wrongs in the eyes of a world that abhorred violence toward women (and rightfully so), Jessie had agreed to memorialize, for the fans who loved him, a man the world thought was dead. A man Jessie was incapable of even thinking about with any semblance of sanity after the revelation, by Josh's own pen, that he had planned to leave her and their children in a final revolting act that Jessie was trying to understand, yet in many ways still seemed egoistic and cowardly despite Josh's self-sacrificial intent.

On stage, Jessie took a step back from the microphone. One of the cameras was panning over the audience. Josh almost choked when he saw that everyone in attendance was on his or her feet giving Jessie a standing ovation, *for just being present*, he supposed. Some were crying, and Jessie had yet to even sing. What really got Josh, though, was that it was crystal clear that the standing ovation—*or welcome*, he reconsidered—was also a show of support for Jessie because she was an expectant mother of three who they thought was now a widow.

Whoever was behind the scenes switching up the images for television and the live stream clicked a mouse and the screen abruptly featured a close-up of Jacob. Standing behind his microphone, a guitar strapped around his shoulders and hanging loosely over his chest and stomach, he bit his bottom lip and held Jessie's gaze. He started to say something to her, but Josh couldn't guess what it was. The shot changed to a wide—a frontal of the stage. Jessie, in black leggings, black boots, and a loose cream sweater maternity top with crocheted lace ringing the neck so that it highlighted the tops of her breasts, swallowed bitterly and gave Jacob a quick nod before she blinked three times in rapid succession, stepped forward and gripped the mic, and ducked her head to focus on some unseen spot.

"Keep it together, girl," Josh heard Arnie mutter, as if Jessie could somehow hear him.

Unable to move, barely able to summon a breath, Josh sent his gal a silent prayer. *I'm here,* he said psychically to her. He wondered where Matt was and whether he and Jessie had made up. On nights like this, Josh was well aware that it was Matt's rock-solid, trusted presence in the wings that often gave Jessie the support and wherewithal to continue. She was thinking the same thing, apparently. Josh let out a little breath when he saw her quickly look to stage right, her eyes swimming, and search for something—someone— off camera. There was a suspended moment when Jessie licked her lips nervously and locked her eyes in place. *Matt's there,* Josh thought. The relief that the realization brought him was expected. Still, it hurt like hell to know that it was not he who was at Jessie's side on this difficult night.

The audience was settling down; a shot to some celebrities in the crowd showed them starting to sit, to wait for the magic they all expected from Jessie Wheeler, with Jacob Ryan at her side. Back to the stage—Jacob was moving to the microphone now, although he was still looking at Jessie. His lips moved. He was counting her in.

The first song was the easiest to get through. It was a *Sacred Peace* special, a popular tune that skyrocketed to the top of the charts around the same time *Sacred Peace* started winning over the gazillion fans who were previously addicted to some other crime-based drama. The quick-fingered live editor switched to a shot of Charlie in the audience. Seeing his good buddy sitting there with Jane on one side of him and Shanda on the other was a jolt. Even harder to bear as the camera panned right were the scared, worried faces of Charles and Dee. Next to them was Jonathon, Josh's father. Giselle, Jon's wife, was gripping his hand tightly, but the snowy-haired man was a rock. Deirdre was the one who broke down before the song ended; Jessie's pain was always her pain. There were tears on Shanda's cheeks, but both she and Jane were sitting with chins raised, taking it all in as best they could. Charlie was suffering. *Sacred Peace* would film for another season, but Charlie's best buddy would no longer be a part of it.

"Jesus Christ," Josh mumbled. If it weren't for Jessie's hypnotic, beatific singing, and Josh's desperate desire to see her, to hear her, he would've gotten up and left the room.

Kalon and Arnie both looked over at him when he cursed. Neither of them spoke, but they exchanged concerned glances. Jessie pulled them back to her when she hit the climax of the song, her sparkling nails glistening under the stage lights, the tiny wet diamonds in her eyes and on her lashes witness to the level of hurt the difficult performance was stealing from her soul.

The second song was harder. A quick glance to Jacob, and Jessie made her way to a grand piano. The song she sang was not one Josh knew; it was being birthed here, tonight, in front of millions. Despite her growing belly, Jessie played the piano herself instead of bringing Christian on board to support her. Jacob and the other musicians left the stage. Not once did Jessie look up from the ivory keys. Not once did she let a tear slide down a rosy cheek. She sang of angels and of a better place, and Josh wondered if he detected a sarcastic bent to her singing, to the way she loosed the lyrics from her lips. The word 'comfort' was repeated in the lyrics, but there was no real comfort for any of them as she sang.

Are you thinking about me? Josh wondered. *Are you missing me?*

In his heart he was certain he was on her mind. In his brain Josh knew he was the object of a confused and frightened anger; it was clearly evident in the subtly unhappy way Jessie graced the ivory keys, in the way her lips quivered and her eyes steadfastly stared at her silent, poised fingers when the song came to its natural close.

Jacob had to call her back to him when he took his place behind his microphone for the last piece. Jessie had yet to look at the audience and she had yet to crack a smile, any kind of smile, even a sad one. She was wearing her hair long and loose. As she slid off the piano stool and tiptoed the few steps to her stand-up mic, she tossed her head and once again fixed her gaze on a spot on the stage. Watching, Josh saw her take a deep breath—*for courage,* he thought—as Jacob started to play the minor arpeggio that would lead them into the final piece.

Even Arnie, when he clued in to the song, recognized the depth of sorrow the last tune would unleash and the tragic energy the world would collectively release when they heard it being played. It was the heavy *Sacred Peace* ballad that was always featured in concerts and at shows with rear projected images to support it. The images, of course, featured Josh and Shanda as their *Sacred Peace* characters.

"She's got some guts," Arnie said to the beach house room in general. He couldn't bring himself to meet Josh's eyes. Kalon did, though. He took a good long look at his recovering patient, and was sorry to see that Josh was shaking.

"Arnie," he said almost under his breath, thumbing carefully toward Josh. When Arnie finally looked over, he found he couldn't look away. It hit him that Josh was in mourning every bit as much as the world watching this show was. Only Josh was mourning himself.

He was mourning the man he used to be, whom Charles and Matt and Charlie and Arnie, and Ulysses by extension, had decreed he could no longer be, if he wanted to remain safe, if he wanted his family to remain safe. Josh was watching himself, as the *Sacred Peace* sheriff, play out on screen in vivid evocative images that, when layered with Jacob and Jessie's song, was unbearable for their reminder of who he once was and of what he was leaving behind. Worse, focusing on Jessie as she sang was a reminder that there was more at stake yet to lose. Love, for one, for a woman Josh was lost in from the time they met; children, for two, including a new baby he had yet to meet.

He held it together, mostly because Jessie was the one everyone was glued to. It was her damp, pale blue eyes and broken heart that an audience of millions was studying in detail, seeking cracks in as the unremorseful cameras came in for close-ups. *If she can do this, so can I,* thought Josh as he watched his wife command the song the way she always did. But he knew her. And so did Arnie. Both were well aware that Jessie's breaking point almost always came at the end of a song that hurt. It always snuck up on her when she brought herself back to the present moment, to the lights and to the audience, to a reality that often just plain stunk.

Jacob knew that about her, too; he knew it as well as anyone and better than most. His eyes were glued to her before he drew the song to a close, before he hit the final crucial, electric note on his lead guitar and stepped back from his microphone. There was a stage tech close by. Without even glancing in the guy's direction, Jacob held out his guitar and the guy came running, his long ponytailed hair swinging as he grabbed the guitar from Jacob's outstretched hand. In four steps, Jacob was at Jessie's side. She was crying now, finally, sobbing, bent over as her protective sphere shattered like glass and exposed her fully and completely to the audience who—at least those in the immediate vicinity, in the Kodak Theater—stood as one and cried along with her as they clapped, whistled and cheered, for Jessie, and for her man, who they all thought was likely dead.

While he was holding Jessie, as he offered comfort and consoled her for something nobody but himself and a few select others even understood, Jacob peered over Jessie's shoulder to spy Matt in the wings, in his usual spot, trying to appear stoic and reserved, but quaking as badly as Jessie, shifting his feet from side to side while he tried in vain to collect himself, to regain some kind of balance on this strange day.

In his Caribbean exile, Josh saw Jacob's strained look. *He's appealing to Matt. Jacob is begging Matt for help.*

In the end, Jacob pushed Jessie away from him, just enough so that he could murmur words of comfort as he held her cheeks in his palms and wiped away the stray tendrils of hair that were now sweat and tear-soaked against Jessie's pallid skin. She was nodding at him, receiving his words of love, and that simple gesture on his part, and of Jessie's obvious trust and adoration of Jacob—their close bond, always and forever a true love of sorts based on a shared capacity for, and love of, music—was enough to secure the public's respect for Jacob once again, during a concert which was supposed to be about awareness of violence against women, and which had become so damn – much – more.

As Josh watched in a sort of stunned silence, Jacob looked over Jessie's shoulder again and gently turned her toward the wings. Not once did she acknowledge the audience, and this time when the camera picked her up in a close up Josh could see the strain in her eyes, in the black shadows under her eyes, in the grim press of her lips, and in the trembling of her fingers when she reached up to knuckle a fist under a misty eye.

She moved toward the wings.

Waiting, Matt reached for her. The camera, ever revolting as it continued its heartless spying, its heartless intrusion into Jessie's pain, followed her. Josh sank deep into the cushion he was sitting on when he saw Jessie approach Matt, turn her head away from him, and cringe as she strode by so that as Matt reached for her he found only empty air.

Still, she turned her head back to him at the last second, after she passed Matt by, and there was fear there, in newly timid, scared eyes. She paused. Matt, wounded by her rejection, stilled for a moment and wiped his own eyes, but when he looked up, he spied not only a camera pointing its unforgiving lens at him, but also Jacob, center stage, searching him, begging for him to go to Jessie, to help her.

Matt turned. Lifting one arm, he placed it carefully around Jessie's waist, and guided her out of the wings, backstage, and to her dressing room.

The camera let them go when Jacob was joined on stage by other performers.

Josh got up, and left the beach house room.

When she got to her dressing room, Jessie went in, wheeled back around, and faced Matt before he got through the door. Suspended between two worlds, he held it and waited.

Jessie planted her feet and puffed up her chest. Her hands shook at her sides as she spat out a new knowing that, during that last song, had cemented itself in her heart. "I'm not going south tomorrow," she declared. "I'll go, I will. But not tomorrow."

A second later, she marched toward Matt, gave the door a hard yank to loosen it from his grip, and slammed it in his face.

Matt stood outside, placed a hand on a hip, used his other hand to anxiously rub his jaw as he stared at the closed door, twisted around to see Sam's curious eyes on him, and slammed a fist against the wall.

After counting to three as he wondered what he should do—go inside and try to reason with her, or give her some space—he stormed away.

Chapter Twenty

At didn't take Arnie, Kalon and Josh long to find a beach café to hang out in when they got tired of each other's company and cooking. Their select Caribbean island was so small that the main village could only support a couple of cafés, one of which seated no more than twenty patrons, and that included the outdoor patio. The larger café, the Salty Dog, which did triple duty as a pub and restaurant, was large enough to allow incognito seating in dark corners. That, too, included the outdoor patio.

It was a Wednesday, a mid-week hump day. Arnie parked the men's shared small car in a dusty nearby lot and headed into the café with his head down and his shoulders tense. The sudden semi-darkness of the little establishment jolted him. The older he got, the harder he found it was to adjust his eyes to the dingy dimness of such places.

Just inside the open doorway, Arnie took off his sunglasses and tapped them against his thigh. He waited a few seconds for his sight to come fully back to him before he gave the mocha-skinned owner a wave and marched outside to a dusty corner. The morning sun was fresh in the sky, just now alighting over the island, cool enough to allow for a comfortable outdoor sit and warm enough for Arnie to wish he could more easily adapt to the locals' way of dress and put on some kind of short pants instead of the hot jeans or track pants he was accustomed to. If there was one thing that set him apart and put him on unwanted radars, it was the jeans. He made a mental note to suck up his pride and stop by one of the small shops lining the main road of the rustic village before driving back to the beach house later. Surely he could find some shorts he could stand to wear.

The owner wandered over and dropped a newspaper on Arnie's table. "How you want your eggs?" he asked outright. This was becoming a usual thing, Arnie showing up alone in the early mornings for breakfast. *Rich Americans,* the guy, Jarvis, had decided when the three rather aloof, quiet men renting the beach house on Moonlight Point first showed up in his place.

Jarvis waited patiently for his reclusive patron to give him his order, even though he could guess what it would be.

"Poached," Arnie said without looking up.

"One of these days you surprise me, no?" A corner of Jarvis' lip curled up into a sort-of smile, or at least what passed for a smile with him. Tall, slim, Jarvis was forty-one, widowed, the father of three boys who were being raised by his wife's parents on a neighboring island. His days were passed at his business. Over the years he'd seen many wealthy men pass through his doors, but this man and his quiet companions were the most reserved. *You all got somethin' to hide,* Jarvis considered as he sidled back into the Salty Dog. In his experience, nobody came to this forgotten island for anything other than to hide. On the plus side, Jarvis was not the curious type. He accepted his customers as just that—customers. The man scrunched up into the far corner of the outdoor patio had, in a short time, already become a regular. Didn't matter why he was there, only mattered that he paid.

Whistling, Jarvis retrieved two eggs from a fridge and got to work.

Outside, Arnie wasn't surprised to see that he was the lone patron in the Salty Dog this morning. Still, he was relieved. He could hear Jarvis whistling as he prepared the order. This was as good a time as any. Cell reception was manageable at the beach house but Arnie wanted privacy for this call. Josh was in the shower when Arnie left the house. Kalon was just laying out a yoga mat on the deck by the pool. They never questioned Arnie's Salty Dog breakfasts. All three were becoming experts at finding things to do that allowed each some highly coveted alone time.

With a glance toward the open, wide space between the outdoor patio and the Salty Dog's interior, Arnie pulled a small phone out of the back pocket of his jeans and dialed. It was a burner phone, for the most part untraceable. He had a collection of these. So did the man he was about to call. They made calls, pulled out the Sim cards and disconnected the batteries when they were finished, and dug out new phones each week. Law enforcement could maybe—a big maybe—trace the calls, but the chance that anyone would bother was unlikely.

It wasn't just Josh that was missing and presumed dead in the supposed plane crash. Arnie, Kalon, Doctor Westfield, the pilot and co-pilot—who had scattered off to far corners of the planet—had to lay low too. Their calls all had to be safely guarded.

Back in Canada, Charles, in the passenger seat of Matt's Audi, answered on the second ring. Matt had drawn the sedan to a stop in a muddy parking lot at Mundy Park in Coquitlam, a treed network of walking trails on the eastern outskirts of Vancouver. "Arnie," Charles said simply by way of greeting.

"Charles."

Matt leaned an elbow on the driver's door and absently chewed a nail as he listened. Arnie had a low, serious voice. His words were easily discernible in the quiet car.

"How's our boy holding up?" Charles barked. Even the mention of Josh gutted him. The loss of Josh as his lead actor on *Sacred Peace* was bad enough. Watching Jessie and the children struggle through the confusion and chaos was heart wrenching.

"Physically, Josh is doing well," Arnie said by way of illumination from his corner at the Salty Dog. "Kalon has him easing back into exercising, small things for now, just to keep him moving."

"And?" Charles asked, as some of the tension in his body gratefully eased.

Matt stilled his nail chewing and bent his head toward his boss as he eavesdropped.

A restrained noise that could have been interpreted as a grump made its way to Canada. "I think he'd be doing better if he knew what his wife's plans were. He's sinking. Every day he sinks a little lower."

Charles emitted a low *pffft* and glanced sideways at Matt, who let out a stuttery breath and shifted uncomfortably in his seat. "I'd like to be the bearer of good news, Arnie, but at this point in time Jessie hasn't shared her plans."

Getting to the point was Arnie's forte. He didn't like wasting time and so almost jumped on Charles. "You don't think she's coming."

"Put it this way. She hasn't packed. Charlie's still in Calgary wrapping

Sacred Peace. Jessie spent last weekend at the ranch with the kids. Dee and Carlotta were with her. Charlie and Jane were there a lot. On Monday they shut the place down for the winter and shipped the horses back to Jack at Southlands, but Jessie hasn't made a move to close things up here in Vancouver. Although at the same time, she hasn't unpacked the few things she was readying before the concert in L.A., either."

"I suppose that can be interpreted as a good sign. How's she feeling?"

"The baby? She'd be feeling better if she'd eat properly. And sleep."

"It's an epidemic." Arnie's wry attempt to lighten the conversation backfired.

Charles' jaw firmed up and he paled. "We need to get her down there."

Next to him, Matt made a disparaging *shuffing* sound and stared out of the window at a lone hiker who was just heading into the Mundy Park trails. The hiker had stopped to read a yellow caution sign that warned about a recent bear sighting in the park. Seemingly unconcerned, the hiker—an older, graying man—adjusted a striped knit toque on his head and marched in anyway.

At his corner table, Arnie leaned over the newspaper Jarvis had left for him and rubbed his forehead. "As you know, Jessie will do what she wants, Charles," he said. "And she'll do it on her own terms. When she wants."

"She needs to be with her husband. The kids need to know their father is alive and well."

"How angry is she at Josh?"

"I don't know that she's so much angry as just sad," Charles said. "And scared. The prospect of going south with the children and with the new baby coming has her feeling cornered. Deirdre isn't helping. She can't keep herself from being emotional in the presence of Jessie and the kids. There's no real win here, Arnie."

"Sure there is. Josh is alive. Morgan has backed off, right?"

Matt perked up. This conversation was a two-parter. The last time they talked to Arnie, Matt and Charles had promised him they'd reach out to his contact, Vaughn, at Brody to suss things out and see what Morgan was thinking. They'd enlisted Ulysses to do the deed, under the pretense of updating Vaughn on what they knew about what happened to Arnie via Josh's medevac flight.

On Arnie's end, a heavy sigh from Mundy Park jolted him out of any sense of new peace and harmony. "What?" Arnie asked, in a demanding tone that left no room for wishy-washying around.

"I'll let Matt update you on what Ulysses found out," Charles said. He handed the phone to his good friend, who took it with a forced inhale for strength.

It took Matt a minute to find the words. When he finally spoke, he told Arnie straight out what Vaughn had shared with Ulysses when the two men connected. The call was made directly to the warden's office because Vaughn's position as a leader in the prison population earned him special privileges, and also because a call direct from the Keating camp after the supposed loss of the well-respected Arnie was considered prestigious. The conversation had been cautious. It wouldn't do to let Vaughn or anyone who might be listening in— the warden included—know that Arnie and Josh had both been secreted away.

"At the time of the call to Vaughn, Morgan was in solitary," Matt explained cautiously over the phone to Arnie. "Stripped, apparently, which translates to freezing. Vaughn told Ulysses that Caulfield has that kind of power. I suppose we can interpret the guard's actions as maybe meaning that Caulfield and Morgan had some kind of falling out."

"Over what? Over Josh surviving the gunshot, maybe?" Trying to wrap his mind around what that could mean, Arnie straightened. He took another surreptitious glance around to make sure nobody was within earshot. From the kitchen he could hear metal on metal, the low sluicing, slicing and scraping of a spatula on a sizzling griddle, he figured. Jarvis was still whistling. *He must be a happy guy,* Arnie thought abstractly.

"Worse. According to Vaughn it was a disagreement over the outcome of the plane's disappearance. I think maybe Morgan, after working with us, has a good idea of what kind of tricks we can get up to. It seems he's not buying it. That Josh is dead, I mean."

A chill ran down Arnie's spine. He rolled up the newspaper and clenched his mighty fingers around it. "So why would Caulfield punish Morgan for thinking that? It doesn't make sense. From what Vaughn told me before about Caulfield, his motivation is to please the inmates. That's why he does what he does, coordinating retribution and vengeance and all that shit."

"We don't know," Matt replied. "We can only guess. Vaughn says there were witnesses to a fight in the gym. There were harsh words spoken about the plane. The fight seemed to have been sparked from some news announcement that Caulfield overheard, a story about how no wreckage was spotted from the air, that kind of thing. The only thing that really didn't make sense was that Caulfield seemed like the one who was the most pissed. He jumped Morgan. Also surprising is that Morgan fought back which, according to Vaughn, he never does. They had to tase him in order to subdue him."

"All right. So Morgan's freezing his balls off in the SHU. Too damn bad, the asshole. Where does this leave us?"

"This is where it leaves us. It leaves us with utilizing some of that movie magic you talked about. We need to get out over Mount Slesse somehow and stage a plane crash. That's where it leaves us," Matt repeated, edgy and tense. "And it's got to happen by spring. It should have happened before, or simultaneously with, our private medevac flight but there just wasn't enough time to pull it together. Charlie and Jon are on it now, working with their stunt coordinator and production designer. I hope to hell he can trust them."

"You can say that again." After an extended silence in which he could hear Matt struggling to even out his breath, Arnie added a hopeful, "That's good, then." He relaxed slightly. His breakfast slid into view before him. Looking up, Arnie nodded a grim thank-you to Jarvis, who saluted, wiped his hands on a white apron tied around his waist, and walked away with a jovial swing in his step. "Get our girl down here, then," Arnie instructed as he picked up his fork. "Let's keep her and the kids on the down low over the winter. By spring maybe we can have some guarantee that things will be final." A thought occurred to him. Arnie scratched his whiskers. Shaving was something neither he nor Josh nor Kalon were bothering with on any regular basis down south. With a shiver he asked in a low, careful tone, "What about bodies?"

Matt inhaled. "Charlie's on it. There will be remnants of clothes, bags and other identifying features. We're staging a fire. Around the plane will be animal prints—animals carry away bones. We'll leave DNA evidence from all of you who were on the plane that we hope will be enough to satisfy our dedicated investigator. Who, by the way, is a friend of mine. Hired of course by Charles and funded by his millions to lead the Feds who, when all is said and done, don't have the budget they need to carry out a thorough investigation, and who will be over the moon to be handed evidence by someone they trust."

"Movie magic. And money. I see. Thank God."

"So all that's left is the hope that Jessie will see fit to go south and join her husband." Matt's stomach wrenched when those words snaked out from between his lips. Lifting a hand, he probed at his forehead with a thumb and two fingers. *And my wedding,* he thought, *which Jessie won't be able to attend. Which maybe is a good thing.* He planned to officially ask Shanda to marry him on Christmas Eve.

They ended the conversation with plans to chat again the next day, at a later time. Matt and Charles were taking Jacob up to the Whistler ski area to shoot a music video. Jessie had grudgingly agreed to come along. The kids, who were being home-schooled for the time being, would be tutored by Patin in the morning and would spend the afternoon and evening with Deirdre and Carlotta at La Casa. The brief break from parenting to go to Whistler, they all hoped, would restore Jessie's flagging spirits and would also provide opportunities for intimate chats.

Starting with Josh.

The next day, Matt was in the Whistler condo kitchen with Jessie and Jacob, putting the last of the dinner dishes away, when Charles' latest burner phone rang. After answering it, with a crook of his finger Charles beckoned Jessie to the living room, to a cozy wing chair by a stone-surround fireplace. He held out his phone. "It's for you."

Taking it from him, Jessie eyed it with a nervous frown. "It's a burner," she ascertained.

Charles forcibly lifted her hand to her ear. "Don't stare at it. Talk."

Watching him, she licked her lips but lowered the phone and held it against her thigh. "Is it Josh?" she inquired with an equal mix of childhood wonder and apprehension. From the kitchen, Matt saw her raise her chin in that stubborn way of hers. He wondered if Jessie would even take the call. Jacob leaned against the kitchen island and caught Matt's eye. Just as curious, he shrugged.

At Charles' quiet nod, Jessie turned her back to him, to all of them, lifted the phone back to her ear without Charles' aid, and let her husband know she was on the line. "Hey, Josh," she managed, swallowing bitterly as she made her way to a small back hallway where she leaned her butt against the wall and slid down to the floor. Hunched over her baby belly, Jessie waited for him to respond.

In the Caribbean, one of the Bayliner's best features was a curved white bench seat that faced the stern, so passengers could gaze dreamily at the boat's wake as they were motored over the water. Josh was perched on the edge of that seat, in the center of the boat almost, staring down at the floor. Working his mouth to find the words to ask his wife what her plans were, he stopped the agonizing over-thinking that was driving him crazy, and tilted his head to Jessie's voice when he heard her say, "I hear water."

"Yeah, uh, I'm sitting on the boat," he admitted, his confession emerging thick and damp. "I'm being lazy. Cell reception's not bad out here by the dock for some inane reason."

Jessie melted. His voice…Josh's voice…Oh God, it was good to hear that so deeply loved dusky voice. She squeezed her eyes tightly shut. Out loud, through rapidly escalating emotion, she mustered up, "You have a boat." It wasn't a question. It was more of a realization. Jessie slapped a palm against her forehead. "Of course you have a boat. You have a motorbike too? Horses?"

Josh's silence was Jessie's cue to push the adrenaline rush at that particular comprehension back down into her body, take a deep breath, and go slow. Just hearing Josh speak again, to her, was enough to remind her how much he meant to her…that this crazy change in their lives was a new chance for them. *He could be dead,* she considered. *But he isn't. But…I dunno if he still wants to be.* The last thought fused a new-old anger, which snuck up on her like a lit stick of dynamite, sizzling its way to a claustrophobic, irreversible explosion.

"No," came Josh's disheartened response at her sarcastic query as he dipped his toes into a tiny pool of water that had accumulated on the boat's bottom, a remnant of the fast spin he and Kalon had taken earlier that day around their almost enclosed private cove. "No horses. No Harley."

The deep sadness in his voice cut Jessie to the core. She shoved the heel of a palm into one closed eye. "No, I guess there wouldn't be horses and Harleys down there. I'm sorry, Josh."

"Not as sorry as I am." Josh was speaking so quietly that Jessie had to strain to hear him. "Look, uh," he said, reaching deep for strength, "I know this isn't the way we need to do this, but…we don't seem to have a choice at the moment. Jess, I…I need to know how angry you are. With me. About what I did."

She paused. "I'm not there," she eventually whispered into the phone. "That oughtta tell you something, Josh."

In the main part of the Whistler condo, all three men knew they should be talking, about anything, really, as long as their voices masked how Jessie's conversation was going with her husband. Frankly, though, none of them felt like saying a word. All were prepared to go to Jessie's aid if she needed it, if she lost it with Josh or if she crumpled into a heap. And all were exhausted by the efforts it was taking to keep her busy, to prevent her from climbing into bed and staying there. Jessie needed to help the children cope; the kids needed their mother to hold her shit together, to stay one step ahead of the darkness that stalked her like a hunter seeking prey.

The guys heard nothing for a bit while Josh was apparently speaking, but Jessie heard him loud and clear.

"Jessie," Josh was saying, "some day you will understand why I did what I did. Why it made sense to me."

She sucked in a breath. "Part of me does, Josh. Really, truly, I half get why you did it. The other part of me wants to rip your throat out and feed it to somebody's goddamn dogs. Slowly. So you feel every bit of pain I feel at the thought of my husband choosing to leave me and our kids behind the way you planned." She wiped a sweaty palm on her thigh, over and over. "That was some Hollywood exit, you bastard. A quick death, I guess it was supposed to be, huh? I should add that a good chunk of me thinks you're a coward for going that route. Where's your sense of honor, Josh? History coulda schooled you on some noble, upright way to die instead. The slow and brave kind, the kind that separates the weaklings from the warriors. You forget to do your research?"

"It wasn't suicide, Jessie. It was never about me killing myself. It was a contract meant to keep you and the kids safe, that's what it was."

"Suicide, shmuicide. A rose by any other name is still a fucking rose. Fuck, Josh, I can't even stand to hear you say the word. All the bullshit I've been through in my life? I admit that I thought of it those times, I considered it. More than once. Back in the Langley house I was pretty damn ready to let go, and with Deuce and his sick little games there was a time when I would have gladly signed off. But I didn't. I stuck it out, I—"

Josh cut her off. He raised his voice, which surprised Arnie up at the pool above and behind him. "You were the only one at risk then, at least in Langley after the kids were returned to me. I wasn't, I was never the only one once we clued into what Morgan had planned for us. The day you were forced into the river with Emily-Grace..." Josh choked. His throat closed over and he couldn't say any more.

Jessie's heart softened but she forced out some of the dark thoughts she'd started mulling over and over the moment she read Josh's hand-written letter. "Don't ever tell me I was the only one at risk back in the old days, Josh. Since the day Sandy took his last breath in my arms I've been too fucking aware of just how much letting other people into my life means that they are suddenly and irreversibly at risk too. Maybe not always phys-ically, but emotionally at least. And why did I leave you back when McCall was threatening us? Huh? Because I wanted you on this planet with me, that's why. I didn't see any hope in living my life without you by my side. I barely saw light when we were apart. If it weren't for Jacob all those times it would have all been darkness." Gathering her wits, Jessie went on. "You know what's worse, babe? Than the idea of ending it all and escaping? I'll tell you what's worse."

In the kitchen, Matt hung his head. He knew what was coming. Charles eased into a soft chair and fixated on the cozy fire. Jacob shuffled his feet and cursed under his breath.

Jessie continued, "What's worse than ending torment through death is being the one left behind. That's what's worse, being left behind with noth-ing but memories to hold on to. Because the thing about memories is that they're intangible, you can't grasp them, they're like clouds that float by in waves so when you reach out to wrap your fingers around them they're just a goddamned nothingness. You can't hold them or smell them or cuddle with them, you can't make dinner and cook and laugh and just touch them like we used to touch each other just when we were passing by, in the kitchen, or in the kids' bedrooms. You can't *make love* to memories, Josh. Jesus Christ, what the hell were you thinking? You selfish, fucking bastard. How could you ever even consider leaving me here alone?"

That was it. That was the bit that broke her, that broke all of them. There was so much at play in Josh's tough decision that it was like some kind of murky soup, all intrigue and secrets and safety and contracts and hard deals and a prison and Morgan and Nadia, still; and it was mean, nasty thugs in an underground parking garage. It was a freezing underwater dungeon and a snow-white puppy and a terrified child. It was another dearly loved man's untouchable fingers and his horrified eyes on the opposite side of a submerged car's window.

It was an unrelenting, stalking fear.

Somewhere in the middle of the entire mess, barely perceptible to those who were not Josh, was a pinprick of light, a light that Josh had, when he arranged the hit, interpreted as hope—not for him, but for his family.

It was almost impossible for Jessie to open up her heart to see what Josh saw, to imagine anything good in an action so reprehensible, so…desperately final.

The crackling fire in the hearth did nothing to quell the sound of Jessie's grief. In the kitchen Matt let a helpless *grrrr* loose. He angled his face out of view of Jacob's stricken eyes.

In the Caribbean Josh was being rocked like a baby on the luxurious new boat. The wavelets were delicate and kind. In lacey, watery bits, soothing whitecaps were gently lap, lap, lapping against the hull. The tranquil sounds were easy on the heart and a balm to the soul.

Josh rallied.

"Matt," Jessie heard him murmur through the phone line. "I wasn't leaving you alone, little one."

"Matt?" Jessie almost spat out the name. Somewhere, a little alarm bell was twinkling, ringing in her ears like a warning. *I need to ease off*, ran through her addled brain. *Josh is alive now. So why is he talking like he can still choose to walk away?* "Jesus, Josh, how fair do you think that is to him? To Matt?" she breathed. "Stop and think about it, babe. How fair would it be to leave him here to pick up the pieces with…" She glanced toward the end of the small hallway where she was sitting. It was desperately quiet out there. It occurred to Jessie that Matt was likely hearing every word passing through her trembling lips. Sucking up her nerve, she stared into the kitchen and finished her sentence. "With a woman who doesn't want him? With a woman who would be spending all her time crying for the man she's lost?"

In the kitchen Matt gripped the edge of the kitchen island and focused on his knuckles. Jacob groaned.

Josh took the admission as an opportunity. He had no way of knowing that Jessie was doing her Jessie-best to quite intentionally sink Matt to his knees. He knew things weren't great between Jessie and Matt; he'd heard they had barely spoken since the night of their fight in L.A. and barely before that, too, since leaving Calgary, but he didn't know how deep the wounds ran between them.

Hopeful, a spark of light flickering in his eyes, Josh said, "So you'll come down here, then. You'll have the baby here. Kalon can handle the birth, Jessie, and there's a midwife in town if you'd be more comfortable with an extra set of hands."

"Josh…"

His heart sank. *Fuck. Fuck fuck fuck.*

"I don't want to have our baby on some random island." Unwanted tears pricked at the corners of Jessie's eyes. Summoning up some fight so she could better stand her ground, she finished with, "I want Deirdre close by. I want the kids to have the security that she and Carlotta can give them. I want Charles and Dee to know this child." Biting her lip, Jessie didn't add that she also wanted Matt close by. With or without Shanda, whether he and she—Jessie—were speaking or not, and with or without the harsh words both he and Jessie had loosed in their earlier fights, he was still, and would always be, strength personified. Now, Jessie laid her free hand on her abdomen and felt the baby's foot move underneath her skin. *You agree, little Sawyer baby,* she intoned silently. *You want these special people in your life.*

"The thing is, Jessie." Josh was struggling. "Right now I can't go back to Vancouver."

"You can't ever come back." Spoken in a deadpan voice, Jessie may as well have been issuing Josh a whole new death sentence. Standing, sliding back up the wall from whence she'd earlier slid down, she made her way to the end of the hall so she could face the living room and kitchen of the Whistler condo. Matt straightened when he saw her eyes land on him. "You can't *ever* come back here, Josh. Ever. And I don't want to go there."

"Everything you just said…" In the Caribbean, Josh's voice was inaudible to Arnie now, who peered down at the boat to see if Josh was still on the phone, he was so quiet. "The thing is, I know you're angry but I also know you still love me. I know you, Jessie. We promised ourselves. No matter what, we said we would never give up on each other." His voice was cracking with the strain.

Jessie snuffed. "Don't talk to me about promises, Josh. Don't talk to me about not giving up."

"On each other," he said, infusing the phrase with a frustrated, desperate need for her to understand. "On us. It's not the same thing as me trying to find a way to give you and the kids a life free of fear. That was bigger than us. That included our kids." He took a breath. "I survived, Jessie. What happened in Alberta is old news. I'm still here; there's a plan in place to help us. I think… maybe you just need some time…"

In Whistler, Jessie and Matt were locked in each other's intense gazes. She almost dropped the phone, the electricity crackling between them was so strong. The only option was for Jessie to shake her head, to try to somehow disconnect herself from handsome Matt's mighty aura. She swallowed. "I do," she admitted softly, a note of hope creeping into her voice. But hope for what? "I do, I…I just need time, Josh."

"So you're going to have the baby there? Away from me."

"Jesus," Jessie cursed, scuffing a toe back and forth across the floor and finally breaking the steel-hardened link latching her into Matt's searching gray eyes. "It was always going to be 'away from you,' Josh. You disowned this baby the second you found out about him. About it."

A surprised gasp fluttered over the line. "Him? You know for sure it's a boy now?"

"Don't change the subject. And no, I don't know for sure. Call it a gut feeling." *And his name is Micah.* Jessie looked back up at Matt. Jacob was on the perimeter of her vision but she barely registered his presence. Her eyes drifted down to Matt's white knuckles gripping the island. *Steady, stable… strength…*

Shoulders sinking, Jessie let her eyes close over. At the same time, she shoved a thumb and forefinger into the outer corners of her eyes. *Sweet Jesus,* she moaned. *What a fucking mess.* It struck her as rather earth-shattering that right now—at this very moment while talking to her husband—the arms she ached to climb into were Matt's. *I'm just scared,* she consoled herself at that seemingly traitorous thought. *It's not a lust thing. It's a trust thing.*

"Okay, Jessie, look," came the subdued voice from the south. "I'm not going to beg you. You're right about the baby, but only because I didn't know how to feel. I found out you were pregnant while Matt and Arnie were trying to revive you, while my daughter was screaming in terror because of what she was going through, just moments after her new puppy drowned. I couldn't think, okay? I couldn't think and I sure as hell couldn't feel. So this is the thing. This is the way we'll leave it, okay?" Exhaling, Josh braced his forehead in his hand. At his feet the puddle was shining, mirror-like and toasty warm in the gorgeous tropical sun. "I don't want you to come here until you're ready. I don't want you to come here unless you want to. Otherwise, what's the goddamned point?"

"Okay," Jessie whispered. "Enjoy ripping around on your new boy toy."

Josh was silent. After a bit he said, "That's all you have left to say to me? That's it?"

Jessie chortled stupidly. "Right now? Hell, yeah. Until you give me a reason to say more, Josh." Jessie let her gaze float back up to Matt. Immobile, he was watching her. She smiled at him, a slow, sad smile that didn't exactly erase all of their harsh words of late, but which seemed to say that she understood where the words came from, and that she hoped he, too, was aware. He blinked unhappily back at her. "Until," she said into the phone, "I no longer feel like I'll be alone if I go down there. Until I feel like I no longer have to hold you up. Because, Josh…" Jessie softened. "These days? Holding up someone else is not an option. I'm having a helluva time just keeping myself and the kids afloat."

She didn't wait for an answer. Letting the phone fall to her side, Jessie dropped it on the floor. After a long, lonely look at Matt, a sideways glance to Jacob, and a quick peek at Charles by the fire, she made her way to the stairs, jogged up to her bedroom, wrapped her arms around her pillow, and cried herself to sleep, where she stayed until Jacob came in a few hours later with his guitar dangling from one hand. In his experience, music was the universal healer.

Jessie got up then and sat cross-legged with her back against the headboard. While Jacob played and ran through lyrics, she chimed in with harmonies, and they passed the deepest, darkest part of the night with trusted friendship and restorative song.

Chapter Twenty-one

*E*mily-Grace tugged at her mother's elbow. "Momma, you look so pretty."

Smiling, Jessie bent down and delicately smoothed lip gloss across her daughter's cherubic pink rosebud lips. "So do you," she beamed. "My beautiful girl is growing up so fast." She turned back to the mirror.

"Nine's not that different from eight, actually," Emily-Grace said wisely, her eyes round and filled with adoration for her mother. "It's just a little more confusing, that's all."

Jessie's eyebrows shot up into question marks. "Confusing? How so, honey?" They were in the washroom of Jessie's old bedroom at La Casa while Jessie dressed for an awards night to celebrate film and television production in the west coast province. *Sacred Peace* was up for a number of awards by virtue of its producers and much of the cast being British Columbia residents. As Josh's supposed widow, Jessie was invited since Josh would be honored tonight, but it all felt fake and unreal to her. She decided she was only going to support Charles, Charlie and, well, grudgingly, Shanda.

Emily-Grace maneuvered her small feet up onto the toilet seat so she could face her pretty momma at eye level. Jessie whirled around to fully face her. "I'm confused about Daddy," the little girl admitted.

"What about Daddy?" It was late November now, more than two months after Josh was shot. As far as Jessie and the entire Keating camp could tell, the children seemed to have relaxed into a comfortable schedule. They were no longer asking the hard questions about Josh and, in fact, Emily-Grace's behavior, without her father around, was much improved. The only one of the three who still wept in his sleep, who woke up with night tremors, was Dylan. The youngest Sawyer had always been joined at the hip to Josh. Thankfully, Jacob took him—and the other two kids—a lot these days. Once again Jacob's easygoing presence was helping to fill the void left by Josh's sudden departure.

Humming softly as she thought about what to say, Emily-Grace wound her fingers tightly in and around each other. She met her mother's curious eyes. "I looked up Daddy on the Internet," she said, and braced herself for the onslaught she felt might be coming.

"What? Why? When?" Jessie was already dressed for the awards night. A brilliant gold Zuhair Murad maternity dress, designed just for her, was her haute couture of choice for the evening. Absently tugging at the short hem, which landed mid-thigh, Jessie faced her daughter with trepidation. The exquisite dress attractively hugged her body; its high neck featured scalloped cutouts for effect, and long, lace sleeves that ended in points over her middle fingers. Earlier, Jessie's hair had been manipulated by a stylist into a sophisticated updo. Her nails were brilliant in a sparkling pearl-cream, and her makeup matched the nails. The lip gloss now was just a final shiny coat. In short, Jessie had morphed into the glamorous mother Emily-Grace only saw once in a while, and whom the little girl was now thoughtfully admiring with a loving gaze.

The baby kicked. With a wince, Jessie looked down and put her hand over her belly before refocusing her attention on her daughter.

"When Patin went to the bathroom I looked on the Internet," Emily-Grace revealed with a touch of shame. "One of the big kids at dance class told me to. He said that they never found Daddy. You know, his...his body. Is that true, Momma?"

Oh, Jesus. You kids are soooo gonna hate me when you're teenagers. "Honey," Jessie started, unsure, "that is true. It is. We've told you kids that, that there is still hope for Daddy."

"On the Internet it said there are no signs of a plane crashing on that mountain, Momma. None at all. It just disappeared from radar, that's all."

Jessie gulped. Extending a hand, she touched Emily-Grace's hair and swept a loose swath back behind her small ear. The way her daughter was looking at her...so much hope in those pale ice-blue eyes...*God, I wish I could tell her,* Jessie sighed. Out loud she cornered right and took them down a safer road. "You miss Daddy," she said, as calmly as she could muster.

Her wise daughter didn't bite. "Momma, I want to know why there's no sign of a plane crashing but people are still talking about Daddy like he's dead." The grim determination in the child's eyes was unsettling.

"It's hard for them to find signs of crashed planes in the mountains, sweetheart," Jessie stated in the end. "There's snow up there, for one, and tons of blizzards, which would cover up any signs. But you and me and the boys," Jessie bent a little and peered directly into her daughter's eyes, "we will pray that we never find signs of a crashed plane. Or if we do, that somehow Daddy escaped and he's okay somewhere. That he can't contact us because it's winter in the mountains."

"He could be hurt, Momma. The kid at dance class said so." Emily-Grace's intense small eyes started to swim. "Is anybody looking for him?"

Jesus, I hope not, Jessie considered, picturing Morgan issuing search and rescue orders from jail. "Yes, sweetheart, don't you worry," she said instead. "Let's you and me just trust Grampie and Matt, okay honey? They're doing everything they can to find out the truth."

"But…what if he is dead? Like, really and truly dead, Momma?"

Jessie swallowed. "I have nothing to say to that, sweetheart. I really don't." And that, finally, was a truth Jessie could live with. "Except that we'll get by. We always do. Sawyer Strong, remember?"

Footsteps hurrying into the room saved her from further scrutiny by her inquisitive child, although Jessie caught herself thinking about Charles' plan to 'movie magic' a crashed plane in the spring. The children would need to know by then that their father was safe. How? How could that possibly work? The only way, Jessie figured sourly as she smiled wanly up at Deirdre at her door, would be for all of them to follow through and join Josh in the Caribbean, and change their names and their lives and leave this glamorous messed up world behind.

Leave loved ones like Dee behind. Sighing again, this time from the depth of her soul, Jessie took Emily-Grace's arm to help her jump down off the toilet.

"Off we go," Deirdre said lightly as her granddaughter snuggled up under her arm for the walk to the stairs. "Isn't your momma radiant, Emily-Grace?"

Emily-Grace didn't answer. She just stared glumly at the floor and wrapped one arm around her grandmother's comforting waist.

A few minutes later, Jessie stood at the playroom door and managed a small forced chuckle at her boys. Sam and Alin were staying with the kids tonight, and were in the midst of building a huge Lego castle. It was so big now that Dylan could barely be seen behind it. David was standing next to Sam, so like Josh in build and in characteristics that Jessie sometimes stared at him for minutes on end; other times she couldn't bring herself to look at him at all. When he turned to her now and smiled, she moved forward and brushed a loose strand of hair behind his ear, copying her earlier movement with Emily-Grace. It was like the simple, repeated gesture could somehow keep Josh closer. It, like the awards night, felt a little false, however. Jessie had not spoken to Josh since the one phone call at Whistler. It was easier to push him away; she just kept telling herself it would only be until after the baby was born. It was easier to navigate her messed up emotions this way. Tonight, the awards dinner would be killer.

"I need hugs," she murmured to her children. "Whose got hugs for Momma?"

An hour later she was seated uncomfortably at a round table with Charles and Dee, Charlie and Jane, Jonathon and Giselle, and Matt and Shanda. They were all a little crowded since an extra seat had been added for Jessie. Wistfully, she eyed Carter and Ashley at the next table, chowing down with some of the *Sacred Peace* crew. Anything would be preferable to sitting almost across from Matt, whom she still rarely spoke to these days. Her driver and usual bodyguard of late was Dan. Since he was the quiet type, Jessie could sink into graceful oblivion in his company. Matt, however, was missed. It was like he went missing right along with Josh, only his disappearance was almost harder to take since he was still a physical presence in her life, a reminder of what she lost and of what she still stood to lose.

The awards got underway with everyone at the table (apart from Jessie) imbibing just a little too much alcohol and cracking jokes that pissed Jessie off since it felt like nobody even remembered that Josh was once a part of their cast, and a part of their lives. The more alcohol they drank and the louder the laughter was, the lower Jessie's spirits sank. The earlier conversation with

Emily-Grace wasn't in any way conducive to making this horrible, false night go down any easier.

"You're all moving on without him," she blurted out partway through the evening, after dinner and dessert were consumed and just before the awards portion of the evening was about to begin. "You suck. All of you." The baby moved its foot, almost stomping on her bladder. Wincing noticeably, she laid a cautious hand over her abdomen.

The table fell silent. All eyes were on Jessie, who grabbed her linen napkin and tossed it onto the table with a petulant huff. Shoving back her chair, she narrowed her eyes at Matt as she leveraged her body upright and issued a sullen demand. "I want to go home."

Without even thinking about it Matt made a motion to stand too, but he froze when Shanda's dainty fingers landed in his lap. He clutched at his own linen napkin, gripping it between suddenly nervous fingers while he waited to see how a mini-showdown he instinctively felt was coming on was going to play out.

Shanda licked her glossy cranberry red lips and gave Jessie a kind of solicitous half smile. "He's been drinking, Jessie," she said evenly. It wasn't lost on her that Matt hadn't been driving Jessie in a while, at least not regularly. This directive from Jessie was clearly a challenge. Nor was it lost on Shanda that Matt had almost instantly vaulted up to respond to the request. *Years of conditioning*, she supposed with a wry grimace.

"And the award you're nominated for is coming up," Jessie bit off in return. "I get it. You want him here to hold your hand if you lose, and to sneak into a stall in the ladies' room to give you a celebratory screw if you win." She followed it up with a stark, unkind, "Should I start calling you Your Highness?"

"Oh, is that how you and Josh do it?" Shanda quickly fired back, skipping over the rude remark about royalty. "You must have christened a lot of restroom stalls over the years."

"Not anymore. Those days are toast," Jessie reminded her, much too calmly for the liking of everyone at the table who knew her well. "Courtesy of the legacy of a wicked woman who wanted my husband so bad she pointed a gun and fired," she went on, raising her chin for emphasis. "At me, by the way, in case you need some education on the subject since you likely weren't so closely following the drama in Josh's life back then. Thankfully, Shanda, your man saw something redeemable in my poisonous character worth saving. Or maybe he was just doing his job."

Considering that, Jessie feigned amazement and placed a reflective finger to her lips. "Oh, that was likely it," she added as a sarcastic afterthought. "Matt gets a paycheck to watch over me, after all." Her head whipped around to Charles. "Didya at least give him a bonus, Charles? After New York? And another one after the Lexus and my daughter's puppy both drowned?"

Deirdre bowed her head. Charlie moaned. Charles' eyes were popping; he looked about ready to erupt. Matt stared under the table, as if he wished he could climb underneath it the way he might have if he were three.

Jessie rubbed a suddenly shaking hand over her swollen tummy. Swallowing bitterly, she forced down an abrupt minor attack of surprise nausea, attributing it to this difficult evening that, when all was said and done, was just an emotional reminder of a man she missed with a desperation that cut her in two.

She couldn't keep herself from adding a quick postscript. It cut through the awkward silence that had overcome the stunned table. "By the way, I'll take that snarky restroom bit of yours as the compliment I know it was meant to be, Shanda, and not as the pitiful jealousy it sounded like on the outside."

Shanda screwed up her courage and fought back. "Um, who's jealous? Do you really want to talk about the green-eyed monster? You can deflect to me all you want, but it seems like jealousy constantly stalks you, Jessie." Next to her, Matt let out an annoyed, not-so-subtle *grrrr,* and fidgeted. Still, he snuck a concerned peek up at Jessie, who allowed herself a quick, sad glimpse of him before they both, rather noticeably, quickly looked away from each other.

A renewed, fiery stare landed back on Shanda. Jessie took a sharp breath. "Seriously, Shanda? You want to talk stalkers to me? I'll win on that one. I had a lot of time on my own to figure out what makes them tick. Well," she added, with a much too casual shoulder toss, "one of them, anyway."

"I noticed." Delicately, Shanda arrogantly pushed a loose blonde curl behind her ear. "How well you understood stalkers, I mean. I ran my hands over that big scar on your husband's side many times. I laid my palms on his warm skin." She held up the index finger of her right hand and purred out a few more details. "If you're the details type and really want to know, this finger—this one right here—traced that scar on Josh's tight body many times. I used to love the way he responded to my touch. With a little shiver, if you must know. Drove me right around the bend. And him too, I think."

"Why?" Jessie countered without hesitation. "Why'd you bother? Did you think you could heal him with your magic touch? You can't, Shanda. I've tried."

"Poor girl. Apparently your touch isn't as magical as you think, Jessie."

Speechless, Jessie's spine curved into a woeful C as she bent over her baby belly in a sort of astounded, bruised wonder. Reaching out, she clutched the table's edge and tried to breathe as, across from her, Shanda raised her hand higher, kissed her fingertip, and held it up toward Jessie so it looked like the number one.

"Round one," she murmured. "I win."

At Jessie's right, Charlie was bristling. He laid his hand over hers as she gripped the table for balance. "Jesus, Shanda. Easy, ladies. This isn't the damn Roman Coliseum. Call back your lions."

Charles threw a furious look in Matt's general direction. "Where's Dan?"

Deflated, done in by the women's verbal sparring, Matt half-heartedly pointed toward the entrance to the grand ballroom of the Fairmont Vancouver, where they were seated for the awards dinner.

This angry rift between Jessie and Matt wasn't serving anyone well. Shanda was still as a statue now on this special night that was meant for her, that put her front and center in front of her peers, that was meant to recognize the hard and tough work she was doing on *Sacred Peace*.

Eyeing Shanda nervously before twisting around in his seat, Charlie saw her grasp Matt's tense fingers tightly. He searched for and caught Dan's eye, and gave him a discreet wave. The bodyguard was poised and waiting. He started striding over, wading through tables populated by elegantly dressed television and film professionals.

Smartly, with a poise and grace they all expected of her, Deirdre rose and touched Jessie's arm. "Jessie, honey, don't go. Stay with us. We all miss Josh, but we're trying to move on. We need to move on. We can't stay in the pain one hundred per cent of the time."

The pale blue eyes clouded over. "Oh, lucky you," Jessie grumped. "Lucky all of you, to be able to push it aside. To push Josh aside." Her gaze, telegraphing a growing fury, dropped onto Matt's hapless form. "Out of sight, out of mind, huh?"

"Isn't it?" The raspy, quiet voice was Matt's. Tossing his linen napkin onto the table, he stood. Raising his arms to the sides, he faced Jessie. "What you can't see and you can't touch, you can easily bury."

"That's what you do with dead men," Jessie steamed, digging her fancy heels into the expensive floor beneath her feet. "You fucking bury them."

Dan, weaving through the last two tables that almost barred his path to the *Sacred Peace* gang, approached the table.

Charles was mortified at Jessie's thoughtless, disruptive behavior, especially since this was a special night for Shanda. "Dan." Snapping his fingers, he signaled to him and pointed to his wayward girl. "Take her home. Now." To Matt, he pressed his lips into a hard, thin line and issued a curt demand. "Back off. This is not the time or the place for the two of you to face off." It struck everyone funny that he did not say a word to Shanda, who was equally as hostile on this supposedly celebratory evening.

Rising, Charles rounded the table to land at Jessie's side. Taking her arm in his, he tried to lead her away but she shook him off, took a few steps backward, and glared at the entire table, each person in turn, lingering a little too long on Shanda. In the end her hurt eyes swung to Shanda's side and landed on Matt again. "You should be ashamed of yourselves," she fumed. "Every damn last one of you." A final look to Shanda, and she rounded up some grace. "Good luck tonight, Shanda," she muttered, not unkindly. "You deserve the win."

With Charles flanking her on one side and Dan on the other, Jessie made her way to the door without meeting the eye of anyone else in the extravagant space. Charles waited with her while Dan hurried off to fetch the car.

"I'm sorry," Jessie mumbled to him. Rubbing her stretched tummy, she whined that she really wasn't feeling well. "It's not about Josh," she sighed, so he wouldn't worry. The thing is, though, it was always about Josh. Every second of every day was about Josh. However, the milliseconds in between those thoughts were generally about Matt, and a desperate need to be held, to feel safe and secure in the arms of someone physically close by whom Jessie knew loved her.

Overtly nauseous now, she blinked sadly at Charles. "I just need some sleep," she explained ruefully as she tried to remain upright. "Apologize to Dee for me. Please?"

"It's fine," Charles replied, taking a quick study of his pale, wan girl. "You were right. We were insensitive. But you were rude and that's not acceptable, Jessie." Backing off, he reflected on the humped-over way she was standing, the way she was constantly shifting her balance from one foot to the other. "Are you certain you're okay? You look a little green. It's not the baby, is it?"

Jessie's heart sank. Intuitively she was wondering exactly that. It had crossed her mind. And she was about to go home. Alone. "I'm fine," she said with an assurance she didn't feel. This was a big night for Charles and his *Sacred Peace* team. A genuine hug softened things between them. "I'll see you tomorrow. Enjoy the rest of the evening I thoughtlessly hijacked on you, Charles."

Dan opened the back door of his sleek sedan. Charles held Jessie's elbow as she slipped inside. As Dan stealthily piloted them away from the hotel, Jessie looked back to spy Matt in the doorway, watching, his hands stuffed in his pants pockets and a look of utter sorrow lining his handsome face. It was everything Jessie could do not to raise a hand and give him the finger, not that he would see it through the window. She sat on her hands instead.

Dan was heading toward the Lions Gate Bridge. Sitting taller, Jessie called out to him. "Wrong way, mister," she said lightly.

"La Casa?" Dan eased off the gas, caught her eye in the rearview mirror, and waited.

"You know, Dan, I just really need to be home tonight. The kids are fine with Sam and Alin. After her night off, Carlotta will be back in the morning to put chocolate chip smiley faces on their teddy bear pancakes. Take me to my own house, please."

Dan eyeballed his cell phone. Regardless of the issues between Jessie and Matt these days, Matt was the guy Dan usually reported to. Well, Ulysses sometimes, and even Charles at times, but really it was Matt who called the shots when it came to Jessie's security. He didn't dare pick up the phone now, though. Jessie was watching him like a hawk.

He turned the car around and headed south toward the UBC neighborhood.

At home, Jessie thanked Dan just outside the back door. "I'm good from here," she said as he turned the key in the lock and pushed the door open. "Go home, Dan."

"Not a chance," he responded rather formally although, since she was his boss, she had every right to order him away.

Jessie pointed to the opposite end of the deck at the far end of the now-covered-over pool, toward the flagstone steps that led up to the driveway. "Go snuggle up with your woman. I'm fine."

"Let me check the house and then I'll stay in the driveway," was Dan's earnest answer. Facing Matt's wrath by leaving the premises was not on the list of options for a favorable outcome this evening. Lately, it wasn't the norm for anyone to stay parked in Jessie's driveway, though. Between the security cameras and the need to help fill Josh's shoes by helping with the kids, most times the team—who really counted as family these days—hung out inside the house. Or with the family at La Casa, usually.

"Check the house, fine," Jessie replied darkly. "But you can survey the driveway and the exterior of the house from your iPad, Dan. I'm serious. Tonight I just want to be left the fuck alone. Capiche?"

Grumbling, Dan closed the door behind Jessie and did a hasty walk-through, growling under his breath at 'pregnancy hormones' and wishing things would get back to normal. *Although,* he chided himself as he opened closets and peered around corners, *there really is no normal when it comes to Jessie.*

Dan called Matt the second he got back into his car. The call went unanswered. Cell phones were on silent at the Fairmont that night. Shanda, at that very moment, was on stage tearfully thanking her long gone co-star for his brilliant guidance and mentorship. Matt felt his phone vibrate in his pocket. Although it crossed his mind that there was a slim chance it could be a Jessie-related call, he was confident that Dan would have just delivered her safely to La Casa. It was likely just Dan reporting in. Matt'd check his phone later.

At home Jessie snuggled into her and Josh's big bed with a Jodi Picoult novel and a glass of sparkling water. By then she was having minor cramps, but told herself the baby wasn't yet due. "Braxton-Hicks," she said to calm herself. "False labor." Unable to focus on reading, she tried texting Matt three times to see how the awards were going—and also just to piss him off and distract him from Shanda, she admitted—but he didn't answer. Successive texts to Charlie also crashed and burned. A raw ache started in Jessie's gut. *Do they even care about me?* she wondered. *Do they miss us at all?* Suddenly the idea of leaving everyone behind didn't seem so bad. Furious at being shut out, she pitched her cell phone angrily across the room. With a protesting splintering-crash it hit a metal leg of Josh's ancient boxy black chair, and lay silent.

"Oh, shit." Slightly amused at her irreverence for the only mode of telephone communication available to her tonight and the next morning, Jessie considered getting up to see if she could somehow resurrect the phone. Picturing Matt panicking when he checked his messages later and tried to respond, she chose not to bother with the phone, and grinned. Widely. "Bastard." She chuckled. "Serves you right."

It didn't take long for her overwrought baby-to-be bladder to start irking the heck out of her. "Three times in an hour," she moaned, swinging her legs over the side of the bed and heading for the en suite bathroom an hour after she got into bed in the first place. "Remind me never to get pregnant again." A sardonic, low-voiced guffaw followed that comment. "Not much chance of that," she chided herself, at the same time sorrowfully reflecting on Josh and wondering how he was holding up. For certain he would be aware that tonight was a big deal in the annals of *Sacred Peace.* He, like Shanda, was up for an acting award that Charlie would have to go on stage to accept for him if he won.

As she waddled toward the bathroom she pondered the fact that Charles was always filling her in on Josh, on the fact that Josh was feeling well these days, that Kalon had hooked up with a local woman, that Arnie was apparently into wearing shorts and was swearing that he would never leave the Caribbean. It seemed like a ploy to keep Josh in her consciousness at all times. Annoyed, she wriggled down her undies and sat on the toilet for yet another pee.

Just as Jessie stood up from the toilet and started to pull up her panties, a warm liquid started to trickle down her leg. Lost in thought about Josh, at first she wondered whether she just didn't quite get all of the latest pee out.

A sudden jolt of awareness got her back on track real quick. "Oh, shit… that'd be my water breaking. You Sawyer babies do like to make your entrances well before your scheduled appointments, doncha? You oughtta waited a few weeks, ya little bugger." Thinking back on her previous births, Jessie climbed into the shower to let the fluid drain for a few minutes, and reached for a soft white towel afterwards. She got her second jolt of the evening when a sudden acute cramp discharged itself into her abdomen. It felt like her womb was splitting in two.

"Oh, Jesus. That was fast." Bending over, she cringed until the cramp peaked and dispersed. A moment later, she recouped her strength and barged into the closet. Tonight's Zuhair Murad was hanging up where she left it. A diabolical grin crossed her face at the thought of showing up at the hospital in it, but she quickly discarded the notion when a new pain sideswiped her. "What is this, the Indy 500?" she asked her unborn child. "This isn't a race, Baby Sawyer!" Pajama pants would do the trick. Blue ones, with sleepy sheep scattered across them like fluffy clouds.

Throwing a new towel between her legs after she was dressed, and grabbing a pad to keep her undies from soaking, which seemed rather futile in the end, Jessie marched penguin-like around the closet seeking a top to wear, and clothes to put into an overnight bag for the hospital. She had a doula available to her, but had zero interest in utilizing one for this, her fourth pregnancy and birth. As far as Jessie was concerned, the hospital would do. Josh wasn't here, and this birth just didn't feel as sacred as the first few. Mostly, it just felt lonely. A wave of loneliness swept over her. Stopping by the broken phone, Jessie bent over her big belly and picked it up. She pushed the 'on' button. Nothing happened. A hopeless black screen stared back at her. The thing was toast.

"Brilliant, Wheeler-Sawyer," she groaned. "You sure messed up tonight."

There was only one recourse—get into the car and drive herself to the hospital. It didn't seem like such a stretch. From here this time of night, traffic would be light. Jessie estimated it would take her about half an hour to arrive at Vancouver General. Josh flashed across her mind. Just as quickly, she pushed him away. There was no time to consider his absence tonight, and what got him there in the first place. She would have to be strong, independent. *I can do this*, she told herself. *He's not here. I don't need him, anyway. I'm tough.* Tears pricked at her eyes.

Heading for the stairs, Jessie doubled over three times before she finally made it outside and up the flagstone steps to the SUV. Backing out of the driveway was easy enough. She wondered if Dan noticed on his iPad via the security cameras that she was on the move. With a half-assed grin, she waved at one of the cameras. *He'll be pissed if he sees me leave,* she thought, *because he'll be wondering where the hell I'm going.* It was after eleven. Dismissing his potential concern for her, she realized he'd likely just think she was headed to La Casa after all.

Swinging the car around to face north, she headed toward Vancouver General.

～ ～

A half hour later, a young blond constable in a Vancouver Metro police cruiser flicked on his lights and cruised to a stop behind Jessie's parked SUV. He ran the plates before he approached the vehicle, which was skewed half-sideways, and which more than one passing motorist had called in to report as belonging to a possibly inebriated driver.

"Seriously?" he asked himself when he realized just whom the car was registered to. Yanking a black ball cap down low over his forehead, he took a hard look at the SUV before he forced himself to walk on shaking legs toward the car.

A sharp rap on the driver's side window startled Jessie, who responded by punching, with one finger, the appropriate button to lever it down. "Jessie Wheeler-Sawyer?" the cop asked, shining his flashlight into the vehicle and almost blinding Jessie.

"Yup," she moaned while hunched over the steering wheel.

"What is it, Ma'am? You're not well, I see." Relieved that Jessie was well enough to speak, at least, the police officer forced his heart rate to a steady, practiced calm.

Jessie was clenching her teeth about as hard as she was clenching the wheel with her fingers.

The young constable was about to order an ambulance when Jessie's pained voice stopped him. "You think I could hitch a ride to Vancouver General?" Laying a flushed cheek on the steering wheel, her tired, strained eyes pleaded with him. "I'm in labor, pretty much." The pronunciation was delivered in a high-pitched falsetto. "If you're thinking about ordering up an ambulance, I don't think this kid's too interested in waiting for more formal transportation."

"Uhhh…" The constable peered in around Jessie. "You're, uh, alone, Mizz Wheeler? Uh, Sawyer?"

"Hell, yeah, haven't you heard? Don't you Google shit like the rest of the world? Heck, my daughter knows more than you do." Jessie angled her head to lean her forehead against the steering wheel now, and groaned loudly. "Oh, Jesus. This part always sucks."

The constable grabbed the outside handle and whipped open the door. "I'm sorry about your husband," he offered. "I just thought you'd have some security with you, or a friend, at least."

Yeah, well, so did I. Taking the arm he volunteered in her general direction, Jessie slid out of the car. "Well, this happened rather suddenly. Like, it was kind of an explosion of amniotic fluid, if you must know," Jessie declared rather crudely. "A trickle at first and then a downright river. This kid's a firecracker, already in a hurry. And as to my security, well, I'm not talking to one of my guys and at this moment the other main dude's likely not too interested in talking to me. Seeing as he's gonna be in shit with guy number one because he left me alone and went home. Even though it was me who, well, rather rudely sent him home." She limped, bent over double, clinging to the young man's arm, to the passenger side of the cruiser. "Oh goody goody, can I sit in back? Are you locking me in? My boys would think it's so cool that I get to ride in a cop car. Can you keep the lights on? What about the siren? What's your first name, by the way?" She glanced at his shiny brass nametag. "Constable Buckley's all well and good but I think we can dispense with the formalities, don't you? In case you have to pull over and touch my private parts while you, owwww! Oh, Jesus! Bloody hell!" Focusing on some quick breathing exercises, Jessie leaned over the hood of the cruiser. After a minute she gasped, "That was a big one. Uh, what I meant to say was while you escort this little Sawyer into the world."

The young constable was beside himself. He had Jessie Wheeler on his arm, about to give birth apparently, and for the most part she was cracking jokes. Looking closer, though, he discerned that she was also trying to discreetly swipe at tears. He stepped up his pace. To her dismay he deposited her in the front passenger seat of his car, ran back to her SUV and grabbed the keys, then vaulted in behind the wheel of the cruiser.

"My first name's Kevin," he told her as he pulled out into the street. "Nice to meet you, Mizz Wheeler. I'll get you to that hospital before the baby comes. Hang on."

He left the lights on and cranked the siren. At his side, Jessie smiled crookedly through clenched teeth and gripped the oh-my-Jesus handle with all her might.

An hour later, just as the film and television awards were wrapping up, Constable Buckley was at the door of the Fairmont Hotel's grand ballroom, nervously adjusting his nylon jacket and repeatedly twisting the brim of the black ball cap he wore over close-trimmed blond hair.

Matt and Charles were alerted of his presence by a server. Both men looked over at the door at the same time. Spying the cop, who was anxiously scanning the room and its chic guests, they bolted for him. Charlie, with a quick, "Stay here" fired in Jane's direction, was right behind them.

The constable led the men out into the lobby. Raising a hand, he said quickly, "It's nothing to be concerned about. Everything's fine. I found your girl parked crookedly on the side of King Edward in a no parking zone," he added, just to be clear. "I transported her to the hospital in my cruiser."

"What? What happened?" It seemed Charlie was the only one with the ability to form and utter words. Charles was shaking—past experiences gifted him with mortal fear at this kind of news—and Matt was struck dumb. Momentarily.

The cop looked at all three of them like they were crazy. "Uh, um, she's in labor. She's having a baby," he explained, as if he needed to clarify that point which, to him, should have been damned obvious. "Frankly," he added somewhat unkindly, hitching his thumbs over his belt, "I was surprised to find her alone. Even people who aren't superstars don't generally try to drive themselves to the hospital when they're about to give birth."

"She should have called," Charles fumed, pacing in a small circle. "She's gone a little rogue lately. Aloof. Likes to do her own thing."

Frowning, Matt held up his phone. Chagrined, Charlie echoed the movement. "She did," Matt said for the two of them. "She texted at least, Charles." He studied the phone. "Not about going into labor, though. Just…other stuff." He wrinkled his eyebrows as he read Jessie's earlier, sometimes off-color texts.

"Thank you," Charles said, reaching toward the young police office in a gesture that the constable interpreted as wanting to shake his hand. The younger fellow complied as Charles asked, "What's your name?"

Hasty, in a quick movement, Charlie took Matt by the elbow while Charles finished up with the police officer. "Look, it's a big night for Shanda, Matt," he stated rightly. "Jane can go to the hospital with Deirdre. Charles and I will drop in after we've finished with the media."

A hurt, questioning look arced across Matt's worried eyes. "I want to be there, Charlie. I should have driven her home tonight; I should have made sure she was okay."

Studying him, Charlie pocketed his hands. "You and Jessie aren't even talking, Matt. You and Shanda, on the other hand, are. But you might not be if you choose to hang around Jessie tonight. Where you need to be for the rest of this night is by Shanda's side."

"Jessie is my job, Charlie. She's my responsibility."

"You're not fooling anyone, big guy." Charlie's words were tough, reflective. Concerned. "Since when does a person's job trump their partner, Matt? Look, it's shitty of me to say, but you lost Julie to the amount of time you spend with Jessie. Let her go. Maybe…" He bit his lip and shut up.

"What? Just spit it out, Charlie."

"Maybe Jessie will go south if you're not around so much."

"I've hardly been around the last few months. I know my priorities, Charlie. I'm kicking my ass for what happened tonight. There's no way in hell Jessie should have been driving herself to the hospital. Who knows what could have—"

"Down, boy," Charlie interjected. "Nothing happened, she's fine."

"Look, we're wasting time. I need to call Dan to find out why the hell he wasn't with Jessie tonight. Finding her alone on the side of a street better not make headline news tomorrow."

Charlie *pshawed* him. "Go easy on Dan, Matt. You know Jessie, you know the way she was feeling tonight. She likely put the run to Dan. I expect he ducked outta there with his tail between his legs."

"You're right, Charlie," Matt responded hotly. "I do know Jessie. I know her better than any of you. And I can guess that right now she's feeling pretty damn abandoned, by everyone."

Charlie did a quick scan of people within earshot, and bent close to Matt. Pointing a finger at him, he laid out the harsh new reality they all had to adjust to. "Her choice, Matt. She chose Josh and so she has to live with his choices. Josh's choices led to his exile. Jessie didn't need to be alone tonight—she could have gone south long ago. Josh won't get this back. His baby is coming into the world without him. He's the one who should be with her. Not Jane or Dee, and definitely not you."

There were sparks in Charlie's eyes. Backing away, he caught Shanda's eye. On the hunt for her man, she was wandering through the doorway to the ballroom, heading into the lobby.

Seething, Matt fired blanks at Charlie, but he did the right thing. Grasping Shanda's fingers in his, he used his free hand to pull his cell back out of his pocket where he'd replaced it. Dan, who had watched Jessie back out of her driveway via the iPad security camera live feed, answered on the first ring.

"She went into labor," Matt told him, his eyes fixed darkly onto Charlie's. "I need to stay at the Fairmont. She's at Vancouver General."

When Matt disconnected, Charlie swung back around and went off in search of Jane and Deirdre to coordinate their travel to the hospital. Dan would meet them there.

Matt felt the air move at his side. Shanda was swiveling around to face him. A barely-there understanding smile from her eased Matt's heart more than words ever could.

"Labor, huh?" she was saying as he tried to focus. Shanda's brow was furrowed into deep lines as she pondered that and what it meant for her and her man. As it sunk in, she went further by saying his name as she wondered what else to voice aloud that might be what he needed to hear. "Matt," she finally said with a patience he later considered he didn't deserve, "I know how hard this is for you. I see you struggling every day because of her. The hold Jessie has over you…"

He *pffftttdd* loudly in a frustrated kind of way. "It's not that, Shanda. It's not a 'hold,' as you call it. You want the truth? It's a helluva lot more than that."

"I wouldn't expect less," Shanda replied, reaching up to give his silk tie a sexy tug. "You two have been through a lot together. Matt…" The fingers stopped moving. "If you need to go, I want you to know that I understand."

What you understand, Matt caught himself thinking, *is that Jessie will never be mine, the same way Josh will never be yours. So I'm safe…with her.* The realization was jarring. It cemented something in Matt's brain, something that said he needed to stay put with the amazing woman who was pawing at his tie right now with delicate fingers he loved to feel moving against his skin, with whom he just might have a future if he played his cards right. Jacob and Kayla came to mind. Whoever thought Jacob could ever walk away from Jessie? Could ever find a love as sweet and perfect—well, even more sweet, more perfect—than what he had with Jessie?

Placing his fingers over Shanda's on his tie, Matt forced a small smile. "I'm where I need to be," he said softly, burying his gentle eyes in hers. "Where I want to be, Shanda."

She relaxed, and bent forward to place her moist lips on his. "I was hoping you'd say that. I have plans for us tonight."

"Ah," he said, his interest in her suddenly becoming much more concentrated. "Do your plans involve a big bed and a bottle of Malbec?"

"I've had enough wine," Shanda confessed sheepishly with a light giggle. "But there might be a bed involved." She winked. "Or the back seat of a roomy limo. You choose."

Slipping an arm around his girlfriend's slim waist, Matt steered Shanda back into the classy, capacious space where the after-awards party was now in full swing. Bending sideways, he whispered in her ear. "Both."

"Mmm," she agreed. "That way we each get a turn on top. Good plan, Matt. I like it."

On stage, a jazz and blues band was playing something mellow and smooth. On closer inspection, the age-old melody of *Amazing Grace*, interpreted in a lazy, respectful blues-style, reached Matt's attentive ears. Seemed like once Jessie came into his life he'd learned to always pay extra attention to what was playing musically in every environment, as if music was some kind of key he had to place into a lock in his soul so it could open up; as if it always had some angelic message to help guide him on his life's path.

Stepping onto the dance floor, he and Shanda floated into each other's arms. When she melted into his embrace and let her eyes close over, Matt's smile, over Shanda's shoulder, lost some of its full-bodied sincerity, and melded into a concern for Jessie that he could not fully hide. The song, about Divine grace, helped a little to offer a much-needed calm, but still he couldn't help but think *I know her the best*. The truth gutted him, though. Knowing Jessie the best also meant that over the last few months, stepping away from her had likely only served to make Jessie feel even more alienated and alone. There was just no easy way to tiptoe around everyone's feelings and think that Jessie was getting through tonight with anything other than the usual awful sadness that clung to her like a shadow.

As he held his kind, attractive, award-winning actress in his arms and swayed to the easy cadence of the old hymn, which wafted around him in a sad, bluesy way, Matt's forced attempts to hide his worry for Jessie worked, for a little while.

In the hospital, where Jessie was preparing to give birth, there was no need to hide her feelings. It was like she had none. The more her labor intensified, the more she sank into the old numbness fueled by loneliness and despair. When Deirdre arrived with Jane by her side, Jessie turned her head toward the wall, and closed her eyes.

Chapter Twenty-Two

Shanda was frisky. By four a.m. she was on her fourth orgasm, and Matt was feeling his age. "Sleep," he mumbled to her afterwards. "I need sleep."

"Why bother?" she asked with a happy, victorious lilt in her equally fatigued, but playful, voice. "You'll be getting up in an hour and a half anyway." It was true. It never seemed to matter what time Matt went to bed; he always got up when his body woke him up, and that was usually by five thirty or six. At the crack of dawn. There was just something about watching the world make its way into another new, glorious day that was beautiful to behold, that offered a serenity that, in this day and age, he often found hard to find.

In response, Matt rolled over onto his side and groaned. Cuddling up against him, Shanda kissed the back of his neck and rifled long fingers through his short hair. "You ought to grow your hair longer," she murmured, the words emerging hoarse and sexy. "Grow it into one of those longer waves the men are wearing now."

"Whatever you say." Yawning, he arranged his pillow in his arms so he could hug it as he slept.

They were just dozing off when his cell abruptly rang. It was on the side table by Shanda's big bed. Extending a hand, Matt groped for it in the darkness. The task was made all that much harder because he was so beat that his eyes barely opened. "Yeah?" he rasped into it. "Charles?"

He guessed right. Charles was on the other end. "Sorry to call you at this time, Matt."

Charles' weary tone was much more effective in bringing Matt to a state of rousing full awareness than eight cups of coffee could ever be. "Is it the baby? Is she okay?" Sitting up, he swung his legs over the side of the bed away from Shanda. Fully alert now, Matt waited.

"Considering how fast this labor came on, it's surprising how slow she's dilating."

There was something else in Charles' voice that Matt caught, something hovering beneath the surface that was obviously troubling the man. "What is it, Charles?" Matt asked as Shanda raised herself up on one elbow behind him. She laid a tentative hand on his back. "What aren't you telling me?" Matt reached for the light switch and flicked it on.

A slow exhale made its way through the line. "She's doing that thing she does. That she's been doing since this whole thing with Josh blew up in our faces."

"Retreating." Matt didn't have to think about it. He knew beyond the shadow of a doubt what Charles was talking about. They'd all seen it coming, worsening, although Matt had kind of wondered on the brief occasions when he was with Jessie over the last few months whether she was mostly just doing it around him—turning away from him, disappearing into longer and longer silences, tuning out, going somewhere where she could be numb for a while and so not feel the intense hurt that came with loving a distant, troubled man during tough times. "She's likely just gone into some kind of zone to help her deal with the pain, Charles," Matt tried, in a vain attempt to ease his friend's mind, although his own brain was firing at the speed of light, wondering how Jessie was really doing, and how he could help her. "You know what she's like—focused and disciplined. She gives birth the same way." He would have forced a low chuckle if Charles didn't sound so utterly defeated. "How's Deirdre holding up?"

"She'd be okay if Jessie would respond to her. I don't know, Matt, that girl…Jessie…" In the hallway of the hospital, Charles leaned his forehead against the wall and sighed, heavy and large. "Lately I've been having these days…I just don't know what to think anymore, when it comes to Jessie."

"Don't torture yourself, Charles." Lowering his voice, Matt stared at the floor. "Jessie's family. She needs you and Deirdre, whether she's capable of reaching out or not."

"That's the thing, Matt. She's really not. Family, I mean. She never was. When she gets like this, pushing everyone away who wants to help her, you can see the old movie playing in her mind, all the abuse she's suffered, starting from when she was a young teenager."

A choking sob came through the line. It shocked Matt, who rose up from the bed, looked over at Shanda, and sent her a disconsolate frown as he started to pace.

Charles had a little more to say. "Sometimes I wonder…all the pain she's brought into our lives…how could it possibly be worth it? Why do we continue to try to love that girl when all she does is push us away?"

"You're not thinking straight, Charles. Don't let her behavior at the awards dinner color your judgment." Flustered, Matt rubbed a palm against his forehead. "You're tired, Dee's tired. It's agonizing to watch someone you love suffer. To know they've suffered, even. Don't be talking about regrets, not when it comes to Jessie. She's overcome a lot. She's given back a lot. And she is your family, regardless of biology."

"I think…Matt, I think it's time to let her go. To give her a push. She needs to put her family back together and figure things out on her own, without all of us stuck to her like fishhooks. I—we, meaning Deirdre and I—need to do the right thing here. We need to let her go. Otherwise, Matt, we're going to go down with her. The last few months…it's like we're going through the motions waiting for the bomb to fall on Nagasaki. She's leaving, we know she's leaving…she's pushing us away while at the same time we're trying to hang on, and all we're ending up doing is drawing out the inevitable."

Stunned, Matt forgot Shanda was even in the room. "Jesus, Charles, this baby's not even born yet. Like I said, everyone's tired—"

Cutting in, Charles said, "Look, I have to go. Charlie's here with fresh tea." His voice was monotone. His spirit was lagging.

Matt heard Charlie mumbling something incoherent to Charles.

Then the actor was on the line. "Matt, go back to pleasuring that beautiful woman of yours. We're under control here."

"Are you, Charlie?"

Charlie paused. "No. Not really. But we're trying." Even tough Charlie sounded completely done in.

To Shanda's dismay, Matt reached for the black dress pants he'd worn to the awards dinner. "I'm on my way."

"There's no point," Charlie said. "She's not dilating, she's going to be a while. There's not a damn thing you can do."

Lowering his voice, Matt jumped all over that. "You're wrong about that, Charlie. As Josh's friend and as someone who has watched over Jessie for a very long time, as well as someone who cares deeply about Charles and Dee, there's a lot I can do. I'll be there in twenty minutes."

With a determined jab, Matt poked the 'end' icon on his phone. Shanda was sitting up in bed now. Frustrated, she raised an arm. "I get why you have to go, Matt. I support you. But I can't help but wonder if you were hoping for a call like this all along."

"Not hoping, exactly," Matt answered as he fished around for his shirt. "But I'm not surprised, put it that way."

"You're used to this. Jumping up at their beck and call."

"I wouldn't have it any other way, Shanda. What I said about family… they're mine. All of them," he added, in case she was at all confused about Jessie's place in his heart.

"I'd ask if you want me to come with you, but I think I know what you'd say."

Matt flipped back around to Shanda while he buttoned up his shirt. Sliding back onto the bed, he cupped her chin in his hand and searched her eyes. "What I said earlier was true, Shanda. My place is with you. Your place is with me. If you want to come with me to the hospital, I'd be honored to have you by my side. If you want to stay here and get some sleep, I understand. All I really know is that I have to go. I've been with the Keatings for a very long time. Having you in my life does not change my relationship with them any more than having them in my life impacts my relationship with you." Getting up off the bed, he grabbed the semi-formal dinner jacket he'd worn earlier. He found it where he hastily left it, tossed over the back of a chair.

"It does, though," she answered him. "When it comes to Jessie, having me in your life has changed everything. The two of you aren't even speaking now."

Matt was heading to the bedroom door when she said that. The comment put a layer of ice over the blood in his veins. Pausing at the door, he said quietly over his shoulder, "We're just saying goodbye. That's how we need to say goodbye, Shanda."

"It's a long goodbye." Her eyes were moist.

"I know. With her, it has to be. But it's coming to an end. I'll call you, Shanda." He started to slip away.

"I love you," she called softly after him.

In the hallway, Matt stopped. "I love you back." For a brief moment he wondered whether he was doing the right thing at all, leaving his girlfriend on a night that was very special to her—after making love to her for the last few hours—to go be with Jessie, who Matt was so desperately in need of letting go. The hesitation was lightning-quick. Matt jogged the last few steps to the door of Shanda's new luxe Yaletown condo and disappeared into the bright, airy, artificial nighttime light of the outdoors.

When he arrived at the hospital, Matt found a glum Charles and an equally disheartened Charlie in a small waiting room down the hall from the suite where Jessie's labor was playing out. He wanted to ask them if Josh knew that his baby was coming into the world, but there were ears everywhere. This wasn't the time or place.

Charlie pointed to the nurses' station. "Go get some surgical greens," he said. "Go see how she's doing. Give my wife and Deirdre a break from the heartache, will you?"

"You sure about that all of a sudden? Me going in there?" Matt didn't move. His intent was clear, though, and it had nothing to do with the request to give Jane and Dee a respite. There was a downturn to his lips when he said it. Alongside his rumpled hair it gave him a stubborn little boy effect.

"I was wrong earlier," Charlie admitted. Staring up at Matt from his slouched position on a hospital chair, he stuck a post-script on the end of their earlier conversations, at the Fairmont and over the phone, which immeasurably changed things for Matt. "She needs you. End of story."

Finally, Matt breathed. *Finally. Finally somebody gets what we mean to each other.* Willful tears nudged at the corners of his tired eyes. Nodding, he let his gaze rest on the wiped out Charles before he took action. Charles was looking up at him with an appeal that Matt could only interpret as desperate.

Down the hall a woman was crying as her labor intensified. It wasn't Jessie. There wasn't a sound coming from her room. Not even music.

Matt was dressed and inside in three minutes flat. His light touch on Deirdre's back was all the convincing the older woman needed to take a break. When she turned, Matt was sorry to see that her face was streaked with tiny little tide lines from tears she'd shed over Jessie's reticence earlier. Jane, across the bed from her, was subdued and equally grateful.

Jessie's fingers, tightly gripping the bed rails, were white. Her eyes were squeezed tightly shut. At the moment there were no doctors or nurses present in the room. Matt was almost surprised to find that, once Dee and Jane made their exits, he was completely alone with her. Unsure of what to expect, he touched her forehead with the backs of his fingers. She was dripping with sweat although, when he came into the room, Matt had noticed Jane lightly dabbing at Jessie's face with a damp cloth.

"Sweetheart," he murmured. "Jessie."

Slowly, she turned to him. The ice-pale eyes Matt adored found his gentle, loving gaze and got lost there. Charles was right. With Jessie, it was always easy to tell when she was in retreat mode, when she went someplace deep inside that could pad her soul with layers and layers of cotton so she could hide until she felt well enough to face the world again. The giveaway was the haunted way she looked out from within as if she were only partially there, as if the remainder of her spirit had left her body and was floating somewhere else—above them, maybe.

Touching her, running his fingertips over her face, Matt implored her to come back to them, to him. "I'm sorry," he whispered as all the old pain he'd pushed aside for Shanda's sake came rushing back. "I didn't—I don't—want to let you go, Jessie. I have to, though. I know that. Do you understand?"

There were tears in her eyes now, floating through the washed out sea-pearl blue. That was a good sign, the tears. Matt allowed a small smile to filter through. "We'll always have Brussels," he sniffled. "You and me. Remember?"

Jessie was incapable of answering verbally. Her eyes deepened into the color of heartache as far as it related to her, and only to her—a crystalline, liquid blue that, when highlighted with points of light gifted by a nearby lamp, had an endless, bottomless depth. She swallowed painfully. And didn't look away.

One by one, Matt lifted the fingers closest to him and wrapped a warm hand around them. "Now," he commanded, taking control, "let's get to work. I was the first person you told about this baby. Now I want to be the first person to meet him."

"Him?" The small word emerged quietly, yet there was a triumphant bent to the way Jessie murmured the simple one-word question.

"I have the same gut feeling you do." Lighting up, Matt leaned forward and pressed his lips to Jessie's. "Sweetheart, whether it's a boy or a girl is irrelevant. This baby is a new start for you and Josh. A baby, sweet girl, is God's way of saying the world shall go on. Your child is a messenger, don't you think?"

Exhausted, Jessie softened through her tears; her face relaxed and a tiny whisper slipped through, a tiny, barely discernible, "Yes." She was coming back to him, to them, to the refuge Matt was offering her, instead of to the one she started hiding in the day the two of them had their first awful fight on the jet. "I needed you," she wept. "These last few months, I needed you, Matt. And you weren't there."

Shaking his head, Matt lifted her hand and held it against his cheek. There were no words big enough for how badly he wanted to hear that, for how desperately he needed her too. Not as a lover, no. Just as a best and trusted friend. "I'm here now," he finally said, his voice dusky and so, so sorry. "We'll have this baby, you and me, and we'll get you back to Josh, Jessie. We'll bring the children to their father. It'll all work out, you'll see. Things have a way of working out."

"Everyone here, the doctor, the nurses, keep telling me how proud they are of me, Matt. How sorry they are about Josh, and how proud they are of me. But I don't feel proud. I hate lying to them. And I hate how scared I am, of… of everything. Of worrying about how Josh is doing. If he's okay. If he's going to be okay. Of how much I miss him. I miss him, Matt. He should be here."

As if on cue, a new harsh pain seized Jessie's abdomen. "Oh, Jesus," she agonized. "I always forget about this part when I'm doing the sex thing trying to get pregnant. Jesus, Matt. Pleasure payback's a bitch, huh?"

"It's a good thing I replaced Deirdre," Matt laughed after the labor pain passed, raising his hand and giving it a good shake for emphasis. "You'd have her fingers broken, girl."

"She's tough," Jessie moaned. "You'd be surprised."

"She's not so tough. Neither's Charles."

Jessie hesitated. "Sometimes, Matt…I just can't…you know…"

"Can't deal? Sweetheart, those two people love you like their daughter. You need to let them be here for you."

"Matt…there's only so much pain I feel I can dump on their shoulders, you know? Only so much worry."

Another contraction snuck up on Jessie. She cursed again and grappled with Matt's fingers until he was certain she might actually break one. Or two. The door swooshed open, and Jessie's usual baby doc, Doctor Wyatt, breezed in.

"You're dilating now, honey," she announced after Jessie groaned and winced her way through the uncomfortable examination. "You'll soon meet the newest member of your family. I'll be back in a minute. Let me spread the good news."

A broad smile was Jessie's response, and it was aimed at Matt. "Good thing you've seen all my private areas before, casanova," she winked. "I wouldn't want to shock you. You should have seen that young constable speed his way here for fear of having to deliver the baby in his cruiser. You'd think he'd want a peek at this." She gestured to herself.

"Uhhh…" Matt made a face, following it up with a half-smile. "Let's not go there."

"Doc Wyatt might ask you to cut the umbilical cord."

"I'm glad you have your sense of humor back, pretty girl." A serious frown upended the smile. "Do you think she might let me do that? Really?"

"She will if I ask her to."

When Doctor Wyatt reentered the room just ahead of her team of birthing professionals, she was surprised to find Jessie's security friend leaning over her, brushing his lips over her face and talking her through another contraction. She was even more surprised an hour later when the newest Sawyer entered the world and Jessie asked her to let Matt cut the cord.

"And?" Jessie asked, breathing heavily after Matt, eyes alight, did the honor. "Boy or girl?"

Doctor Wyatt was holding the baby while a nurse suctioned out the tiny mouth and nose. A great baby wail filled the room. The doctor looked at Matt and raised her eyebrows.

He grinned. "It's a boy," he said to Jessie. "A little fighter, I think. Or a singer. Your intuition was spot on."

"He's tired of me whining and sulking. He's telling his momma to get her shit together once and for all." Jessie was radiant when the doctor placed the baby on her belly for a quick inspection before whisking him away. "Hello, little Sawyer. Little mini-Josh. Welcome to this crazy world."

"Do you have a name picked out?" Doc Wyatt was fighting back tears. As far as she knew, this child would never meet his father. She half expected Jessie to say she was calling her baby Josh.

Jessie's eyes met Matt's. He was lifting the child's fingers, silently counting them, but he stopped when he felt Jessie's eyes on him. "Micah," she announced, burying herself in Matt's tender gaze. "Unless you and Shanda want that name, Matt. Since it's a name that means something to your family."

Matt wanted to ask if Josh knew, if Josh was in agreement over the name. But Matt's heart, and his pride, won out. "Micah. I'm honored, Jessie. So damn honored." Bending down to her, he kissed her forehead. "Thank you."

"So are we friends again, Matt? Is this just a temporary truce or can we actually be friends again?"

"We were always friends, sweetheart," he told her. "The best kind of friends. Always."

"And forever?" Jessie whispered, losing herself in his soft gray eyes.

Matt was still. This night, or at least the last few hours of it, was already etched on his heart and in his soul. There could be no other perfection than the way Jessie was looking at him now with such love and devotion, with her new baby—named in honor of him, for his grandfather—a brand new witness to their deep, shared love. It didn't preclude Josh, no; he was a part of it, of her, of what made her special. Jessie's capacity to love, to forgive, far overshadowed the pain and the fears Charles wearily mentioned on the phone earlier. Not even seeing Jessie in haute couture glittering with diamonds, an orchestra at her disposal, singing from her soul, could come close to this extraordinary feeling.

An aura of divine golden-white light glowed around them. There was a sacred perfection in this moment, in Micah's birth and in Matt's part in it. It wasn't about sexual love or lust; it was a simple knowing that Matt and Jessie were united far beyond the realm of most good friends, because he was her protector, and because she let him in.

Bending once again to her, he pressed his lips to hers and whispered quietly so the others in the room couldn't hear, "I love you, Jessie. Desperately. Never forget that. Now I am going to go and let Deirdre come in and meet her new grandson. And sweetheart, with your permission, I will make a call on your behalf."

"To the Caribbean?" Jessie's eyes filled up again.

"You bet. Is that okay?"

"Oh, yeah, Matt, that's okay. And…" She grasped his hand.

"Um-humn?" Matt was already thinking about what he would say to Josh.

"Tell him, um," Nervous, Jessie looked around her. Nobody was listening. "Tell him I love him. Okay?"

He didn't hesitate. "Yeah. I will. I'll see you in a bit, Jessie."

"I love you too, Matt. Thank you for coming. Thank you for being here. I hope Shanda's not mad."

"Shanda had four orgasms. She'll deal." Matt was beaming as he started toward the door.

"Ewww, Matt. Seriously? TMI, honey." But Jessie was laughing. And secretly wishing she could have a few of those of her own with her husband lying next to her, snuggling close, burrowing his face into her neck as his fingers probed and explored. "So much to look forward to," she murmured softly to little baby Micah just as Deirdre tentatively made her way into the room with Charles tiptoeing in behind her.

"Grammie and Grampie," Jessie glowed, "meet Micah."

Sleepy-eyed, Micah looked up at the couple who rescued his mother so long ago. A tiny gurgle was his welcome; relieved smiles from Charles and Deirdre were their greetings back. This woman was not the one that had been moping around Vancouver the last few months. This woman, their rescued girl, was the picture of hope.

It was Matt's doing. It was his renewed presence in her life, his strength, his final willingness to push the rest of them aside and do what needed to be done. The respite was, to Charles' and Dee's knowledge, just a temporary one. They could only hope that the ache of loss Jessie would feel when she left Matt, when she left them all, to go south to her husband, would soon be replaced with fulfillment—the fulfillment that bringing her family back together would bring.

The fulfillment that having Josh back in her life in a way that they could move forward without fear, would bring.

It was a tiny grasp at a future that, for all of them, would most certainly be worth living.

It was a giant leap of faith.

Chapter Twenty-three

"It's a boy, Josh. You have a new son."

Matt was sitting in the Audi in Coquitlam's Mundy Park gravel parking lot, which was an isolated place that served well as a regular base for calling Josh on untraceable burner phones. A few keen walkers were out this morning but they'd parked and left their cars for the natural beauty the Mundy trails offered. Now, Matt was alone, apart from a vacant white SUV and a low, black Beamer.

No sound came through the line right away. Matt let Josh gather his wits and take his time summoning up a voice strong enough to carry on a conversation. Eventually Matt filled the silence with, "She was tough as nails. As always."

"He's healthy?" The eventual distant question was husky and unsure.

"Yes. Robust and awake when I left the hospital an hour ago. He weighed in at 7 pounds, 7 ounces."

"Emily-Grace won't be impressed." Josh kept his first few sentences short. He was still trying to comprehend this new baby, one that his wife labored through to birth without him present.

"Your daughter will be over the moon, Josh. Her little brothers already adore her. One more boy will elevate her to royalty, in their eyes."

Josh wandered across the living room floor to his bedroom. In B.C., Matt heard a distant door close with an easy *shuffft*.

A white wicker rocking chair in the far corner faced an outdoor patio that led off the bedroom. Josh sighed down into it and raised a hand to paw anxiously at his three-day whiskers. He'd finally shaved his growing beard.

"She name him already?" His life back in Canada felt so damn outside the life he was living now, as if it was a distant memory, a fictional world. An unreal world. Somewhere in the back of Josh's mind he considered the new baby and how remote his paternal relationship with this new child was, from the moment he learned of its existence. "I don't remember...we never talked about names," he confessed as he caught sight of Kalon and Arnie down at the dock below the house. They were taking the Bayliner out for a spin, to give Josh some peace to digest the news. Arnie had answered the phone and was the first in their southern locale to hear about Micah's birth.

A lump in Matt's throat almost prevented him from saying anything more. When he finally shared the baby's name, Josh caught on that it had some kind of special meaning he himself was not privy to. Either that, or Matt was just overcome for a thousand other plausible reasons.

"Micah," Matt stated in due time, with a determined but emotional flair.

"Micah," Josh repeated, testing the name on his tongue.

Immediately Matt jumped in with, "It means 'gift of God,' Josh. It's a good name."

Without meaning to, the hackles on Josh's back flared up. "You help her pick that name out, Matt?"

It was a perfect morning. After the chaos of the last while and the distance from Jessie—outright hostility between them, actually—Matt was still feeling the peace and love of Micah's birth, at how blessed he felt to be at Jessie's side while the child, named in honor of him, of his family, took his first breaths. In front of Matt now, just outside the car, was a natural refuge—trees dressed in splendid colorful late fall foliage, low shrubs and bushes native to this part of naturally beautiful British Columbia. Birds were dipping and soaring overhead, calling out to each other as they played in the light breeze and teased chattering squirrels leaping gaily from branch to branch, their athletic abilities put to the test on swaying branches against the backdrop of a flawless indigo sky. Yet, on the other end of the phone, was the man who should have been present at his son's birth. The tension Matt detected coming through the line was well earned.

"Look, Josh," he said, "I know you're aware that Jessie and I have been on the outs since we left Calgary. You should know that she was alone last night. She was with us at the awards dinner but she went home early." Matt gave Josh a rundown of the previous night's unpredictable events. "The thing is," he said afterwards, "none of us are happy about the way things are right now, but you'll soon have Jessie and the kids with you. The name Micah is a family name—my family. My grandfather's name was Micah. Michael was named for him. It's Jessie's way of saying that goodbye isn't forever. Of keeping us connected. That's all."

Running through Josh's head were all kinds of thoughts and images, scattered, twisted and broken, shards of colored glass that he twisted in his mind like a kaleidoscope against the blue-white light of the seamless Caribbean sky. Fractured beliefs and judgments and pictures, they were jagged at the edges but serenely beautiful within, illusions and dreams of a time gone by. *I want her back,* was written across the sky just beyond the kaleidoscope in Josh's mind's eye. Something mystical was at play here, something Josh only understood because he could read Jessie, and he was well aware of just how close she was to Matt. Her unilateral choosing of a name meant to honor Matt said legions about where her mind was these days.

"You need to bring her down here, Matt," he said over a growing lump in his throat. "Please. Soon."

Perking up, Matt straightened in his seat. He started a nervous tap-tap-tapping on the steering wheel. "As soon as she and Micah are well enough, strong enough to go, we'll travel them," he stated, more affirmatively than he felt. "Or should I say as soon as Jessie and Deirdre feel strong enough to say their goodbyes."

In the Caribbean, Josh stuck a foot out against a virginal white ottoman and gave his chair a rock. It creaked happily in its warm, breezy home, counterpoint to the uneasy burden of Josh's fretful heartbeat. "Matt, I'm going to say something to you that I hope you don't take the wrong way."

"Okay." Suddenly apprehensive, Matt stopped his incessant tapping.

Josh heard the line go quiet. He, too, stopped his restless moving. The rocking chair stilled. "Matt, I will never judge you or Jessie for what you mean to each other. This whole thing…trying to figure a way past all of Morgan's shit…I meant for the two of you to be together. You know that, right?"

"Josh, don't…we need to move forward here. Don't go back down that road." It was like talking through a tube, a tiny tube. Suddenly Matt's voice felt foreign and strange. There were nights when he couldn't sleep that he pictured himself with her, still. In bed, holding her, making love with her. Even with Shanda at his side, Matt let Jessie and the children color his thoughts. Now with Micah…

Fuck it. Fuck it all. Matt's head was weighted now; a great exhale preceded a forward move where he laid his forehead on the steering wheel.

Josh heard it, the great weariness of his good friend, of a man finally allowing himself to feel the incessant fatigue of lost desires, of always having to be the better man—the best man.

"I want her back, Matt. I want her here by my side, I want—I need—to see my kids. To meet this new little guy. At the same time, buddy—I need you to know that I get it, man. I know how much this hurts you. How much it's gonna hurt."

"Jesus Christ, Josh." No more hopeful *I'm gonna be strong for Josh shit.* No more *I'll be the good guy and hold Jessie's hand and call her husband and mold this family back together the way I've always done, like they're all putty and I can just stick them back together.*

With his honest confession, with his truths, Josh had taken their conversation—which hurt Josh too, a lot, for what he was missing—and given it a veracity that cut through Matt's gut the way a vicious dagger once sliced through Josh's spleen.

Struggling, Matt searched for a way to equal the score, to bring himself back up to a place of equanimity where he could, for the sake of self-preservation, feel safe again, or at least feel like he could function. "You're some guy, Josh," he said in the end. "You, of all people, should be spitting bullets at me right now. I got to be with her when your baby was born. I got to hold her hand and tell her," he rasped, "and tell her I love her. You're going to have a very angry and confused woman on your hands. You've got bigger shit to worry about. Yet you get it, don't you? You get what all of this is costing me. I don't think anybody else even cares."

"It's costing everybody, Matt. What I did…Jesus, Matt, look what Arnie lost. Lucie was good for him. He can't go back to Vancouver any more than I can. Look what Charles and Dee will lose."

There was nowhere left to go but to pound at the truth the way a miner strikes at rock. This time, these few minutes alone to talk to Josh, to really get a sense of how he was feeling, of what certainties were still floating around his scared brain, was sacred. Matt sucked in a breath so he could stop the whimpering in his heart and regain control over his emotions. But he dove in deeper, prefacing the difficult stuff with a history Josh well knew. "Josh, I want you to know that your trust, if things had worked out differently, means a lot to me. It means everything, actually." He gulped out more hard truths. "Jessie and me, we're a team. We've been a team for a very long time; I've seen that girl grow into her own light, and a lot of that, the real hard-core part of that at least, came from you. Until you came along she was just going through the motions. I'm sending her back to you because she needs you, and your children need you, Josh. But..." He drifted off.

"What is it, Matt?" Josh asked. "Just spit it out, buddy. I can take it."

"Josh, I—I need to know that you're okay. That you won't do anything else," Matt swallowed, "that might hurt her. That might hurt them. What Jessie needs, what your kids need, Josh, is strength."

A long pause was followed by a forced grunt that Matt interpreted as Josh clearing his throat and reaching for the words. "It wasn't like I wanted to let go, Matt, to leave them. You need to know that. Please help Jessie understand that. It was a bargain, that's all it was. A way to save them, to give them a chance at the kind of lives that I know they want, that they deserve."

Josh hesitated before starting up again. When next he spoke, it was like his voice had lost a layer of substance. "This is what they're getting by coming back to me," he said. "A half-assed, broken man who will be spending his life longing for dreams that can never again come true. If it's strength they need, I don't know if I can deliver, Matt." Clearing his throat, Josh finished with, "When I said I get how much it's gonna hurt you, how much it's gonna cost you, I also meant that I know you get what you're sending her back to. And that's not cut and dry, Matt. It's fifty-fifty. I know she loves me, and I want her back, but I also know I'm no longer who Jessie signed up for."

On high alert now, Matt immediately countered. "Don't be stupid, Josh. If somewhere in that 'woe-is-me' stupid head of yours you are thinking she might still be better off with me, you're wrong. And it pisses me off to sit here thinking that you're off somewhere playing God and feeling damn sorry for yourself. Pick yourself back up and be the man we all know you can be. And please don't ever remind me again how close I got to having her, because you ought to know by now that the only things that would be left of Jessie if you were gone would be tears and sorrow."

"You know what I think? I think you're wrong about that, Matt."

Matt closed his eyes and recalled the angry words he and Jessie threw around at each other on the Keating jet the night of Josh's rigged false plane crash. *I need strength and stability...I'm scared.* Josh was right. He was too damn right. In Matt's mind, Josh's honesty counted as something, though. It counted as understanding, which translated as a cry for help, which translated to hope, and hope was Jessie's mantra. They'd just have to throw it back at her for once.

"Time," Matt said calmly, relying on a reserve of strength he was surprised to find he had. "It heals, Josh. Your family needs to live in peace. This new little baby of yours is truly a gift from God. He's a new beginning for all of you. He's a sign; he's the hope you need to pick up your lives and move on. But you have to promise me that you will try."

A low creaking came from the Caribbean. In the distance a motorboat was heard revving up its engine and heading out of the cove to open sea. Over the engine's smooth roar were voices, happy male voices rejoicing at this pleasurable time on the waves under a perfect cobalt sky.

Josh smiled. "I think my boys are gonna love our boat," he said.

Staring past the Audi's steering wheel down to his feet, Matt held his breath. "Micah might need to grow into it. He's a little small for speedboats yet."

"He's a few hours old, right Matt? My new son?" Josh was sounding more hopeful now that the conversation was on a more even keel, now that they were on safer ground. Rocking peacefully back and forth, he was watching his friends lift their faces to the glorious salty breeze.

"Yeah. Just a few hours. He's brand new, Josh."

"Brand new," Josh echoed.

"Before I forget, I'm supposed to tell you she loves you."

Josh hesitated before he spoke again. "Matt?"

"Yeah, buddy?"

"I know this will never be enough…but thank you, man. Thank you."

Unable to answer, Matt let the toes of his desert boots drift in and out of focus. Josh was not the complicated man he was sometimes made out to be by Charles, by Ulysses, by Deirdre. He was simply a man who understood life at a level most people did not. He was simply a man who wanted the best for his family, even though sometimes the best, in his mind, was not always what his family would perceive as the best.

They signed off with gruff, emotional voices that layered the distance between them with mutual respect. With an optimism that the birth of the new Sawyer baby brought to their difficult words, Josh went about his day with renewed energy and hope, starting with a light jog down to the dock and a wave to Kalon and Arnie to swing back around to pick him up.

At Mundy Park, Matt waited a while before he switched the ignition back on. Instead of going to Shanda's or to La Casa, he piloted the sleek sedan home to his condo by English Bay, switched his clothes to black gym shorts and a gray-green athletic T-shirt, and headed to his treadmill. Forty minutes later he stepped under the healing spray of a warm shower, leaned his head against his forearm on the tiled wall, and said a prayer for baby Micah.

"May you live a life of happiness and joy," he murmured, closing his eyes as the water offered its usual post-run ritual cleansing. "And may you always stay safe."

For that's what it came down to, for Matt, a man accustomed to considering the safety of Jessie and her family for longer than most people stayed married. Today, safety meant planning to send Micah away. It meant letting the new baby's mother go. It meant new lives and a fractured existence for all of them, for all who loved Jessie and her children, and for the man who would now have to reach deep to find the strength to care for them.

Arnie would be with them for a time. But no one knew what his plans were, or where he would go once Jessie and Josh settled into some kind of normalcy in their southern beach house. For all Matt knew, Arnie might take off on some kind of adventurous round-the-world trip. He would want to leave Jessie and Josh on their own, to figure out their new lives in the kind of solitude they would need to get past the hard stuff.

A new-old agony eviscerated Matt. Turning, resting his back against the shower wall, he slid to the floor and thanked God for Shanda to help ease the ache.

Chapter Twenty-four

When Christmas rolled around a few weeks later, nobody, least of all Josh, was surprised to find Jessie still in Vancouver. Micah was just over three weeks old. Flying, at least on the private jet without its risk of viruses floating around, was an option, but in the interest of establishing a secure, comfortable routine for the baby, and in the interest of having Grammie and Grampie nearby, Jessie chose to stay put for the time being.

Matt and Charles exchanged nervous looks when Deirdre decided to take advantage of having Jessie around. It was Christmas Eve; the close-knit group of friends and family were enjoying a light dinner at La Casa when Dee set her fork down with a casual elegance and nonchalantly posed a thought.

"I had a call, Jessie. An offer came my way I thought you might be interested in."

"Oh?"

When Deirdre prefaced her questions with 'I had a call,' Jessie generally anticipated a work thing. Which meant a travel thing. Which meant an 'away from the kids' thing. Spooning a bite of Carlotta's heavenly decadent chocolate mousse between her lips with one hand, cradling a sweetly sleeping Micah in the other arm, Jessie said, before Dee could get another word in, "Oh gosh, Carlotta, this is so creamy. It's heaven!"

Carlotta was at the table with them, her gardener man at her side. She beamed.

Deirdre smiled politely and drew her girl back to the question at hand. "Jessie, honey, a last minute opportunity has come up for you. I think you should do it."

"Hmm? And that being?" After generously licking her spoon, which got a small smile out of Matt across from her, Jessie winked at him and intentionally let the silver utensil clatter noisily to the bowl.

Startled, Deirdre jumped, following it up with a serious reprimand in the guise of a frown.

Graciously waving a hand, Jessie blushed at Matt and rolled her eyes before she said, "I'm sorry, Dee. Really. Continue."

Shanda was seated next to Matt. She laughed softly at Deirdre's narrowed eyebrows. A little on edge tonight, Shanda was being slightly more amenable to Jessie than normal of late, which Jessie found interesting and which she chalked up to her own imminent parting. Kayla was next to Jessie; on Kayla's other side was Jacob with a squalling baby Lily in his arms.

"Take her for a walk and she'll fall asleep," Kayla said to him.

"In a minute," was Jacob's reply. Everyone around the table was curious about what their matriarch had to say. Jessie's future departure for the bright blue skies of the Caribbean was looming now that Micah was already three weeks old. This offer, as Deirdre called it, seemed remarkably well timed.

Expectantly, they all looked at Deirdre.

"The call was from a board member of the Sakura Music Prize," she explained. "They would like to interview you. It would seem your life lessons in relation to your music might be inspiring to some."

Jessie sat back. She cocked an ear. David and Emily-Grace were down the hall in the playroom, alone for the time being, having been excused from the formal, stilted adult dinner which they found tremendously dull. David's laughter reached Jessie's ears. Relaxing, she refocused on Dee. "Life lessons. Meaning they want to boost their ratings by asking me about my dead, um, my missing husband." She stole a quick glance at Matt. Dylan was snuggled into his body—sound asleep, everyone at the table hoped.

A low tut-tut from Deirdre and a grunt from Charles were reminders for Jessie to be cautious. Dylan didn't stir, although Matt looked down at his little face and cuddled him closer to his strong, broad chest. Reproachful, he eyed Jessie warily.

With a grimace, she moved in her seat and shifted her gaze back to Deirdre.

"When do they want to do the interview?" A few seats down, Lily's whining was increasing in volume. Neither Kayla nor Jacob moved.

"They can do it at your convenience, honey. I suggested mid to late January."

The table went silent. Nobody bothered scratching an ear or dabbing at his or her lips with a linen napkin. Lily even stopped fussing after Jacob adjusted her to lean more upright, belly-first, against his chest.

Charles clenched a hand into a fist before he loosened it to pick up his après-dinner brandy. "Deirdre, we should have discussed this," he admonished. "I'm sure Josh is getting anxious to meet his baby son."

"Josh can wait." An even deader silence took over the room. Jessie was the one who had spoken. At the heavy quiet that greeted her statement, she looked around at the others. "Guys, think about it. It's a good opportunity for me to affirm that Josh is, uh," she glanced at Dylan, "um, well, you know. Morgan will see the interview, or if he doesn't, for sure he'll hear about it."

"We removed you from the Grammy Awards." Charles took a sip of the warm liquid before he continued. "The reason being was that we thought it was too soon, Jessie. With the baby, and with the move…" He let the thought fade into oblivion.

Deirdre picked up. "I was too busy organizing your Christmas to remember to talk to you about this, Charles," she rebuked with a haughty tone that was rarely, if ever, aimed at her longtime husband. "Besides, the request came in last minute. And," she shrugged her sophisticated shoulders, "in truth it came out of my lunch with Elaine Sorenson last Friday. She knows someone who knows someone who is on the board. It was one of those opportunities that I couldn't say no to at the time. But Jessie can most certainly decline the offer if she doesn't feel ready or if she's in a hurry to join Josh." The last bit was spoken with a sad little lilt.

Pouting, Jessie sank deeper into her seat. "I'm not in a hurry. I mean," she gulped, "I want to see him, like, I desperately want to see him, to be with him. But this seems like too good of a thing to turn down. Further pushing Morgan's buttons in a way that will give us more security can't be a bad thing, right?"

Nobody could argue with that. Charles huffed while Deirdre sat taller and preened.

"You'll come with me, right Matt?" Pleading with him, Jessie chewed thoughtfully on her bottom lip. He was directly across from her at Deirdre's fancy shmancy dining room table. It was easy to lock eyes. "One last kick at the can."

The harsh quiet was, this time, more of the shocked kind. Matt hesitated, although his gentle eyes disappeared for a time inside Jessie's inquisitive baby blues. An arc of rainbow light spanned the table and seemed to join the two; in truth it had never left them, but tonight it was weeping. The closer Jessie and the man who watched over her got to being parted, the more dense the unshed tears became. The more they metaphorically dripped, like colored water from melting popsicles on a blistering summer day.

Charles broke the awkward silence. "If you want to do this, Jessie, then we will also firm up a date for you to travel south. As much as we'd like to, we can't prolong the inevitable any longer."

A hushed, "Merry fucking Christmas," was Jessie's tongue-in-cheek response. Dejected, she was saddened to see that Charles wasn't any happier about having to make the pronouncement than she was about hearing it.

Shanda chose the long, soundless gap that followed to make an announcement she thought might cheer them all up. Secretly she proclaimed to herself that she had an alternate mission in mind as well, which became clear to everyone present the moment she gave voice to her thoughts.

"So," she said, jiggling in her chair, "speaking of Christmas, I got my present early."

Straightening, Jessie braced herself for the news of this 'gift,' and set impenetrable eyes on Shanda. Kayla knew what was coming. Carefully, so as not to dislodge Micah in Jessie's arms, she clutched Jessie's elbow. Across from Jessie, with Dylan's small body held close, Matt stared at the edge of the table, took a lengthy sip of wine, and held his breath.

"Matt and I got engaged tonight." The way Shanda said it, liltingly, like a small bird perched on a branch singing the praises of new blossoms in spring, grated on Jessie almost more than the actual words.

It was a victory song.

Clearly.

Jessie stilled. She couldn't bring herself to look at Matt. He, however, touched a nervous finger to his cheek, where he absently scratched a non-existent itch, and let his eyes filter up to Jessie's.

It's okay, she was telling herself. *He's not my man. He's just my strength.*

It was like everyone at the table, hiding under dim, romantic candlelight, was waiting for her cue. Either that or they were all on edge awaiting a classic royal Jessie Wheeler meltdown.

She surprised them all. The smile may have been somewhat forced, but underneath it was a sincere wish for Matt's—and Shanda's—happiness. "Congratulations," Jessie whispered. "Truly, Shanda. There is not a better man on the planet."

Once again, Jessie's words brought forth a wordless chasm—the stilted, stunned kind.

"Sure there is," a small voice to Jessie's left managed. "My brother, for one." Withdrawing her hand from the crook of Jessie's arm, Kayla pushed back her chair and rose, leaning over to remove her infant daughter from Jacob's arms at the same time. "Sweetheart," she said to Shanda as she moved, "you have impeccable taste."

Grimacing, Jessie cringed and closed her eyes. That, too, was a dig. It was no secret that Shanda's first choice was Josh—at least, in the old days it was. Who knew where Josh fit in Shanda's mind these days now that she had a taste of beautiful, kind, stable Matt?

Opening her eyes, Jessie met Matt's downhearted gaze. *Once again I fuck up,* Jessie hammered herself. *Once again I stand in the way of your happiness.* She tried to smile but it came out lackluster and lopsided. "You'll come with me to Stockholm, right, at least?" she asked. "So we can say goodbye." Micah stirred in her arms. An adorable baby gurgle lessened the tension around the table.

Matt let his gaze drift sideways. Without saying a word, he was asking for Shanda's permission.

She didn't answer. It was not a surprise to have to overtly observe the level of trust and friendship—and outright love and devotion—between Jessie and Matt here, tonight, when so many endings were upon them. What hit Shanda, though, like a bolt of lightning, was that asking them to part was like having to physically tear apart the unseen cord that joined them together.

Down the table from Jessie, Jacob was silent and still, as well. Charles and Dee were swigging back their booze as if it was water, as if an unquenchable thirst had come upon them. The desert kind. The hopeless, dry, sand-filled, rough sandpaper desert kind.

And Jessie and her children had yet to even leave Vancouver.

"Oh, Jesus," Shanda mumbled, almost falling back into her chair. She touched Matt's thigh. It was enough of an answer for him. Looking back at Jessie, he nodded.

Her eyes were swimming. Standing, as Jacob reached past Kayla's vacated seat to help ease her chair backward, Jessie sent Carlotta what she hoped was a genuine smile. "Thank you, Carlotta," she said, with a natural honesty she didn't have to search for in order to find. "Dinner was lovely. As always."

Grateful, Carlotta lifted her arms and reached for Micah. "Let me hold that baby," she said with a look to her good friend, Deirdre. "Before I have to get ready for church."

Walking over to her, Jessie helped Carlotta adjust Micah in her arms. "I'll be upstairs," she stated in appreciation for the reprieve. Carlotta intuited Jessie's feelings almost as easily as Matt. It was evident that Jessie needed a bit of time alone to compose herself, to gather her wits. To her credit, she bent and gave Shanda a gentle hug before she left the dining room. Matt would have to be more informally congratulated later. His engagement to Shanda was not a shock to anyone. What it said in terms of separation and parting, and his readiness to move on, was not a surprise either. But that didn't mean that Jessie—or anyone else—was really ready to accept the finality of what it signified overall, or how it filtered down to how the rest of them were feeling.

In her old bedroom upstairs, Jessie sucked back an onset of great gulping sobs that threatened to destroy her makeup—and which quelled her attempts to keep her shit together—on this night, this usually magical night that today just felt suffocating. She was gripping the edge of the counter in the bathroom, squeezing her eyes shut and then opening them to watch her tears land in great big plops in the basin, when she heard the bedroom door close. Footsteps—a man's—made their way into the washroom. Strong hands grasped Jessie's waist and turned her around to face him.

Jessie didn't have to look up to know that the person who chose to come check on her was Matt. His hands were familiar; his fingers were often clutched in times of fear or stress, and sometimes just in times of peace, like on the jet during the many flights they took alone, or with Deirdre along as manager and chaperone and overall spokesperson at Jessie's engagements.

Now, Matt pulled Jessie close and buried his nose in her hair. "It doesn't change anything," he murmured. "It doesn't change a damn thing."

"What?" Jessie wept. "You marrying Shanda, or me leaving? What doesn't change?" Backing away, letting her trembling fingers land at his waist, Jessie sniffled. "It changes everything, Matt. Everything's changing. Again."

There was no more to say. They stood together, touching, united, sorry, until Matt thought his absence might be lasting a little too long, was too conspicuous, and he felt he should go.

Twisting behind to reach for a Kleenex, Jessie raised a hand and dabbed at his wet cheeks before he left her. "You did the right thing, baby," she proclaimed with a confidence she couldn't quite muster, her eyes damp and far too bright. "It's time. Shanda is a wonderful, wonderful person. You make each other deliriously happy. I know that. I can see that."

"Thank you." Briefly a bright light, like a lighthouse beacon, swept across Matt's eyes. It disappeared again as he backed away from Jessie. "Your blessing means everything to me."

Jessie let the soggy tissue fall to her side as Matt moved out of reach.

Uncertain, he stopped at the bathroom door. "Your place is with Josh," he said simply.

Picturing Josh at the southern beach house without his family at Christmas, Jessie relaxed when a warm fuzzy zipped inside and touched her heart. "He's paying his dues, isn't he, Matt?" she whimpered.

Shaking his head, Matt's eyes turned solemn, a darker gray than usual. "Don't do that to him," he said. "Don't make all of this something he's accountable for. Raise him up, Jessie. Don't bring him down."

"That's what he needs, huh?" she asked softly, eyes expectant and wondering.

"No," Matt answered, surprising Jessie with the intensity of his tone. "That's what he deserves."

Slipping away from her, Matt shoved a finger into the corner of one eye and then the other so Shanda wouldn't see any evidence of just how hard this night was turning out to be. He loved her, but he wasn't sure his new fiancée would understand, would be able to grasp, just how deep his and Jessie's blood ran in each other's veins. The only person likely to get that, at all, was Jacob, who acknowledged it with a manly clap on Matt's arm a few seconds later at the bottom of the stairs.

Thankfully, in the hustle of getting the kids ready for church twenty minutes later, both Jessie and Matt were able to escape more scrutiny. It was Christmas Eve—Emily-Grace and David were wired and didn't seem to be missing their absent father, which irked Jessie, even though she knew that sometimes the occasional tension in their home came from Josh's presence. Dylan was awake now, standing in uncharacteristic silence in front of his mother as Jessie retrieved his coat from Jacob's outstretched arm. Bending down in front of her son, Jessie was touched to see that, at least tonight, Dylan wasn't doing as well as his older siblings when it came to missing Josh. She discovered that hard truth quite by accident while forcing herself to chatter idly with her children as a way of disguising what was really hurting tonight.

The little guy was rubbing a small fist over and over his still sleepy eyes.

"It's a kids' mass," Jessie told him, trying to comfort him as she started to button up the navy blue formal pea coat Dee insisted Dylan wear to church. "I'll bet Santa Claus will be there after the service, in the hall downstairs."

"I hope so," Dylan yawned.

"Are you gonna ask him for that video game you told me you want?" Glancing around, Jessie smiled gratefully at Jacob when he handed her a pair of soft blue mittens that his grandmother had knit and sent, amongst other thoughtful homey things, in a package from the States.

"Nooo," Dylan was saying, as he held out a hand so his momma could shove a mitten onto it, "that's not what I'm asking for. It's David that wants the video game." He was a little surly.

Focusing more closely on him, Jessie furrowed her brows. A panic hit. The stores were closed. Christmas was tomorrow. A new worry—a mother's worry—accosted her. Running Dylan's Christmas list through her brain, she wondered if she'd missed something. "I see," she said in the end. "So what is it you're asking Santa for, Dylan?"

Next to her, Jacob too, bent down, lips turned downward in concern.

"I want Daddy to come home." Only when he was being silly and showing his confusion did Dylan ever call Jacob Daddy. The fact that he had two fathers was only understood on some peripheral level. To Dylan, Josh was Daddy. A slow tear trickled down his flushed little boy cheek. "I miss Daddy," he said.

Dazed, Jessie thumbed away his tear. If there was ever a reason to get her children moved to the Caribbean, this was it. *Damn, I wish I could tell you the truth*, she thought, and wondered if there was something at all she could say that would help ease her tired, confused little boy's broken heart. Really, in the end, there was only one thing.

"I miss Daddy too, sweetheart," she murmured, and brought him close so she could kiss his little ear, his soft cheek.

Jacob took Dylan from her and lifted him. Recognizing the warmth and love of a man he also knew as a father, but whom Dylan separated from Josh in the way he also separated Steve, Charlie, Matt and the others from Josh, Dylan let himself be held and comforted while, her hand at his back, Jessie eased in for a group hug.

Even after all these years, Jacob still smelled like green apples. Breathing him in, Jessie sighed and considered how happy he was these days, with a new baby in his life, with Kayla—a Sawyer, of all people—at his side, and with the stress over his violent attack on Jessie easing in the world at large. There was love between them now, genuine and safe love, even more so after their little healing threesome the night Jessie learned of Josh's actual intentions with the professional hit.

"Hold him close in church, Jacob," Jessie asked of him now. "He needs you tonight."

"'Course," Jacob replied, reaching out to touch Jessie's cheek with the backs of his fingers, balancing Dylan with his other arm as he did so. "Don't you get into any shenanigans here alone. You're breastfeeding, remember?"

"Yes, oh magnificent one." Saluting him, Jessie giggled and grabbed Kayla's arm as she was passing by with Lily's carrier dangling from one hand. "Kayla and me will celebrate with a big ole bottle of Jim Beam when we both stop breastfeeding."

"That'll be Baileys for me," Kayla winked. "Or maybe a nice full-bodied Shiraz. The whole bottle. Git yer own."

A few minutes later, the happy rumble in La Casa's front foyer ceased when Jessie closed the arched mahogany door behind the backs of her family and friends. She was staying home with baby Micah while the others went to church. Truth be told, she could have joined the rowdy crowd, but there were a few reasons to stay behind. One, she wasn't up for facing anyone outside of their usual circle tonight—Charlie and Steve and their families, who were expected to be at church, not included. For certain there would be some paparazzi present, and other curious onlookers, and no way did Jessie want to face them. Dan was meeting the gang at the church. Between him, Matt, and the other guys, the children would be well protected from long lenses and nosy stares as well.

Another reason to stay behind was the opportunity to make a solitary Christmas call to Josh. Ignoring Matt's—and Charles'—vehement requests that she not make calls to her husband while she was at La Casa, Jessie picked up Micah in his carrier and tiptoed down the hall and turned right. She landed at the music room, in Charles' La Casa studio. Ulysses would be coming by to keep an eye on the place while Jessie was alone with the baby. He'd be here in about twenty minutes. Not that he would interfere with her, but Jessie wanted no extra ears around while she talked to Josh. Some things were meant to be sacred.

Josh was expecting the call. He answered on the first ring.

"You have a Christmas tree?" Jessie teased without saying hello.

"We do," he informed her. "It's even got lights. Two. If citronella candles underneath it count as lights. It's decorated, too. Kalon's got the touch."

"Let me guess. It's a palm tree. How'd y'all hang the ornaments?"

"Wouldn't you like to know?" There was a smile in Josh's voice that Jessie found very comforting. "I guess you'll just have to make your way here, little one. So you can see for yourself."

"Soon," Jessie promised. "I'll be there soon."

There were things to talk about—Dylan's Christmas wish, for one, which gutted Josh when he heard it, and Jessie's consent to do the Sakura Music interview. To appease Josh, she told him that she and Charles would sit down right after Christmas and finalize plans for the move to the Caribbean beach house.

"It's going to be really different for you, having me and the kids around," she said. "Enjoy your sleep, Josh. And that relaxed peace and quiet you're soaking up every day."

"I'm bored crazy," he replied with a dry taste in his mouth. He was sitting by the pool in the moonlit dark, his fingers wrapped around a cool ginger ale. Arnie was at the Salty Dog singing Christmas carols, for all Josh knew, and Kalon was with the new woman he was seeing. "I'm losing my mind."

"We'll keep you busy." Somewhere in Jessie's brain an alarm bell twanged. "Maybe we could get a camera and practice. You like editing, we'll make our own films."

"Harumph," he grunted. "As if."

"Tell me how you really feel," Jessie complained. "Sulk wart."

"What'd you call me?"

Even over the phone, Jessie could hear Josh brighten. Laughing, she tormented him until it was time to go, when she heard Ulysses' clipped footsteps coming down the hall. It was time to feed Micah, too—the baby was being rather insistent about it, actually. Jessie held the phone out so Josh could hear his son say goodbye as well.

"Another singer in the family?" Josh was doing mental arithmetic…a few weeks, hopefully, and they'd be at his side, his family. It was hard to even picture. Butterflies started flitting around his stomach. Happy ones.

"He's got a set of lungs, yep, maybe." Neither had the energy to remind each other that their children would likely grow up as far removed from the entertainment biz now as any child would. For the umpteenth time that night, Jessie cringed and closed her eyes. When they signed off, she was playfully rolling her eyes at Josh's instructions on how to lay out the kids' Christmas gifts. "Next year it's all yours," she informed him. "How many gifts can you get under a damn palm tree, anyway?"

Sullen again, Josh didn't take the bait.

Jessie apologized, bit her lip, and they said their goodbyes.

After saying hello a few minutes later, Ulysses retired to the media room to give Jessie some privacy. Hunkering down on the couch at the far corner, Jessie fed Micah, returned him to his carrier, and was sound asleep when Dylan bounced onto her lap just over an hour later.

By the time the kids were in their jammies and tucked into their La Casa beds, Jessie was tuckered out but too wired to sleep. Charles and Dee helped her lay out the children's gifts before offering sweet, cherished hugs and trundling off to bed with yawns and promises of a memory making time the next day.

Micah was a fixture at Jessie's side. Wandering into the music room again with him in her arms, Jessie spoke to him as she picked out a few notes on the baby grand. "I need music," she grumbled. "How'm I supposed to play when everyone's asleep?"

Ulysses had taken up residence back in the media room. The handsome black man was snoring when Jessie snuck by him a few minutes later.

She was giggling. "Dan'll love me," she mused. "It's always him that gets in trouble when I sneak out." Another thought careened across her mind, this one far more diabolical and far less kindhearted. "Matt'll be pissed."

Correct on both counts.

Ulysses bounded up when he heard a big truck roar to life outside. He was wired to hear those things, sounds that were unexpected at particular times. Running to the door, he swung it open just on time to see Josh's King Ranch, which Jessie had taken to driving when she was alone or with only a child or two in tow, tear off down the lane.

Furious texts to her went unanswered. At two a.m. he finally sucked up his pride and punched in a call to Matt.

Matt was also wired for the unexpected. Shanda was slumbering next to him, her body coiled into his and one arm wrapped lazily around his body. She woke and switched on the lamp on her side of the bed while he fumbled for his phone.

"What?" Matt scratched his head when Ulysses illuminated him on Jessie's newest disregard for established security protocols. "Seriously? That…" He didn't say what he was thinking. He just growled.

When he ended the call, Shanda was sitting against the headboard with her arms crossed. She'd gotten the gist of the harried conversation. "Look at it this way," she said far more calmly than the situation warranted. "Soon she will no longer have you wrapped around her little princess finger."

Matt was already up and pulling on jeans. He stopped his frenzied movements for a fraction of a second at Shanda's mean-spirited gibe, then zipped up his jeans, avoiding her eyes altogether.

Shanda crawled forward on her hands and knees so she could more readily get in his face. "I give her credit for having nerve, Matt. She sure knows how to push your buttons. How to get you to come running. I can't wait until—" Wise enough to know when to back off, she bit her tongue.

About to fasten his belt, Matt paused for the second time. He was wise enough to discern that this little stunt of Jessie's would not in any way be favorable from Shanda's perspective. It was Christmas Eve. He and Shanda had just gotten engaged. A fight wasn't on the agenda. Coolly, he said quietly, "It's Christmas, Shanda. Jessie's likely gone home to cuddle up in hers and Josh's bed. I just need to know she's okay. I need to wake her up and send her back to La Casa so she's there when the kids wake up in the morning."

"Seriously? Matt, come on. Give me a break here."

"What?" He scanned the dimly lit room for his shirt, which, Matt remembered with a certain remembered pleasurable twinge in his groin, came off in a hurry last night.

"She's a mother, Matt! And if she was any kind of decent mother she'd be there now with her kids. Sleeping, preferably, so she won't be toast when she's with them all day tomorrow."

Matt stilled. "You're crossing a line, Shanda," he warned. "Nothing about this Christmas is normal for Jessie. She gets anxious and can't sleep. She has terrible nightmares. She goes for drives when she's losing it—sometimes it's the only thing that settles her. And to set your mind at ease, I'm sure the last thing she wants is me on her tail."

"You, Jessie, and tail. In the same sentence. How perfect." With a scowl, Shanda sat back against the headboard. "Fine. Go."

"Trust me, okay?" Watching her for further signs of the green-eyed monster, Matt couldn't suppress a small smile. Shanda was adorable with her messed-up blonde hair and the flimsy silk lingerie he'd given her just before their athletic session in bed earlier. Chuckling, he rested his hands on the bed on both sides of her hips and gave her a long, lingering, sweet kiss. "I'll be back," he said with authority. "As soon as I can be. I'm sure she's up at the UBC house. I'll just cruise up and shake her butt and probably fight with her as usual, then I'll be back. Keep the bed warm."

"Say please."

"Please. And thank you."

He closed the door quietly behind him on the way out.

Jessie wasn't at the UBC house. Matt called Ulysses from the driveway. "No King Ranch here," he griped. An old dark fear wound its way up the backs of his legs. *No way,* he growled to himself. *No fucking way is she getting away with this, scaring the hell out of us like this.* A parallel comment snaked its way into his brain. *This better be nothing. She better be okay.* Morgan crossed his mind. Matt had to bend over and try not to puke. He'd tried calling Jessie but she wasn't answering. And she had Micah with her, Ulysses had said. "Jessie fucking Wheeler," Matt cursed, angrily placing his hands on his hips, "where the hell are you?"

As if by some psychic coincidence, his cell rang just as he was whipping open his door and sliding back into his car. "Jessie?" he hollered into it.

A grateful voice was on the other end. "It's Scott, security at the Keating Building on Robson, sir. I'm glad I didn't wake you."

Matt's radar jolted up. "The Keating Building? Is everything—"

Scott was as aware as everyone in the mainstream media about the trials and tribulations of the small Sawyer family. He didn't hesitate to cut Matt off. "Everything's fine, sir. It's just that Josh Sawyer's truck pulled into the garage about ten minutes ago. I thought you'd want to know that your girl is here. I've never seen her alone here this time of night, or alone during the day at that, and seeing as it's Christmas, which makes her appearance here even more strange, I thought I ought to try to reach you."

Thank God. Matt exhaled, a long, slow exhale that set his heart rate back at a pace closer to where it ought to be. Aloud he said, "She has the baby, right?"

"Affirmative. She's got one of those baby carriers hooked over her arm. A convertible car seat, I gather."

"You're watching her on the security screen? Not eyeballing her in person?"

"Yes, sir. I'd be happy to go find her, though, sir, to make sure she's okay, if you wish. She appears to be going into the studio on the thirty-first floor. I can keep an eye on her for you if you want to go back to sleep."

"No need, Scott." The flustered feeling in Matt's gut at not finding Jessie home was slowly settling. "When Jessie's feeling down she does three things. One, she shuts people out and goes it alone. Two, she takes drives. Judging by the time she left North Van and now, I'd say she's got the driving part out of her system. Three, she plays music. Keep an eye on the hallway to be sure she doesn't take off. I'm on my way. I'll be there in twenty minutes. I need to see that she gets back to La Casa okay."

In his heart Matt felt certain Jessie would, indeed, plan to be back with all of her children before they awoke in a few short hours. Still—he couldn't resist. This was an opportunity. A tiny thrill replaced the earlier fear. *Jessie… music…magic…* He would, quite happily—and heartbreakingly sadly—make himself her private audience tonight.

Not to his surprise, she was singing *Oh, Holy Night* when he landed on the thirty-first floor. Hands in pockets, he made his way through the open glass door that led from the lobby to the interior hallway, passed Jessie's office on the right, and walked soundlessly toward the studio further down. The lobby's open glass door alone was enough of a clue to let him know exactly where Jessie's head was at on this night when she was surely feeling disconnected and alone.

Tiptoeing closer to the studio as quietly as he could manage, Matt stood outside its heavy open double doors and let the dreamlike enchantment of the treasured carol—a very personal middle of the night solo—wash over him. Jessie was singing into a mic, accompanying herself on an acoustic guitar with melodious light strums and pretty, bell-peal style fingerpicking, which gave the carol a contemporary, almost country music feel. When she hit the famous high C, Matt almost crumpled at its flawless satisfaction as rendered by Jessie's honeyed robust, passionate, stirring voice. This was one of Christmas' most revered carols. Many times Matt had heard her sing this piece, but tonight it felt like she was singing just for him, for the exquisite enjoyment of his ears and his soul alone.

When Jessie brought the carol to a moving, eloquent close, Matt stepped into the studio and faced her.

"Oh, Jesus," Jessie muttered, backing away from the mic and swinging her guitar off her shoulders with a casual practiced and experienced ease. "I should have known Ulysses would call you. You oughtta know by now Matt, that sometimes I don't want to be found."

"Tough. You're found. And you're forgiven." Matt stood before Jessie in peace this night—this holy, perfect night—and let the tiniest smile touch his lips. His eyes were twinkling stars.

"Ah." A wide flush surfaced across Jessie's already semi-embarrassed pink cheeks. She could sing for thousands at once, or millions if you considered television and live streaming, but knowing that she'd just sung for Matt alone raised her music to an entirely different vibration. This was a spiritual night. A blessed energy passed through Jessie, a radiance that felt absolutely holy.

Lifting a finger, Jessie pointed at her buddy. "*Oh, Holy Night* won you over. You're in a mystical, healing state of mind. Must be my lucky night."

"Couldn't sleep, huh?" he asked, ignoring her teasing. She knew him; she could read him. It was true—there was a peace in Matt's spirit now that he was eyeballing her in person, now that he knew she was safe, and happy enough, although happy these days was a relative thing.

"Nope, couldn't," she admitted. "Truth be told, I napped while you guys were at church. And now, Matt my dah-ling, I really have to pee. Can you watch Micah for me?"

"Of course," he replied, with a contented sigh and a relaxed wave. "Go. Do your thing."

When Jessie came back from the ladies' room, she found Matt reclining comfortably on the studio's black leather sofa with her new baby boy snuggled adorably in his arms. The baby was awake, and was staring up at Matt with the reverence of a child getting to know his father.

"He thinks you're his daddy," Jessie whispered as she leaned over Micah and smiled. "I guess you kind of have been, right from the day I first told you about him. You were always watching out for me, making sure I ate the right stuff and all that. Making sure I slept," she giggled, since it was now three-thirty in the morning. "Good thing I'm not pregnant anymore, huh Matt?"

"Yeah, good thing," he answered wryly. "Speaking of sleep, do you plan to be awake when your other kids get up, Jessie? It is Christmas, remember?"

Grumbling, she sat back against the leather couch, drew one knee up to her chest and laid her chin on it. "It doesn't feel much like Christmas to me, Matt. I'm sorry, I don't mean to go all Scroogey on you, but apart from singing this beautiful old carol tonight, it just doesn't. And it never will anymore, as long as we're living in the goddamned Caribbean. Palm trees. Yeesh. Christmas isn't Christmas unless it smells like Christmas. Do you and Shanda have a real tree or a fake tree?"

"Artificial," he corrected her, as he drew a finger along the outside of Micah's tiny lips to try to get the serious little guy to smile.

"You'd have a real tree if you were with me, Matt. Josh knows the rules. He's probably loving all the freedom he has down there. No honey-do list for him these days. You and Shanda gonna have a big wedding?"

"How much coffee'd you drink?" Matt grinned over at Jessie, who lightened noticeably.

"None. Breastfeeding, remember? I admit that I did steal some chocolate peanut butter balls from Carlotta's stash in the kitchen, though. Maybe there's caffeine in those? Killed me not to suck back a mug of Bailey's and coffee along with them."

"Well, this little guy's wide awake and seemingly happy." Turning Micah so he lay on his back on Matt's thighs, Matt let the baby grasp his thumbs. "Strong little guy," he said, picturing the little fella growing up in some distant land. Matt's shoulders caved and curled forward. "She doesn't want a big wedding," he said, referencing Jessie's earlier question. "She just wants to get married."

"Is she...does she worry about me? About me and you?"

"To a point. She trusts me."

"The thing is though, Matt..." Chewing on a corner of her lip, Jessie turned her head to the side so that one cheek rested on her knee. "It's not always just about sex, is it?"

He chuckled lightly. Jessie caught an undertone of raw emotion there, but Matt was more relaxed than earlier that night at dinner, and afterwards in the upstairs washroom. "I'm a man. It's always about sex," he joked.

"Shanda doesn't need to worry. I won't jump you in Stockholm." Solemn, Jessie raised her head and searched Matt's eyes. His serious expression made her rethink what she just said, but she rallied. "Depending on when we go,

I might not even be ready for sex yet, Matt. Four kids, ya know…saggy boobs and all…" She drifted off.

One quiet blink later, and Matt looked away. Lifting Micah off of his lap, he placed him back in the carrier by his feet. Unsure, Jessie watched him secure the baby, who protested Matt's decision to move him by waving his tiny fists in the air.

"I remember when you and Jacob were trying so hard to stay away from each other," Matt finally said. "You enlisted him to help you record the first *Sacred Peace* album. I came in here and found the two of you sound asleep in each other's arms, here on the couch. Fully dressed, I might add. I was impressed at your ability to stay true to Josh with someone you loved the way I knew you loved Jacob."

"Love," Jessie smiled. "I will always love Jacob, Matt. And I will always love you." The admission was enough to choke her.

Reaching for her, Matt pulled her into his arms. They stayed that way, together on the couch, lying down, holding each other close without succumbing to the need to kiss, dozing off and on until Micah, who also fell asleep, woke. Micah's protestations grew more fervent. Jessie had no choice but to let go of Matt so she could feed her son.

Afterwards, Matt followed her. He stared at the ass end of the King Ranch all the way to La Casa on that magical Christmas Eve night, thinking about how right it felt to hold Jessie just for that last little while. In some ways it ground the hurt even deeper—Matt was completely unable to reconcile within himself the chaos that came with wanting Jessie with the truth that she would always belong to Josh, a man Matt considered a friend. Just as the sun was peeking over the horizon, its gorgeous pink-orange promise blanketing, in glowing wonder, the many houses and buildings of North Vancouver, he pulled to a stop next to Jessie in Josh's big truck.

At La Casa, he took Micah's carrier from the big truck and walked a tired Jessie inside, where the children were just waking up, wondering where their mother was as they dragged a happy but weary Deirdre and Charles down the wide, curved stairway.

Only then did Matt remember Shanda. Hauling out his phone, he mused over the blank screen. No messages. Either that was very good, or very bad.

Leaning forward, he pressed his lips to Jessie's forehead with the promise that he and Shanda—hopefully—would be around later to see the kids' gifts.

Letting him go, Jessie watched her good friend shove his hands back in the pockets of his bomber jacket and duck back inside the Audi.

Turning back around, she spied Charles watching her.

"It's all been worth it," she said, softening at the tenderness in his eyes. "All of it, Charles. You know why? Because the bad really makes you appreciate the good. That's why."

Holding out an arm so she could squiggle underneath, Charles walked Jessie into the formal room where Dylan was shaking a wrapped present so hard that Jessie feared he might break it. "Merry Christmas," Charles said as he led Jessie to the tree.

"Merry Christmas," she smiled back in return as, outside, Matt steered the Audi out to the street, and drove away.

Chapter Twenty-five

*B*efore she planned to flick her jeep's left blinker on and head toward Downtown via Cambie Street, Shanda dropped into Elysian Coffee on West Broadway. She needed to grab hot beverages for herself, Jacob and Kayla before popping in for a visit at the couple's spacious False Creek condo.

Vancouver on this early February day was sodden and gray. Rain poured from the heavens. While she was waiting for her order at Elysian, Shanda was fascinated when she looked beyond the café's large front window to see the tires of someone's vehicle almost completely awash in cold, dirty water. Mini whirlpools engulfed the back tires of the silver sedan, soaring up and around the rubber as if the water was annoyed that some idiot had parked in its path. The force was so strong that Shanda would not have been at all surprised if the back end of the car was actually lifted by the water. Josh came to mind—the day he took his unscheduled ride in a glacier fed Alberta river. She shuddered, and turned away.

Ten minutes later, after handing a Guatemalan La Soledad drip coffee over to Jacob and a comforting lemongrass tea to Kayla, Shanda dropped tiredly into a seat at their kitchen island. Baby Lily was napping; the happy couple was standing behind the counter preparing the ingredients to make a hearty thick butternut squash soup for lunch.

"Can I help?" Shanda asked, lifting her chai latte to her lips for a sip.

"It's under control. Thanks, though." Kayla nudged Jacob with her elbow and handed him a chef's knife she retrieved from a drawer. He took it in trade for a kiss. Pinking up, Kayla let a hand drift lovingly over his back before she leaned over a lower cubby to grab a stone baking sheet.

Jacob winked at Shanda. "I came into this relationship as the guy who always orders take-out. She's got me whipped." Lifting the knife, he sliced an already peeled butternut squash into large pieces. Soon those were diced into cubes that Kayla lifted and put on the baking sheet to roast.

"Didn't um, I mean, doesn't Jessie cook?"

The question, edged in a voice a tad sharper than the chef's knife, stopped Jacob's and Kayla's meal prep. Both of them looked up. Shanda's lips had a definite downward twist to them.

Jacob glanced at Kayla before answering. "Josh does a lot of their cooking. Jessie can put a meal together but when she and I were a couple we ordered out more often than not. We got pretty good at baking chocolate chip cookies, though. My grandmother taught me in New York when I was a kid. They've become a staple." He wrinkled his nose. "What brought that up? Jessie and me are old news."

"She just put her man on the jet with Jessie. Yesterday." Kayla raised her eyebrows and jauntily set a hand on a hip. "Jessie's flying south in a week, Shanda. Let her have this goodbye. Let Matt have it."

"Should I be worried?" The question popped into the air so quickly that Shanda actually voiced it from behind her takeout cup. To Jacob and Kayla on the opposite side of the island, she appeared childlike and frightened.

"Of course not," Kayla offered by way of hasty consolation.

Next to her, Jacob set his knife down on the counter and leaned slightly forward on both of his hands. He fixed a straightforward frown on his face as he watched his guest slowly set down her cup.

"What?" Shanda asked. She tightened the hold on her latte.

Shooting an apologetic look to his wife next to him, Jacob said, "I think it depends on what you consider worry-worthy."

Shanda swallowed. "That really doesn't help." A dainty set of fingers came up to rifle nervously through her short blonde curls.

Kayla leapt anxiously into the fray. "Don't listen to him, Shanda. Jessie and Matt have managed to spend a lot of extended time in each other's company without jumping into bed together. Including, by the way, after they did sleep together. She's got a newborn. Sex is the last thing on her mind, trust me."

"Too much information sharing." Grinning wholesomely, Jacob wrapped an arm around Kayla's shoulders so he could pull her close and press his lips to her hair. To Shanda, he said, "Thankfully we're past that stage."

"Agh, men." Sinking lower into her seat, Shanda sulked. "That's the thing, though, guys. It's not even so much them sleeping together that I'm worried about. It's how close they are. I'm not going to relax until Jessie gets on that plane and heads to the Caribbean. Or maybe not until she and Josh have managed to get through at least six months together." Looking up, she immediately paled. "Oh damn, Kayla, I'm sorry. That wasn't very nice of me."

"Maybe you want them to fail. Josh and Jessie, I mean." Hurt, Kayla spoke quietly. "Why don't you run down south right now, while Jessie and Matt are in Stockholm, and see if Josh needs some comfort, Shanda? It only seems fair to me since we all know Jessie will keep Matt attached to her hip these next few days."

"Easy, wifey." Jacob was watching the two women with thinly veiled curiosity, his deep blue eyes darting back and forth between the two. "Shanda, do you want me to candy coat this for you? Where you're at when it comes to Jessie butting in on your relationship with Matt? I can, if you want me to. If you think you can handle it, though, I really ought to give it to you straight. You deserve to know what you're up against here."

"What?" Kayla gave her husband a light push and backed out from under his arm. "Jacob, there's nothing to tell. Don't be giving Shanda some kind of warning that's only going to make her feel worse."

"It's not a warning," Jacob countered, as Shanda sat up a little taller and slowly started twisting her takeout cup around and around. "It's a truth. One that I think Shanda already understands on some level." To Shanda directly, he said, "You're gonna have some pieces to pick up, girl. But you'll get your man back. Let me tell you why."

Blinking nervously over at him, Shanda tilted her head, and listened.

⌇⌇

"I'm not gonna melt."

Sinking back against a mirrored wall, Jessie stared at a tiny red and blue diamond pattern on the expensive Persian rug that lined the floor of the mid-sized elevator she and Matt were riding in.

239

Matt swung around at the waist to face her and took a good long look before taking a step backward and leaning back against the opposite wall, so that he could study his girl and see how well she'd weathered the last two hours.

"The hardest part was all the waiting. Like, all through January. Wondering how bad it was going to be." Jessie tossed her hair with a fatigued, lackluster shrug. This day, February 5th, was the earliest a very smug Deirdre was able to coordinate Jessie's Sakura Music interview. It was over now. At least, as of fifteen minutes ago, the on camera part was over. The fallout was just beginning.

Letting her gaze drift up to Matt, Jessie appraised his casual work blazer and jeans vibe. Shanda's influence on him was apparent. It wasn't so much that the GQ—Beckham feel had changed, it was more of a subtle thing, like the way he was wearing his hair longer and gelled over to one side instead of in the little spikes Jessie was accustomed to teasing him about. Slouching further against the elevator wall, she bit her bottom lip and turned her face to the side.

"You've got every right to check out of dinner, Jessie. Deirdre expected it."

"I couldn't do it," Jessie admitted. "I couldn't sit with those people one more minute with all their base flattery and false pretensions and act like I don't know that I'm some kind of psychology experiment, Matt. Some circus freak, even, brought out to entertain the masses with my hopeless stories of unwanted sex and my husband's problems with addictions and this whole latest lie that we're all living, where everyone looks down on me with their endless pity and sorrow."

He threw up his hands. "You don't have to convince me. I know it was hard sitting there under those lights and telling your story, but you do know, sweetheart, that you've managed to inspire a lot of people with your courage. By funneling your pain into your music." Raising a foot, Matt crooked a knee and rested the base of his polished shoe against the wall. At the same time, he lowered his hands and shoved them in his jean pockets.

Jessie was floating somewhere between all-out misery and hopeless dejection. The interviews with Shawna Coupland were always hard enough on her, but this one—two hours long, bound to be edited into its lowest common denominator, in her opinion, of key emotional moments—was pure torture.

"They were my final public words, I suppose," she said darkly before glancing up at Matt with a sigh and a shuffle of her feet. "They can edit out their favorite life-sucking bits of this one and tweet them up the yin-yang, and use them in my eulogy some day, I don't care. I'm glad it's over, and I'm glad Charles and Dee saw fit to let me out of dinner. I hope they have fun with their new bloodsucking buddies. I'm getting drunk."

Baby Micah was in his carrier at Matt's feet. A small upturn to one corner of Matt's lips telegraphed that he knew better. He didn't have to say it. Jessie was breastfeeding. Drinking herself into oblivion like she might have done in the old days after such a grueling interview was not an option today.

Jessie allowed herself a small smile too, at Micah's fisted protest and demanding cry. "And by that I mean I intend to binge watch Netflix and breastfeed my baby. Preferably with you sucking back a few beers at my side in blatant, unremorseful honor of my inability to join you."

"I'd be happy to, but I draw the line at doing your smoking for you," Matt half joked. "Although you won't mind if I sneak out for some weed later. I'll do my puffing on the outdoor deck."

"I'm generally not that disciplined. Damn, I shoulda brought my breast pump along on this trip. That's why I pump breast milk; that's the whole purpose! So I can inhale the good stuff when I need it."

Throwing back his head for a good laugh, Matt considered Jessie just as the elevator ground to a halt and the door slid open. Sure, the interview was a tough one, lighting upon all aspects of her life from a child on up through sad and happy times. Josh would have to be on her mind now, since he was a big part of the more painful questions, but Matt knew Jessie well enough to know that she would not regress to smoking weed ever while breastfeeding. If anything, she would snuggle under the covers for a long sleep before soon heading back to Canada and having to pack up what remained of her home before moving to the Caribbean to be with her husband.

He picked up Micah's carrier just as the baby opened his mouth and sucked in some air that he released in a loud, effusive wail. "Someone's losing patience," Matt remarked casually, waving an arm to signal Jessie to leave the elevator before him.

She took his cue, but just outside she stopped and reached for his free hand. Without even pausing to consider it, Matt let his fingers wrap around hers.

"It wasn't so much the interview that sucked," Jessie confessed to him as they walked toward her large suite at the end of the hall. "It was knowing that now that it's over, I can't put off going south any longer." Despondent, she slumped all the way down the corridor.

An elderly couple walked by and stopped to coo over the baby, which bought Matt some time to collect his thoughts and consider what to say. The couple obviously had no idea who Jessie was, although they'd all met earlier in the dining room at breakfast and had exchanged a few pleasantries, in English, once the couple clued in that their hotel neighbors were English-speaking Canadians.

"What a beautiful little family," the woman said now in a warm timbre reserved for the well brought up charm school elite type. "You're a very handsome couple, the two of you, with your sweet little baby." She and her husband tottered off toward the elevator, leaving Jessie and Matt speechless.

Once the shock passed, Jessie giggled and tucked her arm firmly through Matt's. "If she only knew how close we came to that, huh Matt? Being a family? I should have told the world today. I should have just let it all out, about Morgan and his threats and Josh's fucked-up attempt at honor, and his hope that you would just walk in and take his place."

They were at the door now. Matt was reaching for the key card—fumbling, actually, his hand was shaking so hard. A calm palm laid itself over his hand and slipped the white plastic card out of his grasp. Before Jessie used it to open the door, she rested her other fingers on the black leather belt at Matt's waist, at his back, just under his blazer.

"I wouldn't have been sorry," she whispered. "I mean, if I didn't have to miss him. Josh. I want him Matt, but…I wouldn't have been sorry to spend the rest of my life with you." She lifted the hand with the keycard in it, and the lock released with a click.

Matt was still, quiet, as he stood with Micah's carrier still firmly gripped in his fingers. Jessie pushed the door partway open and waited for Matt to look up at her. When he did, she was sorry to see that the lines on his face had deepened, the tiny ones that etched out from the corners of his eyes. Within, they contained a loneliness that Jessie understood on a very personal level.

"It's like I'm living two lives," she murmured. It struck her that, apart from sex, she and Matt were every bit like a husband and wife. "We've shared everything, you and me. Me and Jacob, Deuce McCall, Josh, Charlie, your divorce, Morgan…and the good times too, all of them. Awards and shows and fundraisers and films…it's like we're divorcing now, Matt. You and me."

A slow nod was his way of responding. Apart from a recorded performance Jessie was expected to shoot as part of the Sakura Music contract, now that the more grueling part of the Stockholm interview had come to a close the hangover of loss was upon them. It hung over Jessie and Matt like vultures waiting on a feed, black and thick and dirty and raw.

Matt pushed past Jessie and stopped in the center of her large suite. Setting down the carrier, he bent and lifted Micah out of it—Micah, the child Jessie named in his honor. Walking to the big window at the far end of the suite, he held the baby to his shoulder and soothed him with a gentle swaying movement until Jessie reached for Micah, and moved to the couch so she could feed him.

～ ～

Kayla had convinced Jacob to get the soup cooking before he talked any further to Shanda about Jessie. The pungent aroma of curry swept on invisible airy waves through the condo, adding a cozy aura to the gray morning as the soup bubbled pleasantly on the stove. They took seats on the soft couch and love seat by the fire, which Jacob laid and lit so it could warm their bodies while their spirits listened. Lily was up now, being fed by her mother, who was comfortably ensconced next to her husband. Tossing a light cream coverlet around her shoulders, Kayla steadied just as Jacob began to speak.

"First," he said to Shanda, "you have to understand that Matt has been with Jessie from the beginning. Charles hired him early on, when Jessie first started to experience success at a high level. They were close then, but only in the way you'd expect lonely people to draw close. Jessie was a fragment of who she is today. For the most part she didn't talk. She didn't share personal thoughts; she basically just went through the motions."

"I'm aware of all that. I know those things about her."

Jacob hesitated. He was about to go deeper. "Matt tell you that?"

Caught off guard, Shanda answered with a cautious, "Actually no, Charlie did. Matt doesn't talk much about her."

"As I would expect. Matt plays his cards close to his chest when it comes to Jessie because…" Sighing, Jacob leaned his head back and stared up at the ceiling. Next to him, Kayla wriggled in closer. "Because," Jacob looked back at Shanda, who was kitty corner across from he and Kayla on a love seat, "she means too much to him. Talking about her would expose how he really feels. He's afraid you'll see right through him, through the façade of self-preservation he's built up over the years."

"He's only with me because he can't have her." Shanda's voice was tiny, unnatural. Unfamiliar to her own ears. Sitting with her legs drawn up and her feet underneath her, it seemed like she was trying to curl up into a ball, to curl up inside herself.

"On the contrary," Jacob answered. "He's with you because he needs you. Because you keep him sane. Because he knows Jessie has the power to destroy him."

Confused, Shanda blinked at him. "I don't understand."

"Neither do I," Kayla piped up sadly. "Are you saying that Jessie destroyed—is destroying—my brother?"

Laying a hand on her thigh, Jacob shook his head. "Josh is not a part of this equation. If anything, Jessie lifts him up. We all know that. We can't count what life has done to Josh because of his association with her as the same thing, because it's not. Kayla…where would Josh be now if he and Jessie never met and fell in love?"

"Probably dead," she whispered, her big eyes wet and watchful. "For years now. Addictions," she added, for Shanda's benefit. "My adorable big brother was in a bad place when he first met Jessie."

"So you're talking about yourself, Jacob," Shanda said with a start. "She destroyed you."

A weighty silence filled the open concept, sizable room. After a bit, Jacob wrapped his fingers around Kayla's, locked his eyes on the strength he got from her hold on him, and said, "Yeah. Hell, yeah. For a long time. And look what I did to her, with all that anger I built up over many years. I hurt her, in a bad way." He caught Shanda's eye and added respectfully,

"And what did she do? She forgave me. Almost immediately." His voice got husky. "You wonder why Matt loves her the way he does? Why he's stayed by her side for so long? Imagine, Shanda, if the rest of the world learned to forgive other peoples' wrongs the way Jessie does. And by that, I mean everyone. On the deepest level, the way it's preached to us in church. The way Jesus did, or should I say does? What a world we would live in."

"I can't imagine she's forgiven Morgan."

"She's trying to. I think seeing her daughter trapped in that car underneath the water made it pretty fucking hard."

"I don't know if she's forgiven Josh for the choice he made that's sending them all away from us, Jacob." Kayla was just being honest. She, as much as anyone, hated to see the beloved Sawyer family on the run.

"Sure she has," Jacob stated confidently. "Jessie will never give up on your brother. And I'm not saying that it will be easy for her, living away from us and watching out for him, but she gets why he did what he did. She's just terrified of losing him. That's where her anger is coming from. Where her fear is coming from."

"You understand Jessie in a way none of the rest of us do."

"I understand Jessie the way your man does, Shanda. I see her the same way Matt does. The same way Josh does. And I would add Charlie and Steve in there, too, if you want the truth. They get her."

"So what about Matt, then? If he's so embroiled in her, how's he supposed to let her go?"

Jacob let go of Kayla's hand and leaned over his knees. Resting his forearms on his thighs he said, as Lily cooed pleasingly in his wife's arms, "The Lexus, when it went underwater, Shanda, destroyed Josh. That's what fueled his choice to try to save his family at all costs. And he didn't even see them in there, Jessie and Emily-Grace, inside that fishbowl where he couldn't reach them." Jacob was growing desperate for Shanda to understand what he was trying to tell her, so desperate that he clenched his fingers together and had to force himself not to crush them. "But Matt was there," he reminded her. "In the water. On the other side. Looking in."

She got lost in his rich blue eyes; somehow they softened and intensified at the same time as the reflection of the overhead fan flickered in them, making Jacob's earnest truths appear that much more vibrant and alive.

"Matt was there," she repeated, acknowledging the terror in a soft, barely there tone.

"Yeah. Powerless for the most part, until Jessie kicked the window out. Powerless to save the one person he'd grown to love and cherish over the years with a respect that goes far beyond the norm. Let me tell you what he sees in her."

Kayla held her breath. Shanda looked over at her. Always there was a mystical element to Jessie, to the way Kayla still caught Jacob looking at her sometimes. It wasn't during the usual, normal run of things when she saw into his soul that way; it was always when Jessie and Jacob were playing music or at church, or when they were with Dylan or even baby Lily, reflecting on the perfections borne of imperfections, of beauty birthed by heartache. Forgiveness on both their parts was what allowed those spiritually complete moments to sneak in. Without it, Jessie and Jacob would still be roiling in currents of pain and in cyclones of hurt.

"Okay, Shanda," Jacob reeled, preparing to dive in. "Other people drink, or exercise, or do drugs, or overeat. Everyone's got a drug of choice. Jessie's is music. You follow?"

"Yes. I'm hearing you."

"So. Who is always at Jessie's side when she plays? Often when she's writing, or when she's rehearsing down on Robson, or when she's playing a big show, who is always close by?"

Her voice got smaller. "Matt."

"Damn straight it's Matt. And it has been, forever. So. What do you suppose he sees?"

"Look," Shanda recoiled, "I know she's talented. I know she's magical, I've seen her. I've seen the way Josh looks at her when she's on stage."

"It's more than that. Listen to me, Shanda." Jacob regained his footing by taking a deep breath. "When Jessie walks on stage it's like she's taking a journey to someplace else. She must have learned to do that back in the Charleston days, at the Renegade when McCall was starting to hurt her. Or maybe earlier, maybe that's how she escaped the pain of her stepfather's midnight visits, by disappearing inside herself when she played music. Like I said, we all have our drug."

Kayla reached out and squeezed his hand.

Continuing, Jacob said, "Jessie's addiction is music, and the stage makes a damn good hiding place to lose yourself in addictions. You wouldn't think it with all those people's eyes on you, but it does, when the guitars take over and you're in this bubble, encased by music. I've been on stage with Jessie many times, and I've gotta tell you, sometimes she's there with me, completely connected and in this beautiful, incredible place, but sometimes, like when things in her life take her down, she's not there at all. I look into her eyes and I can't see her, I can't find her. She's there, I mean physically she's there, and she's strumming the guitar or playing the piano, and her lips are moving, she's singing, but she's not there, not really. It's like she's this transparent shell—her body, I mean. Her soul is someplace else, floating alongside or up above or where the hell, I don't know. Her eyes are almost vacant, if I can see them at all. Oftentimes they're closed."

Spellbound, the girls bent closer to listen. It seemed Jacob was somewhere else now—he was on some random stage with Jessie, seeing her again in his head, the way he often saw her on troubled nights.

"Jessie, when she's like that, when she's lost in the music that way, when she's so fucking lost that she may as well be alone instead of in an arena with twenty thousand fans, is so perfect that she appears divine. I'm not kidding. She has an energy, a golden-white aura that I can sometimes see. It surrounds her and encapsulates her and it's within her. And it's like a drug, seeing her that way, with the music lifting us up and her in this safe place, in this place that we know is safe for her, that protects her, that guards her, that watches over her. It's like a drug because it draws us to her; it's like a drug because it's a real high seeing her that way, in that protected sphere that somehow elevates the rest of us."

Shanda was shaking her head in disbelief. "I know what you're gonna say," she whispered as Kayla stared at her husband in a kind of mesmerized shock.

"Matt sees her that way," Jacob went on, further enlightening the girls. "He's seen her that way many, many, many times, but you know what, Shanda? He's that for her too. He's that safe place too, that energy, that magical, mystical aura that's such a part of Jessie, that's so wrapped up in protecting her, in keeping her safe, that he, too, is uplifted when he is with her. When they're together, sometimes I'm pretty sure they don't know anybody else is even in the room. Their energies meld into one another and they become one and the same. It's not all Jessie's power over him. He has a power over her too."

Kayla's small voice brought Jacob back to them, to her. "Do you still think of Jessie that way, Jacob? Like she's a drug?"

Glancing sideways at her, Jacob was almost sorry for having to tell the truth. But Kayla was his wife, and they kept no secrets from one another. "Yeah," he admitted quietly. "'Course I do. Kayla, a drug like that…" He shook his head. "It's a helluva addiction. Hard as hell to walk away from. But I did. I broke free, I did it in a very bad way that I will never be able to reconcile myself with, but in the end I did it. I let her go. With Jessie's help. With your help, with your acceptance of me. I still see her that way, yeah, hell yeah, but from a safe place now."

He turned to Shanda. "Matt's still in it. He's still a part of her. He will always be a part of her. But there's a light on the other side of his addiction. And it's pretty damn sweet, Shanda. It's called love, and it's damn worth the pain to get there."

"You said he's part of the addiction. How the hell's he supposed to walk away? Do you see now why I am so scared?"

"Distance. That's how."

"They've tried that before. It didn't work."

"Ah," Jacob smiled. "True. But Matt wasn't head over heels in love with a beautiful actress then. Addictions notwithstanding." He lowered his voice and took her elegant fingers in his callused ones. "Shanda, he didn't have you."

Lily echoed her agreement. Kayla handed her infant daughter to Jacob to be burped, and got up to go check on the soup. Shanda sweated her fear away with a sad smile sent across to Jacob, and a light, hopeful touch on the small baby's back.

Chapter Twenty-six

A choking scream from Jessie's bedroom brought Matt running. He'd been dozing on the sofa in front of the varied stunning city night lights of busy Stockholm, and the terror stricken scream skyrocketed his relaxed pulse into a pounding, relentless overdrive. Vaulting into Jessie's room, he launched himself to her side in a second flat and did a super quick risk assessment. She was alone—no diabolical malcontent had somehow snuck into her room. *Thank God.* She was lost, though, in some nefarious place in her mind, the victim of yet another unforgiving nightmare that was holding her captive in its hoary grasp, that was strangling the life out of her via some vivid horror scene playing out in her creative, busy mind.

Carefully, so as not to shock her awake, Matt eased his body down on the bed next to Jessie. She was actively struggling with some invisible foe, choking and gasping and writhing in her sleep, trying to take hold of her dream, trying to regain some kind of control. Starting with breathing, it seemed.

Lying alongside her, resting on one elbow, Matt took a tentative hold on Jessie's left bicep. Crying out, moaning in her sleep, she tried to beat him away. In the end he had no recourse but to give her a solid shake to wake her up. Soothing her, murmuring her name, Matt eventually got Jessie to calm down.

As she awakened, the world spun back into focus, but as always with strange hotel rooms in distant places, it took a while for her to realize where she was. When reality snapped into place the way a puzzle piece fits into its spot, Jessie laid eyes on Matt. Still choking, she dove into his embrace and lay there, tremendously relieved that she was in his arms, safe and protected.

Hulking sobs accompanied her first words. "I want to be with Josh, Matt, I do, I really do, I love him, I love him, but I don't know how I'm supposed to be without you!" Lifting her head up from where she'd buried it against the soft blue cotton of his T-shirt, she enlightened him on her nasty dream. "I was in the car again, in the river, but I was alone! I was alone, just me, staring at the window, kicking at it, but it wouldn't break and the Lexus was filling up again and," she sobbed and placed her palms against his cheeks as his eyes started to swim, "and then the window finally gave and all that disgusting muddy water started running in again, and it knocked me back against the passenger door and I couldn't—I couldn't breathe! I couldn't get a breath that wasn't full of water! You weren't there! You weren't there, Matt!" Unable to stem the panic that lingered even after waking, Jessie started pounding on Matt's chest. "You're always there when I need you! You're always with me! How'm I supposed to go it alone, Matt? How?"

"You won't be alone," he reassured, pulling her close. Wrapping his arms tightly around the shivering body he knew well, Matt closed his eyes and rocked the woman he'd watched over for so many years, the one he had to let go so she could find her own way with her chosen man. "You'll have Josh," he murmured as Jessie's breathing slowed, as the rasping coughs subsided into sniffles. "You'll have Josh."

Easing Jessie's face away from him, Matt became aware that his right hand had somehow found its way up the inside of the back of the lace-trimmed white tank top she wore to bed. Without even realizing it, he was rubbing her warm skin in the most natural way, as if they were accustomed to being together this way, lying on a bed, him in his bare feet and jeans, her in her panties and light top. She was watching him, peering intently into his worried eyes with her own forlorn, deeply saddened moist baby blues, gently palming his beloved cheeks as if to assure herself that he was here, and real, and touchable.

Distracted, his mind wandering back to that horrific day in the river, Matt let his hand drift down the inside of Jessie's top to her lower back. Pressing his palm to her body, rubbing a little harder, he lost himself in her fretful, searching eyes, and soothed her with his touch.

Almost unaware that he was even doing it because it felt so natural, Matt let his hand slip inside the waist of the back of Jessie's panties; he exerted just the tiniest bit of pressure, bringing her hips close enough to him so that he could sense the heat of her through his jeans. Taken aback, Jessie felt a hardness in his body start to pulsate against her. Desire shot through her, rocketing at the same time through Matt's groin. It shocked both of them with its intensity, with its powerful urge to take control. A sudden, inadvertent moan from between Matt's lips caught him off guard, and he tilted his head back and let his eyes close over so he wouldn't have to see shock on Jessie's face, so he could push her sweetness against him just a moment longer, so he could let his breath go ragged with need and longing.

A quick breath escaped Jessie's lips and her eyes fluttered closed. Gasping, she pressed her lips to the little hollow at the top of Matt's chest and clutched a handful of his T-shirt with one hand. With the other hand she put a little pressure on his back, and she thrust her hips more forward. Hard.

Instantly, her breathing quickened.

Wise enough to acknowledge that where they were headed would have repercussions both would likely regret, Matt forced his eyes open. "Oh, Jesus," he breathed, mortified, as he eased his hold on her and started to back away. "I'm sorry, Jessie. I'm so fucking sorry."

Lightning fast, her hand darted away from his back and she grabbed his wrist instead. "I'm not," Jessie pleaded, her voice soft now, the fear wrought by her chilling night terror transferring to something far, far better. "I'm not at all sorry."

"I can't…we can't…"

"Matt, baby, we're alone here." There was a desperation in Jessie's eyes that it hurt Matt to see. He knew its name—loneliness. Always, with her, it was loneliness. "Nobody knows," she panted as she drew a set of trembling fingers down his cheek, "and nobody has to know. You and me are one. Wherever life takes us…" She sighed heavily. "I want this night with you, Matt. I want one last night to feel safe in your arms."

Swallowing past the ache, Jessie let her left hand float down to Matt's waist. Sliding her fingers underneath his T-shirt, she moved her hand over his tight abs, over his hard chest, his warm back. Panting harder now, she wiggled a little downward so she could shove the soft cotton shirt upwards and press her mouth against his body, over the slight trail of hairs that led down to a part of him she was almost desperate to put into her mouth, to taste, but first—upwards, up Matt's gorgeous body so she could luxuriate in the sweet pleasure of teasing him, of extending his pleasure by sucking on a nipple, first.

Tonguing him, playing there, emitting soft moans while lightly pressing her teeth to him, Jessie let a hand slide down to Matt's jeans so she could unfasten his belt. Looking up for a moment, she lost herself in his sad, scared eyes. "This is not about Shanda, Matt," she groaned, starting now to press her hips rhythmically against him, "and this is not about Josh. I need you tonight, baby. I fucking need you. So fucking bad."

He didn't answer, except by touch. Matt's crisis of conscience went the way of the dodo bird. With a sudden movement he gathered Jessie's hair in one hand, tipped her lips up to his, and let his tongue capture the first exquisite taste of her, of the woman he loved for so long that he couldn't remember when it began, when it first started, except maybe for the very first day he laid eyes on her—a wounded orphan child with gifts in music and acting that were already, by then, beginning to entrance a world who needed her kind of love, her kind of hope.

I'm going to soak her up slowly, Matt determined, letting his eyes close so he could enhance senses other than sight. *I'm going to love her right, and I'm going to make it last.* There were sounds in the darkened room—not the baby, no, Micah was sleeping peacefully in his travel bed close by. The sounds, Matt was almost embarrassed to realize, were mostly coming from between his lips, although a few little ragged ahhhs and moans were escaping Jessie's mouth now as well. *Sweet Jesus,* he thought as he clutched her to him so he could more hungrily probe that perfect mouth, those sweet pink, often pouty lips, *what am I doing? What am I doing?*

As quickly as they assaulted him, he pushed those traitorous thoughts away. Jessie was right. They would soon be parted. Tonight was not the time to get hung up on who might get hurt because, overall, the two people most apt to get hurt, who were most certainly getting hurt when Jessie joined Josh in the Caribbean, were him and her—Matt and Jessie.

She was going for it. Jessie was into this, into him, into saying goodbye this way. Her hand was inside his pants now, reaching for him. Gasping, Matt grabbed her wrist and stilled her movements for a moment.

Thinking he was stopping her, Jessie stilled, too. Backing away just a tiny bit, she moved her hand up and clutched his wrist instead. Her eyes were on his, half-lidded and dusky with wanton desire; watching him, she pressed his hand to her panties, encouraging him to cup her, to play there, if he so chose. Rubbing her hand on top of his, she pushed against his fingers, begging him to continue this midnight game that had emerged from fear and from what would have been certain death had her earlier nightmare been real and Matt not have been there when the Lexus rolled and sank.

"Oh, God," she gasped, desperate to separate the intrinsic beauty of this sacred act from the impending loss, in just a few short days, of this man she loved.

Matt's hand was inside her panties now, probing, searching, soaking up the hot wetness of her, and so Jessie rolled half over onto her back for him so he could have more room to play. Grunting now, letting his body take over, Matt fingered her, in and out, in and out, tormenting Jessie with promising, tiny waves of pleasure.

"More, sweetheart," he begged as she thrust herself up against his hand, as she wrapped a hand around his penis and squeezed and ran a thumb over him. "Open yourself up more for me."

For Matt, there was no time even to steal a few choice licks of her; this need, tonight, came on too sudden and was too insistent. Grunting, aching, Matt couldn't deny how bad he wanted Jessie. A few moments later the lacey panties dangled from a feminine ankle and were kicked aside. Jessie parted her legs and helped bring Matt toward her, and so he took what was offered and went inside that beautiful body— the treasured soul—the one welcoming him with desperate thrusts and eager, reckless mewls. He was quicker than he wanted to be, but he sensed a whole sweet night ahead of them, offering private adult playtime that, once this first frantic thirst was quenched, would be amenable to slower, lingering pleasures.

Jessie, too, wanted more, she wanted a good, sweet suck of her favorite part of him, but instead she came hard onto him, pushing her hips up against Matt as he released his exquisite burden into her. They lay there together afterwards, panting, him rocking her and laying gentle kisses by her eyes, on her neck, her shoulder; him tenting her in his arms the way he dreamed he could for so many past interminable, lonely nights, knowing all the while that although Jessie's heart in many ways belonged to him, he was trumped by a lonely, solitary man who was longing for his wife to join him in the salty, sunny Caribbean.

Matt pulsed inside Jessie for a long time, still moving his hips against her, letting his breathing come back to its more regular pace, relishing the last few waves of bliss, before he raised his face away from where he'd finally buried it in Jessie's neck. Studying her, he let some of the tension at her anticipated reaction ease when he saw that she was watching him with softly glowing eyes moist with tenderness and love.

"I love this," Jessie murmured to him. "I love this, Matt. Being with you this way."

Easing himself out of her, separating his body from hers, Matt blew out a small *pffftt* and lay on his side so he could still play with the body he adored, and with the breasts he now had free access to.

"I have baby belly," Jessie teased, twining her fingers through his and letting him take the lead and move his hand wherever he wanted to on her body. "I apologize. I need a little more time to get back into shape."

"You're perfect," he whispered. "So goddamned perfect, Jessie."

"Sorry about the leaking breast milk. I don't think it turned you off at all." She giggled.

"It was erotic as hell," he chuckled, and bent forward to lick a tiny bit of breast milk trailing down the side of her breast. He made a face.

"Not your preferred beverage? We're quite the pair," Jessie laughed. "Matt…" Turning her head to the side, she peered into the light hazel-gray eyes she loved. "We fight like crazy, we drive each other nuts, and we make love like animals. I meant what I said earlier, baby. I honestly don't know how to live without you in my life. What if—"

His fingers landed on her lips. "No," he cut her off, with an authority that said he knew intuitively what she was going to say. "It's not an option, Jessie."

"What?" she asked, testing him. "What was I going to say?"

"You were going to ask me to come to the Caribbean. To watch over you and your family. I can't do that. I can't do it anymore."

She pouted. "Because you have Shanda now."

"Because I can't share you. Not with Josh. With Charlie, maybe, I wouldn't have cared so much, but—"

Jessie's hand darted out and swatted him. "You dork," she reprimanded. "Charlie would not appreciate that underhanded comment."

"Let me finish." Grabbing her fingers, Matt gave them a small twist. She yelped. "Josh loves you so much, Jessie. You have to stop worrying. Give him some credit."

"Oh, this from the man who helped me undress my husband in the shower so I could wash the urine and vomit off of him. Lovely. Just walk away, Matt. Live your perfect GQ life with gorgeous Shanda and make beautiful little babies. I'll continue to pick up the pieces of my fucked-up existence alone."

He was quiet as he contemplated that. In the end Matt said without looking at her, "You will. You'll do just that. Willingly, I might add."

"I told you already." Now Jessie's voice was small, that of a hurt child. "On the jet that night. I told you that maybe I am ready for some stability in my life, Matt."

Matt almost stopped breathing.

"It's what Josh wanted," Jessie managed. "I think he would still want that. For me. For our children. He wants what he thinks *he* can't give us. He was the same way with Jacob. Josh has always known where he fits."

"Josh is the best man of all of us, Jessie. He's the most honest of all of us. He's the one with the guts to hurt the way he needs to hurt. And for the record, he wants you back. Please don't allude to any kind of a future for you and me again. All that will do is drive the dagger in deeper, okay sweetheart?"

"I can't stand this." She was crying now, not overtly with sobs and choking gasps, but with her trademark big tears, one of which Matt spotted and kissed away as Jessie turned back onto her side and faced him. "I want a choice, Matt. Nobody is ever giving me choices."

"A choice?" He almost laughed. "You want to be able to choose between me and Josh, Jessie? You don't think either of us know which way that would go?"

"Give me a chance," she begged. "Give me a chance to choose. You might be surprised." An idea struck her. "Let's take some time, you and me. Let's just go away and take some time, to see how we do, Matt. Nobody would even think twice about it. Not that anyone has to know right away, anyway. We'll tell them it's business. We'll just fly away somewhere and be together, you and me and Micah for now, until we can sort things out more formally."

Stunned, Matt licked his lips before he answered. "This is your nightmare talking," he ascertained, his voice a low rasp. "This is your fear talking, Jessie. Josh will be okay. You'll see."

"This is the thing, Matt," she said, reaching for reserves of strength so she wouldn't lose it in front of him. The nightmare…being in that submerged vehicle again…alone this time, without her daughter, without Matt there to save her…was what was indeed sinking her now. The icy, cold fear was crawling up her arms and legs again, a living thing snaking along her body trying to get into Jessie's soul so it could destroy her. "I don't know if he will be okay. You cannot guarantee me that he will be okay. Jacob was right all those years ago. Wasn't he, baby?"

In his heart, Matt wondered. But there was one thing Jessie was forgetting, now while she was barely hanging on after the horrid interview today that dredged up so many bad memories, so much fear; and after the nightmare that threatened to undo her sanity entirely. She was forgetting something that he felt she should be reminded of.

"You love him," he said. "Look me in the eye, Jessie, and tell me you don't love him. Then maybe you and me can have a future together."

"Sometimes," she countered, as the big tears continued to trail sideways down her cheeks, "love hurts far too much, Matt. And sometimes maybe it's better to let it go."

A muffled snuffling came from the direction of Micah's travel bed.

"There are children involved here, Matt," she continued, as if cued by Micah's audible reminder of his presence in her life. "Children who are more important than me. Children who need their grandparents close by, their friends, regular schooling instead of tutored home schooling, swimming lessons, dance classes, opportunities. Dylan needs Jacob, hell, Emily-Grace and David need Jacob, and they need Kayla too. Charlie, what about Charlie? Don't you see, Matt? There is so much more at stake here than a man who is hanging on by one goddamned thread. I couldn't see it then. But I see it now. I see it in the eyes of that baby who Josh expressed zero interest in from the time Micah was conceived. I want Josh back, Matt. I do. I really do. But maybe what I want isn't what's best for me, for him, or for our children. Maybe what I want isn't enough."

Micah was starting to wail now. Matt said a silent prayer, bent his lips to Jessie's forehead, and pressed them against sweaty wisps of hair. "God, what I would give to have you. Forever."

For once, he didn't end his thoughts with a resounding 'but.' The way she spoke of them together, and the reasons why…hell, Jessie almost made it sound possible. A minuscule optimistic part of Matt bounced into vision and shouted 'hope.'

Lifting himself up off the bed, Matt padded over to Micah. Jessie watched him hoist her baby up, soothe him with gentle murmurs, and carry him into the bathroom, where she had a little change station set up. A few moments later, she eased herself up against the big bed's headboard and accepted Micah from Matt's outstretched arms. Bringing him to her breast, she helped Micah latch on so he could feed.

Matt settled next to her, wrapped an arm around her shoulders, and let Micah wrap his tiny fingers around his much bigger index finger. As the moonlight washed its pale hope over them in this far distant country with its strange language and freezing climate, Matt laid his head against Jessie's damp curls and ached for the future she spoke of, and wished beyond hope that there was a way it could come true.

～ ⁓

A part of Matt started to really believe Jessie had a point and was maybe able to let Josh go, for all the reasons she gave him, after they extended their stay in Europe and, for all intents and purposes, acted like the couple the elderly pair down the hotel hallway believed they were. Deirdre and Charles were of absolutely no help in pushing a pin into the new balloon-like illusion. Both were wordless observers who did not offer overt opinions, but instead silently wondered what Jessie was up to. In their hearts, neither truly believed she could let Josh go.

Still, they were baffled as to what to think, how to feel.

"We waited a long time for her to come into our lives," Deirdre said to

Charles after they said their goodbyes in Stockholm. Jessie still had the performance video to film, plus Charles and Dee considered that maybe it wouldn't be a bad thing to give Jessie and Matt some extra alone time together before the upcoming planned parting. "I don't want Jessie and the children to leave us. Do you, Charles? If she and Matt…" She couldn't continue.

Charles was as lost as Deirdre when it came to how to feel. "I'd hate to see my lead actress on *Sacred Peace* crushed," he muttered, but only half-heartedly. Might it be possible to keep Jessie and the kids close at hand instead of sending them into exile with an unpredictable, often troubled man? The thing was… that man had proven his love and his loyalty, time and again, not just to Jessie and the kids, but to Charles' series, too. As far as Charles was concerned, Josh was his and Deirdre's son-in-law. There were rocky times, yes, but Josh's devotion to Jessie and their children was never in question. Offering himself to Morgan in order to save his family was an incomprehensible, yet honorable act, in Charles' mind, albeit almost far too unbelievable to even wrap his brain around. To him, now, Josh was hard to read, and Charles, like Jessie, couldn't predict which way Josh would turn or where he would land. But neither could Charles with any sense of decency just let Josh fade into the ether, despite how much both Charles and Deirdre revered Matt.

Matt and Jessie got a little careless on their third day alone in Stockholm. They went to a hockey game, taking little Micah with them in a snuggly carrier cuddled into his mother's chest. Idly, 'due to their distance in a foreign country' they later said in their own defense, they got a little too relaxed in public. Someone snapped a picture of them when they dropped into a busy café after the game where, in order to sit, they had to share a seat. Matt was behind Jessie on a big chair, his hands laid casually on her hips and his breath in her ear whispering sweet sentiments that made her both laugh and blush, while Micah cooed contentedly in the snuggly. The young girl who took the photo happily tweeted that Jessie Wheeler seemed to be moving on after her husband's death. Matt's identity was a mystery to the photographer, but he was quickly identified by the tweeting public as Jessie's longtime security.

Shanda was beside herself when she got wind of the viral photo of her fiancé striking such an intimate pose with Jessie and the baby—his eyes half-closed, his lips brushing her ear. As far as she knew, Matt and Jessie were only staying an extra few days in Europe so Jessie could be filmed singing the song to complement the Sakura Music interview. That part was true, the filming did happen but in truth, by the time of the hockey game, it was long over. When Shanda punched in a call to Matt, he avoided taking it, and didn't reach out to Shanda until a time when Jessie was in the shower so she couldn't overhear. All he said to Shanda was that he would soon be back in Vancouver and that he would come see her upon his arrival.

Josh saw the tweet, too. The sheer happiness on Jessie's face didn't initially upset him—it relaxed him, at least at first, partly because he trusted Matt and partly because after all they'd been through, Josh needed to see a sparkle in Jessie's spirit. There was something serene about spying peace and joy in those sea-pearl blue eyes.

After scrutinizing the tweet, Josh bypassed Arnie at the pool and jogged down the steps to the wooden dock. He hopped lightly onto the Bayliner, pointed its bow westward and took a wild spin at top speed through the calm indigo sea. Turning his face up to the salt spray as he careened recklessly through it, Josh whipped the wheel around in circles, crashing repeatedly through his own watery wake as if he were scratching lines through his choppy past, erasing and modifying his own life in some hollow attempt to outrun his mistakes and the things that hurt. During the entire crazy speedboat ride which Arnie, arms crossed and breath held, watched nervously from shore, Josh sang at the top of his lungs—some basic crude country and western ditty about beer and boots.

It wasn't until that night in the solitary darkness of his bedroom that reality caught up with him and he awoke in a damp sweat, his stomach clenching in some intuitive knowing that Jessie's plans to come south could now be threatened. Springing up, Josh just made it to the toilet before retching miserably into it. Jessie was overdue in their new Caribbean island home. All along she had said she was coming, but there were intimacies evident in the Stockholm tweet that Josh picked up on more closely after taking a more serious look after his crazy boat ride—Matt's fingers on Jessie's hips, the loving smile in his half-closed eyes, one of Jessie's hands over his, her body relaxed into the curved sanctuary he was providing with his own strong physique, his arm wrapped around Micah's small frame—around Josh's child. By the time he had gone to bed earlier, real fear had started digging its sharp blade into Josh's chest; it burrowed under his skin and, like a tick, gave a wrenching twist that made it near impossible to extricate.

Matt was that fear. He was always a part of Josh's plan, meant to be a safe, secure refuge in Jessie's life and in the lives of Josh's children once Josh was gone, but it was hard to reconfigure where the man was supposed to fit into their lives now.

Leaning over the toilet, white-knuckling the sides, Josh fought against this new anxiety. *I deserve it,* he thought. *Look how happy she is with him. Look at Micah, how safe he is with Matt's arms around him. How loved he is.* Shanda crossed his mind. Wasn't there a wedding in the offing? What about the other Sawyer children—Emily-Grace was old enough to understand the image, if she happened to lay eyes on it. She had always loved and respected Matt; the man was already a father of sorts to her. The tenderness in the photo would confuse the heck out of her.

But I'm the tornado in their lives, Josh self-countered as he retched. *Matt's the calming breeze. I'm lost, as far as my kids know. Maybe it would be better for all of them if I stayed that way.*

Josh let his hands slip down the sides of the basin and laid his cheek on the cool tile beneath his body while, in the small bedroom at the back of the jet, as Jessie travelled home to Vancouver, she pushed thoughts of her husband aside, brought Matt to her, and made love in a shadow of uncertainty, but with a promise of hope.

Chapter Twenty-seven

The next day, in the front foyer at La Casa, Jessie touched her lips to Matt's and said, "When Emily-Grace, David and Dylan finish their school stuff with Patin, Sam and Alin are taking them skating. I'm going up to the UBC house to grab my skates so I can hang out with them at the rink while you and Charles meet. I'm bringing Micah with me. I need to pack a few more things for tomorrow while I'm up there. That okay with you, handsome?"

There were plans afoot to sneak away again the next day for a full five days this time, somewhere tropical, since Jacob and Kayla were taking the older three children for the next few days—Jacob's grandparents were visiting from New York and wanted to spend some time with the kids. Winking playfully at Matt now, Jessie extended an invitation. "Come see me after your meeting with Charles. It's early yet. We've got some time before I need to meet the gang. Plus it'll be chaos tonight when everyone else lands with their kids."

Happier than he had been in a long time, Matt took Jessie up on the offer. "Sounds like a plan," he returned, his eyes lighting up. "Everyone's coming for dinner?"

"Yep, Steve and Charlie will also be at the rink with their kids and are coming over afterwards. I'll see you in a bit, Matt." She bent forward for a second kiss.

A rustle from down the hall startled Matt into backing off. "We should take it easy here, Jessie," he warned, resting a hand loosely on her hip as she sank into a sulky pout. "There's no point in confusing everyone."

"Confusing them about what, Matt? How we feel about each other?"

"Where this is going to land. That's what."

Jessie took a step back so she could take a closer look at Matt. He was nervous, uncomfortable, but underneath his concern was a glow Jessie hadn't seen in a long time. Edgy herself, she threw in a quick question. "Have you talked to Shanda yet, Matt?"

A slow shake of his head preceded his answer. "I don't know what to say to her, Jessie. It all made sense in Europe. Here…I want it to make sense, but I'm not sure it does, you and me. Not with…" He bit his tongue.

"You were going to say 'not with Josh still around.' Weren't you, Matt? Do you ever get the feeling that Josh is just as confused about all this? Nothing's worked out the way he planned."

"That could be a good thing, Jessie. You and him could use some time away from everyone to reconnect."

"Awww hell, Matt. Give us a chance, you and me. Please? Let's just go away tomorrow and take some time to see how things play out. At this point Shanda doesn't need to know it's not business."

"I can't keep her hanging on, Jessie. It's not in any way fair to her. And it's not fair to Josh."

Jessie sighed. "All right. Look, Matt, nothing has to be decided this instant. It's not like either of us will have a spare second today, and didn't you say Shanda's got an audition for a film this afternoon? You and me, we deserve some alone time together. We need this trip so we can sit down and make sense out of things."

"I don't know if we're going to find any answers, Jessie. The more time you and I spend together, the harder it's going to be to walk away."

"Matt…please, stop this." Jessie grabbed a handful of Matt's aviator jacket and pulled him close. "This is what Josh wanted. We're just giving him what he wanted."

"I know you're scared, Jessie. You think I don't know that?" Matt's voice was dangerously low. Lifting a hand, he untangled Jessie's fingers from around his jacket. He brushed his lips across the back of her hand and, with his searching eyes, implored her to listen, to understand. "You think I don't know that you're playing some kind of game with me right now? A 'let's just teach Josh a lesson' game? No matter what you're telling yourself, you're giving him a taste of his own medicine. You're shoving 'us' in his face and yelling 'look at me. Look how happy I can be without you.'"

"How can you say that?" Throwing his hand away, Jessie moved backward so quickly that she staggered and had to catch herself against the stair railing. "Josh made his own bed here, Matt. He pretty much pushed me into yours."

"Which is all well and good if that's where you want to be, sweetheart. In my bed, I mean, if that's where you really want to be. Forever. For the rest of your life. While Josh is still on the planet."

"For the rest of my life? Well, you're older, so you're likely to go first." Jessie's tongue-in-cheek dig fell flat.

Matt didn't even blink. "I know you, Jessie. You're operating from a place of fear."

"So go. Go, Matt." Jessie waved a dismissive arm at him. "Get the hell away from me. Don't bother coming up to the UBC house for your free fuck. I'm sure Shanda would happily oblige you, anyway. Although I've got a few little tricks I can pull out that can make you a very happy man, Matt. All that whoring. Starting at age twelve, you know the drill. I learned a lot."

"Oh, for fuck's sake, Jessie. You think that's what it's about for me? Sex? Get over yourself. You're not that good." As he said it, Matt cringed. Their bedtime liaisons were still new and fresh. And they were…that good. Lying down holding her, just simply holding her as she snuggled into his body, was enough.

"Great," Jessie yapped back in a characteristic burst of her usual high-horse princess anger. "Whoring is the only thing I think I really am good at, and you just burst that bubble on me too. Get the hell away from me, Matt. I've got stuff to do at home."

Taking off down the hall, she left him standing tensely in the bright, expansive front foyer of La Casa, shoulders stiff and one hand repeatedly rubbing the two-day whiskers Jessie had begged him to let grow. *Such an un-Matt thing,* she had teased him in the small bedroom on the jet yesterday. *Let your hair down a little. Relax.*

When Jessie returned, she had Micah in his carrier. By then Matt was outside opening the door of the King Ranch, preparing to take Micah from Jessie's hand so he could place the carrier in the back seat of the truck.

Surprising him, Jessie fired him a stubborn 'F-you' look, and stomped over to the SUV instead.

"Always playing games," Matt muttered under his breath, exhausted from the effort it constantly took to read her. Approaching Jessie after she buckled Micah in, he roughly grabbed her biceps to prevent her from jumping in behind the wheel and spinning out in a godawful fury. "I'll be there," he told her. "Give me an hour."

"Don't bother coming up," Jessie steamed, trying to disengage his vice-like grip from her arms. "Unless you're ready to accept what you mean to me, Matt. You," she asserted, stabbing a finger into his chest hard enough that he winced. "Just you. Separate and apart from my sad, tormented husband."

Matt wanted to say *I dare you to look Josh in the eyes and say that. Take one look into those deeply loved, troubled eyes and tell me I even exist.* But at that juncture, a small part of him was still desperate to believe Jessie, or maybe to believe *in* her. He wanted her to himself, and he still prayed he could have her. It wasn't until he got to the UBC house later, a lemon tea peace offering suspended high in his hand for her, that the first real, true seeds of permanent doubt snuck in.

What he found there sent him careening back down a lonely road.

When he wandered into the house, he could hear her crying. Upstairs, Matt stood in the hallway and didn't move for a long time. From his vantage point he could see that she'd piled a few items in the center of the bed—some toiletries, and a few clothing items like panties and socks. Something in the center of these was glistening. Closer scrutiny revealed Jessie's engagement and wedding rings, which at first jumpstarted Matt's heart and gave him hope that Jessie was ready to make a change this big, that she was putting the past away. Something else shiny and bright lay abandoned nearby. Matt recognized it as the locket Josh gave Jessie their first Christmas together, the one with the tiny painted miniature of the two of them fastened carefully inside.

His mind was in a weird fog. It wasn't really a surprise to find Jessie emotional now. Matt expected she would have a hard time coming back here, but she'd seemed so happy these last few days, so content at La Casa yesterday and today, at least until he and she had their little spat in the foyer of the sunny home. Yet, emotional was one thing, but the kind of soul-baring crying coming from her spirit now was the kind that ripped a person in two, and that included any person, such as Matt, who might, perchance, find himself in the direct vicinity of such inconsolable, gulping sorrow.

From the hallway, training his eyes on the direction of the sobbing, Matt picked out that Jessie was in the large walk-in closet next to the en suite washroom. The light was on, shining rather brightly overall when compared to the single lamp illuminating the bedroom from a nightstand. There were clothes in the closet, hanging from white racks and folded in cubbies—dresses, yes, and—Matt squinted so he could bring them into focus—

Ah. Jeans. Shirts. Vintage button-down shirts.

Josh's clothes.

Letting his gaze drift downward, Matt saw Jessie huddled just underneath the clothes. His heart did a double take when he spied the woman he'd watched over for so long clinging to something large and white; *something heavy*, he thought. Jessie didn't see him. Her face was buried in it.

It was a thick new motorcycle jacket, a butter-soft white leather one with a red racing stripe running down the center of each arm, and a stand-up half collar. Jessie'd given it to Josh for his birthday in April. It was meant to be worn when riding the Harley. Matt didn't have to stretch his imagination to discern that, in Jessie's mind, the jacket may as well have been Josh himself, so embroiled was her husband's essence in his beloved big bike.

Backing out of his spot near the entrance to the bedroom, out of the hallway, Matt took his crushed heart back down the stairs. He left the lemon tea on the kitchen island. Outdoors, he sat in the driveway for a long time before he forced his Audi into reverse and backed out into the quiet street.

He and Jessie would still take a trip tomorrow. Today, she might notice the tea he left her, but she might not. Maybe she wouldn't know that he spied on her, that he was witness to a pain that great, one that was meant to be carried alone so it wouldn't burden anyone else. Or maybe he wanted her to know that he was there. That he, too, was now suffering, with a truth that Jessie seemed unable or unwilling to face, a truth that clearly said he, Matt, was right all along. That Jessie could hide behind him all she wanted to, and they could likely enjoy a good long life together, but that really, truly, she belonged with her husband. She belonged with Josh.

Swiping a forearm under his nose, Matt sucked in a breath, pointed the Audi toward Shanda's place in Yaletown, and carried on with the dignity and integrity expected of him, of the man who watched over Jessie Wheeler-Sawyer.

Of the man who used to be detached enough to do his job right.

Chapter Twenty-eight

The playroom at La Casa was littered with toys. As expected, everyone descended on La Casa after a shared two hours at the rink—Steve and Sophie, and Charlie and Jane—even Jacob and Kayla had popped into the rink for the last while. They all had kids in tow. The hum of excitement that took over the pretty Spanish villa was genuine in its sincerity, even though a low undercurrent of fear and questions buzzed below the voices.

Steve and Charlie ganged up on Jessie the first chance they got, while an unusually quiet Matt was helping supervise the kids in the playroom in his strange role as protector/temporary father figure.

They were washing the pots and pans, Charlie up to his elbows in suds while Steve and Jessie dried. After feeding the large rowdy, animated group, Carlotta was enjoying a well-deserved break.

Charlie started by hanging onto a pot that Jessie was trying to take from him. "What's this I hear about you and Matt taking off tomorrow for a few days together? And I heard that from Shanda, by the way. Who heard it from Matt this afternoon."

"What'd he tell her?" Jessie couldn't meet Charlie's eyes. Yanking the pot out of his grasp, she stared at a skewed, distorted reflection of herself in its shiny metal. At her side, Steve couldn't bring himself to speak.

Charlie made a frustrated popping sound before he illuminated Jessie. "He told her the two of you need some alone time to say goodbye."

"Oh. He was supposed to tell her it was business." Sickened, Jessie stopped drying. Charlie grabbed the dishtowel from her and dried his hands on it. When he was done, he forced the pot from the death grip she had on it and practically dropped it onto the counter, which startled Jessie and made her jump. Glaring up at him, she let out a high-pitched accusatory whine. "Was that really necessary, Charlie?"

"What's up, Jessie? With you and Matt?"

"Not your business, Charlie." Pivoting around, Jessie turned to go but Steve grabbed her arm and jumped into the fray.

His growl was enough to stop her in her tracks, but apart from trying to yank her arm free, she didn't look at him. "Jessie, don't be stupid," he said. "You think you and Josh came this far to walk away now?"

"Maybe I should have walked away a long time ago," she retorted. "And had some stability in my life. In my kids' lives."

"Is it your career? You're afraid to give that up?" Steve's career was on fire. He was so busy that he rarely spent time in Vancouver these days. If anyone understood how hard it would be for both Jessie and Josh to suddenly reverse their lives like they were heading down a switchback on a mountain pass, it was him. Charlie got that, too—Charlie, who was already mourning the loss of his lead actor while he finalized scripts for the third shooting season of *Sacred Peace*.

"You're sleeping with Matt again." Sparks danced in a dangerous arc across Charlie's serious eyes.

"So what if I am? He's everything to me."

"And how fair is that to him? He's a goddamned lifejacket. A life preserver in a storm. Cut him loose, Jessie. You can do this move."

A quiet mewl snuck out from between her lips. She wiped damp hands on the thighs of her leggings. "Hell, yeah. I can do it. I'm just not sure if I want to." Facing her friends, she said, "It's everything. Everything, guys. The weight of…of everything. What I'm losing, what we're all losing. What we've already lost."

"You're letting Morgan win." Steve fell heavily back against the counter, the dish towel he was using hanging limply at his side.

Charlie went deeper. "Josh won't get past this latest shit without you, Jessie. You know that."

"Duh, Charlie, Josh caused this latest shit. On your set. Short memory, much?"

Raring up for a fight, Charlie threw her sarcastic haughtiness right back at her. "How the hell can you still be angry at him? How much of this was his fault, huh Jessie? Take it back to the day he found out his entire family was kidnapped. How much of that was Josh's fault?"

"Ahhhh, Charlie!" she cried. "I'm so sick of blaming and hurting and being angry and worrying! I just want to feel happy again."

"You're happy with Josh," Steve cut in. "Deliriously. Stop fucking poor helpless Matt around—"

"And Shanda," Charlie fumed, all too happy to gang up on Jessie on Josh's behalf. "You never think about who you're bowling over. You just take and take and take and push away any thoughts of who you might be hurting."

"Do the right damn thing here." Like a big brother telling his younger sister to get her shit together, Steve's demand was final.

Pissed at this conjoined effort to push her in a direction in which she was literally terrified to go, Jessie was gearing up for a nasty rebuttal when she heard a noise behind her. Whipping around, she saw Matt wander into the room, his hurt eyes as serious as she had ever seen them. Cradled in one arm was Dylan, choking back sobs and wiping a hand over damp cheeks. David was at his side, clinging to Matt's left hand but using his free hand to repeatedly shove long hair back behind his ear. The visual reminder of Josh disarmed Jessie every time she saw David copy his father's actions. David's cheeks were glistening in the light. Whatever set the boys off, it was bad enough to bring on waterworks.

Jessie hunkered up her shoulders and adopted a stoic mask on her pinched face. Uncertain, she let her eyes float up to meet Matt's, wondering, at the same time, how much he'd seen at the UBC house earlier that day. She'd spotted the lemon tea, but it was still sitting where he left it, on her kitchen island at home, untouched, left to grow stale and cold.

Charlie, Steve, and Jessie were silent. All of them were nervous as they considered just how much Matt might have just overheard, although both Charlie and Steve almost immediately chucked their concern into the waste bucket and hardly cared. Shanda's worried voice on the phone to Charlie that day pissed him off enough to not give a shit about how Matt was feeling right now. The guy should have known better than to fall prey to Jessie's fear and land back in bed with her. Both Charlie's and Steve's major concern was for Josh, their good buddy, whom they both missed and worried about on a daily basis.

Jessie reached for Dylan. Her young son turned from her and buried his face in Matt's warm neck. "What happened?" she finally asked, choosing to rub the little boy's back since he didn't seem too interested in taking more comfort than that from her at the moment. Jessie bent down to David, her usually quiet boy, although when all was said and done, all three of the Sawyer children generally operated on a low volume, so accustomed were they to hushed voices and worry and fear.

"Dylan didn't like what I did." Bravely, David clung to Matt's hand and faced his mother with an angry resolve.

"Mmm?" Jessie encouraged, eye-to-eye with him now as, next to her, Dylan tucked his hands under his belly and sobbed quietly into Matt's comfy neck. "What did you do?"

A big sigh from his toes to his nose was David's way of saying *I'm done talking about this.* Turning to Matt, he let his forehead rest against the trusted big hand, if only to avoid looking into his mother's always-sad eyes.

That was warning enough for Jessie to know that whatever happened between the boys, it was beyond the norm of their usual brotherly scuffles. "It's okay, David," she said. "I won't get mad, I promise. I'd just like to understand. So maybe I can help."

David's voice was muffled and small, like it was being spoken from inside some dark tunnel. "I took his truck from him. The one that looks like Daddy's."

Jessie's heart skipped a beat. "Ummm….why, honey?"

"I didn't want to see him playing with it. That's why."

"Why not?" Now Jessie was speaking in a low tone, afraid of the answer she instinctively knew was coming. She couldn't look at Matt. All through dinner she could barely meet his eye. This now, with her children, was an extension of everything that swas already messed up with Matt; intuitively that knowing was creeping over her like a web, sticky and unrelenting, trapping her inside so that she was slowly becoming immobilized.

"Because," David elaborated, clenching Matt's big hand with both of his little boy ones now, "I hate that stupid truck. I hate it!"

If he were older, Jessie was pretty sure her son would have inserted a sincere 'fucking' in there after the word 'stupid.' *Stupid fucking truck,* she thought. *Stupid fucking Josh. Stupid fucking Morgan.* "Honey," she said to David, trying to detach him from his death grip on Matt, frustrated because neither of her two older boys seemed to want her at all, "Dylan likes the truck because it reminds him of Daddy. He needs the truck."

"Dylan's stupid. He's just a baby. He needs to grow up." Openly sobbing now, which was something David rarely did, he started to tremble.

Tears pricked at Jessie's eyes. She shifted her weight, and one knee cracked. "Ouch," she exclaimed softly.

Matt, looking down at her, wondered whether she was referencing the stiff knee or her sons' mutual pain at the loss of the man they both revered.

In a thick, heavy voice, out loud Jessie said to her son's back as she started rubbing one palm up and down it, to offer what comfort she could, "How about you kids just stay little, okay David? How about we all just believe in unicorns and magic dust a little while longer, okay?" Inside, a new fury was inserting itself, seeding and growing, and it was aimed at Matt for making her a part of this new pain, one that he was mercilessly shoving in her face that said *You see? Your boys need their father.*

Standing, knees creaking, Jessie slumped sideways into one of Deirdre's high leather chairs and grumped furiously at Matt. "I know what you're doing," she scolded him, "and just so you know, you suck." Inside she said, *you fucking suck,* but in the presence of her sons she held her tongue.

"It's bigger than us," Matt responded uselessly. "All of this. It's even bigger than a wife crying her heart out with her husband's motorcycle jacket in her arms."

Jessie's mouth opened and closed. Nearby, Charlie and Steve straightened.

"When there are kids involved, it's bigger, Jessie," Matt went on. "But not bigger the way you said it was in Stockholm. You've got it backward. It's time you saw Josh's actions for what they really were."

"What?" she cried, in the heat of the moment pushing her sons' pain aside in order to sort out her own confusion. "What, Matt? Are you gonna say that what Josh did was some kind of sacrifice? I know that already. Y'all keep hammering me over the head with that one." She rolled her eyes. "For me, for our kids, right? But why? So in the end he can prove that he's better than me? That he's a better person because he's willing to give up his life for us? Let's see how well that holds up a year from now when he's miserable because he's not working, while the roles he aches for go to Ryan Forester!"

"Jessie. Watch what you're saying."

Charlie's cautionary voice from behind her made Jessie stop and think. Twisting around to look at him, confusion colored her face. Charlie pointed to David who, when Jessie spun back around, was staring at her with a child-like innocence and hope that broke her heart.

"Ahhh!" she groaned, driving her fingers into her hair in frustration. Lowering them, she covered David's ears. Quick to respond, Matt did the same with the small boy in his arms. "It's him on one hand and all of you on the other." Jessie's eyes were flashing. "Think about what you're asking from us, from Josh. Think about the new weight he will be carrying on his shoulders. You think he's strong enough for that? To bear the brunt of dragging me and the kids away from all of you?"

Clipped footsteps rounded the corner and ended up in the kitchen. Stopping at Matt's side, Charles frowned and placed his hands on his hips. "Jessie," he chastised, "I could hear you down the hall. What these children need right now is hope, not more worry. You used to be good at dishing that out. What the hell happened?" Dylan, upon hearing his grandfather's voice, sighed and leaned over so Charles could take hold of him and gather him in close.

"Oh, for God's sake," Jessie griped. "Morgan happened. And Nadia happened. And Josh happened. Y'all need your memories rewired. They suck." She ran a hand through David's hair and sat back, saddened, when the little boy recoiled at her touch.

Throwing her a frustrated look, Matt reached down and lifted David into his arms, in Dylan's place.

"That's enough." Charles' reproachful stare was final. "It's time you moved forward. The rest of us are trying to."

Aghast, Jessie shouted, "By shoving us under some goddamned proverbial rug? Our whole entire family? That's your idea of moving forward? I can't do it! I can't fucking do it! You'll all still have each other! What'll we have? Nobody! Nobody, Charles!"

"Jesus," Charlie muttered behind Jessie. Skirting the island, he took her hand firmly in his. "To the music room. You're being banished until you cool down. And yes, I meant to say banished. Or exiled or tossed away, those words would work too. You ought to be getting used to the idea since your record seems to be stuck on that loop."

Shifting Dylan in his arms, throwing up a hand as Jessie started to move past him, Charles issued a final demand. "The language you choose to use in your own space is up to you, Jessie. In my house, with your children present—my grandchildren—you need to edit your words before you speak them. Expletives are not welcome here. Not when small ears are listening. I don't care how hard this is on you. It's ten thousand times harder on a lot of others, on others who are waiting for you to make up your mind. Burrowing back under the covers and delaying the inevitable accomplishes nothing."

"I'm here, aren't I?" she spat at him. "I'm in *your* kitchen, after making you how much money in Stockholm? Your little whore goes and makes you a ton of money that you don't even need, and then she comes home only to be reminded that this place is no longer her home, that she doesn't belong anywhere anymore! She's in oblivion, caught between two worlds, caught between two—" Jessie was going to say 'men,' but the steady tears streaming down David's cheeks stopped her short. With his left cheek resting against Matt's shoulder, he was scrutinizing her with a look of sheer disappointment and confusion washing over his face as if, for the first time, he was seeing the deepest flaws in his mother's character.

Shaking Charlie off, Jessie stormed out of the kitchen, grabbing the King Ranch keys on the way. Unsure, Charlie looked past Matt to Charles, who shook his head.

"Let her go," he said. "Let her drive it off." Charles was trembling. A hard look to Matt followed. Thoughts ran between them, tough, aching thoughts, thoughts that, for the children's sakes, needed to remain unspoken.

"I know," Matt said quietly anyway, in answer to what he easily guessed Charles was thinking. "I know, Charles." Handing David over to Charlie, he followed the thought up with, "Take him, please. Read him a happy story. Something with a happy ending, Charlie, please."

"No trucks," David demanded, his young voice holding far more spite and anger than a small boy's words ought to. "No fucking trucks."

Nobody moved.

After a bit, Matt ran his fingers through the hair at the back of David's head, upside down, shoving it upwards, as if he needed to feel the child's scalp, his essence that, for all of them, was such a visible reminder of Josh. "David," he said calmly, "we don't use that word in this house. You know that's a bad word. You heard Grampie tell your momma that she shouldn't use it, either."

"Fine," David declared from Charlie's shoulder. "But then we can't use the word truck, either. Truck's a bad word too. I hate that word."

In Charles' arms, Dylan stilled.

"Not for long," Matt said softly. "Soon, boys, truck will be a good word again." Unable to meet the eyes of Charles, Charlie or Steve, Matt shoved his hands in his pockets and left the house. He was a few minutes behind Jessie, but he didn't try to find her; he didn't text or call or search her out at her downtown condo or back at the UBC house, or even at the studio on Robson. Instead, Matt pointed his Audi toward Yaletown, toward Shanda's luxurious condo. He stayed there only a short time; eventually he made his way to his own sterile place overlooking English Bay. It was there he tossed and turned in restless sleep.

Outside, a silvery moon rose over dusky Vancouver, and whitewashed its people with light.

Chapter Twenty-nine

At didn't strike Jessie as odd when Matt texted and told her he was staying at his place. It just struck her as sad, as if they were starting to unravel now at a hurried, fast pace. She wished they'd stayed in Stockholm, maybe to travel around to explore the Scandinavian countries that, when she toured them in the past, were just a blur of anonymous cities. If it weren't for the desperate need to see her children, Jessie would have stayed, with Matt in her bed and Josh pushed somewhere deep inside where the idea of him living a lonely life in the Caribbean wouldn't hurt so damn much.

Around five a.m., just after she put Micah back down, a warm body crawled wordlessly into bed behind her. There was a time when Matt would not be accepted upstairs in La Casa's living quarters at all. Now, with the UBC house mostly packed up and the Sawyer family living in North Van with Charles and Dee, Matt took a chance, and wrapped his arms around Jessie.

Reaching back, Jessie laid a hand on his hip, just to let Matt know she was okay with him not being with her earlier, and that she was sorry about the nasty words that passed between them yesterday. In her heart she felt he had maybe gone to see Shanda, to lay some things out straight, but she didn't have it in her to ask.

His voice was gruff when he spoke to her. *He's tired. Absolutely done in,* Jessie thought, sharply reprimanding herself for being the cause of so much pain for this trusted, dear man as she felt she was for all of the people in her life now, and—well—for pretty much always.

The words he said aloud were breathed into Jessie's ear. Her eyes fluttered open when she heard them. There was an intensity to what he was asking;

for some inexplicable reason Jessie felt his question had a hidden meaning, even though it seemed disguised in a half-awake attempt to get some sunrise sex going.

"Do you touch yourself sometimes? When you think of me?" he was asking, his voice gruff but sure, as if this was something he not only wanted to know, but that he needed to know. Jessie couldn't see him since his back was to her, but if she could, she would have seen that Matt's eyes were closed, that the way his head was tilted into hers—a little above so that he was almost looking down—was his desperate way of holding onto her, of memorizing her. His body was curled into hers; Matt had drawn his knees up so that Jessie was, in some ways, inside him, inside the gentle curve and slope of his chest, his hips, his legs. Unbeknownst to her, he wanted to keep her there forever, lost to everyone but him—so she could be his, and his alone.

It was an illusion, this hopefully endless dreamlike perfection of their few days together, of this impossible future that both Jessie and Matt thought they desired. It was based on fear, on a long shared history, on the need to feel safe, and on the need to protect. Underlying all was a deep, abiding love.

What made it an illusion was also love. The deep aching kind. And it had a name—*Josh*.

A little surprised at Matt's erotic, seductive request, Jessie shifted over onto her back. With sleepy eyes, she blinked up at him. Matt let his eyes flit open; they were light in color, pale and troubled. Moons devoid of source energy. Bereft lamps with barely a flicker of flame left for warmth.

As usual, Jessie's nighttime wear these days was tank tops. They were both under the covers, but slowly, enticingly, she pushed the duvet and sheet down around her hips as she gazed at him.

Careful, cautious, as if he didn't know how she would respond, Matt lifted Jessie's right hand and laid it over her white panties. He rubbed his hand hard overtop, and swallowed as Jessie went along with him, as her fingers relaxed on her body and cupped herself. Matt's touch was light after that, gentle; with a slow, precise movement he floated his fingers upwards to the bottom of her tank top. Carefully grasping the hem, he moved first one side up so it sat just below her breast, and followed the movement up with the other side. When he was done, he tipped his face up to her and lost himself in the inquisitive, drowsy eyes he loved. Slowly, his eyes locked on Jessie's, he pushed her top up further, over one breast, and then over the other, never losing her gaze even as he reached for her free hand, lifted it, and laid it over her left breast.

"Show me," he demanded in a hushed whisper, his own tired eyes growing dusky and hard in the early morning mid-winter grayness. "I want to watch you. Come for me, sweetheart."

"I will," she almost squeaked back to him in anticipation as she parted her legs for his pleasure, "I'll come for you, baby. But you have to come for me, too." In a deliberate, gradual movement, she started to rub herself over her panties, using all of her fingers as Matt, raised on his side, leaning on his left arm, nodded his assent, and let his hand float over hers as she moved.

As Jessie's body heated up, she wriggled her hips, allowing her knees to butterfly open wider. Of their own accord, small mewls left her lips, sporadic, and blissfully sweet to Matt's ears while he watched Jessie massage her breasts, arching her back to increase her pleasure as she brought herself closer to orgasm. He kissed her fingers, her nipples, tongued her there, helping her along as she panted under his loving gaze. For both of them, the sweetness of this kind of mutual lovemaking was increased tenfold by virtue of Matt's spoken need, by virtue of his eyes on her body, and his hand going occasionally to himself as he grew hard watching his girl respond to this little game, as he watched her half-lidded, wanting eyes open and close and land on him as his hips, too, started their own undulating, rhythmic movements.

"Come for me, sweetheart," he begged, his breath hot on her body as he kissed and teased her. "Please, come for me. I need to see you. I need to feel you, to hear you."

Matt took Jessie's fingers in his, lifted them to his lips, and put them in his mouth so he could suck on them, so he could wet them before moving them back to her body and forcibly slipping them inside her panties. He let his fingers linger there, and let out a long, ragged *ahhhh* when he touched her, when his hand pushed hers aside so he could cup that hot, damp part of her. His body curved in on itself with the ecstasy of touching Jessie again this way as he whispered, "Is this for me, sweetheart? Is this for me?"

"Y-yeah," she managed, gasping, aching. "It's for you, baby. You ready? You want to go in?"

She didn't wait for his answer. Rolling onto her side, Jessie stopped ministering to herself and slid down Matt's body so she could place a hand on either side of his hips. He cried out when she took him in her mouth; then there were no words left to either of them. All that remained were guttural animal sounds, and primal instincts to love and be loved, in this, Jessie's old room at La Casa, inside a home that Matt had, for years, considered probably more of a home to himself than his own house; where he came and went as he pleased, but never to Jessie's bed where, now, he was making sweet love with her just down the hall from his employer.

When the tidal wave was upon them, cresting its way to a final need, Matt roughly hoisted Jessie away from him, pulled himself to his knees, and dropped down between her legs. The low grunts that escaped his lips were unrecognizable to him. This lovemaking was of an intensity borrowed from the hands of time, borrowed from an ending Matt didn't want that was rushing toward him with the speed of a rocket. In one rough grab, moaning and breathless, his chest heaving, he had Jessie's damp panties in his fingers; after yanking them down hard and fast, he wrapped his strong arms around her thighs, gave her a wild pull to bring her closer to him, and sank his wet mouth down onto her body.

As Jessie writhed and cried out underneath the experienced darting and licking of Matt's tongue, under his primitive moans vibrating loudly and helplessly against her, as she rocked her way to climax his earlier words echoed in her brain, catapulted inside her head—a pleading, frantic need he'd voiced as, "Come for me, sweetheart. Please, come for me."

She did. She came hard for him, sensing but not knowing for certain that he, her beloved protector, was playing some kind of game with her. Not knowing that this beautiful intimacy, this astounding, primeval pleasure—a coupling born first of need and then of friendship, infused with complete and rapturous love—was a hard farewell.

"Oh, God, Matt," Jessie cried after he moved upwards and, with one quick movement, sank himself deep into her, eliciting even more waterfalls of pleasure that zinged up and down her body, igniting every pore with fire and sending her heart rate through the roof, "Fuck! Oh, fuucckkk!!!"

When it was over there were tears, a lot of tears, accompanied by choking gasps, because Matt was rocking Jessie against him, holding her hard, quivering body as close as was physically possible, whispering little *sorrys* that she thought were for the bitter words of yesterday, and not for the burning anger to come.

The tears were Matt's. The sobs were his.

Pressing him to her, digging her nails into his back to keep him close as his convulsions slowed, Jessie was frightened; fear crept up her legs and threatened to negate the exultant, soaring endorphins that 'coming for him' had unleashed with such perfection.

"Hey, I've got you, Matt, I've got you," she murmured repeatedly into the coveted hollow of his neck and shoulder as he trembled in her arms. "Always, baby," she breathed. "You've had my back forever. I've got yours now, too."

For some odd, inexplicable reason—maybe because for so many years she was accustomed to holding another man this way after making love—somewhere in the hollow reaches of her soul, Jessie felt a stirring that brought Josh to mind. Josh, with his soulful, molten chocolate eyes; Josh, sweet and tender, a man instantly loved by animals—innocent creatures that knew a man's soul better than anyone. Josh, her husband and the father of her children (even if one was biologically, in reality, another man's son).

"Oh, God," Jessie breathed again, nascent tears of her own threatening to spill over onto Matt's cheeks, to merge with his. "Oh, sweet Jesus."

It seemed wrong, unfair, that after such a powerful coupling with Matt, the old familiar longing for Josh could come back so fast. Jessie snuggled her nose into Matt's essence, in the sweaty, musky male scent of his hair, by his ear, and disguised the yearning in short, quick gasps as her eyes, too, leaked tears of pain.

When young footprints started down the hall later, Jessie and Matt had recovered and were prepared, and were listening for the children, so Matt eased out of bed, dressed quickly, and headed to the shower in the guest room next door. He slipped off the bed without a word to explain the watershed that the morning's sunrise lovemaking had unleashed.

All through Carlotta's healthy breakfast of oatmeal pancakes, Matt barely talked and hardly met Jessie's eyes as he helped the kids with their needs. His aloof behavior concerned Jessie enough that, when she appealed to Deirdre with a look of serious concern, the older woman replied wordlessly with a knowing, creased brow. Jessie was just moving toward her to whisper a quiet, "What's up with him?" when Dee got called away by Dylan, who was throwing a little boy tantrum at the way Emily-Grace was cutting up his pancake.

The usual morning chaos at La Casa that day deflected at least some of what was bothering Matt, or at least pushed it aside based on necessity. By the time Jacob and Kayla landed to pick up the three older Sawyer children, Sam and Alin had also arrived. They ducked into Charles' office where Matt, Ulysses and Dan were by then knee deep in discussion, a discussion that Charles told Jessie was the security team 'just touching base.' Clearly Jessie wasn't invited, but she was busy enough with the kids that she shrugged the unscheduled meeting off.

Matt was the last to emerge from Charles' space. Red-eyed, serious, and bone-weary tired, he strode alongside his equally stooped boss up the long, finally quiet main hallway, scratching at new, unshaved whiskers as he walked, his eyes following the morning sunshine toward the curved mahogany door where Jessie was just setting down a small travel suitcase as she waited, perplexed, a growing uncertainty settling into her belly.

"See you in a few days, Dee," she was saying to Deirdre as Matt and Charles took hers and Matt's travel things out to the Audi. Backing out of Deirdre's embrace, she finally asked the hard question that was floating around her head all morning. "Do you think something's up? Matt's not himself."

Deirdre responded with a careful, "I'm sure he's fine, honey. Give him some time."

"I'm not getting a good vibe, Dee," Jessie replied, reaching to take Micah from the older woman's arms to settle him into his carrier. "I think he was with Shanda last night."

Deirdre's response came back edgy and sharp. "He owes it to Shanda to tell her what's happened, Jessie, between you and him. He's a man of integrity. Being with you, a married woman, while he's engaged to Shanda, would tear a man like Matt up inside."

Oh. But not me, flashed across Jessie's mind as, inwardly, Deirdre's unspoken words assaulted her. *Matt and I getting together wouldn't tear me up inside because I'm an old whore, let's remember that. Sex comes easy to me. Sex without considering consequences, without considering who gets hurt. Matt wouldn't have done shit without this old whore to entice him, to…seduce him.* She guffawed at that, knowing it was what Dee likely thought, that Jessie had 'come on' to Matt in Stockholm and not the other way around, since Matt was such a 'stand-up guy.'

The old familiar mask of shame placed its unwelcome smokescreen over Jessie's face, landing just on time for Matt to come back in and take Micah's carrier from her hand.

"Ready?" he asked, meeting her eye for pretty much the first time all day.

Jessie almost collapsed. Unsure of what to say or how to feel, she was shaken by how drained he looked when she was this close to him. She searched his eyes as if they were the secret window to his soul, as if they could be the answer to what was bothering him. Swallowing nervously, she watched him carry Micah over to the car, then abstractly touched a finger to a lip before glancing worriedly back at Dee for a rueful, final look.

"I don't have a good feeling, Dee." The echo of her earlier thought was uttered almost soundlessly, as if saying it out loud might somehow meld it into Matt's aura. Spinning slowly around on one heel, Jessie started for the open door.

Deirdre clasped her hand and exerted some pressure to get Jessie to stop moving. "Honey…I have to ask you…what about Josh?"

The tough question, posed just as Jessie was heading out of town with Matt, was unexpected. The pungent, leathery smell of Josh's leather jacket yesterday sprang back unwarranted. Jessie recalled slipping to the floor in the closet at the UBC house, burying her tears in the soft, welcoming leather. She almost lost her balance in stark, visceral remembrance.

The aristocratic Deirdre sensed that she had overstepped her boundaries, but she drew herself up tall, thrust her shoulders back, and didn't let go of her girl's hand.

"You haven't said anything before this, Dee." Jessie's voice was dangerously low. "In Stockholm, and here yesterday and this morning, you never seemed outwardly concerned about Josh. Why bring him up now?"

"You need to be sure, that's all, honey. Matt's got a heart. And it can break."

"I see. So it's not Josh's heart that's on your radar. It's Matt's." It wasn't lost on Jessie that she was now defending her husband instead of Matt. Confusion landed on her face with a haunting perplexity, in pink blushes that spotted the tops of her cheeks.

Rarely did Deirdre raise her voice with Jessie. When next she spoke, in an assertive 'listen, and listen well' tone, Jessie was almost too astonished to react. "These men you love, Jessie, they're not toys," Deirdre started. "Taking up with Matt would please Charles and I a great deal, I admit in part because it would keep you and our grandchildren close by. Life wouldn't have to change the way it would if you go to Josh. But Jessie, avoiding your husband for the wrong reasons, using Matt to hide behind the same way you hid behind Jacob when life got tough, is not going to serve anyone well in the long run. Not you, not Matt, and certainly not Josh."

Both Matt and Charles overheard the warning. For a few long, extended breaths, everybody froze. Jessie was, at the best of times, stubborn and hot-tempered, and these days were not the best of times. Yesterday in the kitchen was proof of that, not that anyone really needed a reminder. They waited to see what ball she would bounce back to Deirdre.

"I'm afraid, Dee," was what Jessie said in the end, her voice no more than a quaver in the mid-morning gray of a damp west coast winter.

With a shake of her head, Deirdre tut-tut-tutted. "That's not enough, Jessie. That's not enough reason to ask a good man like Matt to end his engagement with a woman that you and I both know he loves. To ask him to turn a blind eye on the solid foundation he's built with her, and to turn a blind eye on his own moral code, just because you're scared."

"But—"

Air palming her, Deirdre finished saying what she needed to get out on this monumental day. It hurt Jessie to see her eyes fill up, to hear Deirdre's words emerge in a thick, hurt ache as she choked up. "Charlie told us that the night you went to Josh in Calgary when he was drinking, you were beautiful with him. The kind of love you have shown that man, over and over and over, even when the rest of us could see nothing in him worth saving..." Dee sighed heavily. "If I thought you were just scared of him going off the wagon again, I'd laugh at you. I'd say 'get over yourself,' because I know you, honey, and

I know that you can handle that about Josh. You love him enough to accept that difficult part of him. I think what you are really afraid of this time, is of losing him once and for all. It's easier to build walls than it is to accept— and live with—the vulnerable parts of ourselves in which that kind of fear dwells, isn't it honey?"

"That's only part of it, Dee," Jessie choked. "Just ask Charles. And anyways, there's no guarantee. With Morgan…"

Deirdre countered hard. Tough-love was never easy, but sometimes, with this wild girl, it was an absolute necessity. "There is never a guarantee, Jessie," she responded quickly, almost pouncing on Jessie's mention of Morgan. "The only guarantee that comes with living is the one that declares an ending. For all of us. Why would you choose to give up one hour with the man you love? One minute, one second? Let me say it again—hiding behind Matt is not acceptable."

Taking a breath for courage, Deirdre dove in deeper by taking them down a path to the right. "You don't think we know, all of us, what he means to you? Matt? We know, Jessie, and maybe that's my fault, and Charles' too, for letting the two of you spend so much time together all these years that you've practically lived out of each other's pockets. For that reason, it's hard to say these things to you. But we would be doing you—and Matt, and Josh and your children—a disservice to let you carry on the way you are without speaking out. Without saying what, in our hearts, we feel."

"Oh, for fuck's sake, Dee," Jessie wailed, stomping her foot in her childish way. "Did you have to say this now? You couldn't just let me have these next few days?"

"Take them," Deirdre insisted. "Take all the time you need, and bury yourself in that man's arms, and in his heart. I hope you can live with yourself down the road, that's all. Because there's no easy way to come back from loving someone as deeply as I know you and Matt love each other, not when you step over that line the way you two have."

"Sex!" Jessie cried. "It's called sex. Or fucking, if you prefer! That's the only thing we were missing all this time, and I gotta tell you, it's pretty fucking awesome to be getting regularly fucked by this man!"

"Jessie!" Charles warned, heating up at Jessie's rather vulgar outburst toward his society wife. Matt, a silent observer, grabbed his arm to stop him from approaching the two women.

"There's no good way for this to end," Deirdre added, giving as good as she was getting. "Remember what happened with Jacob…"

"Jacob? Really, Dee? Jacob and Matt are two completely different people, with completely different roles to play in my life. Anyways, I'm so fucking sick of endings. Take your goddamned endings and shove them up your lily-white ass." Fuming, Jessie thrust her hand down and away from Deirdre's. Eyes sparking, she spun around and headed for the Audi.

Matt was shaking when he slid in behind the wheel. Just before he did, he caught Charles' eye. A slight nod passed between the two men, a nod that neither of the women noticed. It acknowledged a thousand things, including the most important of all—friendship, and trust.

Charles walked over to Deirdre and pulled her trembling body to him. Jessie and Matt both watched through the rearview mirror as the power couple disappeared from sight.

"Oh, puhhh," Jessie smoldered, sliding down lower in her seat and staring out of the window as Matt headed south toward the Lions' Gate bridge. "Jesus, Deirdre. You couldn't just let us have this, huh? For fuck's sake."

The silence in the car threatened to do them both in entirely. Annoyed at Matt's continued gray funk, Jessie flipped on the radio. She and Matt listened to The Peak all the way to the airport, both unable to find words adequate enough to cover the gamut of unruly, unwelcome emotions that were suddenly storming around their restless hearts and minds.

Chapter Thirty

The Vancouver day heated up when the sun came out a few hours later, morphing into an unexpected day of promise filled with the assurance that within a month or so gorgeous pink cherry blossoms would burst into flower. Soon the treasured blooms would line the city's streets with the kind of buoyant, natural cotton-candy art that lifts spirits and lightens souls. Kayla took advantage of the gorgeous weather, enlisted Jacob to stay with Lily for some father-daughter bonding, and called Shanda to go for a run.

They were winding down, jogging past Matt's building on the west side just past lush Stanley Park, watching sailboats navigate seamlessly around cargo ships bobbing contentedly in English Bay, when Shanda lifted a water bottle to her lips and slowed to a brisk walk. Kayla stopped, bent over her knees as she caught her breath, then caught up to her friend, sucking on a water bottle too as Shanda started to speak.

"Matt came over last night," she said rather matter-of-factly.

Kayla floundered. She and Jacob were floored by the newest development in the Keating camp. Neither expected things to ramp up with Jessie and Matt quite the way they had. "I'm really sorry, Shanda," she sighed. "I can't imagine what you're going through. I can't imagine how my big brother is going to react when he finds out. He tries so hard, and he just gets hurt and hurt and hurt again."

"So you know they've been sleeping together," Shanda said. "I guess we predicted they might go back there. Cling to each other that way."

Kayla glanced over at Shanda and wrinkled her nose. The attractive woman was far too calm for one who had likely just been soundly dumped.

"Look, Jessie's a handful," she admitted. "She's pissed me off more times than I can count, and in my opinion there's no defending her actions. She's a solo creature, she always has been, and she always will be. Her Highness doesn't always see the repercussions of her actions."

"She acts on fear, Matt says, as much as she spouts otherwise. She lets it take control of her." Shanda took a sideways look at her running mate. "Aren't you being a little hypocritical here?"

"What, L.A.? Jacob and me, the threesome?" Kayla shrugged. "You heard her that day. She needed a respite from the pain. Me and Jacob gave her that respite. It was a one time thing. Josh hurt her pretty bad. He threw everyone for a loop that day. It wasn't just about her, that night."

Skipping over the Josh part, Shanda elaborated on the first part of Kayla's admission. "That's what Matt says he's doing. Helping her through the pain."

"Jesus, Shanda," Kayla said, overtly startled at Shanda's seemingly composed acceptance of this latest harsh development. "You must be a goddess if you're taking all this in stride. Either that or you're one of those people that keeps all the shit in and then violently, suddenly, erupts." She stopped walking, thrust a hand down onto a hip, and faced her friend. "I don't suppose you're planning some diabolical revenge, are you?" Morgan shot through her mind. All of a sudden Kayla felt like puking, and it wasn't because of the energetic sprint at the end of the run.

"I don't need to take my revenge," Shanda replied softly. "I hate to say this, because I know you care about her, but Jessie's about to get what I think she deserves, Kayla. Let me just say she'll have her time to mourn. And then for your brother's sake, I hope she pulls herself together."

"For Josh's sake? Shanda? What about Matt?"

"He'll be okay. He'll be just fine." Shanda resumed her comfortable quick, post-run pace.

Kayla trotted along behind for a few seconds, before running ahead of Shanda and jogging backward so she could face her.

"What do you know that I don't know?" To herself, she pleaded, *Please please please.* The image running through her mind was that of her brother alone and lonely in this new exiled life he was forced to live.

A slow curve started in the corner of Shanda's lip. Lifting the water bottle to her mouth, she took a few good gulps before lowering it, wiping a few excess water drops off her chin, and meeting Kayla's eyes with a dangerous glint in her own. "I get why Matt went back down that road with her," she confessed. She stopped walking again so Kayla could draw to a halt as well. There were a gazillion people on the scenic path today—Kayla barely avoided bumping into two or three cyclists, although she was good-natured at ignoring the curses they tossed in her direction. "I can't say I'm surprised that it happened. He's a good, kind man. He loves her. He really does. She's confused as hell, and he opened his arms to her. But as long as I live, Kayla? I hope I never have to lay eyes on Jessie Wheeler-Sawyer ever again."

Shanda wasn't the rock Kayla thought she was. Knuckling a quick, escaped tear away from one pretty eye before she raised her chin, she bypassed Kayla, and started jogging once again.

～ ～

The first clue Jessie got that her world was going back into some sort of messed-up spin cycle was when the small Cessna four-seater airplane she and Matt were taking on the last leg of their journey dipped its wings over a bleached white beach house nestled into a cozy cove on a pristine cobalt blue bay. It wasn't so much the beach house that got to her, or the dipped wings, which seemed like some kind of signal (*I've watched way too many movies,* she told herself); no, it was the speedboat docked at a wooden pier that got her heart racing. It was yellow and white, and the name Bayliner was stenciled in large letters on the bow.

Lots of people down here have Bayliners, she thought to herself as she started twisting ringlets in her hair. *It's a well-known pleasure boat brand.* Still, it was evident that the island Matt was taking her to was not large—it was an isolated paradise, he'd told her on the jet, which they left two islands back for the smaller island hopper. There were not, as far as Jessie could see, many other large homes on this island. The ones within view were isolated and lonesome looking. Saliva collected in her mouth. She almost forgot to swallow. Next to her, Matt wrapped his fingers in hers and exerted some pressure. He was sweaty, and still too damn quiet for Jessie's liking. Inwardly, she tensed.

The boat's a coincidence, she said over and over, afraid to look at Matt. *It's okay. It's fine.*

Someone had left a small local car for them at the tiny airstrip beyond the local village. After thanking their pilot, Matt secured Micah in the back seat and started to walk toward the hood so he could skirt it, and slip behind the wheel on the driver's side. Jessie was standing by the passenger door, watching him. She grabbed his arm when he moved to go by her.

"Hey," she said, demanding his attention, her flimsy mid-thigh white cotton sundress blowing in the island breeze. She flipped her sunglasses up on top of her head and frowned. "You need to start talking to me, Matt Kelly. I don't like this silent treatment. It sucks big time." Reaching for him, she tried to grab his sunglasses so she could remove them and see his eyes, so she would have a better sense of what he was thinking, of what he was feeling, but he wasn't having it.

Matt gripped her wrist and yanked her hand down. "In the car," he demanded brusquely before striding away.

"What the hell?" Jessie muttered, a new panic overtaking her. Slowly, she put one leg into the car and then the other, and then she pulled her door shut. Matt was already behind the wheel, firing up the dusty little car by the time she got settled. It was a standard transmission. Whipping it into gear, he spun the tires and pulled away from the earthy airstrip.

Twenty minutes later, still not speaking, he slid to a stop outside the white beach house that Jessie had spotted from the air. Reality rocketed between Jessie's eyes when she saw, for the first time in more than four months, her old Downtown Eastside friend, Arnie. He was sitting on the outside stoop, waiting for them it seemed, since he didn't appear in the least surprised.

"Oh, Jesus," Jessie breathed. "Jesus Christ, Matt. You fucking fucked up fucker. I fucking hate you." Closing her eyes, she forced the wetness that was quickly accumulating in each scared baby blue to stay put. One set of fingernails dug deeply into the back of the other hand. She didn't move.

Matt didn't move either, at least not at first. Arnie wasn't coming any closer; the stoop he was sitting on was about six feet from the door of the house. Clearly he was simply waiting for them to make their entrance. Watching him, Matt spoke quietly. "I saw you yesterday at the UBC house. With Josh's leather motorcycle jacket in your arms."

A slow tear escaped anyway. Angry, Jessie fisted it away and tossed her head with spite drawn from some inner resolve of strength. "So," she seethed, "you pulled a Josh Sawyer and made a unilateral decision to dump me down here. So you can go back to fucking Shanda and I can start to rot. That's what that was about early this morning? The whole 'do you touch yourself when you think of me' bullshit? Committing fucking me to memory, were you?"

Saying nothing, Matt laid a hand on the door handle and made his exit. Standing next to the car, he planted his expensive shoes a shoulder's width apart in the warm Caribbean earth and dropped both hands to his hips. His gaze was focused staunchly on Arnie, who remained seated at attention, but still.

With a bitter resolve, Jessie allowed her eyes to open. Micah was starting to fuss; she would need to feed him before his cries became open-mouthed wails. Part of her wished she were him so she could just open her mouth and scream.

Arnie looked good, all tanned and robust. Somewhere, niggling in her soul, Jessie realized she was glad to see her old friend. A hug from good ole Arnie would sure be nice right about now...

Down at the house, a roguish, tanned figure stepped slowly out of an open doorway into the bright sunlight. Barefoot, in his usual faded jeans— entirely too hot for this scorching day—Josh appeared, nervously ducking his head and hiding behind long, ragged layers of sun-highlighted chestnut hair. Sucking in a breath, Jessie straightened. She let the breath out in a long, slow exhalation and stopped damaging her skin with her fingernails. Opening the car door, she stood and took three steps forward, resting one hand on the hot vehicle for balance, before seeing Josh look up and, from a distance, meet her eyes.

Without meaning to, Jessie gasped and lifted both of her hands to her face. Covering her mouth, she moved past the front of the car around to the driver's side, and stopped in front of Matt, her back to Josh and Arnie.

Lifting Matt's sunglasses off his nose was easier this time, because he didn't fight her. He let her see his eyes, let her see into his soul, into exactly how damn rotten he was feeling. There were tears in his eyes now, too. Choking, gasping, Jessie lifted a hand and smudged them away with a thumb.

He spoke first. "You and Josh..." Matt shook his head slowly from side to side. "Deirdre was right. I'm a good place to hide behind. And I think," he shifted his feet in the dirt, "I think I was hiding behind you too. It felt safe there. With you. Like I could protect you so much better as long as I had you close by." He sniffed, and looked away to catch his breath, his wits, before he spoke again. Jessie gave him the time he needed, and placed his sunglasses on the top of his head. At the same time, she lovingly ran her fingers through his longer Shanda-inspired hair. "I think what I've had to realize, Jessie," he added, struggling to remain in control, "is that there's one thing about you that I can't protect. That I've never had control over. Not really." Lifting a hand out of a pants pocket, he placed it on her chest, over her heart.

"Nobody ever gives me a choice." Jessie laid her hand over his, but didn't let her eyes leave his. "Not the kind of choice I want, anyway. Why, Matt? Why now? Why couldn't we have tried?"

"Because, Jessie. You need this man. And he needs you. And I need…" He gulped. "I need to not live every day of the rest of my life wondering whether I did the right thing by taking you away from him."

"Like you won't be wondering now, wondering whether or not you and I might have had a chance?"

Matt let a thumb trail down her cheek. "You're forgetting, Jessie, that I've had years of watching you with Josh. Of watching the two of you duke it out sometimes, but always coming back together and getting lost in each other. You may not know it now, kid, but when the pain starts to go away, as every day gets easier, you'll see that Deirdre is right, and that I'm right. Your place is here with your husband."

As Jessie digested that, unable to counter in any way that made sense, Matt took a deep breath for strength and turned to lift Micah's carrier out of the car. He set it at their feet and lifted the baby out of it as, in the courtyard below, Josh straightened. Holding Micah close, Matt brushed his lips against the tiny forehead before handing him to his mother. "Jessie, look, two weeks, okay?" he said. "Give it two weeks. If it's just not working, if you're miserable and need a rescue, then or anytime after that, you can come home. I can always come get you if you need me to. Okay?"

Numb, she sniffled, and nodded.

Matt sighed. "Josh and Arnie have a stash of unregistered, untraceable burner phones, and I put a few more in your bag this morning. In the meantime, Charles and I talked. We're bringing Emily-Grace, David and Dylan down in a week, after you've had some time to adjust. Dee will be with us; when we fly home the next week, you can come too, if you need to. This isn't final. You're not in exile."

"I needed some time to prepare, Matt. You just…all of you…you're dumping me off like a bag of garbage." There were more tears, now. Proud, tossing her hair again in her angry way, Jessie held her child close and stared daggers at the man who had watched over her forever, it seemed. Who saved her life—twice.

"Go," he whispered, pulling her close and running his fingers through her hair, trying to soak her up just one last time, that beloved lavender scent and the fresh, sweaty smell of her in the tropical heat. "Go introduce that baby to his father. Find it in yourself to forgive Josh for what he did. Find it in yourself to completely understand what kind of honor and true, true love it takes for a man to sacrifice himself in order to save what he loves the most."

"Sacrifice? Is that what you're doing too, Matt? Because I don't want you to. I don't want you to go. I love you."

"I love you too," he returned. Running his lips along her face, by her eye, down her cheek, Matt cupped her chin, let his mouth land at her tender, pink lips, and kissed Jessie with as much passionate love and truth as he could muster.

And, because after that there was nothing left to say, and no courage or strength left to say anything anyway, Matt walked around the car, removed Jessie's bags and the baby's things, then got back into the car and started the engine.

It was Arnie who walked up behind Jessie and took her trembling shoulders in his, who turned her around to face the beach house. He held her, but only for a moment. He nodded at Matt, saluted him, and watched as Matt backed out of the yard and turned the car around.

Later, Jessie didn't recall whether Matt stayed close by to watch her reunion with Josh. She couldn't recall the sound of the car puffing its way back down the road. Arnie stayed away from the house for a few minutes. As far as Jessie knew he went for a walk to give her some time, or maybe he jumped in with

Matt for a catch-up, she had no clue, because all of a sudden her mind was completely focused on her husband.

Josh didn't come toward her; he was witness to the passionate kiss by the car and knew that he would have to wait for her to come to him. He was well versed on the fact that Jessie and Matt's relationship had quite abruptly leveled up. Arnie had sat him down for a talk last night, and Matt himself had shared some inklings of deep feelings over a phone call yesterday, although Josh didn't really get the gravity of the change that had transpired in their lives until he was witness to the impossibly hard goodbye.

It seemed like forever but was really only a moment before Jessie stood unsmiling before him on trembling legs in her virginal white sundress, with girlish flip-flops on her feet, a hot, breezy wind in her hair, and trails of indignant, dejected tears on her cheeks. Protesting the sun and with a growling belly, Micah, in his mother's arms where Matt had placed him, was demanding attention.

A slow smile lightened Josh's troubled eyes. Tentative, he reached out a finger and touched his son's baby-soft face for the first time. "Hello, little Micah," he murmured. "It's nice to finally meet you."

"He's hungry," Jessie pouted, fighting for control of her emotions. Josh, in front of her, was so fucking adorable and sweet and sexy and sad and worried that she thought she might collapse. Worse, he was real, so damn real, and alive and healthy now, and tanned and muscular, and his eyes were filled with love, the real, true, solid dependable kind, not the frightened, secretive kind she knew from back at the ranch the summer before he was shot. "Oh, God," she gasped, and leaned into him, temporarily forgetting Matt and how much it would soon hurt to realize how gone he was now, from her family, and from her life.

Josh took his wife in his arms and breathed her in. He breathed as deeply as he could so he could absorb her essence the same way Matt did before he let her go, as if the two men were melding their energy in her aura. Too, it was as if what Matt gave back to Jessie was, at least in part, now being taken by Josh; it was an exchange of sorts, a truce and capitulation by one man, a clear victory by another, with a scared, lonely woman lost and floating somewhere in the middle.

When Josh's arms encircled Jessie for the first time in months, her knees gave way. She had the sense to hold onto Micah, but with the fingers of her left hand she clutched at her husband's T-shirt and dampened it with her tears. All the while she cried, she felt tremors rock Josh's body too. Words were reaching her ears—Josh's voice, soothing, calming. "It's okay, Jessie. It's okay now. We're okay."

Strength personified.

He followed it with, "I won't let you down anymore, Jessie. Never again. You'll see. I promise."

Standing back, still in Josh's strong arms but giving him a little space, Jessie fisted away the last of her tears, relinquished Micah to his father, forced away her sorrow and walked, in the safety of Josh's shadow, into her new home.

Chapter Thirty-one

Meals were quiet in the Caribbean beach house that week. Outings in the speedboat were quiet, wanderings along the shore were quiet and lazy afternoons by the pool were downright silent. At least from Josh's and Jessie's perspectives they were. Kalon spent most of his time in town with the woman he met at the Salty Dog; he didn't dare bring her to the house in the odd chance that, once she saw Josh and Jessie together, something would click and she would recognize them. Arnie found things to do, like hanging out at the bar talking with Jarvis. There were locals around but he was careful and didn't want to take a chance on really getting to know anyone else.

Near the end of the week, the day before Charles and Dee were expected back with the children, Arnie plunked down by Jessie at the pool. She was sitting in the shade, reclining on a big chaise, sipping on a cold sweet tea that Jacob once showed her how to make—Talia's Nashville legacy—and generally avoiding Josh who was, at the moment, in the bedroom rocking Micah, putting him down for a nap.

Arnie got right to the point. "You haven't had much to say this week."

Jessie set her glass down on a table at her side and adjusted the gold sarong she was wearing over her white bikini. She, too, didn't mince words, although she avoided Arnie's eyes when she spoke. "Have you been talking to him?"

"To Matt, I presume? Yes. Some."

Looking down, Jessie started idly scraping at flaking polish on a left fingernail. Irritated, she grumped because there was nothing in the beach house that could remove the old polish, no acetone of any kind, and none in the rustic village. It seemed nobody in the immediate vicinity wore any kind of nail polish, regular or gel or otherwise. She was stuck with what she had, at least until Deirdre arrived with a rescue kit. "Is he okay?" she asked.

"Not really, no," Arnie said. "But he will be."

"You know what my problem is, Arnie?" With a light scoff, Jessie let herself meet her friend's concerned gaze. He was facing her, sitting on a chaise a few feet away from Jessie, the one Josh just vacated with baby Micah in his arms a few moments ago.

Arnie treated her to a careful half-smile. "We all have problems, Jessie."

"Well," she harumphed, "mine is that I fall in love too easily."

"I don't see that," he counseled wisely. "It took years for you to fall under Matt's spell. To get caught up in his aura."

"No, it didn't," she disagreed, with a vehemence that surprised Arnie. "It just took years for me to act on it. I had other distractions. Matt and I were connected from the first moment we looked into each other's eyes."

Arnie had to be vigilant with what he said. Raising his head a little so he could see better, he peeked cautiously over Jessie's shoulder to the open sliding door of the master bedroom where Josh was rocking Micah. It was only about ten feet behind Jessie's left shoulder, angled out to a more private part of the deck. Jessie saw Arnie look guardedly toward the bedroom; she twisted around so she could see behind her as well. The door was clearly in sight. Colorful orange and green patterned curtains wafted on the rise and fall of the day's tropical gusts, but Josh wasn't visible.

Sighing, she turned back around and started grating at the cracked nail varnish again.

Arnie aired his thoughts. "Matt loves you deeply, Jessie. He's a good, honorable man who is smart enough to recognize that now is just not the right time for the two of you to be together. This lifetime may not provide the time. You need to see that too, and let him go."

"It's not like I don't love Josh, Arnie. That's the thing. I fell so hard and fast for him that I've been blind. Charles and Dee knew it, Charlie knew it, Jacob knew it. Even Kayla recognizes that her brother has tough issues that a lot of women would have left behind a long time ago."

Tough, streetwise Arnie's voice got soft. "And all of those people you just mentioned also long ago recognized the capacity you have for loving him through the difficult times, Jessie."

"You walked out on him." In one quick motion, Jessie hoisted her body back so she could sit taller, and she latched her heated eyes on Arnie's. He was sorry to see that the usual loving sea-pearl blues were suddenly impenetrable gunmetal gray stone.

"Yes, I did." He recoiled. "He was asking for something I couldn't see to give him. I could see no way out, Jessie. Josh was the only one of all of us who was willing to take a risk that big. Your husband understands love, Jessie. He understands sacrifice."

She deflated. The eyes lost their intensity and faded into a dejected cerulean blue. At the same time, Jessie's shoulders slumped forward over her body. "Sometimes I can see it that way," she said. "Sometimes I can't." Jessie dropped the hand with the cracking polish that she'd been fiddling with and used her other hand to reach for Arnie's fingers. Entwining her more delicate fingers around his, she added, "I will say, though, that I think Josh looks better, Arnie. More at peace here in this incredible place. But honestly I can't see it lasting. I'm already going crazy down here. There's nothing to do. He will want to get back to work. But he can't."

Trying to remain agreeable, encouraging, Arnie said, "You need your guitar, girl. Dee's bringing it."

"We have no piano. What will the kids do? They'll have no friends to play with, and no way will I be able to get Emily-Grace in the water, not after what happened to us. No dance lessons, no people who love them, nothing." She raised their entwined hands and tapped on Arnie's thigh for emphasis. "What about you, honey? What about Lucie? She thinks you're dead! What about all those people on the Downtown Eastside who count on you to help them? They held a candlelight vigil for you. Did you know that?"

"I'm touched. I really am, Jessie. But you know something? I needed a break from the sadness too."

"A hard guy like you? Pshaw! You're a brick wall. Sadness bounces off you before you even feel it, Arnie."

"That so?" Grinning, he gave her fingers a squeeze. "Not when it comes to you, Jessie. You have a way of getting under a man's skin. That's why it has to be up to you to let a certain man go."

"Back to Matt, are we?" She *pfffdddd*. "I miss him, Arnie." The baby blues were watering now. "Can I tell you something?"

"Of course." His rueful grin flipped upside down and gave his heart a good wrench at the same time.

Jessie's eyes were pleading, begging, when next she spoke. "Matt told me to take two weeks. He said I can still come home if I want to."

Arnie paused. "No, Jessie. Don't. Please. Give yourself some time. That's not nearly long enough to try to get close to Josh again, not after..."

"Sometimes I think I'm being selfish, Arnie. Other times I think I'd be doing the right thing, for me, for our kids, to go back to Matt, to build a life with him. That I've been selfish all along trying to hang on to Josh, to a man that unpredictable." Conspiratorially, she leaned sideways and whispered, "We haven't even made love. I've been here almost a week and I can't bring myself to touch him that way. So many scars…most of them because of me." Glistening, Jessie's eyes were like the pool laid out in front of them now, mirrored and hard, as if with one good pinprick they'd ripple and open up and pour water from the heavens, if she allowed herself to feel, if Jessie allowed herself the guts to let Josh back in.

"What are you scared of, Jessie?" Arnie's big shoulders tightened as he listened. He knew all about allowing oneself to get close to Josh, and about how much it hurt to walk away from him, as he did when Josh was so desperate back in Calgary.

Jessie scratched her chin as she thought for a minute, and eased back into the center of the chaise so she could reflect on the peaceful pool before her as she talked. "I'm scared that he'll get bored, that it'll lead to him getting angry. That he'll start drinking again, or using, maybe. Take his frustration out on our kids. I don't know…we have a lot of years ahead of us. We have a new baby, which means a lack of sleep and frayed nerves."

Arnie cut into her fears. "Did you know that when you came to see me that day so long ago on the Downtown Eastside looking for a gun, that I was feeling useless? That I was drinking?"

Surprised, Jessie's eyes darted back to him. "I remember seeing bottles around your place. I just figured you'd had some people over, or that Lucie was drinking. It didn't mean you were drinking."

"I was. A lot. I was going through a time that I just felt adrift. A lot of alcoholics occasionally go off the wagon, Jessie."

"You've always said you were clean from the time you gave up drinking. I don't know why you'd lie about that."

"Pride, kid. That's why. Nobody likes to let others see the cracks. And," Arnie let go of Jessie's hand and playfully tweaked her nose with a finger, "I don't think that's what you're afraid of, anyway. Not really."

"I see. So what in your almighty opinion am I afraid of, Arnie?"

"I'm in agreement with the others. You love him too much. Josh. You can't stand to see him hurting, because it hurts you too. And now with the children starting to get older, you have to watch them hurt too as they begin to realize their father is not perfect. But worse," Jessie wriggled uncomfortably under Arnie's truths but held his gaze as he added, "loving someone that much is like its own death sentence. You spent years before you met Josh being closed to other people, not letting anyone in. It's easier to start slinking back into your secure little hidey hole than it is to open yourself up to Josh again. The second you bring him back to you, the second you let him back in, you're vulnerable again. Big time."

"And I'm safe with Matt. I know that, Arnie. Just thinking about Josh breaks my heart. Seeing him on the ground writhing in pain trying to breathe after he was shot…and finding out that he set it up himself…" It took Jessie a few minutes to get her breathing back under control after airing that excruciating reality to the world. The old anxiety had a way of sneaking in and taking her hostage. After a moment, she continued as Arnie listened with both ears wide open, "I swear to God. I want to do it, to be here for him, and you're right, of course you're right, and Matt and Deirdre were right too, but I think what everybody keeps leaving out, what everybody's forgetting, is that I'm not that strong. Yeah, I preach forgiveness and I swear I get why he did it, I do, but all of you need to stop and give your heads a shake. Arnie," Jessie swung her legs off the side of the chaise so she could face him square on, "this isn't over. Hiding out down here doesn't change a damn thing! One day we will be recognized and Morgan will find out that Josh is still alive.

It's like it was with Deuce McCall! Only worse, because even if Morgan dies some day there will still be other minions around to carry out his vicious vengeance. We'll be looking over our goddamn shoulders for our entire lives if I stay with Josh. Me, him, and the kids. All four of them! This is what all of you are forgetting. This is why I'm so damn scared to let him back in. This is what breaks my heart when I look at him, when he stands before me in his rumpled T-shirts and messy hair and the saddest eyes I've ever seen on this entire goddamned planet."

Standing, Jessie had one last thing to fire at her Downtown Eastside friend before she walked away. "And nothing your guy Vaughn at Brody Pen can discern or learn from Morgan now holds any ground for our future. Everything's subject to change the first time one of our kids makes a mistake and lets the truth of who we are slip. By the way, tell Vaughn he's never getting his song. He engineered this deal for my husband, right? Through Lucie and through Vaughn's woman, Murphy? No song for him. Ever."

Turning toward the house to go, Jessie stopped short and took a frantic step backward. Sucking in a breath, she froze and curled her hands into fists at her sides. Blinking, swallowing repeatedly, her pulse almost stopped at the sight of Josh in the open arched doorway of the beach house, watching her, listening.

Josh was leaning against the center arch, hands shoved deep in his pockets as he watched her step backward, as he watched the comprehension that he'd just overheard her wash over Jessie like a tidal surge on a stormy day. His expression was fixed, but it wasn't hard and stony like hers was earlier, instead the liquid chocolate eyes Jessie so deeply loved were organic, moving, like little rivers flowing daintily over polished pebbles that glistened in the afternoon heat.

"You're wrong," he said to his wife as, behind her, Arnie stood and wondered what he could possibly do to help make things better between this couple that he and a lot of others cherished so dearly. "I don't have the saddest eyes. You do."

Jessie rocked back on her heels and let the truth of that sink in before she answered. When she did, she raised her chin and spouted back, "Only when it comes to you, Josh. Somehow I manage to be happy around other people."

"What is it you're really saying, Jessie? That I'm finally too much for you?" Lifting a hand, Josh rifled it through his long hair and, with a nervous lick of his lips, dared her to be brutally honest.

"What I'm saying, Josh—" Jessie stopped, as if she wasn't sure she should pull the trigger on the disgraceful bullet that was rolling around and around on her tongue. Blankly, she stared at the aforementioned sad eyes and wondered if the hurt with which she wanted to disembowel the man who owned them could possible equal the hurt he unleashed on her on a horrifying September Alberta day.

Arnie recognized Jessie's nasty, threatening tone and the closed fists, and so he closed his eyes and groaned before she even continued. "Don't, Jessie," he warned uselessly. He knew she wasn't holding back when he saw her throw her weight staunchly, evenly, to both feet so she had solid ground to stand on.

Jessie let 'er rip with a force that choked Josh and sent him under cover of their bedroom for much of the rest of the day. "What I'm saying, Josh," she repeated, for emphasis, "is that when I have sex with Matt and he comes hard inside me, so fucking hard like he really, really wants me, my heart doesn't break into a million pieces like it does with you." She thumped a hand against her chest for emphasis. "That's what I'm saying. A hundred thousand pieces, maybe, but not a million. I can't do it. I can't love you that way anymore. It was hard enough with Matt. Love just hurts too goddamned much."

Stomping past him, she gave him a hard shoulder shove when she went by. Josh almost stumbled, but he caught his balance and whipped around when Jessie, completely ignoring the fact that Josh had just gotten their baby down for his nap, raised both hands to her head, clutched great clumps of her hair, and screamed, "I need a drive! I need a fucking drive!"

The only car they had was in town in Kalon's care at the moment, and even if it was close by, it was a stuttery little thing with a crappy stereo. Jessie was gasping now, in the midst of a real classic Jessie Wheeler meltdown. Frantically pacing the room in small and large circles, she was losing her battle with this latest anxiety.

Josh didn't hesitate. Narrowing his eyes, he marched to the kitchen, yanked open a junk drawer, and grabbed a set of keys with a spongey yellow duck attached to them. Striding angrily toward Jessie, he thrust them into her hand and forcibly wrapped her fingers around them. "There," he stormed at her, "drive. That little yellow duck? It's meant to keep the keys floating in case you decide to toss them overboard. You remember how to operate a speedboat, right? We had one that blissful summer we spent on P.E.I.?" He started to walk toward the bedroom, leaving her staring at the keys, stunned, but then Josh whipped back around. "She's got a helluva stereo in 'er, Jessie, but you better get used to country music. It's either that or spicy Cuban down here. And you can't use your iTunes cuz of the GPS. My bad. Sorry. Country or Cuban. Take your pick." The door slammed hard behind him. A second later, Micah started to howl.

"Oh, for fuck's sake," Jessie wailed, looking up from the keys to see Arnie shaking his head in a forlorn, hopeless way. Jessie started for the wooden dock but halted when Arnie started to move toward her. "No! I don't want company!" Raising a hand to sternly air palm him, she flushed, embarrassed, when he opened the lid of an outdoor storage bin and tossed a life jacket at her.

"Be home in time for dinner," he ordered without gusto. "I'm making pasta."

~ ~ ~

Two hours later Jessie still wasn't back, but from the rocking chair in the bedroom where he was chewing his nails in frustration, Josh could see the little boat bobbing near the right side point of land in their little cove. Obviously Jessie'd figured out how to put the anchor down. He could see her reclining in the center of the back seats, feet up and face tilted up to the sun. Guilt made his belly cringe when it occurred to him that the sunscreen he usually kept on the boat had been inadvertently removed to poolside the day before. Josh actually found himself half wishing Jessie would get sunburned so she would have a different kind of pain to focus on for a few days.

His wish came true when Jessie straggled home red and burnt an hour later. It would be full out dark soon; the sun was starting to say goodnight by dipping behind pink puffed clouds, and the willowy wings of ocean birds were coasting on a fresh evening breeze. Arnie, Josh and Kalon—who was home for dinner—were silent companions, tiptoeing around each other when Jessie was back in the house. Micah, however, was furious. His

301

hungry little belly wasn't impressed with his mother's stubborn tardiness. The men were all relieved when Jessie finally took him to her breast.

That night, Jessie and Josh slept in the same bed, but back to back. When Jessie got up at one in the morning to feed Micah again, almost too sunburnt and sore to hold him against her body, Josh got up too, retrieved a bottle of aloe vera from the en suite washroom, and dropped down onto the ottoman in front of the rocking chair. Squeezing green gel out onto his fingers, he patiently smoothed it onto his wife's burnt skin, melding it into the tears on her cheeks as she remorsefully telegraphed a succession of silent *sorrys,* with the saddest eyes Josh had ever seen.

Chapter Thirty-Two

An apprehensive truce reigned over the uneasy beachfront household when, at noon the next day, Charles and Deirdre landed at the door with the three oldest Sawyer children. The news that they would see their long lost father today was brand new to the kids—on the jet, Grammie and Grampie lovingly told them he was alive, that their mother was with him, and that their daddy could hardly wait to see his children.

All three were nervously clinging to Grammie and Grampie when they left the cars and made their way into the outer courtyard. Chiding herself for looking past her babies for Matt, whom Jessie simply expected would be along on this trip, Jessie had to force herself to refocus when he didn't appear. Kneeling, she took all three kids into her arms at once.

"Where's Daddy? Where's Daddy?" Dylan was vibrating with anticipation.

Jessie smoothed back his dark Jacob-curls. "He's in the house, sweetheart. He wanted to give me a minute with all of you in case you had any questions before you see him."

"Does he look the same?" David was doing his best mini-Josh imitation, switching his weight anxiously from one foot to the other while peering at his mother from behind long layers of chestnut hair. Jessie wondered whether Micah would also always resemble his father in appearance and mannerisms. A sudden tug pulled at her heartstrings. Dylan would always be the odd child out, with his curly hair and cobalt blue Jacob-eyes. Oddly enough, he was also the child most attached to Josh. He would need Josh more than the others would, likely, as time went on, or would he end up pushing Josh away as the world got tougher on him for being Jacob's child? Jessie shook her head. Those questions and hard accusations might never come up again. Life in exile might offer them that one small perk.

Standing, Jessie felt Emily-Grace lean into her as her small fingers wound around her mother's. Behind her, Deirdre and Charles ushered the two boys inside. Jessie saw Sam and Alin coming down the walk with suitcases in hand. Beyond them was Carlotta, and beyond her? Only an endless, empty, blue tropical sky.

Matt hadn't come on the trip.

A bitter taste filled Jessie's throat. She almost gagged.

Emily-Grace wiggled her fingers to get her mother's attention. "Momma, Stella said her daddy told her we're not going to see them again for a while. That we're gonna live here. Are you or Daddy making a movie here?"

Reeling at that bit of news, Jessie fired a few invisible daggers at her good friend. *Charlie, you suck,* she fumed. *You couldn't have waited until my daughter was gone before her world was shattered?* "No movies. No work," she said aloud. "Just a holiday of sorts. Daddy's here, baby. Isn't that something? We're so lucky to have found him again. We're so lucky that he's okay."

"So his plane didn't crash." Emily-Grace was trying to wrap her mind around the impossible.

"Apparently not." Jessie swallowed her hurt over Matt's inability to face her, and pivoted around so she could lead her timid daughter inside. "I guess miracles do happen."

"God was watching out for him, Momma. God does that. He watches out for us. He knows what's best."

Stopping in her tracks, Jessie looked down at her daughter. There was a satisfied air in Emily-Grace's countenance, in the way she was allowing a small smile to form on her rosebud lips. Struck dumb by her child's gentle wisdom, Jessie tousled her darkening blonde ringlets. "Sweetheart, you are so wise and beautiful and sweet," she murmured adoringly. "I cannot tell you how much I've been missing you. I'm so glad you're here." *I'm so glad I can hide behind you now, and behind my boys.* Steeling her courage, Jessie started playfully swinging Emily-Grace's arm. Giggling, bouncing with excitement, her daughter stepped inside the house.

Inside, Dylan was already clinging to his father like a baby monkey to its parent, his small face buried in Josh's neck. Josh was crouching on the floor. A low, muted whimper was vibrating against his skin. At the same time as he held Dylan close with one strong arm around his little boy waist, he was pulling David close, too. Discreetly, Charles, Deirdre and the others treaded quietly around the little family.

Jessie felt Emily-Grace's fingers slip out of hers. It only took a few steps for the firstborn Sawyer child to make her way across the warm terracotta tiles to land next to David and wrap her arms around the father who often confused her, but whose existence she mourned when he was 'missing' and whom, to her and to all of them, was larger than life.

"Daddy," she moaned, "Daddy." Again and again. "Daddy, Daddy, Daddy…" Plaintive, like a kitten. She turned to Sam, who was setting bags on the floor. One of these was a cushioned pet carrier. "Look how big Fluffy is now," she wept to her father. "Sam, can we take Fluffy out now?"

Alone now, Jessie pressed her hands into her hurting belly and leaned back against the wall by the front door. Across the sea of small faces, bags, and generally happy confusion as Fluffy, barking wildly, entered the fray, she met Josh's moist eyes. Their family was reunited yet again, complete in its disarray and in the perfect love of children. He offered her a sad smile but swallowed it back when he saw Jessie's strong façade crack; she turned away from him, pressed her sunburnt forehead to the wall, and cursed inwardly, kicking the wall with the toe of one flip flopped foot as she tried to suck in the frustration wrought by Matt's intentional absence.

"I'm going with you when you go," she bit off to Deirdre, who approached and laid a concerned hand on Jessie's back. "I can't do this. I can't live in exile down here, away from everybody. Matt said I could come back to him."

"Hush, Jessie," Deirdre warned as, nearby, all of the adults—including Josh—froze. "Not so loud, honey."

Charles stepped soundlessly up behind them and touched his wife's arm.

Jessie saw him there, but her grief was too great to warrant discretion. She wanted Josh to hear. As he crouched on the floor with their three children in his arms, the children they all lied to in order to carry out the unplanned, devious 'part two' of the deal he brokered with Morgan, Jessie broke. Grasping Deirdre's elbows, she said in front of everyone, "I choose Matt. I choose Matt, Dee. I hate it here. I want to go home."

Charles pushed past his wife. He was tired, he was aging, but he was a man who, his entire professional life and likely a good part of his childhood, demanded respect. The way he was looking at Jessie now, with a determined resolve imbued with pity, took her breath away before he even spoke. And when he spoke, he shattered her.

"Matt's married, Jessie. He married Shanda yesterday."

Jessie pushed Deirdre away from her. "No. He wouldn't. He told me that he would come and get me, that he would…that I could call any…any time…" She started to stutter, to stammer, to struggle for the words. Both hands came up to her face to cover her pain. "F-for rescue. He said he'd rescue me. He said. He promised."

Deirdre saw Charles start to speak again. Recognizing Jessie's peril and the limitations of Jessie's capacity to accept how desperately her life needed to change, she sent her husband a guarded warning.

Immediately, Charles softened. "I'm sorry, sweetheart," he said. "I'm truly, truly sorry." The producer's staunch back was to Josh.

In Charles' eyes, Jessie saw truth. At the same time, she let this latest defeat get the best of her.

"I hate him!" she cried. "I hate him!" Her eyes locked on Josh. "I hate you too! I fucking hate you! You and your stupid plan! Look where it got us, Josh. Look where we are! In God-knows-nowhere!"

One quick movement, and Jessie was out the door. Throwing off her flip flops, she took off running in bare feet.

Charles spun around to Sam. "Go," he demanded. "Stay back, but go with her, please."

It was a good hour before Jessie came huffing back to the house, with Sam keeping pace just behind her the way Matt used to in the old days. Her mind and heart had settled somewhat during the course of the run, with the knowing that her baby needed her. Her older children crawled all over her when she got back, confused once again but intuitively knowing there were bigger things at play than their young minds could comprehend. Still, she had nothing to say to any of the adults present. With the exception of the children, who could only urge a trancelike word here and there, Jessie was back in her private cave.

Later that day, in early evening, she laid Micah down to sleep and took the opportunity afforded by privacy to give in to her grief. The afternoon run had been more about rage. Lying on the big bed she shared with Josh, Jessie let hulking sobs overtake her. Most of their group had taken the children down to the dock to walk the shore and collect shells. Josh remained, with Arnie at his side as they washed and dried the last of the dinner dishes.

Hearing Jessie crying, Arnie wiped a dishtowel over a wine glass and gestured toward the bedroom. "Go," he said. "Jessie might not act like she wants you, but she does, Josh. She needs you. I'll join the children and the others on the beach. You'll have some time to yourselves."

Josh shoved the dishcloth into the sink. He nodded, and gave the cloth a royal twist. It leached its wetness out where it belonged, and the excess water went spiraling down the drain. Inhaling for strength, he clapped a hand on Arnie's arm and padded off toward his bedroom.

To her credit, Jessie didn't push him away when he lay down behind her. She didn't acknowledge him at first, either, though.

"Shhh, little one," he murmured into her long, tired curls as he spooned her quaking body. "I wish you'd let me help. I wish you'd let me in."

Jessie was inconsolable. "Why would he do this to me? Why? Why would he abandon me again? I can't do this without him. I'm not strong enough to do this without him. He knows better. After the last time we were apart, he knows better!"

"This is the thing about Matt," Josh started, easing his way into helping by shuffling his body closer to his wife's and tenderly twisting strands of her hair around and around his finger. "From the beginning, you've trusted him, right Jessie? Always? And he's never let you down. He's always done the right thing by you. By us."

"That's why it hurts so much. He's leaving me here alone to pick up the pieces, to…" She sobbed harder and buried her face in the pillow. "To try to help you, when I can't even help myself these days. I don't know whether I'm coming or going. I don't know where all of this is going to land!"

"That's the thing, Jessie," Josh whispered, laying his cheek against hers.

"Nobody really does, except for this one thing—Matt wouldn't leave you here if he didn't think he was doing the right thing. If there was any doubt, he would not leave you here with me."

Sniffling, forcing the greatest of the sobs to come to a hiccuping halt, Jessie lifted her head off the pillow. "He trusts you," she choked. "He trusts you."

"And you. And we owe it to him to grant him the same respect, Jessie. He knows what he's doing. Matt's always known what to do, even when it means he has to get hurt too."

"You think he's hurting too? I can't stand it. I can't stand it, Josh." Jessie ducked her face back into the pillow and choked out a few more sobs.

"Oh, Jesus, Jessie. Of course he is. Of course he bloody is. He doesn't get to hold you. How fucking lucky am I?"

A sarcastic sniffling laugh made its way to Josh's ears. "You're not so god-damned lucky. Look at me. I'm lying here crying over Matt and you're taking a hit to your pride trying to comfort me. You're not lucky at all, Josh."

"Oh, yes I am," Josh smiled as Jessie turned her head back to the side so he could lay his cheek against hers again. "My family is all in one place finally, and my wife is in my arms letting me comfort her while she hurts. All that's left is for her—you," his voice grew more tender as he brushed his lips against Jessie's wet cheek, "to muster up some of that famous Jessie Wheeler-Sawyer courage and become brave again. So you can learn to trust me again too." His smile tickled Jessie's cheek when he murmured, "I know you love me, beautiful girl. I accept that what you have with Matt is real too, and I sure as hell don't deny that it hurts. At the same time, I acknowledge that it was me that orchestrated it. Wasn't it? Because I trusted him to look after you, and he was just doing what I asked him to do in the first place. But, Jessie?"

"Mmm?" She was quieting now, listening, slowly opening up her heart to let her husband back in.

"I'm glad he's not here," Josh continued. "And I'm damn glad he married Shanda. Because I want my wife here in my arms where I can love her properly without Mr. GQ around to distract her from loving me back. So we can get on with living that normal life you've always coveted."

"Normal? Josh…babe, nothing about life down here is normal. Nothing. And I don't see that ever changing."

Josh hesitated, but only briefly. Something stirred in Jessie's body while he kept laying his fluttery little kisses on her cheek, by her eye, and lower; as he pushed her hair aside so he could brush his lips across her neck. Shortly, she angled her face around to him so she could meet his probing, searching lips face on. With Jessie's mewling assent and her body's full cooperation, Josh took her fast, a little roughly, as he regained ownership of what he felt wanted to belong to him again but which, in fact, was really always his all along.

Chapter Thirty-three

"Daddy, Daddy, watch what I can do!"

Jessie was putting a load of laundry in the washing machine when she heard David call out to his father. Normally David was their quiet child, but all morning he'd been vying with Dylan for his daddy's attention. It was around eleven—everyone was already out at the pool, either in the water or hanging out poolside. The day was hot, "Damn hot, in a good way," Sam said to Arnie earlier. Overhearing, Jessie let herself smile at Sam's enthusiasm for the tropical climate. Vancouver in mid-winter was generally rainy, gray and damp. *I need to reframe my thinking,* she'd chided herself at the time. *Lotsa people would be on their knees in gratitude for a hot, sunny winter down here.*

Scooping up a stray pair of Dylan's shorts from the floor, where they'd fallen as she was transferring clothes from the basket to the washer, Jessie stole a sneak peek through the laundry room's small window at her family in the pool. Dylan was in Josh's arms. Slippery and vibrating with happiness, Dylan twisted around and leveraged his bare feet on his father's bent knees. With a happy roar, Josh propelled him upwards, so Dylan got to half-dive, half-belly-flop in the warm swimming pool. Laughing, Josh fell backward and grabbed David, who was furiously kicking himself around on a child-sized body board, trying to get Josh to watch him.

"Easy on your father," Deirdre called to Dylan when the little boy surfaced. "He has parts that hurt. Easy!"

"I'm okay," Josh said to Dee, ducking his head, embarrassed.

In the laundry room, Jessie clutched a rumpled T-shirt to her chest and rocked back on a heel. As Josh stood upright in the pool, she let herself pick out the bullet wound scar on his chest. Puckered and round, it was healed over but, to her, it would never reconcile itself as something that was over and past, the way she felt Josh seemed to be trying to do as far as the horrendous hit was concerned.

"We can't live in the past," he'd said to her last night as they lay snuggled up with each other on their bed after making love. "We have to move forward."

"This from the man who not all that long ago couldn't see a future for himself at all." Wryly, Jessie had rolled over onto her back and found a spot on the opposite wall to stare at.

Josh hadn't answered, except with a roll onto his side toward her, a light touch on her cheek and his comforting breath on her ear and on her neck. Nothing he could think to say could ease a pain this big. But he was trying. Every day he put one foot in front of the other, and now that his family was here and there was distance between Morgan and them—and Charles reporting that according to their resources at the prison it seemed largely believed that Josh was dead, and so Sawyer-related activity in Morgan's corner seemed to have quieted as a result—there was hope again.

The bullet wound…thinking about it now as she did the laundry, Jessie had to look away from her husband's oh-so-touchable broad, tanned chest. She finished putting the load in the washer, added soap and fabric softener, and started the cycle. As the machine filled with water she wiped sweaty palms on the light sundress she was wearing over her bikini, and padded barefoot out to the pool.

Emily-Grace was sitting on a chaise, doodling in a sketch pad. Jessie plunked down behind her and loosely wrapped both arms around her daughter's neck.

"Aren't you going in the water?" she asked hopefully.

"Nope. I'm staying out here in the shade with Fluffy." Deep water, despite the fact the oldest Sawyer child was a competent swimmer, was not Emily-Grace's friend. It hadn't been since the day the family's Lexus was so heartlessly submerged in the cold Alberta river. A forlorn twist formed on Emily-Grace's lips. She laid a hand on the small dog's head and bent down to kiss its fur.

She was remembering Snow, the lost puppy, but Jessie didn't have the heart to bring up that awful day. "You don't need to put your face under, sweetheart," she said gently instead. "Daddy or Alin can stay right by you."

"Nope. I just wanna draw, Momma." A fervent swoop of a yellow pencil crayon created a circular swirl in the sky.

Looking over her daughter's shoulder to the sketch pad, Jessie relaxed. Emily-Grace was evidently as happy as Dylan and David today. A bright sun boasting a radiant smile was shining down upon a lot of happy people who Jessie assumed rightly were the clan gathered here today.

In the pool, Josh handed his boys over to the care of Sam and Alin. Arnie and Charles were in the kitchen conferring over something or other—the heat, Josh hoped, uneasily eyeing them. Deirdre, with Carlotta as her shadow, stayed by the older boys, hovering, worrying, and occasionally laughing. Micah was asleep in the master bedroom. While watching the boys, Dee had a baby monitor swinging from a hand as she moved.

Approaching Jessie and Emily-Grace, Josh bent down to scratch the puppy's head.

"Daddy," Emily-Grace complained, "you're dripping on my picture!"

"Emily-Grace," Jessie started to warn, but stopped short when she looked up to see Josh smile down at his daughter. He bent to brush his lips against their little girl's soft cheek, being careful to sidestep the chaise so his pool-wet body wouldn't damage her drawing. Surprised, Jessie leaned back against the chaise when Emily-Grace dropped her yellow pencil crayon and drew both skinny arms up and around her father's neck.

"I missed you so much, Daddy." The little girl sighed happily. "I'm so, so glad you're found."

"Me too," Josh said, his heart fluttering with this unexpected embrace from his usually reticent child. "I'm glad we're all together again, sweetheart. Fluffy included." Chuckling, he ran his fingers through the puppy's fur, his happy grin widening even further when Fluffy emitted a puppy-style murmur of contentment and rolled onto her back for a coveted belly scratch.

"Animals love you, Daddy," Emily-Grace said, half in awe. Eyes wide, she watched her father lightly scratch the puppy's belly. "I love you."

A sweet shimmering light passed through Josh's eyes then. A silent observer, Jessie swore the universe was handing her and Josh a moment to remember, the sacred kind that, in its perfection, was telling them that all was finally well. It was like a falling star, it was that quick—it arced across Josh's liquescent eyes in a fireworks burst of ecstatic, elated radiance; silvery sparks accompanied by imagined joyful, sizzling sound. Its message to all of them was *I'm glad you're here.*

Jessie swallowed back a new thick lump in her throat and soundlessly agreed with the universe as her husband bent to her too, and treated her to a perfect, sweet kiss. She made sure to bend her face up to him so his lips would land on hers instead of on her cheek or forehead. Grasping his bicep, she held on and extended their kiss until she felt Josh's kiss morph into a smile. Letting go, Jessie watched him with a mixture of love and bewilderment. She hadn't expected him to be so calm and accepting; she hadn't expected to see peace in Josh's eyes here in this lonely exile. More so, his easy approach to his family's return to him was rubbing off on the children, on all of them, really. Emily-Grace in particular was a different child now that she had her daddy back. It was almost as if she knew, on some intuitive level, how close she came to losing him for real this time.

A harsh ring from the burner phone Charles was carrying around jarred Jessie back to reality. Swinging her head around, she sucked in a breath. Catching Josh's eye after she realized whom Charles was talking to, was sobering.

Josh bit his bottom lip and studied her, a calm acceptance in his eyes.

"S'okay," he said, leaning diffidently on one bare foot, drips from his straggly wet long hair puddling on the deck beneath his toes as if to communicate hurts that he couldn't bring himself to say, or perhaps that he knew he brought upon himself. Touching Emily-Grace's arm, he chose to remain on neutral ground as, behind their daughter, Jessie could barely bring herself to breathe. "Come swim with your brothers and me," Josh urged his little girl, his voice low and husky. "You can hold on to me the whole time. I promise I will not let you go."

The trust he offered her on this hot day was sorely needed. It was a step toward normality, to the time 'before,' when Emily-Grace was not afraid of water, and when the dog at her side was much tinier than this one, and was a different kind of white—a pure, first love snow-white kind. Emily-Grace extended a hand, latched her eyes onto her beloved father, and let him lead her to the edge of the pool, where five steps down were all the steps Josh needed to immerse him to his waist in this, the shallow end.

"Huh," Jessie thought, running a fingertip over her bottom and then her top lip. In front of her, Josh lifted his daughter and carried her further into the pool toward the center where the boys were frolicking happily with Sam and Alin. Emily-Grace was clinging to her daddy, tightly, trembling a little, even. But she was trusting him—his strength and sense of duty as a father—to keep her safe.

A voice at Jessie's side startled her. It was Charles. He was holding the phone toward her. "Take it," he demanded, leaving no room for her to decline, even though a very large part of her wanted to.

Hesitating, Jessie stared at it as it free-floated, almost, in his fingers. It seemed like some weird, strange thing, but it held a voice she coveted and desperately missed. A soul-connection she craved.

"Make your peace," Charles added, declaring, in his small myopic vision, that he thought it could be possible to heal a hurt this big simply by swapping a few words over a run of the mill cell phone that, in its untraceable plain-ness, announced just how much things had changed.

Turning her head, swiping a suddenly shaking hand through her hair, Jessie made herself peek up at Josh through long, damp eyelashes. He was watching her, waiting to see what she would do. It was a bizarre moment for Jessie, seeing her husband holding Emily-Grace, standing in the center of a flurry of boyish water activity—effervescent splashes and jubilant hollers—while pondering whether or not to take a call that surely meant Matt was on the other end.

A tiny, almost imperceptible nod accompanied by lips pressed in a thin line was Josh's way of saying *Do it.*

I don't know what you expect, Jessie breathed back to him as she sucked on a lip and pondered him, standing there immersed in water with their children all around him. *Do you think it's that easy to just let him go?*

Without looking away from her husband she took the phone, then swung her legs over the side of the chaise and stood, losing eye contact with Josh by striding definitively into the kitchen, and bypassing Arnie on the way, who supportively squeezed her hand as they passed.

"So," Jessie snarled into the phone after she moved through the front door to the courtyard and finally lifted it to her ear, "I guess by 'rescue' you meant saving me from you. Seeing as you went running back to Shanda the second things got tough."

Matt's breaths were audible although it took him a few beats to muster the courage to speak. Jessie near collapsed when the usual tough timbre of his voice emerged thin and lusterless. Letting her eyes flutter shut, she sank down on a stone wall near the upper driveway and laid her forehead in one hot palm. "Hello back, Jessie," was all Matt could manage in the first minute of their renewed connection.

"Pleasantries are not uppermost in my mind right now, Matt." There was no real anger in Jessie's tone, though—just hurt. Seeing Josh with the kids, watching him return to himself down here in this island sanctuary, making love with him, finally, which was largely due to Josh's patience and tender understanding about Matt overall, was eroding Jessie's need for Matt and replacing it with the love and desire she so desperately missed with Josh. All that remained was destroying the old bridge she had with Matt, and building one anew. Her voice softened. "Either Shanda doesn't know the truth, or she's one helluva understanding woman."

"She knows the truth."

"Ah. So, understanding it is."

"She's forgiving, Jessie. Like someone else I know."

"You and me, Matt..." With a deep sigh, Jessie started absently picking at a loose thread in the hem of her embroidered sundress. "God, we really had something good. Didn't we?"

"We did, sweetheart. We really did. Just not...good enough. You had too much to lose."

"I'm doing better now, Matt. I mean, Charles might not have said so to you because I kinda lost it yesterday, but Josh and I...we sorted a few things out. He seems so much more at peace here than I expected."

"Sorted some things out," Matt repeated. At Mundy Park in Coquitlam, he was leaning against the front of his car staring at the trees, pondering where Jessie was exactly and wondering what she was wearing, what she looked like. Was there a light in her eyes? Judging by her voice and her willingness to talk to him, he thought maybe she was, as she said, indeed doing better. Still, he couldn't keep a jealous edge from creeping into his voice. "So I guess you had an orgasm or three. I'm happy for you." Even now the memory of holding her, whispering to her, begging her to 'come for him,' was so recent, so real, that it shocked Matt with its intensity. That slender, adorable body writhing and moaning in his arms, whimpering and begging him for release…

Matt shivered. "Jesus," he cursed almost silently. He hung his head and his shoulders drooped. Never again…never again could they go there, him and her.

"I miss you," Jessie whispered, glumly toeing the dirt with one bare toe. "Your handsome mug. Your arms around me. Not just your sexy body, Matt. I'm going to miss the old days, doing shows and having you there in the wings always ready to come to my rescue if I needed you. Well," she sighed heavily, "you used to be ready to come to my rescue. I guess a lot has changed."

"Sweetheart," he started, coping as best he could with an impossible situation, "I will always be here for you. You know that."

"I know, Matt, I do, I just…You know, it was Josh who set me straight. He told me to trust you. The funny thing about that is that it kind of came with learning to trust him again, too."

"Arnie told Charles he's doing really well. I wouldn't have left you with him if I thought you or the children were in any danger, Jessie, and I don't mean that just in physical terms."

"My heart too, huh? My poor old beaten, bruised heart?" Tugging at the loose thread, Jessie let her lips curl further downward. It was like the more she pulled at the thread, the more her whole spirit sank.

"Yeah, your heart, kid."

"Reality hasn't sunk in yet, Matt. Nothing about this place is normal. It's a fantasy hideout. One of these days the kids will get bored and some great hole will appear in Josh's illusory world. It's like he's stopping time for a while; like he's living in this pretend or imagined place in his mind that negates the truth, that makes him forget what he's left behind. Including Morgan and his threats. And I think what will bring it all back will be the kids. It'll be the kids getting bored and missing everyone," she gulped, "that will reignite the truth of what Josh, too, is missing."

"You're talking about work. About acting."

"Hell, yeah. I know my husband, Matt. This play world of his seems to have won him over for a while, but I can't help but wonder for how long."

Hesitating, Matt rubbed his chin before tossing in, "I have an idea. It's not…perfect, it still won't fill the gap you're talking about, but it might help with the kids, with keeping them entertained, I mean."

"Oh? What are you thinking, babe?" The endearment snuck out. Wincing, Jessie shrank back into herself.

A long, slow exhale followed by a heartbreaking sigh didn't make her feel any better when it reached her ears. "I'm going to pretend I didn't just hear you say that." In the park back in a rainy, cold Canada, Matt swung around and got into his car so he could stay dry. Flipping on the ignition, he cranked the heater up and wished to hell Jessie was sitting next to him instead of in some foreign paradise a gazillion miles away. The radio was on low. Sitting back, he raised his face to the moon roof, above which ominous grey clouds were rolling over, suffocating him with a heavy, menacing gloom. Water droplets landed directly above him. He felt like he was in a fish tank. Or in a submerged car, maybe.

He shrank lower into his seat and tried to breathe.

The clouds. Wafting above the city, to Matt it felt like they were in his head, aligning themselves with the acute sorrow that seemed to constantly swell up in his mind, as it had since the second he first spied Jessie crumpled in a heap in her closet at the UBC house hugging Josh's leather motorcycle jacket to her chest.

"I'm not sorry." Calling her back to him, to her tender voice, Jessie added, "We will always mean something to each other, Matt. We're not like others who have affairs. Even Josh, and I guess apparently Shanda, too, get that about us. About how much we mean to each other. And why."

"You're right." A tiny, minuscule waft of gray cotton lifted from Matt's mind, taking with it a teeny bit of the constant hurt. He smiled, just a tiny little up-curve of one corner of his lips to start, but it was something. "All right," he rallied. "This is what I was thinking, Jessie. Listen up."

"There's the Matt I know. Saucy, demanding, bossy. I'm listening." Lightening up too, Jessie let her spine straighten. A white butterfly floated lazily past. Her eyes brightened as she reached out a finger to trace its zig-zaggy pattern in the air.

"Prince Edward Island."

"What?" Jessie let her hand drop to her side.

"Jessie, I…before, uh, a few weeks ago, I mean, I…I bought a house there. On your island."

"On P.E.I.? Oh." Reality snuck in and gave Jessie a good hard zap between the eyes. "Jesus, Matt." Comprehension washed over her. "For us…for you and me. And the kids."

"At the time, yes. But now…" A quiet *pffftt* echoed its way to the Caribbean. "Why not for you and Josh? A fresh start, somewhere a little more, well, normal, as you say, than that isolated place where you are now. The kids could still be home-schooled for their own protection, until they're older and can understand the gravity of how important it is to never reveal the truth of who all of you really are, but in the meantime you can take them places. To public pools so they see other kids and can continue their lessons, skating, camping, dancing, all that normal stuff you always whine about."

Smiling, Jessie could hear a new, hopeful tone in the voice she adored. "I don't whine. I am SO not a whiner. Don't speak of whining and me in the same sentence. Please."

"Yes, your highness. Sir. Ma'am." Matt cranked up the volume on the radio. One of his all-time favorite Jessie Wheeler tunes soaked the car with love and longing. "Jesus, I am going to miss watching you sing," he complained, enclosing the yearning in the satisfaction of having had the sweet pleasure, over many years, of doing just that.

Jessie brightened. "Dee says I can still do some shows, Matt. Once things settle down. I hope you'll be there—in the wings, I mean. Watching over me like always. And I hope Shanda doesn't mind if I hold you, for a really long fucking time. That's all. Just hold you, babe."

From the depths of his soul, Matt murmured his consent. It emerged victorious, wholesome and full. Inside, he cried in sweet relief. This could have gone so badly. Jessie could be miserable, as Charles had half-predicted aloud that she might be when he answered the phone earlier. Jessie could be begging, crying, screaming, throwing things, or maybe not have taken the call at all. Instead she was calm, at peace on some level, Matt thought. Reasonable. She was being reasonable, talking about the future—a future with him in it—in a way that seemed possible, once the big hurts stepped aside and let them move on.

It's Josh, Matt said to himself as, in the car, Jessie's tune on the radio flowed weightlessly into the corners the same way it filled his heart. *Josh is the calming voice in all of this. Josh knows what he almost lost. He knows this new life, 'post-shooting, post-Morgan,' is a gift.*

There was really only one thing left to say before they could talk details. "I love you," Matt murmured into the phone, sinking even deeper into his seat and reveling in the fact that the woman whose moving, poignant ballad was flowing around and through him, in him, loved him back.

In the tropics, Jessie's cheeks pinked up before she smiled. Softly, she returned the love. "I love you back, Matt. Truly, madly, deeply. Always."

In front of her, the white butterfly took another float around, as if it was looking for something, as if it was searching. Lo and behold, a few seconds later a second white butterfly joined it, and they went off together, wings seemingly flapping easier now that they had found each other again. Surprising herself, Jessie let her mind flit to Josh, to telling him about what Matt was talking about now, a house in Prince Edward Island. A life in Prince Edward Island. Her mind half-tuned Matt out and drifted to lazy hand-in-hand sunset walks on island beaches in summer; snow forts and snowmen in winter; crisp, crimson, ever-changing autumn leaves in the fall; tiny new buds, new leaves shooting forth on trees in the spring.

"Thank you, Matt," she said in the end before they had to force themselves to say 'so long' for now. It was not a stretch to know that, once she and Josh gave their consent, Matt would dive into this project, into making sure every i was dotted and every t was crossed so that the little Sawyer family could live in peace—at long last—on Jessie's much-loved east coast island.

Chapter Thirty-four

When she wandered back down to the house and out of the open, arched space to the pool, Jessie was astounded to find Emily-Grace taking dolphin rides on her father's back, letting Josh take her under the water, even, as she clutched his shoulders. The little girl came up sputtering and laughing, the terror of the river not forgotten, but temporarily removed in favor of safe playtime in a family pool with a dearly loved daddy, and people she loved and trusted all around her.

"This is too good to pass up," Jessie said to the warm tropical air, hoisting her sundress up over her head and stepping into the water. A few strokes later, she was not far from Josh's side. Dylan launched himself into her arms, David started hollering, "Watch this, Momma, watch this!" and it occurred to Jessie that, at this particular moment in time—one of the sweetest, ever—she couldn't care less if she ever acted in a film again or set foot on another stage.

Josh could read her mind; always and forever, Jessie and he were united in that serene, mystical way. One small dive and he was right beside her, a wide grin lighting up his eyes. Emily-Grace joined David on the body board, and soon Dylan was hanging onto the end kicking his feet furiously as Sam took hold of the front to steady it, and as Alin placed a hand around Emily-Grace's waist for comfort and extra assurance.

It felt like old times.

Jessie turned around in the water and lifted both arms so she could circle them around her husband's neck. "I feel like I'm seeing you for the first time," she murmured, her sea-pearl eyes filling with love. "I feel like we've been reborn."

"We have," Josh said, holding her at the waist and drawing her close for a kiss. "At least, one of us has."

Reaching up, Jessie touched a finger to his lips and frowned. "No bad stuff," she whispered tenderly. "Only good from here on in."

"You got it," Josh agreed. He didn't say anything else, but Jessie could tell by his curious eyes that he was wondering how the call with Matt went.

"It was fine," she breathed, snuggling her lips against his neck. "It was good that we talked."

"You and your Matt," Josh sighed. He pulled her close so that their bodies were aligned. "I'm glad you had some time with him, Jessie. I really am. Both of you…I think you needed it. I think you needed to know."

To know what? Jessie thought. *Heartache?* She sighed into her husband's neck and left that thought unspoken. Shortly, she lifted her head and fixed a mischievous gaze on Josh.

"What?" he asked, leaning forward for a kiss. He followed it with, "I know that look, Jessie Wheeler-Sawyer. And I don't always like what follows it."

"Um, Josh?" Alight, Jessie abstractly touched a nervous finger to her lip and cocked her head to one side. "How do you feel about shoveling snow?"

His loud groan alerted Deirdre, Charles and Arnie to some unknown factor at play between Josh and Jessie, but they all relaxed when they saw, for the first time in a while, a silent, unspoken, beautiful light pass between the couple. It arced between them the way all great loves arc between lovers, uniting them, revealing true love at its best, with colorful rainbow prisms and magical unseen butterflies and easy, carefree, wafting breezes.

Close by, the Sawyer children played in the water, oblivious to the heavy silences and oppressive worries that so very recently were such a part of their daily lives; oblivious to the great man their mother had to leave behind in order to bring their family back together; oblivious to all the hard stuff that hurt. It was easy; all three children stopped splashing at once to ponder their parents as Josh and Jessie held each other and tenderly kissed. All three would remember, in the years to come, that these were their favorite childhood times, the times when their mother and father were as lost in each other as rainbows disappearing in mist; when sweet kisses were accompanied by serene, hopeful, dewy eyes; when their own existences were so plainly explained as having come from great love as if they were always meant to live this way, exiled together in a far-off place where hope reigned eternal, and where love triumphed above all.

A muffled gurgling got Deirdre's attention. Lifting the baby monitor, she almost called out to Jessie to tell her that Micah was waking and was likely in need of a diaper change and a feeding, but she couldn't do it. Deirdre, like the children, like Charles and Sam and Alin now too, was transfixed. Tiptoeing, Dee made her way to the far end of the pool, where she met her husband's eye. On chaises nearby, Carlotta was now reading, and Arnie was snoring.

No words were necessary. Charles' and Dee's glowing faces said it all. One day many years ago a very good friend had introduced a silent, homeless waif to them. A wise knowing in their friend's eyes had communicated simply, "She's special." Back then, even Jack Deacon had no idea what gifts Jessie held, or what incredible magic she would, over many years, bring to the world.

She gifted the world music; she gifted the world honest roles in films that challenged viewers, that moved people, that provoked thought and discussion, and that changed the way people thought, about themselves and about the world around them. Through these, through music and film, she gifted an honest love, and a capacity to forgive that, even when it was sometimes tough to do so, seemingly knew no bounds.

But she gave so much more to Charles and Deirdre, who considered Jessie their own. As far as they were concerned, she was their daughter, and her children were their grandchildren. Today by the pool they were both humbled at the love they saw pass between Jessie and Josh—as short a time ago as yesterday they were reduced to wondering whether the fracture that Morgan and Nadia originally broke open between them a few years back had widened to a point where it could not be fixed.

Clearly now, there was peace in Jessie's eyes. In Josh's arms when things were good, she was the most transcendent, happy creature on the earth. In his arms she was complete.

"The baby's awake," Dee said to Charles, smiling happily as she drifted past. "Micah needs his momma."

Charles yawned, stretched, rose, and followed her into the house. "Let's give her a minute," he said. "You can change him first."

"It's time you learned, Charles." Deirdre was as giggly as a schoolgirl.

Laughter trailed behind the older couple who, not all that long ago it seemed, couldn't even imagine this kind of joy—the kind that came on the delighted wings of children—in their lives, at all.

In the pool, Josh pushed a few wet strands of Jessie's hair out of her face. "I think Micah's awake," he said, with one last press of his lips to hers. "I'll go get him."

"You're too late," Jessie stated decisively, turning Josh's shoulders so he could look toward the arched columns at the back of the house. "Grammie and Grampie are on it."

Josh winked playfully. "The senior mafia strikes again. Maybe we should enlist them into babysitting so you and I can take ourselves a little boat ride." A low, throaty, sexy growl snuck between his lips. "Last night was pretty sweet, beautiful girl."

"We did say five…" Raising her eyebrows into curves, Jessie waited for Josh's expectant response.

She got it in less than a second.

"Can I at least get used to Micah first? He's not even three months old!"

"Kidding! I'm covered. No more babies just yet."

"Sleep first. Then one more baby."

"Sex—you know, for practice—then sleep, then one more baby. Fair enough?" A light swat accompanied the remark.

"One track mind," Josh laughed. "Soon, little one. We'll finish our amazing family off the way we planned."

"Promise?" It seemed too good to be true.

"You bet."

It was only a few minutes before Charles appeared with Micah in his arms. Deirdre was right on his tail, lecturing him on being the kind of old fashioned man who was not capable in the kitchen, and even less capable when it came to changing the diapers of wiggly little babies who sometimes peed on their caregiver while they were being changed.

"Oh, here we go," Jessie groaned in jest at their playful bickering as David threw his arms around her neck and begged her to come play. To her son, she said, "Momma needs to go feed your baby brother, sweetheart, but I'll come back in the pool after. Daddy can play with you for now."

And so the day went on, and the next day and the next and the next, until Charles and Deirdre, with Carlotta and Sam and Alin in tow, had to fly back to Vancouver to supervise their businesses and to feed the media fire that had flamed up at Josh's supposed 'passing' that, by now, was finally starting to trickle down into benign, glowing coals. As always, their departure was tearful on many counts—the women, at least. Soon their small cars puttered out of sight.

Prince Edward Island had occupied a lot of the discussion over the past week. Watching the car disappear around a distant bend, Josh laid a casual arm around his wife's shoulders and pulled her to him. Micah was between them, in Jessie's arms; the other three Sawyer kids were engaged in a rousing game of tag in the empty field across from the beach house. Arnie and Kalon were behind them, wandering back through the courtyard down to the house.

"So," Josh said to Jessie as he considered their reinvented lives in P.E.I., "this name thing. What do you think?"

"Changing our names? I'm more interested in seeing you with a full beard. It'll be like that film you made back around the time David was born. The frontier one. Sexy as hell."

"Beards are trendy again," Josh offered helpfully.

"Yeah! Only because you started that trend! Doofus." She poked him in the rib.

"So I was thinking Toby MacDonald. We could be MacDonalds. There're lots of those in P.E.I., right?" So he could join in the game of tag with his kids, Josh started toward the field, inadvertently bringing Jessie and Micah along with him.

Frowning, Jessie shook her head. "Nope. That name is on my contact list, on my cell phone. Someone good at tech research might clue in, even if I change phones."

"Oh yeah—forgot about that. I think I also gave that name to Alin at one time. She likely has it on her phone, too."

"So…Gallant is another common Prince Edward Island name. Not Gawl-lawnt, like some people say, it's more of a slang version, Gal-lant. Like the bug. Although, now that I think about it, most Gallants are descended from the Acadian people. And we don't speak French."

"Okay, how about, hmmm, let's see, MacDonald is Scottish, and I could likely pass as Scots when my beard grows in."

"Dork, this isn't the 1300s. Pretty sure you don't need a beard to pass as a Scotsman these days."

"Whatever." Josh laughed and said, "What about MacPherson? MacRae? MacWilliam."

"McIver. Mc. Not Mac. Maybe that's the Irish version?"

"Why?"

"I dunno." Jessie shrugged. "Old George had a friend named Joe McIver. He spoke highly of him. It kind of has a ring to it, don't you think? And we know it's an island name, as they say." She nudged him. "Whaddaya say, Joe?"

"Josh, Joe…is it too close?"

"It's a J name," Jessie replied with confidence. "It's important that you remain a J." Her girlish pout reappeared.

Josh could see that this necessary exercise was getting to her. With Charles and Dee taking their departure, it seemed the talk of changing names was losing its initial thrill. When they started it, Josh thought it might be kind of fun. At Jessie's solemn look now, he was regretting the decision to take her down that road just yet, but Matt and Ulysses had work to do in order to reinvent the entire Sawyer family. They were already asking for their choices so they could create identification, including passports, driver's licenses, and provincial health cards.

"What about me?" Jessie asked, rallying, moving Micah to her other shoulder and bravely facing Josh just as they reached the kids. "Who should I become? I need a name with some meaning behind it too."

"Well…" Stopping to take a close look at her, Josh sucked thoughtfully on a lip. "Do you think a J name might be too obvious? Might lead people down the wrong path?"

"Maybe. But I love us as J & J. We'll always be J & J."

"So let's stay J & J. Nobody will put that together anyway. Not when we change our hair and stuff. What about…Jasmine? You could spell it Jasmyn. That's pretty."

"It's too pretty. I need to be more, um, ordinary."

"You couldn't be ordinary if you tried, Jessie," Josh chuckled.

"You know what I mean. I need to fit in. It should be a popular name."

"J names, hmmm. Jane would be weird since we have a friend named Jane."

"Not like we'll ever see her anymore," Jessie sighed. "Jenni. With an i."

"Might be too close to Jessie. How about Annie Hayden?"

"Ha. Funny guy. Did that, bought the T-shirt. Jasmyn, then. You can call me Jazzy. That'd be fun. How are we gonna handle this with the kids?"

"In bed I'll call you Jazzy. That can be your…" Josh gulped. "Uhhhh…"

"Jesus, Josh," Jessie groaned. "Tell me you weren't going to say my hooker name. Or something equally revolting."

"Sorry." Josh looked over at the kids. "I'm gonna go play tag with our rug rats. We can wrap this weird chat up later."

"Yeah. You do that. Jesus."

Always, it seemed Jessie's past was not far behind. In this short discussion Josh had managed—without intending to, Jessie was sure—to bring up her incognito time in Scotland as Annie Hayden, and her sketchy time working in the black box studio with Caryn and Eric on the Downtown Eastside. She had made tons of films over the years, had taken on many new characters, but these—the ones that inherently demanded strict attention relating to her survival—were always the toughest.

"Jasmyn," she thought, pushing the hard past aside and rolling the new name, the new identity, around on her tongue. "Joe and Jasmyn. Joe and Jasmyn McIver and their passel of rug rats, are moving to Prince Edward Island."

There were a lot more questions to be answered, a lot more details to come. Matt, of all people, would continue to work this new life out for Josh and Jessie. He still had power over Jessie; he still had dominion over her. He had a large part to play in orchestrating her life. What he didn't fully have, and likely never would, was complete and final closure after their deep love for each other had leveled up into a brief sexual relationship that, for a magical time, made forging a life together seem possible.

What Matt also did not have was the strength to fully walk away. He'd done that in the past. He'd removed himself from Jessie before, not once but twice, and not just in distance, but also via communications as well. The pain of those separations was bad enough then. Now, bearing that kind of heartbreaking weight was absolutely incomprehensible. This time, Matt would stay in touch with Jessie. He had to.

Thinking about him, Jessie cuddled Micah close and watched her family run gleefully around. With his long hair cascading down to his shoulders, Josh zipped in and around his kids with reckless abandon, teasing them by darting away just as they reached for him. There were yelps and hollers, all happy and jubilant, and the occasional childish cry of, "Momma! Come help!"

There would be other days in which to consider all the moving related issues. There would be solemn, moonlit nights in which to mourn a much-missed man whose love and strength were, at many times in Jessie's life, the only things that kept her sane.

For now, Josh and Jessie had their family intact, and a tropical paradise in which to play.

And so it was, as the sun set later that day—as the Sawyer children snuggled in for bedtime stories with a momma and a daddy who were present and attentive—that a new Sawyer family was already being birthed. Josh and Jessie were about to become Joe and Jasmyn McIver, and together with their children they were about to play, when all was said and done, the biggest, most demanding, roles of their lives.

～ ～

The End.

～ ～

Thank you!

If you liked this book, please take a few moments to leave a review on Amazon or Goodreads, and consider sharing your thoughts on social media. Self-published authors like myself count on your support to help us continue our writing journeys!

Have a wonderful day ☺

Susan

Join the *Drifters* family by signing up at **www.susanrodgersauthor.com**. As a welcome gift, I'll send you a free bonus/deleted chapter from book one, *A Song For Josh*. Happy reading!

www.susanrodgersauthor.com

Facebook: search **Susan Rodgers, Writer** and **StillTheWatermovie**

Twitter: **@srbluemountain**

Instagram: **SusanDrifters**

Pinterest: **Susan Rodgers**

email: **fatcat@pei.sympatico.ca**

Susan Rodgers' first novel *A Certain Kind of Freedom* was a Finalist in the Writers' Federation of Nova Scotia Atlantic Writing Awards for unpublished manuscripts. Her short story from the novel of the same name, published in two anthologies, has received rave reviews, as have the Drifters novels, Susan's all-time favourite books to write.

Owner/Operator of Bluemountain Entertainment, Susan is a 'Diploma With Honours' graduate of Vancouver Film School. She produces mostly documentary style client films and short dramas with plans to one day shoot a Feature Drama based on the novel Atlantic Blue.

Formerly a Museum Curator, in winter Susan lives with her partner Steve and her striped cat Oliver (Lucy Maud Montgomery once said the only good cat is a striped cat) in Summerside, Prince Edward Island, Canada. In summer, she hides in a small trailer in Darnley, P.E.I., where she writes novels, paddles kayaks, and crafts sandcastles on the beach. She makes frequent trips to Vancouver to visit her son Christopher, where she enjoys life in the hippie city while listening to great music and sipping on good espresso.